D0099290

City
~of~
Bones

Tor books by Martha Wells

The Elements of Fire
City of Bones

Chapter One

Somewhere else, in a room shadowed by age and death, a man readies himself to look into the future for what may be the last time.

The day was long, and Khat was bored with bargaining. He leaned on one pole of the awning and looked out into the dusty street, ignoring Arnot's wife, who was examining their find as if she had never seen the like before and never wanted to again.

"Two days, no more," Arnot's wife finally said, mopping the sweat from her brow with a corner of her scarf and feigning disinterest.

Khat shook his head, irritated at this display of deliberate ignorance. His partner Sagai raised an eyebrow in eloquent comment and said, "The lady has a mischievous sense of humor, and Arnot is an honorable man. One hundred days."

Khat smiled to himself and thought, *The lady is a thief, and Arnot is a rat's ass.* More dust rose in the narrow street outside as pushcarts trundled by, piled high with wares destined for markets on the upper tiers. The sun had started its downward progress into late afternoon, leaving the high canyon of the street outside Arnot's shop in shadow. The heat was still stifling under the patched awning and must be far worse in the shop's cavelike interior, dug out of the black rock of the city's backbone, where Arnot himself sat on his money chest and listened to his wife bargain.

The man in the shadowed room cups the fragments of bone in one hand. They are only a focus, because the power to see beyond time is inside his thoughts and his blood and his living bones, not in the dead matter in his hand.

The woman's laughter was a humorless bark. She said, "Nothing is worth that."

The article in question lay atop a stool, wrapped in soft cloth. It was a square piece of glazed terra-cotta floor tile, made particularly valuable by the depiction of a web-footed bird swimming in a pool filled with strange floating flowers. The colors were soft half-tones, the purplish-brown of the bird's plumage, the blue-green color of the pond, the cream and faded yellow of the flowers. The subject matter, a waterbird that hadn't lived since the Fringe Cities rose from the dust, and the delicate colors, impossible even for Charisat's skilled artisans to duplicate, marked it as Ancient work, a relic of the lost times more than a thousand years ago.

Piled all around under the awning were the rest of Arnot's wares: serving tables with faience decoration, ornamental clocks, alabaster vessels, tiny decorative boxes of valuable wood, and junk jewelry of beads, lapis, turquoise, and carnelian. There were few Ancient relics out on display here; the quality would be inside, away from the untutored eyes of casual buyers.

"We know what these tiles are fetching on the upper tiers," Sagai said with reproof. "Don't treat us like fools, and our price will be more reasonable." He folded his arms, ready to wait all day if necessary.

With an ironic lift of an eyebrow, Khat added, "We only come to you first because we're such good friends of your husband."

There was a choking cough from within the shop's dark interior, possibly Arnot about to launch into an attack of apoplexy. Arnot's wife bit her lip and studied them both. Sagai was big and dark-skinned, the hair escaping from his headcloth mostly gone to gray, his blue robe and mantle somewhat frayed and shabby. He was despised as a foreigner because he came from Kenniliar Free City, but all the dealers knew he was a trained scholar and had studied the Ancients long before circumstances had forced him to work in Charisat's relic trade. Sagai's features were sensitive, and right now his brown eyes were liquid with humor at Arnot's wife's predicament.

Khat was krismen, and even lower on Charisat's social scale than

Sagai, for he had been born deep in the Waste. He was tall and leanly muscled, longish brown hair touched by red, skin browned against the sun, and a handsome face that he knew from experience was no help with Arnot's wife, who was just as much of a professional as he and Sagai were.

But Khat could tell she was starting to weaken. He pointed out more gently, "They're buying these on the upper tiers like cheap water. You could turn it around in the time it takes us to walk back to the Arcade."

"Or we can take our business elsewhere," Sagai added, frowning thoughtfully as if he was already considering which of Arnot's competitors to go to.

Arnot's wife ran a hand through her stringy white hair and sighed. "Twenty days."

"Forty," Sagai said immediately.

There was a growl from the shop's interior, a crack and a sound of the shifting of massive bulk that seemed to indicate Arnot himself was about to appear. Arnot's wife rolled her eyes and folded her arms over her tattered gray kaftan.

The man closes his hand on the fragments of bone, thinking of their former owner and how unwillingly he parted with them.

Arnot appeared in the arched doorway, glared at the two men from under lowered brows, and advanced toward the tile. As he reached for it, Khat said, "By the edges."

Arnot regarded him a moment in silence. Legend said krismen eye color changed according to mood. Khat's eyes had lightened to gray-green. Dangerous. Arnot lifted the tile gently by the edges, and turned it, so the light filtering through the red awning caught the colors and made them glow almost with life. The tiles were one of the few relics that even the cleverest forgers hadn't the skill to copy; before the rise of the Waste, that tile had graced some Ancient's fountain court, and Arnot knew it.

The dealer considered, then set the tile gently down again. He nodded approval to his wife, and she dug in the leather pouch at her waist for tokens.

Something made Khat glance out into the street.

Three men watched them from the edge of the awning. One wore the robes and concealing veil of a Patrician, and the other two were dressed in the rough shirts and protective leather leggings of wagon dock laborers. An upper-tier Patrician down in the market quarters of the Fifth Tier meant one thing—Trade Inspector.

Arnot's wife, caught in the act of passing over the brass counters, each representing several days of artisan's labor, froze and stared at the intruders, her gray brows coming together in consternation. Sagai had his hand out, Khat and Arnot were obviously giving their countenance to the deal, and the merchandise lay in plain view on the stool.

It took them all several moments to remember that there was nothing illegal about what they were doing.

Smiling, the man looks up at his companion across the table and says, "It's an intriguing game, where one player sees the board and the other is blindfolded."

"Yes," she replies. "But which player are we?"

Arnot nudged his wife, and she dropped the counters into Sagai's palm. Sagai tucked them away inside his robe, and exchanged a look with Khat. Their expressions betrayed nothing; it would have been a mistake to show any kind of fear.

Arnot took his wife's elbow and steered her toward the door of the shop, a protective gesture Khat was surprised to see from the cut-throat dealer. Arnot growled, "We close early today."

Khat exchanged a look with Sagai to make sure they were both thinking along the same lines, then stepped out from under the awning. One of the dockworkers moved to intercept him and said, "Are you Khat, the relic dealer from the Sixth Tier?"

The man was smiling at him unpleasantly. He was big for a lower-tier city dweller and blond, his short-cropped hair greasy with sweat and blown sand. The one who hung back with the Patrician was short and stocky, wearing a red headcloth. He carried an air gun slung casually over one shoulder. The copper ball beneath the stock that was the gun's air reservoir had been recently polished, and the skeleton butt had shiny brass fittings.

Khat didn't answer, and Sagai shouldered his way gently past the dockworker before the man could react, saying, "Excuse us, gentlemen."

Khat followed Sagai up the narrow canyon of the street. Walls of black rock and mud brick rose up on either side of them, with narrow doorways on the lower levels and shallow balconies and windows on the upper, some with cheap tin shutters painted with desert flowers or luck signs. Clothes hung out to air festooned some of the upper floors, and sewer stink was suspended in the still, hot air. The three men followed them, though not fast enough to be actually chasing them, and the rifle wielder did nothing overtly threatening. Sagai muttered, "And the day was going so well, too."

Trade Inspectors would never have let them walk away. But Khat and Sagai had no Patrician clients and no reason to expect any, with rifle-wielding guards or without. " 'Was' is right," Khat answered, irritated. Their pursuers were still too close for them to dodge down any connecting alleys.

The street widened into an open court, where a fountain carved into the shape of an upended tortoise shell played and the sewer stink was not quite so bad. There was still no opportunity to bolt. Grim now, Sagai said, "They know your name, obviously. They may know where we live. We'll have to talk to them."

Khat couldn't think of a better idea, so he took a seat on the fountain's wide edge to wait for their pursuers to catch up, and Sagai rested one sandaled foot next to him.

Women in light-colored kaftans filled jugs and buckets at the fountain and lingered to talk, old men sat on the stone balconies above them and smoked clay pipes, and a shrieking gang of children tore by, scattering a peddler's collection of baskets and stampeding some stray goats. An old woman sat on a faded red rug near the fountain, telling fortunes by burning fragments of bone in a brazier. The old man who kept the fountain casually strolled toward them and shook his clay bowl of coins and tokens suggestively, reminding them to pay before using the water.

The Patrician and the hireling with the rifle stopped several paces away, the blond man coming nearer to confront them. Khat lounged at ease on the fountain rim, and Sagai regarded the man's approach with polite interest. None of the other inhabitants of the court fled at the sight of the possible altercation, but the women who had not been disturbed by Khat and Sagai's presence at the fountain found reasons to move on, and the water keeper retreated across the court.

The rifle's odd, Khat decided. It was an upper-tier weapon, used by lictors assigned to court officials or paid vigils. Even bonetakers and cutthroat thieves could only afford to carry knives. Presumably the Patrician could have hired the dockworkers and given them the weapon to defend him, but it was hard to believe he would be quite that trusting. It was more likely that the pair were private vigils as much accustomed to the upper tier as their master. *And who are they protecting him from?* he wondered. *The septuagenarian fountain keeper maybe, or the beggar woman telling fortunes?* This was only the Fifth Tier, not the Eighth. Still smiling, the blond man spoke to Khat. "I'm Kythen Seul, and I know who you are."

On the table is an iron bowl half-filled with hot coals. The bones will be burned there as the man looks past the slow turning of time. He does not know the reason for this except that a symbolic death by fire seems to aid the process.

His companion watches.

Well, Khat hadn't tried to hide it. He said, "Then why did you ask?" He felt his theory was confirmed. Seul spoke Tradetongue too well for a dockworker. Khat looked over at the Patrician, who seemed to have a slight build under all that heavy cloth. His inner robes were rough silk without beadwork or embroidery, the outer mantle of tougher cotton, and the long gauze veil was wound around his head and over the lower half of his face. Not ostentatious, unless you considered how far such materials had to be ported across the Waste to reach the Charisat markets. Khat wore a light shirt over tight trousers and soft leather boots, with his robe folded back and tied off around his waist, and to anyone accustomed to the robes and heavy veiling affected by Charisat's upper-tier nobility, this was practically undressed. The krismen needed less protection from the sun than he did relief from the heat; it was cooler out on the Waste than it was on the black stone of Charisat's streets in the afternoon.

Seul displayed his tolerance of uppity krismen by ignoring the question. He glanced pointedly at Sagai and said, "Your friend can go."

"Oh, but we have business still to do together," Sagai said, as if he thought it suggestion rather than command. "I prefer to stay."

Seul's eyes hardened, but the smile didn't disappear. Khat was beginning to dislike that smile. Seul inclined his head back toward the Patrician, and said, "The Honored needs a knowledgeable guide to take him to the Ancient Remnant on the Tersalten Flat."

Sagai frowned. "The one to the west?"

"Yes."

Khat had done this before, but usually for scholars from some other city or the Academia, and he didn't feel accommodating today.

"If you already know where it is," he said patiently, but with the patience usually reserved for a child, "why do you need a guide?"

"I don't need a guide." Seul's voice took on a testy edge. "I prefer one."

"And you want me to suggest someone?" Khat looked mildly confused. As a way to drive someone wild he had found this was second to few, especially when what the person was trying to tell you was as plain as daylight.

"No, I want you."

Khat smiled back at him for the first time, a particularly krismen expression that revealed pointed canines and had an unequivocal meaning. "The whorehouse is down that way." Out of the corner of his eye he saw Sagai glance briefly skyward, as if asking the air spirits to witness what he had to deal with on a daily basis. His partner had also unobtrusively rested a hand on the knife hilt concealed by a fold of his robe.

Seul's smile came close to evaporating, but he only said, "The Honored doesn't ask for free service. He intends to pay."

Before Khat could answer, Sagai interposed, "Might one ask why?"

"He's curious." The smile was back with renewed strength. "He's a student of the past."

The man drops the bones into the glowing coals in the iron bowl, and they yellow, then blacken as the heat takes them, and thin veins of smoke rise into the still air of the time-darkened room.

"Not the future?" Khat asked, and then wondered why. The old woman hadn't moved from her rug near the fountain, where she muttered to herself and burned bone chips to look into the future. Perhaps he had been thinking of her.

Amazingly, Seul stopped smiling. "The reason isn't important. He'll pay ten gold reals."

Khat heard Sagai's snort of disgust. He said, "Is this a joke?"

The man's eyes shifted from the krismen to Sagai and back. "It's a fair price."

"It's more than fair," Khat agreed. "But I'm kris. I can't get a trade license to own Imperial-minted coins." In Charisat and most of the other Fringe Cities, citizenship had to be bought, and noncitizens couldn't own or handle minted coins unless they bought a special license to do so, which was almost as expensive as citizenship itself—

and sometimes not worth the trouble, since Trade Inspectors paid special notice to sales made with minted coins. Trade tokens were a holdover from the old days of barter, and worthless without the authority of the merchants or institutions who stamped them. If a city became too crowded and faced a water or grain shortage, it could always declare all trade tokens void, forcing noncitizens to leave or starve in the streets.

It was better than the early days after the Waste had formed, when the Survivors had struggled for food and safety on the ruins of the Ancients' cities, killing any outsiders who tried to encroach on their water sources, but to Khat's mind not much better. Foreigners, even foreigners from other Fringe Cities, were still viewed with suspicion, and if you were poor you stood little chance of ever amassing enough trade tokens to buy citizenship. Or if you were krismen, and were simply not permitted to buy citizenship or special trade licenses. For any price.

"I meant the equivalent in trade tokens," Seul said.

Khat consulted Sagai, who shook his head minutely. He looked back at Seul and said, "All right. I'll guide him."

Seul nodded, his hard eyes expressionless. Perhaps he was surprised to come to an agreement so easily. "I know where you live. One of us will meet you there at sunrise." He turned back to the Patrician, spoke with him a moment, then all three retreated up the street.

Watching them go, Sagai sighed. He said, "So you've gotten yourself hired for some uncertain and suspicious purpose by an upper-tier relic dilettante. You have some clever way out of this, I assume?"

As Khat stood, the beggar woman caught the hem of his robe and said, "Tell your fortune, pretty?" Because of the cloudy film over her eyes she was nearly blind. He dug distractedly in a pocket for a halfbit trade token and dropped it onto her frayed carpet, and told Sagai, "He knows who I am, where we live. How can I refuse?"

The woman took more bone fragments from a stained cloth bag and rubbed them between her palms, preparing to drop them into her brazier. Some fortune-tellers unscrupulously used rat or lizard bone. Most bought what were supposed to be the bones of executed murderers or stillborn babies from the dealers on the Seventh Tier, but those were more often from murder victims, killed by the dealers' own bonetakers. Purists in the trade believed that only krismen bones gave a true casting of the future, and, being one of the few kris in Charisat, Khat occasionally had difficulty keeping his intact.

Sagai was capable of infinite patience. It was one of the reasons he and Khat got along together so well. Finally, Khat met his friend's skeptical eyes and said, "He wants to go there for a reason. Maybe he knows something I don't."

"Betrayal," the beggar woman whispered, startling them both. She was holding her hands in the wisps of smoke rising from the coals, the burning bones. "Betrayal of you, betrayal by you."

In the death-shadowed room the coals have already cooled, and the bones are ash.

Sagai was still registering disapproval when they reached their own court down on the Sixth Tier. It was ramshackle and poor, and its fountain was only a small basin up against one wall, but the clay-coated tin shutters on all the second- and third-story windows glowed with Sagai's colorfully painted designs, and some of the neighbors lounging around the court greeted them cheerfully.

Their house, consisting of three rooms set one atop the other and a fair share of rooftop, had been owned for a time only by the widow Netta and her two children. Netta was well able to take care of her own affairs, but a large family of cap makers from the next court had taken a fancy to the house, as well as to Netta's daughter, and had continually tried to force the widow out. She had taken in a pair of young street entertainers to help her hold on to her property, but the struggle to keep the cap makers out went on so long they had little time to practice their own livelihoods. It was not until Khat and Sagai, and Sagai's wife Miram, had moved in that the cap makers had chosen discretion as the better part of valor. Netta had boasted that all the two relic dealers had had to do was sit out on the front stoop and all enemies had fled. Khat and Sagai hadn't told her that they had also gone to the cap makers' house late one night and beaten the libido out of the three eldest brothers.

The other neighbors in the court were mostly street entertainers or peddlers who worked the fringes of the Garden Market, and it was a good arrangement, with no other relic dealers nearby to generate competition or theft.

"He could still be a Trade Inspector trying to trap you somehow," Sagai argued as they crossed the court. "That Seul fellow did offer you coin."

"Then I'll be honest," Khat answered, reaching into the door hole to pop the latch. "I'm always honest."

Sagai snorted. "No, you think you're always honest, and that is not the same thing at all."

This side of the court had been in shadow as the sun moved behind the bulk of the city, and the room would have been almost cool except for the press of bodies. The floor was covered with children of various ages: Netta's youngest, barely able to walk, Sagai and Miram's three small daughters, and the baby boy whom Sagai had vowed would be the last child born to them in Charisat. Libra and Senace, two young men who did a juggling act in the market, were sprawled on the faded matting, counting the copper bits they had been tossed that day. Copper could be weighed and exchanged for trade tokens, another way noncitizens could get around the Coin Laws.

The widow Netta sat on the narrow bench carved out of the wall, fanning herself and Miram, who was at the low table separating a tray of colored beads into individual glass bottles. The two youngest children were helping her in this task by struggling for possession of her lap. When Miram and Netta could afford to buy the metal thread they needed, they made jewelry from the supply of beads Miram had managed to bring with her from Kenniliar, and sold the product to one of their neighbors who kept a market stall.

Miram looked tired and frazzled from the children, but still smiled up at them as they came in. "Well, are we wealthy yet?" Though Miram hadn't made a serious study of the Ancients, she had picked up an interest in the subject from Sagai. Her education hadn't been nearly so extensive, but her ability to read and write Tradetongue occasionally let her do a lucrative business in reading legal documents and writing letters for their neighbors.

"No, but we're comfortable, at least for today," Sagai said, and put the result of their day's trading on the table for the others to look at. There was a small box etched with floral designs and made of *mythenin,* a hard, silvery Ancient metal that made up most of the relics found intact. There were also some pieces of smooth stone of a rich blue-green color in round settings of the same metal, that might have been anything from jewelry to pieces in some forgotten game.

Charisat's metalworkers and gemstone cutters were acknowledged as the best across the Fringe and down to the cities of the Last Sea, but even they couldn't manipulate liquid metal like the Ancients.

Khat settled on the seat next to Netta. Water jugs filled most of the cubbies, and pegs pounded into the clay-smoothed walls held the few copper cooking implements Netta owned and the oil mill and grain grinder every household needed. The position of honor on the only shelf was taken by her grandmother's copper tea decanter.

Sagai was telling the others about their adventure.

"That's worrisome," Miram said, with a critical glance at Khat. "To go into the Waste when you don't know what this person wants." She was younger than Sagai, and had come from a well-to-do family in Kenniliar who had not entirely approved her choice of a learned but poor husband. When Sagai had decided to come to Charisat, he had tried to convince her to stay behind until he returned with his fortune, or at least enough coin to buy himself a place in the Kenniliar Scholars' Guild. She hadn't taken the suggestion well at all. She didn't like Charisat, but she preferred it to living with her disapproving family in Kenniliar and wondering every day if her husband was alive or dead.

"In the Waste, that Patrician will be helpless," Khat pointed out. Miram didn't entirely approve of Sagai working the relic trade because she thought it was dangerous. Khat couldn't argue that point with her; she was perfectly right, it was dangerous. She didn't entirely approve of Khat sometimes, either, and he had to agree with her on that score, too. "I can walk out of it alive, and he can't, guards or no guards."

"His guards could shoot you," Netta pointed out helpfully. "They don't carry a gun for their own amusement."

Khat didn't answer. He knew that drawing the attention of an upper-tier citizen was not particularly good, but the last thing he wanted to do was tell them his real reason for accepting the commission.

The door flew open suddenly, and their neighbor Ris stood there, panting. The painfully thin, dark-haired boy had obviously been running. After a moment he managed to say, "Lushan's looking for you, Khat."

"Since when?"

Ris collapsed on the floor and pulled the crawling baby into his lap to tickle. "Not long after noon. I heard it from one of the fire-eaters outside the Odeon."

Netta got up to rescue the squealing child from him. "Outside the theater? I should tell your aunt."

"She knows," the boy retorted. Ris and his family lived in the next house over, and his father was a street entertainer who performed in the Garden Market. Last year a pair of drunken slummers had smashed his harmonium and therefore his livelihood. After some time, Khat had been able to repair the instrument, replacing all the fiddly bits of metal and wire by trial and error, and Sagai had polished off the job by painting the case with delicate scrollwork. Since then, Ris had carried messages and run errands for them.

"Lushan again?" Sagai said, frowning. "What can that misbegotten creature want?"

Khat leaned back against the wall and managed to look unconcerned by the news. "I'll go see him later. He could have some deals to throw our way."

"And why should he favor us?" Sagai objected, but the baby was hauling itself up on the hem of his robe, distracting him. Pulling it into his lap, he still added, "I don't trust him. But then, you can't trust anyone in our business."

Khat wished his partner hadn't phrased it quite that way.

Khat strolled down the theater street on the Fourth Tier, enjoying the retreat of the day's heat and the long twilight. Colonnades paved with colored tile sheltered peddlers and gave entrance to the shops, and the street was crowded with folk in search of an evening's entertainment. It was growing dark, and lamps enclosed in perforated bronze pots were being lit above the doors of the wealthier establishments of the goldsmiths, lapidaries, bakers, ironsmiths, and wineshops. Many of the lamps were inset with red-tinted glass, making the available light murky indeed, but hostile ghosts and air spirits were supposed to avoid red light. Gamblers hawking for games and especially fortune-tellers squatted outside the doors haloed by the muddy bloodlights, for security as much as for a way to see what they were doing.

Knowing he still had some time to waste, Khat bought a flower-shaped dumpling from a stall and sat on the steps of the Odeon, near the prostitutes who were working the theater crowd. The ebb and flow of the mass of people in the street held endless fascination.

There were robed and veiled Patrician men, Patrician women with their faces unveiled but their hair hidden under flowing silk scarves or close-fitting cloisonné caps, all with servants trailing them. Litters draped with silks and lighter gauzes carried Patricians too exalted to even walk among the throng.

The crowd from the lower tiers was less colorful but more active, some turning to climb the steps to the pillared entrance of the vast theater at Khat's back, or continuing down the street to the wine-shops and food stalls, and the ghostcallers, fakirs, and clowns performing in the open-air forums. There were wide-eyed visitors from other Fringe Cities and the ports of the Last Sea, babbling to each other in the different dialects of Menian and to everyone else in pidgin Tradetongue.

There was a shout, and one of the foreigners fought his way out of the crowd, dragging a struggling boy. *Caught a thief,* Khat thought. Then a group of men dressed in the dull red robes of Trade Inspectors poured out of a nearby shop and surrounded the pair. One of them held up what looked like a piece of scrap *mythenin,* and the boy began to yell denials. *No, caught an idiot trying to bypass the dealers and sell a relic for coins.* Khat sighed and looked away. From the boy's threadbare robe and bare feet he doubted he was a citizen. *Soon to be a dead idiot.*

The boy was a fool to be caught by such a common trick. Everyone knew that Trade Inspectors disguised themselves as foreigners and tried to buy illegal relics or offered Imperial-minted coins to dealers who did not possess the right licenses. Sagai's notion that the Patrician who had approached them was a disguised Trade Inspector wasn't just an idle suspicion.

As the others hauled their captive off, one of the Trade Inspectors stayed to scan the crowd on the steps, searching for possible accomplices or just anyone foolish enough to look guilty. Khat didn't betray any reaction besides idle curiosity, and the man turned to follow his colleagues. You couldn't be too careful, even though at the moment Khat hadn't anything as incriminating as a pottery fragment on him. The Trade Inspectors took special notice of merchants or relic dealers who were not citizens, and Khat didn't have the option of becoming one, even if he could raise the fee.

Tradition said the Ancients had made the kris to live in the Waste because they feared it would spread to the end of the world. Khat's people were born with immunities to desert poisons, with the ability to sense the direction of true north on a landscape where it was death to lose your way, and with pouches to carry babies, when humans were forced to give birth live, in mess and inconvenience. But the Ancients were dead, and their plans hadn't come to fruition. The Waste had taken much of the world, but it had stopped before the Last Sea and left the coast untouched. The kris were forced into the deep Waste, and the people of the Fringe Cities, especially the Imperial seat Charisat, plainly did not want them inside their walls.

More lamps were lit above the Odeon's doors as the natural light died, and one of the male prostitutes gently suggested that if Khat wasn't going to buy anybody he should get the hell out of there. Khat left without argument; it was dark enough now.

The great hall of the theater was huge and round, the dome ceiling high overhead a vast mosaic of some past Elector ascending to the throne. The stage was circular and in the center of the hall, with the audience a noisy flowing mob around it. Wicker couches and chairs were scattered about, and the tile floor was littered with rotting food and broken glass. The air was stifling, despite the long narrow windows just below the dome that were supposed to vent the heat. The farce being performed was an old familiar one, which was just as well because most of the audience were here to talk and throw things at the stage.

As an added distraction a fakir was performing in the crowd. He was young for the trade, but had managed to extend a rope nearly twenty feet straight up before beginning his climb.

Khat fought his way around the edge of the crowd, then was hailed by a loud group of rival relic dealers. "We heard about that little trinket you and Sagai sold Arnot today. Any more where it came from?" Danil asked. She was a lean, predatory woman who sold relics on the Fourth Tier. Her narrow eyes were artificially widened with powders of malachite and galena.

Khat leaned on the back of her chair and said, "Traded, traded to Arnot. It wouldn't be legal for me to participate in a sale."

Some of the men wore upper-tier veils, but of much cheaper gauze than real Patricians wore. Most were already drunk, and one laughed so hard at this that he rolled off his couch.

Danil's seductive smile became strained. She didn't like the others interrupting her probing. "Why are you here tonight?" she asked, a little too sharply. "Another buyer?"

She was too far off the mark for Khat to worry. He grinned down at her. "Just came to see the show, love."

He left them laughing at one another's jokes and made his way to the back wall, where an alcove hid a spiral stair used to reach the private balconies. At the top there was a service passage inside the wall, which gave the private servants and those the theater employed access to the balconies without venturing out on the open gallery reserved for wealthy patrons.

The passage was cramped and lit by oil lamps, which stunk and made it hot. Khat passed a variety of people on various errands, none of whom paid him any attention. This corridor was used by many who wanted their business kept inconspicuous. He found Lushan's balcony without difficulty, since there were two private vigils armed with iron-tipped staves standing outside the servants' door. They let him in without a word.

The round balcony was protected by a high copper-mesh screen, and the noise of the crowd rose up around it. The floor was covered by woven matting dyed brilliant colors, and a clockwork-driven fan moved back and forth on an ornate metal rack overhead, stirring the sluggish air and the incense that was thick enough to drown in. Lushan lay on a low couch, a servant girl wearing a plain undyed kaftan in kneeling attendance on him. He had thin light hair, and was dressed in a gold-embroidered mantle of dark blue that didn't hide his impressive corpulence. One of his eyes was small, alert, and greedy; the other was unfocused, staring at nothing in particular. He never wore a veil around his servants, and he never wore it in meetings with Khat. It was not a good sign.

Watching Khat thoughtfully, Lushan took a cup of delicately painted translucent ceramic from the wine set on a low alabaster table and said, "You came promptly for once, my boy. I hadn't thought you had much sense of the passage of time."

"I didn't come for your job. You know I don't do that anymore." Khat leaned back against the wall beside the door, because Lushan would go gormless if he touched anything anyway, and though he liked heights, the place gave him the unpleasant sensation of hanging in a cage over a great unfriendly mass of people. "I've got the coin you think I owe you."

Lushan's mouth set in a thin line. He put the delicate cup down on the table with an audible click. Khat winced for its sake. People who had no concern for beautiful things had no right to have them. "And how did you manage that?"

"That's not your business, is it?"

The servant refilled the wine carafe and replaced it on the table, carefully wiping it with a cloth to prevent any sweat from her fingers being transferred to Lushan. The upper-tier Patricians of Charisat were insane about touching anyone in public, as insane as they were about wearing veils or covering their hair or looking at theater through a metal screen to prevent the lower-tier crowd from accidentally seeing them. This was particularly alien to Khat, who had been a child in the kris Enclave on the Waste, where there was even less privacy than in the lower-tier courts, and you could get a thick ear for refusing to kiss the most wrinkled granny-matriarch. *As if anyone in their right mind wanted to get within touching distance of Lushan.* Khat had long known that while the wealthy broker might have as much minted gold as a Patrician, he hadn't been born one, and was only mimicking their manners. After all was said and done, Lushan was only a thief with clean hands, whose special talent was getting other people to dirty theirs for him.

"You are my business," Lushan said, his good eye cold and contemptuous. "While I found the buyers for the relics you . . . liberated from their current owners, it is you the Trade Inspectors would be most interested in. You've been very profitable to me in the past, and if you think I'll let you go so easily . . ."

"You're good with threats and promises. Don't think I haven't noticed." Khat let his eyes wander over the dome's mosaic, the view much better here than on the floor with the plebs. The border pieces were old, far older than the center with its not-terribly-inspired rendition of an Elector's ascension, and were probably scavenged from whatever structure had occupied this site before the theater. Charisat and the other Fringe Cities were depicted as islands in shallow freshwater seas, the way they had been over a thousand years ago before the Conquest of the Waste over the Land. The artist had peopled the seas with strange and colorful swimming creatures and dotted the mild blue skies with large bladderlike air bags that carried passengers in baskets slung beneath them. This section of the mosaic was undoubtedly valuable. The discoloration around the cracks told him it couldn't be removed from the wall without destroying it, which was a pity.

"If you think I'll let you go so easily, you're much mistaken," Lushan was saying. "If you don't continue with your part of our arrangement, I'll have a conversation with a certain Trade Inspector I know who will—"

"And when he hears about your part of our arrangement?" Lushan hated to be interrupted, which was why Khat did it so often.

"Foolish boy, why should he believe you?" Lushan's smile was malice itself.

"He doesn't have to believe me. But he'll have to believe the Patrician."

"Patrician?"

"The one I'm working for now." The lie grew, blossomed. "He's inherited a collection of Ancient relics, and I'm valuing it for him." When Khat was younger, he had found it difficult to get used to the idea that he could lie to city dwellers while looking straight at them, and the shifting color of his eyes would tell them nothing. Now he didn't have that problem. "I told him you wanted me to work for you, but he said—"

"What?" Lushan's voice grated.

"That I wouldn't have the time. I'd hate to have to tell him different. You know how they are."

Lushan slammed the cup down on the table, cracking it and spilling wine onto the matting. The servant girl winced. "You will tell him nothing, you bastard kris."

There was no point in staying any longer. Khat stepped over to the flimsy door in the copper screen. "I'll send someone with the coin. It may be a few days. I hope you don't need it to pay your bill here." The second cup in the set came flying at him, and he ducked out the door.

A short flight of steps led up to the brass-railed gallery running above the private balconies. The great dome curved up overhead. Below, the milling crowd was applauding the fakir, who had now climbed to the top of his magically stiffened rope and was standing on his head, supporting himself with one finger on the frayed end. Khat ran along the gallery, ignoring outcries as he was spotted by wealthy patrons in the other balconies below. He reached the first vent, which was long and only a few feet wide, starting about eight feet up the wall and ending just before the base of the dome. Khat jumped and caught the bottom of the sill, pulling himself up onto it.

The night air was wonderfully fresh after the heat inside the theater. The flat roof spread out below him, and the rise of the Third Tier was behind him, blocked by the height and breadth of the dome. There was a shout behind him, and he scrambled out of the vent and landed down on the slate-flagged roof.

He crossed the wide expanse, surefooted on the slick surface, the warm wind pulling at his clothes and hair. No one came after him. Lushan would not want to draw attention to himself by sending his vigils, and the theater owners would only care about getting the intruder off the gallery and away from the private balconies; they wouldn't be much concerned with how he left, as long as he did.

Khat reached the waist-high wall formed by the uppermost portion of the theater's pediment and leaned on it, enjoying a unique view of the street below, and thought, *I'm glad that's done.* He had been an idiot to get involved with Lushan in the first place, which Sagai and the others would certainly point out to him if they knew. But not knowing was the only protection for them, if Khat had ever been caught stealing relics from the upper tiers.

It only remained to see if the mysterious Patrician lived up to his part of the bargain. *Or if I live through it,* Khat thought.

There was an agitated stirring in the massed folk near the theater's steps, and after a moment Khat spotted the cause. Three Warders moved up the street below, cutting a path through the crowd, their brilliant white robes and veiling reflecting the flickering lamplight and drawing attention amid the bright colors of the rich and muted tones of the poor. *After Lushan, maybe, with an Imperial order of execution,* Khat thought hopefully, but the trio passed the steps of the Odeon without pausing.

Warders were the special servants of Charisat's Elector, protecting him from poisons and assassins and destroying his enemies in the other Fringe Cities. Rumor said that if someone wanted to kill the Elector, the Warders could pick the thought right out of his head. They could cloud an onlooker's eyes to hide themselves even when in plain sight, and make ordinary people see things that weren't there. Khat was not entirely sure he believed everything that was said about them, but he considered them another one of Charisat's less endearing oddities.

Before the three Warders on the street below could pass out of sight and out of mind, one of them suddenly broke away from his companions.

Startled, Khat watched the rogue Warder rush wildly across the street and seize a man out of the crowd. The Warder shook the unfortunate despite his struggles and screamed incoherently into his shocked face. The people in the street milled in confusion, half trying to escape, half trying to get closer. The Warder dragged his victim toward the colonnade, slamming him up against a pillar, his head striking the stone with a sharp crack that made Khat wince in sympathy.

The other two Warders reached the rogue one and wrestled him away from his captive, who slid limply to the pavement. Then the mad Warder tore himself free, sending one of his companions staggering.

He seemed to hesitate, standing as if paralyzed, staring down at the man who lay helpless in the street while the other Warder tried ineffectually to pull him away and the crowd stirred and muttered in fear. Then a white light suffused the ground under the limp form, and the unconscious man's clothes were in flames.

Khat felt the hair on the back of his neck rise as screams echoed up from the street. The bystanders started back in panic, and the other Warders managed to seize the mad one again. They hauled him away despite his struggles this time, and several figures leapt forward to smother the flames with their robes. Finally they were able to lift the body and carry it out of the street.

For years, Khat had heard rumors of incidents like this, but this was the first he had actually witnessed. Everyone knew the Ancients' magic made people as mad as sun-poisoned beggars, but the Warders practiced it despite the inherent danger. The street fortune-tellers, ghostcallers, fakirs, and kris shamen used only natural magics, simples and healing and divination, and even they sometimes went too far and ruined themselves; the older powers that Warders played with were far more deadly. Khat shook his head grimly and looked toward the horizon and the black still sea of the Fringe rock in the distance. *And they think the Waste is dangerous.*

Chapter Two

KHAT LEANED BACK against the low rail of the steamwagon's platform and watched the world rattle past. From horizon to horizon the Waste stretched forever, the flowing waves of tan, gold, and black rock glowing like gilded metal under the oppressive heat of the late morning sun. The weirdly shaped boulders were a sea frozen in stone that grew steadily higher as the wagon trundled along. Before they reached the Remnant the rock of the True Waste would be several times the wagon's height, riddled with chambers and canyons and tunnels and made dangerous by the predators that lived in the soft sand beneath. It was no wonder the people of the Fringe Cities thought of the Waste as a living entity, bent on eating away the last of the habitable land as it had conquered the Ancients.

Here and there the spiny tops of jumtrees were visible, waving gently in the hot wind. Their tapering trunks stretched up almost sixty feet out of the gorges or sinkholes, wherever there was a mid-level sand patch deep enough to hold their roots. They bristled with sharp thorny twigs, but the pulp inside the trunk retained large amounts of water, if you knew to cut your way in to it.

The Ancient road beneath the wagon was as straight as a carpenter's plane, cut from smooth black stone that vanished beneath the rougher rock lining the edges. The heavy iron wheels of steamwagons were already wearing ruts in it as the lighter wooden windwagons and those driven by human labor had not; soon this and the other old roads would be ruined for any kind of travel. *Then what will the silly bastards do?* Khat thought. The roads and the Remnants had been the last true works of the Ancients, completed after the seas had drained away and lakes of fire and molten rock had still dotted the Waste. There were scarcely any Ancients about now to rebuild trade roads destroyed by the Empire's own folly.

Charisat had made itself the ruling city of the Fringe by its position on the hub of twenty-seven of those Ancient trade roads, the only safe routes of travel through the Fringe of the Waste. When the other cities didn't comply with Imperial dictates, Charisat simply blocked the Last Sea grain caravans from their trade roads. Its influence didn't extend into the Low Desert, where the Ilacre Cities and other smaller dominions held sway, but the only city in the Fringe that hadn't fallen into line was Kenniliar. Kenniliar Free City had its own trade route to the Last Sea and had fought to keep it open, holding out from sheer stubbornness until Charisat had given way.

Charisat was visible in the receding distance now as a mammoth pile of rock, a massive crag out of which a city was carved, a great mass rising in eight concentric tiers to the topmost pinnacle that was the Elector's palace. Dark with black rock and mud brick on the lower levels, Charisat grew lighter as it grew taller, until the First Tier glowed white under the brilliant sun with limestone and marble. The rocky outcrops scattered nearby hid mine shafts that fed the independent forges and the huge metal works on the Seventh Tier which produced everything from copper beads to steam wagons. It might have been a city of the dead now; they were too far out to see the activity around the wagon docks at this side of the base, and the pall of coal smoke was torn away by the hot constant wind before it could dull the sky.

The stocky vigil with the red headcloth had come for Khat that morning as the krismen was sitting on the edge of the basin in the court watching the keeper count yesterday's water payment. The man was still made up as a wagon dockworker—stained shirt, battered leather leggings, and the incongruous air gun slung over one shoulder.

"The tokens," Khat had said, looking up at him.

Netta's youngest child wobbled unsteadily out of the doorway, bread and grain paste still smeared on his face, and tried to climb into Khat's lap.

The vigil smiled down at him, a false expression of good comradeship. "He says he'll pay you after."

The widow herself appeared in the doorway, saw the strange man, and reached instinctively for the stout club she always kept near to hand. Khat said, "It's all right, Netta." He lifted the squirming child out of his lap and nudged him back toward the doorway.

Netta withdrew, shooing the boy ahead of her and glaring balefully back at the vigil. Netta wasn't really a widow, though she wore the title like a badge of honor; her husband had left the city shortly before her second child was born. There was some bizarre Charisat prejudice against widows, but it was apparently nothing compared to the prejudice against women whose formal husbands abandoned them. This had made Netta almost as wary of strangers as Khat was.

To the vigil Khat said, "No, he would have sent at least half of it with you." *How else,* he thought, *can I be tricked into a false sense of security?* He also wondered who the man meant by "he," Seul or the Patrician. It was difficult to tell who was running things.

The vigil's face turned cold. "Are you calling me a liar?"

"No," Khat said, waited a beat, then added, "I just want the tokens he gave you for me."

The old fountain keeper snickered. Sagai came out and leaned in the doorway, eyeing the impasse, and said, "Just as well. Now you don't have to waste the time. There's business aplenty for us in the Arcade."

The vigil's face didn't change, but Khat could almost see the wheels turning like the works of a glass-cased clock. Finally the man said, "You mean the trade tokens." He burrowed in a pocket, came up with a handful of trade tokens, and counted them out, one by one, into Khat's outstretched palm. There were six ten-day tokens, each worth ten days of artisan's labor, the equivalent of half the amount of Imperial minted gold Seul had promised.

The vigil's face bore no ill feeling, and Khat decided, *This one's dangerous.* Khat had handed half the tokens to the fountain keeper, who counted them twice and marked them off on his tally stick. He stood to give the rest to Sagai, saying, "Find me something pretty in the Arcade."

And Sagai, never one to drop a moral lesson, had said, "It will certainly buy you a pretty funeral."

Now the sun burned into the Waste, and Khat shifted, trying for a more comfortable position, then gave it up as useless effort. The metal of the steamwagon's platform was hot, from the sun and from the boiler only a few feet away inside the housing, and the warmth was creeping unpleasantly up through the folded robe he was using as a seat cushion and the thinner fabric of his pants. He could even feel it through his boot leather. The action of the steam-driven pistons made the iron wagon shake like the world's end, and the hiss and rattle of the boiler was deafening.

The wagon was high, about twenty feet off the ground, with a platform in front for passengers and cargo, and a smaller elevated platform behind where the carter who worked the steering perched. The housing covered the boiler and the coal bin and the pistons which turned the wheels, and the aged stoker who kept the whole cumbersome thing moving. Khat would have much preferred a windwagon, which, while shaky and erratic, at least was fairly quiet.

His employer couldn't be enjoying the journey either. The heat had already driven the Patrician up onto a precarious perch on the railing. He wore faded brown robes that made him look like a poor merchant, but even in this heat he still kept his gauze veil. Khat had his sleeves rolled up; he wouldn't need the protection of his own robe until the sun was at its height.

As Khat was thoughtfully eyeing him, the Patrician's outer mantle slipped aside, and the krismen saw he was wearing a weapon. For a moment Khat thought the man had a knife in an ornate metal sheath of the kind carried by travelers from the Ilacre Cities. Then he saw it for what it was.

It was all he could do to keep his expression neutral and drag his eyes back to the road and the rocky landscape. The Patrician casually twitched his robe back up to cover the weapon. It was impossible to guess if he was aware of Khat's reaction.

The man was carrying a painrod, an Ancient relic housing what scholars believed to be a tiny arcane engine. It was a foot-long metal tube with an odd rounded lump on the end, its surface covered with etched designs or studded with semiprecious stones. The weapon was not common; most citizens of the lower tiers would have taken it for a fancy club, if they noticed it at all. As an experienced relic dealer, Khat knew better.

Painrods were not sold on the open market. The rare relics could only be legally owned by Warders. *He might be a less-than-legal col-*

lector, Khat told himself. He knew from personal experience that Patricians could get anything they wanted, in or out of Imperial law. But the man was probably a Warder. *Fine. Here I am with a Patrician wizard who earns his water doing dirty business for the Elector, and who could go mad any moment and try to kill everyone in sight.* That thought made the rising Waste rock look inviting, if not downright friendly. The smartest thing he could do now was to jump off the wagon and walk back to Charisat. Khat didn't move. He needed the rest of the promised trade tokens to pay off Lushan.

Still watching the Patrician out of the corner of his eye, he considered the painrod's price as a relic on the Silent Market and decided it was worth at least eight hundred and fifty days of artisan's labor, if not more. Khat wondered if the Patrician could be persuaded to part with it, and in the event of that unlikely occurrence, if he could take it apart without waking the tiny arcane engine that lived inside the metal body and killing himself.

The vigil who had come for Khat that morning climbed around the wagon's housing and onto the front platform. He glanced at the Patrician perched on the railing and then at Khat sprawled inelegantly in the corner. He said, "How much further?"

Khat reluctantly hauled himself up on the railing. "A few miles. You should be able to see it when—"

He was turning forward as he spoke, to point to where the Ancient Remnant would be visible above the ridges and waves of rock. Suddenly the vigil was behind him, grabbing a handful of his hair and shoving him down into the rail. Khat ignored the painful grip, too busy twining an arm around the rail to keep from going headfirst over it and under the front wheels of the wagon. The vigil said, "If you've been lying to us, kris, you'll wish . . ."

It was usually only the Patricians who assumed that lower-tier noncitizens lied out of habit; this vigil must have worked for them so long he thought like them. Khat decided to forgo the rest of his lecture. He was bent over the railing, and the vigil stood unpleasantly close. He snapped his elbow back into the man's groin. As the vigil fell away, Khat straightened up to take a seat on the rail, long legs hooking around the corner support. The vigil was doubled over on the floor of the platform, vomiting. Khat smiled at the Patrician, who had stiffened visibly, his hand resting on the painrod. The krismen said, "It's a few more miles. You'll see it as soon as we top the next rise."

The Patrician said, "I don't think that was necessary." It was the first time he had spoken, Khat realized. His voice was husky and oddly soft. Short for a Patrician and slight, and keeping to his veil despite the heat in the road's canyon. *Behaving like someone with something to hide* . . . To make him talk more, Khat nodded at the vigil, who was showing some signs of recovery. "He has a very upper-tier attitude for a dockworker, don't you think?"

The Patrician hesitated, and then the steamwagon's stoker crawled over the top of the housing to glare suspiciously down at them. A bent old man in a leather apron, he nodded at the vigil, who was still recovering on the platform floor, and said, "It's extra to clean that. Who's going to pay?"

After a moment the Patrician relaxed, dug under his mantle for a coin, and tossed it up onto the housing. The stoker collected it in disgruntled silence and withdrew.

Kythen Seul came around the housing to stare at the scene, and Khat waited, wary but outwardly at ease. But Seul only gave the Patrician a sour I-told-you-so glance.

The wagon topped the rise, and in the distance across the sea of rock was the blocky shape of the Remnant.

Another mile gone, and Khat had pulled his hood up and begun to doze. The heat of the Waste dried the eyes, tightened the skin, and seared each breath of air. It was nearing the point in the day when all rational people slept.

The Ancient Remnant had been visible for only a short time, where it stood high above the rocky sea, a giant stone block with gently sloping sides looming above the top level of the Waste. From this distance it might have been an unusually level plateau. Not so startling when compared with some of the greater flights of architectural fancy among Charisat and the other Fringe Cities, but its stark, solitary presence here was disquieting. Now they were closer, and the rock of the Waste rose high on either side of the road, blocking the view of everything but the sky, which was a blue so bright and blinding it might melt anyone who touched it.

Iron clanged like a bell as something struck the wagon. Khat opened his eyes and saw a canister roll across the platform, spitting sparks.

He was instantly on his feet and yelling a warning. Vaulting the railing, he landed hard on the smooth stone and scrambled for shelter. He reached the rubble lining the edge of the road just as another firepowder bomb landed beneath the steamwagon's wheels. The two explosions came one after the other, and Khat covered his head, trying to burrow further into the sand. Hot metal fragments peppered the ground around him; some landed on his back and he rolled over, scraping them off before they could set his clothing on fire.

The steamwagon was slumped forward, one of the front wheels blasted out from beneath it and the driving chain broken. The housing gaped open, and clouds of steam and smoke billowed out. The old stoker was sprawled unmoving on the road, his skin fire-red from the released heat of the ruptured boiler, and the carter was draped over the wheel on the crazily tilted back platform. Khat couldn't see the Patrician or his vigils anywhere.

He cursed, knotted his draping robe around his waist, and crawled back through the rock away from the road. He couldn't see the pirates, but he could hear the skitter of pebbles, loosened by feet climbing over the tops of the boulders. Belly flat to the hard-packed sand, Khat kept crawling. It was hard to say just how much trouble he was in. Pirate bands varied widely, with the less dangerous being formed of escaped criminals and the poor of the Fringe Cities. Unable to pay for water and forced out because of it, they joined the pirate bands if they survived the initial exposure to the Waste. Others were formed of people who were barely people anymore, the descendants of Survivors who had unwisely left their ruined cities after the Waste had formed. They were the most desperate and the most dangerous. They had nearly decimated the kris Enclave until all the lineages had united to drive them off, and now the pirates killed each other for food when they couldn't raid caravans on the trade roads.

But this band must be desperate indeed, to risk an attack this close to the well-patrolled outskirts of Charisat.

There was a scrabbling on the top of the boulder behind him, and he froze. A dark form leapt over the open space above and kept moving.

Khat changed his course slightly to stay parallel with the road, following it further into the Waste and away from the city, the direction the pirates were not likely to search for survivors in. Then a gap in the rocks showed him others had had the same idea.

Two forms lay sprawled in an open space between the boulders, and the ground beneath them was the loose sand of the bottom level of the Waste, dangerous with burrowing predators. The stocky vigil with the red headcloth was dead, the back of his robe rent into bloody fragments by shrapnel from the steamwagon. The other was the Patrician. He lay facedown, a crumpled bundle of cloth, but Khat could see from here that he was still breathing.

Khat pushed himself up enough to see the wreck of the steamwagon through a gap in the rock. Tattered figures swarmed over it, trying to get down into the housing and the small cargo bed beneath it but hampered by the superheated steam still escaping from the boiler. In moments they would realize the passengers had escaped and begin a search. Khat knew he should skirt around the dead and dying and keep moving, but the prospect of acquiring a painrod distracted him silly. Survival instinct warred with the thought of possessing so rare a relic, and temporarily lost. Khat started forward.

His hand was on the painrod on the Patrician's belt when movement in the corner of his eye alerted him. He turned just as a dark-clad figure knocked him backward over the corpse of the vigil. They rolled in the soft sand, struggling for the weapon.

The pirate shoved his weight down on Khat's arm, forcing the painrod toward the krismen's side. Khat twisted frantically, but the painrod grazed his ribs, and the pirate shifted his grip enough to trigger it. Khat's muscles spasmed as fire seemed to jolt through his body, and he cried out with the last breath of air in his lungs. He was helpless for an instant, unable to move, and the loss of control was terrifying. The pirate was straddling him, and he couldn't see anything of the man's face past the concealing hood and layers of dirty rags. The stinking robes were stained with old blood and sewn with whitened bone fragments and lengths of human hair, still attached to pieces of dried scalp.

A figure loomed above the pirate suddenly, wrapping a wiry forearm around his throat. The pirate gasped for the breath so suddenly cut off and fell backward. Khat dug his hands into the gravelly sand and managed to sit up, panting desperately for air. As the pirate wrenched away from the slight form of the Patrician, Khat drew the knife from his boot sheath. The pirate flung himself at him, and he slashed sideways, catching him in the throat. The pirate recoiled and collapsed, twitching helplessly, his blood staining the sand.

Khat was still trembling from reaction to the painrod. He looked around and saw the young Patrician had staggered to his feet again.

His veil had been torn loose, and he . . . *No*, he corrected himself, *she*. The idle suspicion he had felt when he heard her speak hadn't been so idle. The hair was blond and cropped close to the skull, the fashion Patrician women followed. The young features were well formed, if narrow, the eyes dusty blue and glazed with pain. Lifting a hand to her forehead, she sat down hard suddenly, and pulled her veil back over her face.

Khat cursed, bitterly angry at himself, at fate, at the world in general. It didn't help. The woman had saved his life and obviously wasn't near enough to death to make abandonment feasible. He put the painrod into a sleeve of his robe and knotted it, then stood and hauled the young Patrician unceremoniously to her feet. Half dragging, half carrying her further into the sheltering rocks, he muttered, "If you had any common courtesy you'd die now and save me this trouble."

This deep into the Waste, traveling on the bottom level would only get them attacked by one of the myriad of poisonous predators living in the sandy hollows and the shade of the rocks. Hauling the dazed and injured woman with him, Khat scrambled up a fall of tumbled stone to the midlevel, where natural trails, tunnels, and caves honeycombed the rock. Faster still would be to climb to the very top, where the stone had been mostly smoothed into gentle waves by the wind, but up there they would be seen by the pirates as soon as they climbed out of the canyon formed by the road.

It was slow going, with the woman's arm over his shoulder, supporting her weight and minding his own balance on the treacherous pathways. They were in shade much of the time, though the sun fell at irregular intervals through sinkholes and the jagged tears in the rock over their heads. Khat kept hoping she would die suddenly, releasing him of any responsibility, but she seemed to have no inclination for it.

They had reached a narrow chimney leading up to the harsh light of the top level when she wrenched back with enough force to make Khat stagger, and demanded, "Where are we going?" Either she was still trying to disguise her voice, or it was naturally deep for a woman.

Too irritated to be gentle, Khat dumped her on the rocky floor of the tunnel and said, "Where do you think?"

She had adjusted her veil to conceal everything except a pair of angry blue eyes. Controlling her temper with effort, she said, "To the Remnant?"

"Clever." The inside of the chimney was rough and easy to climb. Khat hauled himself up into it and said, "Now come on."

He reached the top, and a cautious look over the edge told him they had beaten the pirates here. Those worthies were probably still searching for wounded passengers along the fringe of the road, knowing anyone city-born would be afraid to venture into the Waste. Khat struggled out of the hole and leaned down to haul the reluctantly following young woman out.

Struggling over the edge, she pulled away from Khat's helping hand and collapsed. Then she looked up and caught her breath. The steeply sloped wall of the Ancient Remnant stretched up more than a hundred feet above them, and the Patrician simply sat and stared, arrested by the sight. The smooth walls were a warm amber-brown that seemed to glow like gold in the heat, and flat stone slabs formed the base, meeting the darker, rough-textured Waste rock only a few yards from the chimney opening. Even from this angle it was apparent that the trapezoidal shape of the huge structure was too regular to be natural, the lines too straight, the rounded corners too smooth and seamless.

Khat crossed the base to the wall of the Remnant, found the one crack that was testament to the age of the place, then counted paces to the left until he found the lip of the circle cut into the smooth brown stone. It was about a foot in diameter, set a few inches above where the wall met the base. It refused to move when he pushed on it, and he had to sit down and shove it with both feet. It shifted finally, stiffly sinking back into the stone.

The wall trembled from the motion of whatever Ancient gears and wheels worked the mechanism, and a ten-foot slab slid sluggishly back and upward, revealing a gaping doorway into the Remnant.

Something stung Khat's hand, and he slapped the little creature casually against the rock. The predator was only about the size of his palm, a jellylike sac covered with spines, deadly poisonous to anyone without a krismen's natural immunity. It had gotten him in the fleshy part of his thumb, and he pulled the stinger out with his teeth and spat it aside before getting to his feet. It would leave a reddened swollen place by morning, and the little bastard wasn't even any good to eat.

The woman was still staring at him, and at the black square of the doorway.

"You wanted to come here, didn't you?" Khat asked her acidly. The bite hadn't improved his temper.

She started, as if coming back to herself after a shock, and twisted around to scan the waves of Waste rock for the pirates. "Will they follow us?"

"Probably." Ignoring her obvious distaste, Khat hauled her to her feet again.

As they passed under the heavy square stone above the opening, she stopped again to gape. This part of the Remnant was a great hollow block, indirectly lit by a clever system of shafts and traps in the thick stone ceiling that let in air and light but kept out all but a little windblown sand. The walls and floor were flat and even, the seams of the blocks that formed them invisible. The only break to their serenity was the hollow square of another doorway in the opposite wall, which led up to the well chamber in the roof.

Khat helped the Patrician out of the doorway and across the floor, to let her down on the first step of the shallow pit. It was about three feet deep and twenty square, with a wide step of bench down to a floor as smooth and unmarked as the rest of the surfaces in the Remnant. In the center was another smaller hole, square with rounded corners, only a foot or two deep and three feet on the side, which was often used as a fire pit by explorers. By the ashes at the bottom, it had served that purpose recently, and in the far corner of the central chamber there was a pile of dried stalks of ithaca, a mid-level plant that made good firewood. Travelers, maybe even a party of krismen, had been using the place as a caravanserai. Pirates seemed to avoid the Remnants, and anyway would have left the place in a far worse state than this bone-dry cleanliness.

The stone peg near the door on this side moved more readily, but the one next to it that locked it in place was stiff with disuse. Arms aching with the effort, Khat managed to give it half a turn, and wedged a loose rock brought in from outside beneath it.

He got to his feet again and stepped back, watching the door block sink slowly into place, shutting out pirates, Waste predators, and other undesirables. The thickness of the walls kept out much of the heat, and now that the door was sealed it seemed a little cooler already.

A yelp made him turn. The Patrician had pulled up one leg of her loose trousers to see that a spidermite had wrapped itself around her calf above her low leather boot. The spidermite's body was only as large as a small coin, but its legs were thick and a good foot long. The venom numbed the bite; it had probably gotten her when she had carelessly lain half-conscious on the sand. Khat let out his breath and stepped forward, drawing his knife again.

The Patrician scrambled back and almost fell off the bench, distracted even from trying to pry the spider out of her flesh.

Khat grinned and sat on his heels to wait. "It's me or him. Take your time."

"You can get it off?" What little of her face he could see was pale, and her eyes above the veil were desperate and proud.

"Not from over here." There wasn't any hurry. The greater danger of spidermites was to unconscious or helpless victims, who could be eaten alive if the creatures were given enough time. Khat picked the dirt out from under his fingernails with the tip of the knife, whistling to himself.

"All right."

Khat started to say that was very gracious of her but was she absolutely sure, but he took pity. He stepped down onto the bench and knelt beside the Patrician, who shifted uneasily at this unwelcome proximity. Using the tip of the knife, he carefully worked it under the spidermite's body. The first pincer popped out, and a little blood welled, but the second broke off in her flesh. Khat pulled the legs free, then slapped the spider's body sharply against the bench to kill it and tossed it onto the floor of the pit. The Patrician watched it, fascinated disgust in her eyes. Khat decided to put off telling her that the spider was going to be dinner later, and pulled the broken pincer out with thumb and forefinger.

She probed the swollen, purple area of the bite and said, grudgingly, "Thank you."

"You're so very welcome. Now." Khat put the knife up, but didn't move away, as she so obviously wished he would. "Why did you want to come here?"

She hesitated, the eyes above the torn veil straying to the walls of the chamber, and didn't answer.

"You know this is the closest Ancient Remnant to Charisat. It's been gone over by experts and amateurs for decades. It's empty. Everything that could be carried off is gone. So what did you think was still here? What did you want me to look for? And more importantly, if I found it, was I going to be left alive to spread the word about it?" She had the audacity to get angry. "I wouldn't kill someone I'd hired."

"Why come to me, then? If you wanted an expert in relics, there's a dozen scholars in the Academia you could've had, if your purpose was legitimate. Why come to a lower-tier dealer, except because he's disposable?"

"I'm a Patrician. I wouldn't have to resort to that."

Her scorn was almost convincing, but Khat thought, *You're fooling yourself. If you didn't kill me, your friends would have.* He was thinking of Seul in particular. But there was no talking to some people.

He got to his feet, trying to think what she could want here. She watched him, still angry but cautious. Khat paced idly and, hoping to provoke a reaction, said, "This is only one of twenty-five Ancient Remnants in Charisat's recognized trade boundary. Sure you haven't got the wrong one?"

She looked away, but he sensed the expression under her veil was anything but bored.

"Of course, the others are just as scraped clean as this. Some are in worse condition. The door slabs don't close all the way, or the sand traps are clogged. In the one to the south the cistern's been blocked." He went to the nearest wall, and ran an appreciative hand over its cool surface. The stone had a peculiar quality, a soft, almost velvety texture. "There are shallow, possibly decorative grooves in some of these walls, especially in the well chamber. And on the floor of the well chamber there's a carved pattern—"

"A pattern?" Her voice held a spark of reluctant interest.

"A pattern of lines, or grooves, where there was inlaid metal, probably scavenged after the Survivor Time. Robelin thought it was silver from the traces left. He also thought the Remnants were built to house arcane engines, maybe as a last attempt by the Ancient Mages to hold the Waste back from the cities." There was a legend about an arcane engine the Ancients had used to keep the sea around Charisat calm, when water had covered the Waste and people had traveled on it in wooden contraptions just like the traders on the Last Sea. If the Ancient Mages had used their engines to control wind and water, it stood to reason that they would have at least attempted to use them to control the fire of the Waste. "But he never could find any real sign that there was anything here. Of course, they could have built the Remnants for that, then died before they put the engines in, but in that case you'd think—"

"You knew Scholar Robelin?"

Khat was used to being interrupted at about that point. Few people except the scholars and the die-hard collectors cared about the whys and hows; most spent their enthusiasm speculating on the amount of coin relics would fetch in the markets. "Yes. I was out here a few times with him. He used to come down to the Arcade . . ." He glanced back at the young Patrician, saw the skepticism in her eyes, and was suddenly angry. "How do you think he learned everything he knew about the Waste? Did you think he sucked it in out of the air in the Academia Garden?"

"If you expect me to believe that an Academic scholar as well-known as he was . . ." She shrugged one shoulder in disdainful comment.

Her words stung, though she couldn't know why. Khat hadn't been allowed past the inner gates of the Academia since Robelin had died. Starting toward the door to the well chamber, he said, "If you want to take a walk, you saw how I worked the door. Tell the pirates I said hello."

A square ramp with a slant a shade too steep for comfort led upward through the solid stone to the well chamber level. There were no air shafts in its steeply sloped ceiling, making it a dark, airless climb. At the end of it the antechamber was unchanged, and still as obscure as anything else in the Remnant.

It was a boxlike little room, lit by reflected sunlight through the tall square door of the well chamber. Its walls were covered with shapes, cut a hairsbreadth into the stone walls, surrounded by spirals and patterns of hairline grooves. Squares, stylized suns, triangles, abstract shapes—Khat had copied them all at one time or another, sometimes selling the drawings to scholars. They were the same shapes that decorated the walls of the antechambers of other Remnants, but arranged in an individual pattern. Whether they served, or once served, some function or were merely decorative was anyone's guess.

Past the antechamber, the well chamber was a wide bowl-shaped room, open to the hot blue sky overhead but set within a forty-foot well in the Remnant's thick stone roof that protected it from most of the windblown sand. In the center was a cistern of water five feet deep and more than half the length of the chamber. It was the theory that each Ancient Remnant had been built on an artesian water source, like the Survivor cities. The system that raised the water from the underground source to this level was as clever as the one that brought reflected sunlight through the shafts to the central room below, or the one that raised and lowered the door. The pattern Khat had told the Patrician about was between the cistern's rim and the door to the antechamber, though the general shape of it was obscured by a coating of sand and dust now. It was made up of overlapping triangles forming a roughly square shape, and was probably only decorative.

The Remnants hadn't been meant for occupation; that was made plain enough by the roads, which were built at the same time—or so the Survivors had recorded—and passed near the structures but never led directly to them. It was a practicality that made Robelin's theories about the Remnants as storehouses for arcane engines all the more believable.

Khat hopped on one foot to get his boots off, then stripped and slid into the pool. The water was warmed by the sun's passage, but still pleasant. This was all the Remnant had to offer: central chamber, ramp, antechamber, and well chamber. Khat had been on the roof of this Remnant many times, as well as several others to the east, and found them as featureless as all the other explorers had before him. If there were other chambers hidden in the thick walls, they had been hidden well.

Before Robelin died, Khat had spent long afternoons at the Academia Garden, lying on the grass and listening to the old man instruct Charisat's wealthy youth in the lore of the Ancients and occasionally interrupting him with a correction. Khat's presence had often startled the more sheltered of the students, which had amused Robelin. The scholar had shocked his colleagues when he had declared that the krismen living in the deep Waste had been studying the Ancient ruins far longer than anyone in the Fringe Cities, and were an untapped resource of potential knowledge. *And he was right,* Khat thought, floating on his back, *but even we've forgotten more than we know.*

It was frightening how knowledge slipped away. The Ancients

had left few written records and an oral tradition with as many holes as a sieve. Most of the useful texts came from the Survivor Time, and were often journals describing the almost impossible task of learning to live in the presence of the Waste and passing on the authors' fears of the unnatural powers of the Ancient Mages and their prejudice against the new race of krismen.

The Survivors had gathered on the sites of the Ancient cities, like Charisat's immense crag and Ekatu's plateau, that were above the clouds of noxious gas and pools of fire that had dotted the Waste then. They had used the ruins for shelter and lived off what was left of the cities' grain stores. Charisat's artesian spring had been near the top of the mountain, still accessible; Ekatu's wells had been buried under tons of rubble. One of the most popular Survivor texts was a description of the unearthing of those wells, written years after the event by a woman scribe who had faithfully recorded everything but her own name. The intensity of that search for water still burned from the faded pages, and in Khat's opinion anyone who could read it without breaking into a sweat simply had no finer feelings. It was copied and circulated more than any other Survivor text; even the kris Enclave, isolated from the Fringe Cities by miles of Waste and years of alienation, had six copies in its archive. The text was probably responsible for any number of young people becoming Ancient scholars. Or relic dealers.

Khat found his thoughts going back to the Patrician woman in the chamber below. *She had to have a reason for coming out here.* And for traveling unobtrusively, on a hired wagon. Obviously she could afford to travel in safety and comfort, with enough vigils to frighten off any number of pirates.

Khat slung himself out of the pool, irritated, and sat on the sun-warmed stone of the edge. From here he could look into the antechamber, and remember all the relics Robelin and other scholars had hauled out to try to fit into those shapes on the walls. Many had been the decorative *mythenin* plates found in the Ancient ruins beneath the crumbling mud-brick houses on Charisat's lower tiers. Those plates had delicate floral designs etched into them if you were lucky, and bringing them out to fit into the shapes in the antechamber's walls had been all the rage among relic collectors for a few years, but nothing had come of it. While some objects closely approximated the shapes, none really fit well into them.

Then he remembered that the only time that stubborn-as-a-stone Patrician had shown any interest was when he had mentioned the pattern in the floor of the well chamber. *That's it,* Khat thought, pounding his fist on the basin's edge.

He struggled into his clothes, a task made more difficult by the fact that he was still dripping wet, slung boots and robe over his shoulder, and started down the ramp.

Instinct warned him as he reached the door back into the central chamber, and he hesitated at the threshold, wary.

The Patrician had gotten to her feet and was limping along the far wall, running her hand over it and stopping occasionally to examine the fine stone more closely. She started when she saw Khat, and her attitude was such a mix of guilt and confidence that he was certain she had done something.

He looked down. On the floor just in the center of the doorway was a short piece of knotted cloth, probably a strip torn from her mantle. There were three knots, each slightly larger than the one before it. Kris shamen used knotted cords in simples for finding pirates or sources of underground water, and fakirs used them to make periapts against death. Warders, perhaps, used them for some other purpose.

Khat bit his lip thoughtfully and considered his options. She was young, he knew. And if she was a Warder, she hadn't been able to do anything to protect herself or her companions from the pirates. The chances were that she wasn't terribly good at being one yet, and he couldn't stand here forever. He reached down and brushed the knotted cloth out of the doorway.

Nothing happened, at least as far as he could tell. He looked up, and saw her eyes were startled. Whatever reaction she had expected, she hadn't gotten it. "What was that for?" he asked her.

She stiffened. "What do you mean?"

As an attempt to brazen the incident out it was unconvincing, and Khat lost the last of his patience. "Fine. Keep your bad granny magic to yourself if it makes you happy. But show me what you brought out here."

"What are you talking about?" she demanded, flustered enough that he knew he had guessed right.

Khat dropped the robe and his boots, and started barefoot across the chamber towards her. He said, "You brought something out here. You've got it with you now."

She backed away, wary. "I don't have anything. You're mad."

The Patrician was surprisingly strong, but still unsteady from her injuries. The brief struggle ended with her pinned to the floor. Khat ducked to avoid a desperate swing that would have hurt considerably if it had connected, and found a flat wrapped package in the inside pocket of her outer mantle. Wrestling it away from her, he rolled out of range and came to his feet, tearing the gray cloth wrapping away.

She struggled to stand, cursing him fairly well for an upper-tier woman. "And I thought you were only defending your modesty," Khat told her. Then the last concealing piece of cloth fell away from the relic, and he forgot about baiting the Patrician.

It was a thin *mythenin* plaque with some kind of crystal glass or quartz seamlessly woven into its surface in long narrow strands. The crystals sparked with color, a red sheen that came alive and brightened to sun color as he turned it in the light, then darkened to green, then blue, then near black and back to red again. The plaque itself was irregular in shape, almost but not quite square.

Khat found he had wandered across the chamber and sat down at the edge of the pit. The Patrician limped up behind him and kicked him in the back. "Ow," he protested, glancing back up at her. Fortunately she had missed the kidney, whether from design or bad aim, it was difficult to tell.

"You knocked me down." Her eyes were furious, and she was holding the disarranged veil over the lower half of her face. Awkwardly leaning over, she made a grab for the plaque.

He held it out of her reach. "You had to show it to me eventually, love, if you don't want this trip to be a waste of time. And there's some dead folk out on the road who wouldn't appreciate that."

She sat down and pulled off her veil, flinging the crumpled gauze into the pit. It drifted gently to the stone floor, a highly unsatisfactory thing to fling in anger. "If you didn't know I was a woman before, you certainly found out then," she said bitterly.

"I knew before."

Her mouth twisted wryly. "When?"

He considered saying he had known it from the first meeting in the fountain court, but if they were being honest now it would be a poor way to start. "Your voice. And I've only seen upper-tier women shave their hair like that." And when it came down to it, she made a thin, awkward sort of boy, but a slender, fine-featured woman. Her skin was light, which in a Patrician was a sure sign of a newer family,

probably Third Tier, but it was sun-darkened from time spent out-
doors.

"Why didn't you say something then?" she asked.

"Your private life isn't any of my business."

"My private life has nothing to do with it. Who would wear a veil
if they didn't have to?" She frowned and ran a hand over her blond
fuzz, as if it felt odd to have it out in the open. "How do you know
how Patrician women keep their hair?"

"I read it somewhere," Khat said, and knew he needed to change
the subject. "Who are you?"

She hesitated, biting her lip, then answered, "Elen."

Khat noticed she hadn't added her household or any other family
affiliation. "Where did you get this relic, Elen? It isn't one of the hundred and seventy-five known types."

She looked hopefully at the plaque in his hands and said, "It's an
actual relic, isn't it? Not some kind of forgery."

"No." Khat turned the plaque over again, trying to stop admiring
it long enough to examine it dispassionately. "It's not a fake. And
there hasn't been a new type of find for over twenty years." He dug in
his pocket and brought out a flea glass, a useful little device no more
than two inches long, made of two finely carved bone cylinders, each
containing a glass lens. Examining the plate through the glass, he
could make out the pattern of finely cut lines between the crystals.
"Oh, you've got something here, all right." Crystal pieces or heavy
glass tubes filled with quicksilver, especially set into *mythenin,* were
known to be remains of arcane engines, or at least the kris and the
scholars knew them to be remains of arcane engines. Khat wondered
if the Warders knew it as well.

"Does it resemble something in here, or fit into something?" Elen
asked, trying to look over his shoulder.

He looked up and waited until she met his eyes. Her mouth made
that wry twist again, and she added, "We thought it might."

Khat stood up, still holding her gaze. "Oh, it could 'fit in' to
something here. This is somebody's secret, somebody's important secret. Still say we were going to part friends when I'd done what you
wanted?"

She spread her hands apologetically. "Yes, but I didn't realize you
would understand, or know so much . . ."

Enough to be dangerous, Khat thought, and started toward the
ramp.

He reached the antechamber and stood in the center, studying the shapes cut into the walls. Elen limped up the ramp behind him and stopped in the doorway, distracted by her first sight of the well chamber. Khat stepped closer to the wall, turning the plaque over thoughtfully. The shape he had chosen looked right but . . . He pressed the *mythenin* plaque in, and it fit like a foot into an old familiar boot.

After a moment Elen shifted impatiently, and said, "Nothing happened."

"Would you have preferred an explosion? Or the Remnant gradually sinking into the sand, maybe?" Khat tried to wiggle the plaque, but it fit too well into the carved depression. And here he was without even a marked string to measure with. "You know, if you'd let me in on this secret before we left the city, I could've brought some measuring tools to see just how closely this matches. As it is, you'll be telling your friends that yes, we stuck it in there, and yes, it looked about right."

"But . . ." Elen came closer, reached up to touch the plaque carefully, investigating the fit with her fingertips. "I thought it would do something."

The idea that relics had mysterious purposes was a common misconception among those whose entire knowledge of the Ancients and the Survivor Time was acquired at the knee of their superstitious and half-mad old granny. "The highest drama in the relic market is when your competitors get fed up with your success and try to kill you," Khat told her. The Mages' arcane engines must have been hideously complex if the leftover bits that Khat had seen were any indication; they might find a crystal-inlaid plaque for each shape in the antechamber wall without having even half the pieces that made up the whole device, and still have no way to wake the thing. Still, it was an invaluable clue to the Remnant's purpose. Robelin would have danced with delight. Khat might feel like dancing himself, once the enormity of it had a chance to sink in.

After a moment's thought, he gently pressed the plaque in the center. With a bell-like tone, it obligingly popped out of the shape into his hands. "But there's no mistaking that it's meant to go there, and that still makes it a major find. You know the Academia will want to buy it. I can do a valuation for you, but an upper-tier dealer will have to confirm it since my mark on a legal document isn't worth anything." He glanced at Elen and saw that she looked more than just disappointed. She looked crushed. "What did you expect?" he asked her. "I can count the number of known arcane relics that actually do something on one set of fingers." *Painrods, for one,* he thought. She probably believed she had lost hers out in the Waste.

"I know." She was shaking her head. *She doesn't really understand,* he thought, *she just thinks she does. They all do.* Immediately proving him right, she added, "It just isn't what I thought it was."

If I was holding that much coin, I wouldn't complain. But some things were relative to your situation. "We can try it again in the morning before we leave. The sun floods this chamber then, and it may tell us something. Of course, it's probably just a decoration. From what the Ancients left behind, you'd think they never had anything but trinkets." A Warder would want to hold on to a piece of an arcane engine; a decorative plaque she might be persuaded to sell to the Academia.

"We're leaving in the morning?" She looked suspicious. "What about the pirates?"

"I'm leaving in the morning. You're welcome to stay as long as you want," Khat said, not liking to admit that in all the excitement over the relic he had forgotten the pirates.

She sighed and rubbed the bridge of her nose. "I meant that if the pirates are gone, can't we leave sooner? I know it's dangerous to travel the Waste at night, but . . ."

At night the predators and parasites that hunted the bottom level of the Waste would move up to the mid- and top levels. For someone without natural resistance to their poison, it made travel of any distance difficult if not impossible. And there were those pesky pirates to consider. Especially now that Khat knew why they had attacked the wagon. "The pirates may not be gone. They didn't get what they wanted, did they?" Khat held out the plaque to her, and after a moment, she took it.

Chapter Three

Outside, nightfall would be bringing some relief from the stifling heat of the Waste, but within the protective walls of the Remnant the only indication that the sun was setting was the gradual failure of light in the main chamber. Khat collected a bundle of the dried stalks of ithaca that had been left in the central chamber to build a small fire to see by. The air shafts in the ceiling high overhead would draw up the smoke and disperse it to the wind.

From the opposite side of the pit Elen watched him build the fire, frowning slightly. "Are there ghosts here?" she asked finally.

Khat glanced over at her. "Sometimes." The city dwellers believed the souls of the dead were drawn down through the surface of the Waste to the still-burning fire that lay just beneath. If your life had been just and modest, your soul had more weight, and sank below the seven levels of fire to the cool center of the earth where the night was eternally calm. The worst souls were the lightest of all, and they drifted above ground, still preying on others as they had when they were alive, growing more evil as they absorbed whatever filth their invisible forms passed through. These were the ones that eventually grew so strong they left the ground behind entirely, and rode the wind as air spirits.

Whatever the Ancients' opinion on the subject had been, it was now lost; the Survivors had believed their gods were dead, killed by the rise of the Waste, like the seas and the Ancients' cities. Little cults flourished throughout the Fringe Cities, worshiping any number of odd things, but most people believed only in ghosts.

It was difficult to tell what Elen thought; something had taught her to school her expression to impervious stone when she wanted to. If she was worried about ghosts, it might mean that she wasn't really a Warder, and had got the painrod some other way. Khat said, "They'll suck your life out of your body like marrow out of a cracked bone." Doubt crept into the oddly unchangeable blue of those eyes. Straight-faced, he added, "But I'm not worried, because they only like girls. Do you want half of the spidermite?"

Persistence was apparently one of her virtues. Her mouth set in a grim line, she tried again. "What about rock demons?"

"They aren't so bad, especially if you drain the blood out before you eat . . ."

"I meant, are there any around here?"

"They never come near Remnants." Khat cut the poison sacs out of the spidermite, and tossed them down into the fire. The contents turned the flames a brilliant blue for an instant. He added, "They're too afraid of the ghosts."

Elen slumped back against the stone bench, unamused. She also refused her share of the spidermite, so Khat cracked the legs open for the pulp inside, and finished it all off himself. A shaman he had known back in the Enclave had vivisected a rock demon once, and shown everyone how the creature had a rudimentary pouch and several other uncomfortable physical similarities to krismen, causing several to speculate that the Mages might have made one or two rather drastic mistakes during their experiments on the Survivors. Imparting this information to Elen could have an interesting effect, but he decided to save it for when she really annoyed him.

After that he stretched out and watched her watching him and pretending not to. He had noticed earlier that she still limped from the paralyzing venom in the spider bite, though she had cleaned away the worst of the blood and dust in the well chamber's pool. She had also wrapped the despised veil around her head in a tight cap to modestly cover her cropped hair, an odd gesture from someone who obviously didn't worry much about conventional behavior. It was a point in her favor that she had managed not to look overtly disgusted while he was eating the spidermite. City dwellers considered anything that grew or lived in the Waste to be unclean. Some extended this prohibition to include krismen, and those were the ones who tended to spit on you in the street. Some found it more to their best interest to exclude the kris from that category. Krismen and the Survivor-descended city dwellers could not breed together. Despite the scarcity of kris in Charisat, most Patricians were aware of this and of the immediate consequence to themselves, that they could take kris lovers without having to worry about any telltale babies appearing. This was especially important to Patrician women, who were expected to keep their class pure. Khat thought that having to worry about involuntarily giving birth was odd anyway. If a kris woman didn't want a baby, she simply disposed of the fertile egg sac when it came out, instead of implanting it in her own pouch or the father's or someone else's. Khat wondered if Elen knew that. Probably, but her face had a calm innocence to it that made you think she didn't know where babies came from in the first place. Such an appearance could conceivably come in quite handy to a Warder.

Surprising him, Elen said suddenly, "Your eyes really do change color. I thought that was a myth, but it's happened three times now."

Khat gave her his best bored-to-stone expression. The comment had the distinctive sound of an attempt at distraction, and reminded him she really hadn't told him anything yet. "Where did you get the relic, Elen?"

She folded her arms, stubborn. "Why do you ask all the questions?"

"So ask one of your own."

Elen watched him thoughtfully. "If you thought I was going to kill you, why did you agree to come with me?"

"Because I needed the tokens. Very badly." Khat had left his knife out after cutting up the spidermite. He angled the bone hilt so the amber bead set there would catch the firelight and turn into a living eye. It was a long, flat Kenniliar steel blade, with a gut hook just below the rounded pommel.

"And why haven't you killed me yet?" Elen asked, more softly.

"Have you given me a reason to kill you?"

"You said you needed money. The relic must be worth"—she gestured helplessly—"hundreds of . . ."

"Thousands of," Khat corrected, using a stick to poke at the fire and not looking up.

"So what stopped you?"

I'm not a murderer, I'm a relic dealer, and I'm trying to stay on the friendly side of the Trade Inspectors, Khat could've answered. *What do you think it would do to my business with the Academia if they found out I took an upper-tier client into the Waste and she was never heard from again?* But he didn't think Elen would accept that explanation. Instead, moved by curiosity, he asked, "What would you do in my place?"

She looked away. "I don't know."

Khat rolled his eyes. "The problem with this conversation is that one of us is still pretending that this isn't anything but an unusual find that's going to make someone a small hoard of coin in the relic market, and someone else is pretending that the other one really believes this. Which one are you?"

Instead of answering, Elen leaned forward and turned back the cloth on the relic. The flicker of firelight woke a hundred jewel-like colors out of it. *Beautiful,* Khat thought, then realized he had spoken aloud. She was watching him. Eyes serious, she said, "I didn't know you would feel that way about it."

Khat rolled onto his back and stretched to cover his confusion, suddenly feeling vulnerable and not sure why. He said dryly, "What a shock. It has feelings."

"And it's far too sarcastic for its own good," Elen said, with a not-quite-smile. "Why were you certain I'd kill you for knowing about the relic?"

Khat hesitated. So she had a painrod. She obviously had access to an upper-tier collection of relics. That didn't necessarily mean anything. *Now who's fooling himself?* He said simply, "You're a Warder."

Elen blinked, badly startled. She licked her lips, said, "I . . ." and stopped, unable to deny it or unwilling to lie again.

Khat sighed, and sat up on one elbow. He had been hoping she would deny it. "Next time you disguise yourself, don't carry a painrod. A professional dealer can smell a valuable relic in a high wind over a charnel heap." Here he was with a living symbol of Imperial might. All Warders had the status of the highest First Tier Patricians, but they were personally sworn to the Elector, and were supposed to carry out his will as if they had none of their own. As one, Elen might hold any number of high offices. She might be a spy, a diplomat, an assassin. What this would do to their burgeoning relationship he had no idea. He knew the Warders searched for evidence of power or talent or whatever they called it among the young of the Fringe Cities, taking those who qualified up to the First Tier of Charisat to come down robed in white. Some, it was said, never came down at all. They searched everywhere for candidates, even the lower tiers, but it wasn't any effort to guess that Elen was Patrician by birth.

"That's why you hid it?" she asked.

"Hid what?"

It was Elen's turn to study the Remnant's heavy ceiling in irritation. Finally, she said, "If I'm not mistaken, we have a truce. I would appreciate it if you could manage to remember what it was you hid sometime before we get back to the city. Or I'll be in worse trouble than I already am."

Khat stirred the ashes in the fire again, considering. If she could hear what other people were thinking, as Warders were supposed to be able to do, she would know where the painrod was by now. She still seemed awfully young to him; that might be why she hadn't used her power on the pirates. Or on him, that he knew of, except for that one abortive attempt with the simple. He asked, "What was the knotted cloth for? Was I supposed to fall over dead?"

"Hardly." She snorted and looked away, perhaps in embarrassment. "It was meant to keep you out of this room. I was sure I had it right."

"It didn't work," he pointed out.

"I'm aware of that."

Her voice was a little tight, and he decided to stop prodding on that point. He reached over and picked up the plaque again. It was difficult to resist it, the crystals winking there in the firelight. "Is this yours?"

"No. I . . . took it. I had to bring it here, to see if it really was what my master believed it to be. Someone had to, to stop them from just talking instead of doing, to make some progress." She rubbed her hands over her face and sighed. "I admit it was, well, precipitate."

"Precipitate. Impulsive. Stupid." There was an example of the difference in their station already. When Khat "took" something, everyone agreed it was stealing.

"Not stupid. Seul felt as I did, that we had to bring it out to one of the Remnants, but neither of us knew enough about them, or relics, to do more than stumble around aimlessly once we were here. I've never even been this far out into the Waste before." She stared into the fire. "It was his idea to hire you. And Jaq was my lictor. He discovered what we were doing and insisted on coming with us." She swallowed, remembering both men were dead now.

That explained Jaq's Patrician attitude. Vigils were paid guards, usually from the lower tiers, while lictors were personal retainers from the lower-ranking Patrician families. They were given to court officials by the Elector as rewards for service. It also explained Seul. *So he was a Warder too,* Khat thought. He was glad the man was dead, though he didn't intend to say so. "The pirates knew you had something worth the trouble of taking. Now, it's death for them to be caught inside Charisat, so someone had to be able to tell them where you were going with it, where to wait in ambush." Some upper-tier merchants were rumored to have contacts with pirate bands, and occasionally to bargain with them for attacks on the caravans of rivals. The attack on Elen and Seul's steamwagon could have been similarly arranged.

Elen shook her head, unwilling to concede the point. "Then why haven't they tried to get in to us? That door block isn't so thick we wouldn't hear them pounding on it."

"Maybe they've left. Maybe they'd like us to think they've left." Elen had made a fine attempt to lead the conversation away from the matter at hand. "Who knew you were coming out here with it?"

"I told you, no one."

"Who did you take it from?"

Her answer was reluctant. "My master. He . . . studies the Ancients. He wanted to bring this here to test a theory, but I knew it was too dangerous for him. I was right about that, at least. So we took it without his knowledge and came in his place."

Khat stared at her, amazed at how quickly the disaster had occurred. He knew Warders were organized into households, with the heads of each household having varying degrees of rank in the Elector's court. It was something like the way the kris Enclave was organized into lineages based on lines of descent, though there was nothing like a formal ruler in the Enclave; everything was decided by council and argument, with the oldest women having the deciding verdicts in most matters. Elen must mean the master of whatever household she came from. If the man came after her, there was a good chance he would need a scapegoat for the trouble she had caused, and she had been thoughtful enough to provide one for him by hiring a kris relic dealer. Perhaps that had been Kythen Seul's intention all along. Khat shook his head. "Elen, you don't know what you've done to me with all this."

Elen looked defensive. "With all what?"

Khat hesitated. She was leaning back against the side of the pit and hugging her knees, still flushed from the shame of admitting all the rules she had broken. Well, those rules were probably important to somebody. To Khat they had about as much weight as the rules governing a game of tables or mancala. A young woman raised on the upper tiers as a citizen of wealth and Patrician privilege and now become an apprentice Warder, and in Imperial favor. No, there was no possibility that Elen would understand. "Never mind," he said. "Never mind."

Later that night, when the fire had burned low and Elen had dropped off into an uneasy sleep, Khat went up the ramp to the well chamber. He hesitated at the entrance to let his eyes adjust. Moonglow and starlight gleaming off the still pool of the cistern were the only illumination. The chambers of the Remnant looked even more unearthly in the stillness of night; it was not surprising that most people believed them to be teeming with ghosts.

Some clever artisan had attached a metal clip to the end of the painrod, and Khat used it to hang the weapon from his belt. He hadn't had a chance to examine it closely yet.

Boots slung over his shoulder, he found the worn grooves in the wall and started to climb. He had done this before, but it wasn't easy in the dark. It was made possible only by the fact that the stone inside the grooves was rough, providing good purchase for even sweaty fingers and toes. He was biting his lip and breathing hard when his hand found the edge of the roof.

Khat lay on the flat stone for a time, resting, feeling the difference in the stone's texture, pitted lightly by however many years of blown sand. The day's leftover heat was like a warm blanket, and only faint light came from the obliquely angled openings of the air shafts. Without the interference of Charisat's eternal glow and man-made canyons, the sky was dark and gorgeous, like a dark-skinned woman wearing tiny gleaming diamonds.

He pulled his boots back on, and groped across the roof looking for the rope. His last visit had been more than a year ago, another roof exploration financed by one of Robelin's colleagues. The rope had been handy then as a second way out of the Remnant, and he had left it behind for his next trip.

He found the section of oilcloth held firmly down by piled rocks and uncovered it, getting stung in the process by a couple of wind-borne insects hiding in its folds. The rope was still coiled neatly underneath, oiled to protect it from the elements, tied to an iron spike laboriously driven into the surface of the Remnant. That had been another discovery. The other surfaces of the Remnant were impervious to any iron cutting tool; the vulnerable pitted roof was the only place where you could drive a spike in.

He uncoiled the rope to the edge of the roof, then flung it over the side. This climb was relatively easy, holding the rope and walking backwards down the steep face of the Remnant.

Khat slid down the wall to crouch at the base, just another rocky lump in the dark. The rope was invisible against the Remnant's surface, and nothing stirred. The Waste was even more like a solidified sea in the stark moon shadows, and this close the heat rising up from it was like the banked furnace of a steam engine. The smooth, flowing rock of the top level rose and fell in waves, bleached colorless, only the dark gaps of sinkholes and the jagged tears of gorges and miniature canyons that led down to the mid- and bottom levels visible.

For a long moment Khat contemplated striking off across the Waste now, going back to Charisat. But left alone, Elen would make for the trade road and be caught by the pirates long before any honest travelers or patrolling vigils wandered by. Or she would try to cross the Waste alone and die.

If she hadn't pitched herself at that pirate, you'd be meat now too, Khat reminded himself.

Yes, and if you get her out of this, maybe she'll even feel grateful enough that she won't set the Trade Inspectors on you, or have you killed for knowing about her relic. Of course, one could always make time to visit Sagai's relatives in Kenniliar Free City, out of Charisat's Imperial jurisdiction. Khat's own relatives were out in the kris Enclave and as removed from Imperial justice as made no difference, but he had no intention of going back there. Not even if his life depended on it.

After a time of sitting in the quiet he began to wonder if perhaps the pirates had gone. But then there was the sound of stone hitting stone, a clumsy step starting a minor avalanche of pebbles. No, they were still blundering about, when they should be huddled into a defensive knot on some relatively safe plateau of the top level. They must have a strong motive for moving through the midlevel after sunset, risking death from the poison of Waste predators, from the ghosts and air spirits that haunted the Waste, and from all the other lethal night hunters. Since he happened to be one of those hunters, Khat felt it was high time to start disposing of the interlopers.

Belly flat to the ground, he crawled forward across the base of the Remnant to the nearest opening, pausing occasionally to listen. He climbed down through the sinkhole, feeling for his handholds carefully. From the crevices that led to the bottom level he could hear the hiss and snap of active nocturnal predators.

Reaching the midlevel, he scrambled through a low tunnel into the twisting, turning passages, making his way in the direction of the rockfall he had heard. He reached a place where the top level had been ripped away, baring a lengthy, steep-sided gorge. The floor was sandy and marked with an occasional low ridge of creeping devil, a long tubular plant covered with sharp spines. It took root continually at one end, inching forward as the rear end shriveled and died, climbing any obstacle it encountered. Odd, but harmless, and it tended to keep away the larger belowground predators. Khat started to climb out of the narrow passage when a faint skittering of pebbles from above warned him.

A tall form in tattered robes appeared at the lip of the gorge, clambering awkwardly to keep from silhouetting itself, then sliding down the steep plain of the wall to the sandy floor. Metal glinted in the man's hand, a weapon held close to his body. He stood still, scanning the rocky walls of the gorge intently. Khat was motionless, considering how to deal with this impediment. He wanted to be able to strike fast: you had to kill pirates quickly, otherwise you might remember that they had been people once, and any hesitation could be fatal.

The pirate stepped forward and stumbled. Snarling curses in a low voice, he stamped savagely on the ground, trying to free himself from something that clung fiercely to his leg. Never one to let opportunity pass him by, Khat sprang. They struggled, and Khat caught a slash on the forearm, then drove his own knife in under the man's rib cage.

After lowering the body to the ground, Khat searched for the predator the pirate had stumbled into and found it a few feet away, scrabbling in the sand to return to its burrow. It was a bloater, a foot-wide, distended, jellylike sac with a large mouth rimmed with tiny sharp teeth. It hunted by burying itself in the sand with only the mouth exposed, waiting for other predators or someone's unwary foot to blunder in. A quick twist of his knife dispatched the creature, and he tossed it back toward the pirate's body so he wouldn't misplace it in the dark.

Khat decided he needed to see how many determined pirates were still out there. He scrambled up the face of the gorge to where he could crouch on a ledge just below its rim, then crawled along it at an angle. Occasional peeks over the edge showed him an empty landscape of silent stone and shadow. He paused once, listening to a faint wheeze-click sound that seemed to come from the folds of rock toward the road. It was an air gun's reservoir being pumped up in preparation for firing, maybe the same air gun that Elen's lictor Jaq had carried, salvaged from the wreck by the pirates. A well-made rifle could fire twenty bullets with no more sound than a sharp exhalation that would be inaudible a few feet away, though pressure in the air reservoir would drop with each shot, decreasing the range.

After Khat had gone a considerable distance along the ridge he reached a craggy area that provided some cover from anyone scouting the top level, and eased up into a crouch.

From here he could see across the slope that led down to the artificial cut of the trade road. After only a few moments' wait, he sensed movement somewhere.

Finally his eyes found them. Below and about half the distance to the road two forms crept over the top layer of rock, one behind the other. Then the one in the back disappeared, suddenly and silently, dropping through a sinkhole down into the midlevel. Khat blinked. It had been so quick even the man's companion hadn't noticed. Then a stealthy form rose out of the same sinkhole, creeping toward the second unlucky pirate. *There's someone else down there.* Another ambushed traveler, a pirate from a rival band? The silent form took the second pirate from behind. But as they struggled quietly in a flurry of robes, Khat saw three more forms closing in on the first two.

As they moved out of the shadow of an upthrust crag, moonlight glinted off knife blades and showed Khat the long, distinctive outline of a rifle barrel. Otherwise occupied, the patient pirate-eliminator below hadn't seen them.

The second struggling form slid limply to the rock, and the approaching pirate with the rifle stopped to raise it as the killer straightened up. Khat yelled, "Look out!"

Echoes distorted his voice, but the quarry dived down the sinkhole and the pirate's shot went wild, the sharp crack of the bullet striking stone reverberating off the waves and folds of rock. Khat slid back down below the level of view, quietly cursing himself. The echo would prevent the pirates from guessing the direction his shout had come from, but best to finish with this and get back to the Remnant. It was far too noisy out here for his own good, anyway.

He made his way hurriedly back along the ledge. As he climbed down to the floor of the gorge he could hear the skittering retreat of the few predators who had come out to nibble on the dead pirate. He would have to finish here and leave quickly, before the smell of so much fresh meat drew more attention than he could handle.

Sitting on his heels on the floor of the gorge, Khat knotted his robe up to make a bag and stuffed in the carcass of the bloater. Not only was he still hungry, but the stomach lining would make a water container for tomorrow's walk back to Charisat. Khat could've done the walk without water, though he wouldn't have enjoyed it, but Elen wouldn't last a mile, even traveling in the partial shade of the midlevel. Something small and overzealous struck him on the ankle and withdrew in confusion, frustrated by the thick leather of his boot.

Turning to the dead pirate, he shoved the stinking robes aside and quickly searched the body underneath. There was a knife, though its balance was far inferior to that of his own, and a pouch containing dried meat, hard little rounds of black bread, and dates. *These are wealthy pirates. First firepowder bombs, now city travel provisions. You'd think they were paid in advance.* It supported the theory that Elen's secret relic was not as secret as she had hoped. He carefully picked out the meat and tossed it onto the gorge floor, where it sank beneath the sand as soon as the belowground night hunters sensed it. With the sort of meat pirates preferred, you couldn't be too careful.

Khat tucked his finds away in his makeshift bag, then rolled the body over. Something fell out of the front of the man's robes, and he picked it up. It was another painrod.

Damn. Can't get a close look at one for years, and suddenly they're falling out of the sky. But why didn't he try to use it on me? Khat turned the weapon over, running his thumb carefully along its length in the negligible moonlight, and felt a split in the metal. *Broken.* And whatever blow had cracked the case had undoubtedly shattered the works of the tiny arcane engine inside. The weapon was still worth several hundred days on the Silent Market. *Doesn't explain how the bastard got it . . .*

He didn't hear the quiet step behind him, any more than the dead pirates had.

Something struck him low in the back, and he doubled over, dropping the dead pirate's painrod. Falling onto his side, he moaned for effect and slipped Elen's rod free of his belt. As the figure bent over him he triggered it and swept it upwards. The man staggered, but the rod didn't incapacitate him, and he caught Khat's arm and slapped the device out of his hand.

Khat twisted and punched his attacker in the midriff, momentarily freeing himself. But as he scrambled to his feet he was yanked back again from behind and a hand clapped over his mouth to silence his involuntary outcry. He bit down hard on it, swallowing a salty mouthful of blood to keep from choking himself. Ramming an elbow backward into his attacker's chest had no effect, and he took a swipe over his head, trying to find the man's eyes and encountering only a tangle of cloth and veiling. He ripped at it, hoping to blind his attacker anyway, and was suddenly lifted off his feet. Before he could brace himself he was shoved into the rocky face of the gorge, one arm twisted painfully behind his back. Whatever had him, it was far too solid to be a ghost, and it was big and very strong.

He kicked backward, striking what he hoped was a knee joint, knowing a broken arm was preferable to a slit throat. With his free hand he unobtrusively felt along the wall, searching for a loose rock, but it was solid as pavement. He cursed himself for not going for his knife in the first place. He was beginning to think that painrods were only useful for their market value, where they could be sold to other idiots who thought they gave some imaginary advantage in hand-to-hand combat.

The pain was making his eyes water, but his opponent didn't exert the final pressure that would snap the bone. The hand was removed from his mouth, the palm bleeding what looked like black fluid in the colorless moonlight. A voice close to his ear said, "You were the one who warned me."

The accent was educated, the voice deep, with an actor's gift for measured tone and timbre. It sent Khat right over the edge into homicidal fury. His own voice tight with suppressed rage, he said, "I swear I'll never do it again." His knife was still in its sheath, but he couldn't get to it without it being patently obvious what he was doing and giving away the location of the weapon.

Sounding amused, the man said, "But why did you do it?"

Khat bit his lip in frustration, then said, "Because, you bastard, I'm not a pirate." He felt unwilling sympathy for Elen; he had handled her almost this easily when he had taken the relic away from her, though he had been far less rough. *And how did he find me?* With the echoes tossing his voice around, his shouted warning could have come from anywhere.

"You don't smell like one, I'll admit. How do I know you're not a new member of their little band?"

"I'm kris; they wouldn't let me in their 'little band' even if I went mad and wanted to join."

There was a hesitation, and Khat tried to shift his weight to give himself some advantage. Then the man's free hand reached around him, felt down his chest and across his stomach. Khat swallowed an inarticulate snarl. The man was looking for the line of rough skin that marked the pouch lip, something no one but a krismen would have, unless he was a city dweller with a well-placed scar. "A little lower," he said acidly.

Finding it, the hand dropped away, and the voice said, "Pardon me, but I had to be sure. My enemies wouldn't employ a krismen. But there is this . . ."

Elen's painrod appeared in the corner of Khat's right eye. Being struck in the head with it would kill him instantly, but maybe this madman didn't know that. It certainly hadn't affected him much. Khat said, "I'm borrowing it from a friend." The hold on his arm had loosened, just a little. Perhaps just enough. And the force holding him against the rock was not quite so strong.

Amused again, the voice said, "Are you?"

As Khat drew breath to answer there was a rush of cool air directly overhead and an eerie whistling. In another instant it was gone. It was an air spirit, brushing dangerously close to them and lifted almost immediately away by a gust of wind. Khat felt the man behind him jerk in surprise. He took advantage of the instant of distraction to shove away from the wall, spinning out of the painful hold and freeing himself. He dived and rolled to put some needed distance between himself and his larger opponent, and came to his feet in a crouch with his knife ready.

The man was across the little gorge already, back by the pirate's body. He was a big, shapeless figure in dark robes, featureless at this distance. He said, "You will have to tell your friend you lost it."

"Fuck off," Khat suggested, still furious, knowing he had been intentionally released.

The other man chuckled, and disappeared back into the rocks.

Khat waited until his heart stopped pounding, afraid the blood rushing in his ears would affect his hearing. He didn't like surprises and meant to do his best to avoid another one tonight. Then he found his bag, added the pirate's broken painrod to the collection, and made for the dubious safety of the Remnant.

Chapter Four

ELEN WOKE SUDDENLY and sat bolt upright. It was a moment before she remembered where she was, that the heavy stone walls stretching up in the flickering firelight were the walls of the Remnant, that the strange shapes the flames cast against them were only shadows. She leaned back against the side of the pit, grimacing as she stretched out her injured leg. The spider bite felt as if a coal from the fire had been buried in her flesh.

Then she remembered again that Jaq and Seul were dead, and forced back the shame with a Discipline of Silence. She needed to make herself think constructively, not wallow in self-recrimination. Seul, at least, had known the danger, and it had been partly his idea to bring the relic here. But Jaq had come only out of loyalty to her, and his death was on her head alone.

A fine Warder I am, Elen thought, disgusted with herself. The strip of knotted cloth should have kept Khat from crossing the threshold back into this room. She had meant to weave a structure of avoidance into each knot, and it had worked no better than a street fakir's love simple. She sighed and rubbed her eyes. It was only fortunate that she hadn't needed it to protect herself. Or not from Khat, anyway.

She had never been that close to a krismen before. She had studied what little was known about them, as Warders were required to do. They were, after all, the creation of the Ancient Mages, though it was accepted now that they were a faulty creation. But she had never met one before.

His skin was a golden brown, and the flicker of the fire had brought red highlights out of what should have been ordinary brown hair. She had heard stories that everything about the kris altered with the sunlight, or lack of it, but the only change she had noted was in his eyes. The odd color transformations weren't too noticeable, unless you looked for them, but the canine teeth that were just a bit too pointed were a disturbing reminder of otherness, of the Waste and its intrusion into the world. And when he smiled wide enough for her to see them, she didn't think the expression was meant to be taken for a smile anymore. That hint of danger combined with a form that was all lean muscle and cheekbones the palace artists would have sighed over made an intriguing combination, despite the fact that his nose had obviously been broken at some point in his youth. One of the stories said the Mages had bred their creations for beauty, though in Khat's case it wasn't so much beauty as a very masculine sort of handsomeness. Elen sniffed disdainfully. From what she could tell, they certainly hadn't bred them for an engaging personality.

She caught herself chewing nervously on a fingernail, and winced. The worst part was that his mind was entirely closed to her. When he had been sitting across the fire from her, she had felt nothing, and she couldn't even sense his presence in the Remnant now. She had known it would be that way, of course. It was one of the reasons the Warders were so certain the Ancients' experiment had failed. If Warders couldn't sense the thoughts and emotions on the surface of the krismen's souls, then they must be without souls at all.

It's a theory, Elen decided. She wasn't sure how much credence she gave it. One of the earlier Master Warders, who had lived a few hundred years after the Survivor Time, had declared that women had no souls, because they had no power. His son, who had succeeded him and undoubtedly had his own set of grievances against the old bastard, had widened the search for female Warder candidates, and trained the first one himself. But even now Elen was the only one of her generation. She suspected it depended on the Warders who did the searching, for if they had done their job thoroughly, they would have found more female candidates.

And a day's acquaintance with Khat had increased her doubt in the theory. Anyone with quite so much . . . personality must have a soul, or some equivalent.

And where is he? Elen wondered. She had assumed he was somewhere else in the Remnant, but it felt so silent, so empty. Human souls left traces on physical objects, on the stone walls of long-used homes, on jewelry worn next to the skin. Even with her poor skill Elen could sense these faint traces, especially in the homes of Warders. But the Remnant held no traces at all, not even from her presence. It was as if that strange golden stone reflected souls as well as it shielded against the heat and light of the Waste. It made the place feel bare and isolated and, curiously, as if it were waiting for something to fill it up . . .

No, that was only her imagination at work, surely. Elen peered at the wall where the door to the ramp was, but it was lost in shadow, and her Sight was useless with the firelight blinding her. She considered searching for Khat, but the bite wound was making her leg ache all the way up to the hip, and what would she say when she found him? That she was lonely? He wasn't terribly impressed with her competence as it was.

She leaned her head back against the stone and closed her eyes, clearing her mind for one of the Disciplines to banish pain, and shutting out the aching emptiness of the Remnant.

Her brows drew together. As she focused her thoughts, she could sense something outside the thick stone walls. Something foul, like an untended sewer, like the miasma of despair and rage and desire that hung over the Eighth Tier. Like the miasma that had enveloped the trade road, just before the pirates attacked, that either she or Seul should have recognized.

Something thumped against the thick stone that closed the entrance, and Elen started. The thump was repeated, and she struggled to stand, wishing she had something to use as a crutch. Now she had to find Khat.

Too tired to make the precarious climb down into the well chamber unassisted, Khat used the rope. As he dropped the last few feet, a voice said out of the darkness, "Where were you?"

Khat spun to put his back against the wall before he realized it was Elen. Recovering his breath, he said, "You wouldn't believe what's going on out there. It's as crowded as the Arcade on Tax Day."

"That's why I was looking for you," she said, her voice sounding worried and reassuringly normal after everything else. "The pirates are trying to get in down below. They're forcing the block up."

"It's about time." Pushing off from the wall, he handed his bag to her. He had left the dead pirate's painrod on the roof, under the rope's oilcloth.

"What's in here?" Ellen had presumably opened the bag and was peering in. "Something dead," she answered herself.

This near to the door of the antechamber the walls were blocking out much of the moonlight, and Khat could see nothing more than her vague outline. He said, "The leather packet's for you."

"Um, what's in it?" Elen asked cautiously, evidently reluctant to reach into the bag.

"Dried dates and bread, courtesy of one of the pirates," Khat said. Elen could have used a stick as a torch to light her way up here. Instead she had limped up the pitch blackness of the ramp and identified Khat climbing down the rope in the deep shadow of the well chamber. *And she can see inside that sack.*

"Oh." Without having to feel around for it, Elen found the packet and freed it from the folds of the robe. "What about the pirates?"

They were walking back toward the door of the antechamber and down the ramp. Khat found his way by knowledge of the route and a natural feel for distances and where things were in the dark. Elen walked as if it was broad daylight. *So Warders can see in the dark, or at least Elen-the-Warder can.* Was that one of the mysterious abilities they were supposed to have? The maniac out on the Waste had had excellent night vision as well. He had taken Elen's painrod, but hadn't bothered to stop for the pirate's because over Khat's shoulder he had seen that hairline crack in the metal. *So maybe it's a mad Warder loose outside. There's a happy thought.* "We have to convince them there isn't any reason to loiter around here."

"Huh." Elen sounded skeptical. "You used that rope to climb down from the roof? What were you doing up there?"

"Looking around. Maybe it wasn't a good idea." He darted a sideways look at her, useless in the dark. "There's someone else out on the Waste distracting our friends. That's why they haven't tried to break in before. They must have thought we were safely penned up, then . . ." *Then I gave in to nerves and warned that bastard out there, letting them know some of us at least weren't as penned up as they liked.* "Then they saw you," Elen finished. "It doesn't matter. They would have come after us anyway."

They reached the central chamber. The fire had burned low, an orange glow in the pit. The grinding that must have woken Elen was loud to Khat's ears too, the grating protest of the block mechanism as the pirates tried to lever it up from the outside.

This Khat was prepared for. "You've got the relic with you?" Elen clutched the inside pocket of her robe protectively. "Then kick out the fire and get back up to the well chamber."

"What are you going to do?"

"We're giving them what they want. We're letting them in." He went to the door block, laid a hand on it, and could feel the faint vibrations from their efforts on the other side. They might not lift the block on their own, but they might break the hidden mechanism by trying to force it. If it broke, he knew the block would slide upward. Apparently the Ancients had meant for no faulty works to trap anyone inside.

"I think I see." Moving awkwardly, Elen scattered the coals and stamped them out. "But they're going to know we've been here from this hot ash."

"I'm not trying to convince them that we were never here, just that we're not here now."

The last sparks died, and he heard Elen's footsteps on the other side of the chamber. Khat gave her a moment or two, then kicked out the rock preventing the peg from turning and ran to the ramp, keeping one hand on the wall to guide himself.

He reached it as the block started to rise, caught up with Elen at the top. In the well chamber he held the rope steady while she climbed it, then swarmed up after her. He pulled the rope up and bundled it out of the way, motioning Elen to back away from the edge. Then he lay flat on the warm stone.

The pirates rushed into the well chamber, halting in confusion when they confronted an empty room. In the yellow light of the battered oil lamps they carried, Khat could see they were a motley assortment. Their robes were dirty and stained enough to have been looted from the dead, and he could smell the bodies underneath from up here. The Tradetongue they spoke was so pidgin it was difficult for him to understand them, but their anger and confusion were evident. One bright lad stood on the rim of the cistern and held his lamp high to look under the water, and Khat eased cautiously back from the edge to where Elen waited.

There was some arguing below in muted voices; then the light faded as someone carried the lamps back into the antechamber. Khat went to the outside edge of the Remnant above the door slab, dropping to his belly before he reached it so as not to silhouette himself against the skyline. The moonlight was bright against this side, and he easily counted nine figures crossing the base back toward the cover of the Waste. Nine. There had been at least twelve in the well chamber.

As he turned back he heard Elen's warning cry. The missing three pirates were climbing the well chamber wall to the roof.

Elen ran forward and kicked the first in the chest. The blow wasn't strong enough, and the man caught hold of her foot. Khat expected to see her tugged over the side, but instead she dropped down and used her other foot to smash the pirate solidly in the face. He released her with a strangled scream and fell backward into the well chamber.

The second had already scrambled over the edge before Khat tackled him. An elbow smashed into his face as they fell, and they rolled dangerously close to the well chamber's drop-off. The pirate made the mistake of trying to lever himself away from the edge, and Khat managed to drive his knife into the man's breastbone. The pirate flung himself away with a cry, only to fall forward, forcing the blade in deeper. Khat looked for the other one, then saw he could take the time to free his knife.

The third pirate lay sprawled on the stone moaning. He had obviously made the mistake of trying to ignore Elen and take Khat from behind. She must have struck him in some vulnerable spot in the neck or spine, Khat decided. The man barely struggled when he finished him off.

Khat glanced down into the well chamber then and saw the first pirate had tumbled backward into the cistern. Either he had hit his head on the edge or the water hadn't been deep enough to cushion his fall; he floated facedown, lifeless.

He looked for Elen then, and saw she was curled into a ball, clutching her calf where the spider had bitten her and rocking back and forth. He crouched next to her and said, "Are you all right?"

"Of course. I'm a trained infighter. I don't lie around by a fountain all day like—"

"Prove it. Stand up. Walk, or dance."

"Stop making fun of me," she snarled.

"I'm not making fun of you, you oversensitive bitch. Let me see your leg."

She pulled her pants leg up with a sob of pure frustration. He felt the area of the spider bite gently. It was swollen and hot to the touch, and he could tell it hurt her, though she wouldn't make a sound. The venom remaining in the bite had formed a lump just under the skin. To hide it, to limp around painfully, and to fight the pirates had taken substantial determination. "The poison's taking on badly. It does that to some people. Why didn't you say something?"

"There was nothing you could do. Poison is a force. I should be able to . . . purge myself of it with my power . . ."

Now she was babbling. "Know everything, don't you?" He couldn't use his knife; it would have to be cleaned in a fire after having dirty pirate blood all over it, and he didn't want to reveal their position to the rest of the world by building one up here. And there was no knowing how long they had before the other pirates returned. He would just have to do it the traditional way. He took a firm grip on the underside of her calf. "Don't scream."

Before she could react he bit through the skin over the distended lump, then pressed it to let the poison flow out. Elen did scream, but deep in her throat, without opening her mouth.

After a few moments she took a deep breath and said reproachfully, "There's blood running all down my leg."

"That's what's left of the poison, love. Don't touch it."

"You could've warned me." He snorted. She said, "All right, I would have reacted badly, I admit that, but still . . . And if they come back, how can I fight like this?"

"Try to walk on it."

She struggled upright awkwardly, and hopped on her good foot, putting her weight gingerly on the other. "It's better," she reported after a moment, sounding surprised. "Sore, but I don't feel as if I'm being stabbed every time I move."

Khat left her to recover and found his robe still on the roof where she had left it. He took out the bloater and used the knife to make a few strategic cuts, turning the thing's guts inside out and freeing the membrane. His nose was bleeding, and the cut he had taken in his earlier fight had torn open again; they were lucky to be so far above the Waste floor, where the predators would've been driven mad to reach them by the smell of blood.

"What are you doing now?" Elen hobbled over to stand next to him.

"Going to get some water."

"You can't go down there. What if they come back?"

"Can't let them trap us up here without water." In the morning, under the sun with the roof like a baking pan. "And I have to get the offal out of the cistern."

Elen couldn't argue with that. Every instinct dictated that a water supply should be preserved.

She waited on the edge for him as he hauled the dead pirate out of the cistern and filled the membrane from the opposite end. There was no sound from the Remnant's interior, but Khat resisted the urge to press his luck and check it for himself. Elen let the rope down for him, and he climbed up again without incident.

She seemed surprised by the idea of searching the two pirates' bodies, but did it with only the mild protest, "They stink." The results were disappointing; the pirates carried two long knives, but no painrods, broken or otherwise, and no other belongings. *As if they knew they might be caught or killed, and wanted to leave nothing to help us,* Khat thought. But that seemed too complex a notion for disorganized pirates.

They waited and watched and listened, and after what felt like an hour, Khat said, "A trick. They never meant the others to come back."

"Strange." Elen lay down and pillowed her head on her arm.

"And how did they know we were still up here? A lucky guess?" He was thinking aloud, and was surprised when Elen answered.

She said hesitantly, "There are ways to tell if living beings are near, and where they are, what their intentions might be . . ."

He waited for her to say more, but she was silent. He had seen her move through pitch dark as if it were broad daylight, so he supposed there might be something in what she said. "Can you do it? Can you tell me where the other pirates are?"

"No." Her voice was flat.

In a tone of false pity, he said, "Oh."

Elen's quick intake of breath suggested frustration and a bitten lip. "It wouldn't be safe for me to do so."

"I see."

"No, you do not." She sat up, wrapped her arms around her knees. "We know the Ancient Mages had power that would make Warders children in their eyes, but so little of what they knew was passed down to us. We can't make their arcane engines, or do any of the great magics they could accomplish. The farther we reach to understand, the greater the risk of damage to the soul. If I had the Ancients' skill I could make the Waste around us an image inside my head and see every spark of life in it and tell which sparks were only living creatures, which were thinking beings. But if I tried that without the right teaching it would put me one step closer to the day when inevitably my power will make me insane, and the others in my household will send me away. Do you want me to go insane?"

"If you did, how would I be able to tell?" Khat retorted, almost automatically. He knew Warders went mad, but in Elen's case it was hard to take the possibility seriously. She was so sane she was annoying.

But the maniac out on the Waste had found him in the midlevel maze quickly enough.

He could hear Elen tapping her fingers on the pitted stone of the roof. In a cold voice she said, "Might we change the subject?"

"Seeing in the dark is one of these Ancient skills?"

Khat didn't think she was going to answer, but the desire to discourse on one's favorite subject, whether the listener wanted to hear it or not, was not a fault confined to scholars and relic collectors. She relented, and said, "It's not really seeing in the dark. It's a sign of the Sight, of the ability to see with the Eye of the Mind. The Sight is what allows us to glimpse the future." She looked away toward the west and the limitless stretch of the Waste. "It's nothing special. It's the first sign of potential Warder talent."

"How do you know all this, Elen? Is there a Survivor text that talks about the Ancients' magic?" If there was one, it had been kept hidden from the Academia.

"No. All the teaching we have is passed from master to student; it's forbidden to write any of it down. Not that there's much to write down." Elen shrugged. "But the words of the Oldest Master, the Ancient Mage who Survived and taught the first Warders, were 'Man was given magic to repel the thunderbolt of what is to come.' That's reason enough for me to keep learning. He also said, 'What magic does is to open the mind to the world, and sometimes the world isn't what we think it is.' He didn't say it in quite those words, but that's what he meant. At least I think so." She sighed. "There's much that will be revealed to me later. I'm young in the ways of power, so they tell me."

There was that amorphous "they" again. They who owned the relic, who were going to be waiting for her, and possibly for him, back in the city. Khat didn't enjoy being reminded of that.

Elen asked suddenly, "Why don't you live in the Waste? Why did you come to Charisat?"

"Why are you a Warder?"

"No, I'm serious. I let you bite me in the leg; you ought to answer a simple question for me."

Khat watched a vagary of the wind sweep a curtain of sand off the far edge of the roof; it sparkled in the moonlight like gem dust, then vanished in darkness. A decade ago the Enclave had become over-crowded, and some families had moved to the caves and tunnels in the outer walls. It must have seemed like a good idea at the time; the warrens in the inner walls of the massive bowl-shaped rock forma-tion that formed the Enclave were growing cramped and unhealthy, and so many had moved to the outer perimeter that they must have felt safety in their numbers. But the pirates had been experiencing an increase in their ranks too, and when the attack came it had been swift, unexpected, and devastating. The Mages had made only forty-one original kris lineages, with forty-one lines of descent requiring careful mating practices. Bad luck, and maybe hereditary foolishness, had always kept Khat's lineage from branching often. The pirate at-tack had nearly destroyed it. He didn't mean to tell Elen any of that. He said, "If I was back at the Enclave, I'd be somebody's secondary husband with six babies to look after. And the archive manages to get a new book just about every twenty years; I couldn't stand that." Nei-ther statement was an exaggeration. Kris mated in threes, and the at-titude everyone had held toward Khat just before he left the Enclave would have kept him from being anyone's first choice. The idea that the third partner in a marriage was the one who did all the work and took all the trouble was outmoded, but Khat felt that it would have been true in his case, since anyone who took him on would have seen it only as a sacrifice and a duty to the Enclave.

He looked over at Elen. Knowing that she could probably see his expression, though her own face was unreadable in the dark, was somewhat unnerving. "So why are you a Warder?"

Her voice was matter-of-fact. "My family were Third Tier Patricians. One day when I was a little girl, the Warders came and said that I had power, that I could be one of them, and they took me away. My father was dead, and my mother didn't object. I was her fourth daughter, and she had trouble enough arranging advantageous marriages for my sisters; there's not much use for fourth daughters." Judiciously she added, "If I had to be married and have six babies I think I'd move to a foreign city, too."

Khat wasn't sure what was prompting him to attempt to lay Elen's soul bare and reveal nothing of his own in the process. Maybe he was afraid of her, even if she couldn't use her magic for dread of what it would do to her. He asked, "Do you trust me?"

A few heartbeats of silence passed. She said, "I suppose I do trust you. I've been in more compromising situations with you today than I would have ever dreamed possible, and you've never made me feel afraid."

Khat struggled to find something in that statement he could construe as an insult and failed. He started to say that her beauty left him underwhelmed, and that since he was disinclined to murder her at the end of their little adventure, rape would've been rather awkward. He reconsidered at the last moment and said, "Forgive me for not being more romantic. I'm too worried about being killed and eaten by pirates."

"They really eat people?" Elen asked, distracted. "That's not just a myth?"

"They really eat people. But to them, I'm not people."

After a moment of silence, she said, "Then we're both in the same rank. I'm a woman, so I imagine I'm not people to them either. Out here I'm just a thing to be used."

Khat glanced down at her, wondering if all women Warders were this bloody minded, or if it was just her.

The first herald of the sun's return was a gentle glow along the eastern horizon. As it rose higher, Khat knew, it would turn the top level of the Waste to molten gold, re-creating for a time how it must have appeared so long ago when it first rose up from hell to destroy the seas. But instead of morning light running like water over the ground it would have been liquid rock, killing everything in its path, forming lakes of fire, spewing gas that choked everyone it didn't burn. Or so the stories said. The stories had never said what caused it.

Elen had fallen asleep, finally, curled up in her robes like a child. The gathering heat was already spotting her forehead with perspiration. They would need to be off the roof before the sun rose much higher.

Since the pirates had never returned, Khat saw no reason not to stick to his original plan and start the walk back to the city. Once they were away from the Remnant, hypothetical pursuers would be unable to track them through the midlevel. It was what might happen after they reached Charisat that worried him.

You've gone soft, he told himself. Living in the city with Sagai and the others, relying on them, had made him weak and careless. Something made him glance away from the sunrise, and he thought he saw a puff of white smoke in the distance near the trade road. In another moment the wind brought him the smell of overheated metal and burning coal—a steamwagon. Khat leaned over and shook Elen. "Get up. More company."

She came awake all at once, alert and wide-eyed. "Where?"

"There's a steamwagon down on the road. Come on."

She followed him to the outside edge of the Remnant above the door slab, both of them crouching close to the roof to make it harder for observers to pick them out against the hazy predawn sky. From here Khat could see at least twenty figures moving openly over the top level, coming up from the road and obviously making for the Remnant.

"Oh, it's them." Elen started to stand, and he yanked her down by the edge of her robe. "They're Warders," she explained, a little breathlessly. "My master must have sent them. He must have sensed I needed help." She shook her head ruefully. "Explaining this is going to be interesting. I've caused him more trouble than I'm worth."

Khat looked back at the approaching party. None of them were robed in pure Warder white, though, like Elen, they wouldn't want to advertise their identity. He felt sweat that had little to do with the early morning heat trickling between his shoulder blades. "Are you certain?"

Elen's expression was confident, and she wasn't dreaming, or crazy. "Yes. I know it's them. It's difficult to explain, but—"

"Then explain it later." He rolled away from the edge, came to his feet, and started back to the well chamber's pit. She scrambled after him and caught up just as he tossed the rope down for her. "You'd better get to them before they tear the place apart looking for you."

Elen hesitated, watching him.

"What's wrong?" Khat asked. She could hardly help but note that he hadn't lowered the entire length of the rope, only the forty or so feet needed to reach the well chamber's floor.

Finally she said, "You don't have to run away. They won't hurt you."

Khat stared at her, incredulous. "Run away? What gave you that idea?"

"Oh, come now." Elen made an exasperated gesture. "You can't wait to bolt. You'll be gone as soon as I turn my back."

"I'm not saying that's true, but if it was, why do you care?"

"You could help us," she said, real urgency in her voice. She really believed she was telling the truth. "We need the advice of someone who has experience with the relics. When I tell you what we're up against—"

"Don't tell me anything else," Khat interrupted. "Will you just climb down and go to your friends?"

"But what will you do?"

He was running out of time, that's what he was doing. "All right. I won't leave. But I want you to go down first and tell them what happened. I wouldn't want them to overreact before you could explain what I'm doing here. Make sense?"

"Yes, but . . ."

"Just do it, Elen."

Her expression said she didn't believe him, but she seemed to realize further argument was useless. She took the rope that he held steady for her and slipped over the edge. As soon as she reached the well chamber floor and let go he dragged it back up.

Khat went back for a last quick look over the outside edge. The group had almost reached the base of the Remnant. *No leisurely walk back to Charisat today.* He was going to have to go to ground somewhere out in the Waste.

He knotted his robe up, then found the pirate's broken painrod under the oilcloth and attached it to his belt. After a moment's thought he decided to leave the water bladder. It would be cumbersome to carry, and he could live without it.

The opposite side of the Remnant showed him an empty landscape without moving figures, Warder or otherwise. He flung the rope over and started down. They would have no reason to surround the Remnant, not knowing there was a second way out.

Khat reached the ground and crossed to the edge of the base. He halted abruptly as a figure stood up from the cover of a loose tumble of rock. Khat dodged sideways and bolted for the nearest sinkhole, more than forty yards away. He knew he was running for his life now. The lip of a narrow gorge was closer, but if he chanced it and found there were no openings into the midlevel from there he would be a sitting target for them. The sinkholes always led to more passages.

He saw two, no, three more moving forms in his peripheral vision, heard a confused shout off to the right. Then someone tackled him from behind. His elbow grated painfully on the rock as he fell. A punch and a kick freed him from his attacker, who had apparently knocked the wind out of himself already, and Khat rolled to his feet. Then something struck him hard, he lost his balance, and the ground slid abruptly away beneath his feet.

Stunned, he lay sprawled on warm stone, the rocky walls around him a blurred haze. Shooting pains through his skull momentarily crowded all the thoughts out of his head. Even trying to blink the sand out of his eyes hurt terribly. He tried to push himself up and saw darkness pouring in at the edges of his vision. The ground swayed alarmingly, and his arms gave out.

It was typical. He hadn't done anything to Elen, except take her painrod, and he might have given that back if the maniac hadn't stolen it from him last night. But in rushing to their young colleague's rescue, the Warders hadn't stopped to inquire about any of that. There were footsteps and the crunch of shifting pebbles somewhere behind him. He made another attempt to lever himself up, to move, anything, but he collapsed again onto the rock.

As the steps drew closer some sense returned, and he let himself slump down onto the stone, not breathing, not moving. Just let them leave him for dead. Maybe they would be satisfied with a bloody and apparently lifeless body. He could worry about surviving the Waste later.

Then a kick to the ribs surprised a yelp out of him, and he knew they wanted more than that.

Chapter Five

$\mathcal{G}$RADUALLY DRIFTING BACK to awareness, Khat realized he lay on his side, on something soft, and he could smell sweat and a faint trace of blood. He remembered he was in trouble. Then someone touched the knot of pain at the back of his skull, and he flinched away from the contact and back into wide-awake.

Elen was leaning over him. "You look awful," she said helpfully. "Your eyes are so black I can't see the pupils. What does that mean?"

"It means I feel like hell." His voice was a dry rasp that startled him. They were in the central chamber of the Remnant, near the lip of the pit, and his own robe had been bundled up to make a pillow, somewhat easing the insistent pounding in his head. He tried to push himself up, and pain lanced down his back. He gasped, grimaced, and moved more carefully, easing away from Elen and just managing to sit up.

The door slab was open to the late morning sun and a warm wind, which had raised the normally bearable temperature of the chamber to a smothering heat. There were two men standing near the open doorway, veiled and robed in dingy white and brown, watching him suspiciously. They looked like ordinary travelers, except one had a particularly handsome air rifle slung over his shoulder. They weren't vigils; vigils didn't wear veils, even upper-tier vigils. They also usually wore leather cuirasses under their robes to guard against stabs in the back, and while some might be armed with air rifles, most had only metal staves, useful in breaking up fights outside wineshops. These men were probably lictors, like the dead man Jaq.

Moving had made Khat aware of all the other bruises and scrapes he had recently acquired. The ribs on his right side ached in a particularly painful way, and he lifted his shirt to see a large purple bruise. He had taken a kick there, he remembered. He looked warily at Elen. "I've never been beaten senseless by Warders before."

"It was the lictors Seul and the others brought. They said they thought you were one of the pirates." She had dark smudges of weariness under her eyes, and her makeshift cap was fraying apart. "I'm sorry."

It was hard to tell if she was really sorry or not; she was wearing her stone face again. Khat noted that his knife was gone, and there was nothing in the chamber around them to use as a weapon. Then what she had said penetrated, and he asked, "Seul's here? He's supposed to be dead."

"Yes. He was thrown clear in the explosion, and the pirates left him for dead. He was able to walk back along the road and reach the city. He brought the others." She turned to rummage in an oilcloth pack and pull out a pitch-coated leather water flask. "Here, try to drink some of this."

Khat accepted the water flask, sniffed it, then took a cautious sip. It was warm, but there was no taste of any of the number of opiates or essences that would have rendered him more amenable to persuasion. It reminded him that his stomach was mostly empty, but in his present condition that was probably a good thing.

Elen was watching him gravely. He touched his face carefully, investigating the swelling along his jaw, wondering how best to talk his way out. "Elen, what's the point of this? I know you have the relic. So? There are valuable relics all over the upper tiers. I don't know anything that can hurt you."

An unreadable expression crossed Elen's face. She put the stopper on the flask and set it aside. "When you said you expected me to have you killed just because I was a Warder, you weren't exaggerating, were you?"

He wasn't sure what to make of that, and fell back on an honest answer. "No, I wasn't."

Something flickered in her eyes, and with an air of weary resignation she said, "No one is going to kill you, or hand you over to the Trade Inspectors, or whatever else you're worried about. My master only wants to talk to you."

That was hardly reassuring, but it did explain why they simply hadn't put him out of his misery immediately. "Talk about what?"

"The relic, of course. What else? You've been going on about it as if it's the discovery of the age."

"Oh, that." If not the discovery of the age it was at least the discovery of the decade, or it would be to the Ancient scholars in the Academia. If they ever got to hear of it. Khat discounted Elen's reassurances automatically. If she hadn't been able to stop the lictors from indulging themselves during his capture, she wouldn't be able to stop her master from disposing of him once he had what he wanted. *Whatever that is,* Khat thought.

A shadow crossed the light as a man stepped through the entrance of the Remnant. As he came toward them Khat's shoulders stiffened with tension. Kythen Seul hadn't bothered to pull his veil into place, not out here where there were only lictors, other Warders, and people of no consequence to see. He wasn't dressed as a Warder, either, wearing a brown outer robe over white, but there was a painrod swinging from his belt. Seul said, "Elen, I told you not to get near him."

"It's a bit late for that, Kythen," Elen said without glancing up.

Seul looked at her sharply. Khat winced and wished he could knock Elen's thick little skull against the nearest wall. He wondered if she had any idea what the penalty for rape of a Patrician woman was, or that her overeager relatives might not believe her when she told them nothing had happened. Possibly she was so poor at lying that the possibility of the truth not being believed had never entered her mind. "He saved my life," Elen continued, oblivious. "I told you that."

The Warder didn't appear pleased to hear Elen defend Khat. Because there was no point in behaving as pathetically trapped as he felt, Khat smiled up at Seul and asked, "Jealous?"

This did not make Seul happy either. He gestured to the two lictors waiting across the room, and they came instantly to stand at his side. He said to Khat, "He will speak to you now, and you will keep your insolence to yourself."

Khat thought that what Seul wanted was exactly the opposite, so there would be an excuse for another beating. He stood up, and the edges of his vision went black, then gradually cleared. Seul watched his unsteadiness with a tight-lipped smile, then started back to the door. With the two lictors closing in around him, Khat went without further comment. He noticed that Elen's limp was better.

Outside on the base of the Remnant the sun was too bright, searing into the dark stone and making the lighter glow gold. The sky was burning blue and cloudless.

More lictors were waiting there, headcloths pulled forward to shield their eyes from the glare, air rifles held ready. There were more Warders standing with them, recognizable by the painrods at their belts.

Seul led the way through the lictors. Their stares were curious or hostile, as if they had never seen a live krismen before, and perhaps they hadn't. Khat had never seen this many representatives of Imperial justice at one time before, and being surrounded by them was not pleasant. As he and Elen passed through them Khat heard a low-voiced mutter, the one distinguishable word being "feral." He doubted the speaker was referring to Elen.

An old man stood at the fringe of the Waste rock, using a small brass distance-glass to look up at the top edge of the Remnant's outer wall. He wore plain robes, but no weapons, and no veil. His skin was a dark honey brown, lined and seamed, and grizzled white hair was tied back from his face. He lowered the glass as they approached; his eyes were a washed-out blue and hard to read.

Elen went up to him, pulling the relic out of her robe. The cloth wrapping slipped a little as she held it out to him, and the crystal sparked with color. She said simply, "You were right."

He reached out to touch the relic but hesitated, his fingers a few inches away. "Where?" he asked, eyes intent.

Elen looked back at Khat. "He knows."

There went any hope of pretending ignorance. Khat squinted up at the sky to accustom his eyes to the glare and said, "The antechamber, right wall from the ramp, third shape up and fourth from the corner."

"It fits precisely?" The old man was looking at him now. Khat did not feel reassured. He had seen buyers who were fanatical about relics, who worshiped the Ancients as gods almost, and it hadn't occurred to him that Elen's master might be such a man. He said, "As far as I could tell."

"Show me."

That was the signal to troop back inside, the old man leading the way. Khat was glad to see that most of the others remained behind, apparently to guard the Remnant's door. Only Elen, Kythen Seul, another young Warder, and three of the lictors followed. The lictors were right behind Khat on the way up the ramp, as if they were hoping he would take advantage of the comparatively cramped passageway to attack someone. The angle of the ramp seemed to make the krismen's headache worse, and he kept one hand on the smooth wall to steady himself.

In the antechamber the old man handed Elen the relic, and she found the correct shape and pressed the *mythenin* plaque into it. The old man stepped up and ran his fingers lightly over the metal where it met the stone, and said, "Yes, it's perfect." He looked back at Khat. "Well done."

Khat managed to keep his expression neutral. *You're very welcome,* he thought, *but it's not as if I invented the damn thing.*

"I am also grateful to you for saving Elen's life."

That he couldn't let go by. "You have an odd way of demonstrating it. If you were any more grateful, I'd be dead."

Startled, the old man smiled. "A mistake only. My men didn't know who you were."

The apology was too easy; it might be sincere, but the man obviously didn't think much of a kris getting knocked around, and he probably couldn't see why Khat should either. Before Khat could say anything else, Kythen Seul interrupted. "There's something you should know." He stepped forward and held out a painrod. "He also stole this from her."

Elen stared at the evidence in alarm, then blinked and took the weapon for a closer look. "This isn't mine. It's smaller, and the pattern on the metal is different, and look, the case is broken." Surprised, she glanced up at Khat, who raised an eyebrow at her. It was, of course, the wrong painrod; Elen's was long gone with the madman last night.

"Where did you get this?" the old man asked him, bemused.

"One of the pirates had it."

Seul did not appear happy with this revelation. With a faint smile the old Warder took the damaged weapon and handed it to one of the lictors. Then he popped the relic out of the wall and returned it to Elen. "I am Sonet Riathen, Master Warder. I have something else I would like you to look at for me."

Khat's throat was suddenly dry. This wasn't just any powerful Warder. The Master Warder was the one who sat at the Elector's right hand, who spoke for all Warders, who was leader of them all. *You're dead and you just don't know to lie down for it yet,* Khat told himself. *But why is he bothering to play with me, as if he means to let me go?* That thought felt suspiciously like hope, and he squelched it firmly. If the old man wanted to pretend both of them were going to walk away from this, it was probably from pure sadism.

Riathen was moving out into the well chamber and the better light, the others following him. One of the lictors gave Khat a not un-gentle push to get him started, and he trailed after.

Riathen pulled his outer robe off one shoulder to free a satchel slung under it. Opening it, he took out a flat, thick leather case. He held it out to Khat, saying, "This book. It is purported to be almost a thousand years old, written by one of the Survivors only a few years after the Waste rose. Is it a forgery?"

Interested in spite of everything, Khat wiped his sweaty palms off on his shirt before taking the book. The leather case enclosing it had been softened to the texture of fragile human skin by time and much handling, but it was nowhere near a thousand years old. The bronze fastening had broken some time ago, and Khat eased it open and carefully drew the book out. The leather cover of the text itself was more promising; it was as brittle as badly mixed glass and cracked even under his careful touch. A design was cut into it, a circular pattern of lines burnished with faded gold leaf. That matched the few other Survivor texts Khat had seen, many of which were badly damaged or incomplete and were kept closely guarded by private collectors or the Academia. What little knowledge the scholars had of the Ancients had come from those texts. There were also hundreds, perhaps thousands of copies and forgeries of Survivor texts circulating through the markets of the Fringe Cities.

The design and the aging of the leather was the easiest part to counterfeit. The original ribbon-ties that had bound the compact mass of yellowed paper had long ago crumbled away, and new ones had been added, probably at about the same time the outer case had been replaced. The new ones were red and not much faded, possibly a sign the book hadn't been removed from the case overmuch. That boded well for its condition and its authenticity. A forger would have felt compelled to add faded or broken ties. Khat felt for his flea glass for a moment and realized it was gone. The lictors had probably stolen it.

He undid the ties carefully, then sat on his heels to lay the book facedown on the smooth stone and unfold it from the back. Someone started to make an objection, was instantly silenced by someone else. Khat ignored both. The first page had completely captured his attention. The book was written in Ancient Script.

Most Survivor texts were written in Old Menian, which scholars knew had been the common language of the vast area where the Waste and the Fringes now lay. Each Fringe City had made it its own during the years of isolation in the Survivor Time, corrupting the original into entirely different dialects. Tradetongue was a mix and match of those new dialects, and if you could read it and didn't lack for imagination, you had more than a sporting chance of being able to read Old Menian, too. Khat had less trouble with it than most, because the Enclave's version of Old Menian was so close to the original as to make no difference at all. The areas of the Last Sea coast and the islands spoke several entirely different languages that had undergone little change since the Waste formed, though so few Survivor texts were found in them, they were scarcely worth learning. But Ancient Script was something else.

Robelin had believed it to be a language not in common use even in Ancient times, something for scholars and law courts and maybe for Mages. There was a passing resemblance to Old Menian, but it was there mainly to confuse the unwary. Each word had three to four different meanings, depending on the context, making it an economical script and difficult to decipher. The few texts that were written in it were the oldest ever found, and in such poor condition they were barely readable.

Unfolding the book took time. Khat paid special attention to the color of the paper inside the fanfold creases, to the places where the weakened paper had torn or crumbled, to the musty sweet smell of the aging inks. He tasted tiny fragments of several different sections, to make sure no new pulp had been mixed in with the old paper. He read enough to make sure the words flowed alternately left to right and right to left, as Ancient Script should, and checked that all the numbers he could find were in the old reckoning as well. Forgetting to translate the numbers was one of the commonest mistakes found in otherwise superb forgeries.

This was not a superb forgery. It was a superb original. Almost from the first touch he knew what he handled here was a jewel beyond price.

Khat looked up finally, and was a little startled to find that his back ached from bending over and the shadows had lengthened. The lictors and the other Warder were leaning on the walls, and Elen was sitting on the edge of the cistern, Seul next to her. Riathen hadn't moved. Khat said, "It's genuine Survivor work." He took a deep breath, and wished he was telling this to anyone but these Warders, who had no need for coin and, as far as he could tell, little reverence for unique relics. "It's in Ancient Script, so the text itself may be even older than Survivor." No reaction; he might have been speaking to statues. He tried again. "This isn't just a better copy of a book the Academia already has. It's new."

"Can you read the old script?" Riathen asked, his face expressionless.

"I can only pick out a few words, and the numbers. But I can tell from the engravings it's original," Khat lied on impulse, and the back of his neck prickled. He had suspected the book was an entirely new find the moment he had deciphered the title, and confirmed it with a brief examination of the text. Elen knew enough about him to doubt that statement, and he waited for her to contradict him, but she remained silent. "You'll have to show it to someone else if you want it translated," he added cautiously.

"No need, I've read it." Riathen smoothed the front of his robe in a preoccupied way, and Khat thought the old man looked relieved.

But Kythen Seul shook his head and sighed in a long-suffering way that seemed to invite attack with some sort of blunt club. "How do you know he's telling the truth, Riathen?" he said.

Khat sat back wearily and rested his arms on his knees. His head was pounding, he hurt all over, and he was doing valuable work under duress that he wasn't getting paid for, and Seul seemed to think the Warders were the aggrieved party. "Take it to another dealer. Of course, you might have to pay him."

Elen's lips twitched in a smile. Khat pretended not to see it.

"Why did you taste the paper?" Riathen asked.

Khat looked away, suddenly self-conscious under that steady regard. "New paper isn't as tart. They rinse the pulp more often now."

Riathen stepped forward finally and leaned down to move one of the book's folds, so gently Khat didn't feel the need to wince. He could make a good guess as to who had handled the book so carefully that it was still in such good condition. Riathen treated it with respect for its age and delicacy, but if he had been a true collector, his hand would have trembled to touch it. The old man said, "I am searching for two more relics similar to those in this drawing. Have you ever seen their like before?"

Engraving, Khat thought. *Not drawing.* The inks had faded on this page, and he had to peer at it closely. One of the figures appeared to be the plaque Elen had stolen. The shape was right, and the artist had been careful to show the ripples of different colors playing across its surface and the lines of crystal. Next to the plaque was an oval shape, faceted, with the stylized design of a winged figure embossed or inscribed into the center. That was distinctive. Ancient depictions of birds were rare, and valuable.

The third piece was a large square block covered with what might be random line patterns or Ancient Script, indiscernible in the faded ink. Near the three figures in neat lettering were the dimensions of each, and the word *mythenin,* which seemed meant to indicate the material they were made of. Khat's brows rose as he converted the numbers, and he did it twice more to make sure he hadn't erred.

The oval faceted piece wasn't unusual in size. It was small enough to fit into his palm. The square block was four feet long and two feet high. It wasn't a known type, but its presence in the Survivor-era book and the *mythenin* comment seemed to indicate that it might be Ancient as well. "This oval is a common type, except for that crest or incision in the center—that makes it valuable. This other, I don't know. Something that size would cause a sensation in the market. Unless the figures here are wrong."

"The figures are accurate."

Khat didn't bother to argue. He had never been able to fathom why people assumed the scribes who had laboriously copied out these texts were infallible simply because they were decades dead.

"I know these relics are somewhere in Charisat," Riathen said. "What would your price be for locating them?"

Khat went blank. He looked over at Elen, back at Riathen. "What would my price be if I didn't locate them?"

Serious, Riathen said, "I assume you're asking about the consequences of failure. I would ask that you keep silent about your dealings with us, but I also understand that that is a usual feature of this sort of arrangement." He shrugged. "You would simply have to trust me, as I would have to trust you."

Khat had difficulty getting his thoughts around the whole idea. Being able to locate relics for them seemed to imply that he wouldn't be dead or in prison in the near future. "I want the rest of what Elen said she'd pay me, plus . . ." No good asking for a percentage of the sale; he was reasonably sure the old man didn't want these to resell at a profit. "Plus two hundred-day tokens for each find, if they're comparable in value to the one I've already seen."

"That's seems fair." Riathen smiled again, and Khat knew the price was probably ridiculously low to him. But it *was* fair, and it would be a fortune down on the Sixth Tier.

Looking up at Riathen, Khat suddenly realized there was someone standing behind the old man in the darker well of the antechamber.

Khat blinked, thinking he had been deceived by the dust in the air or the reflected glare of the water in the cistern. The man standing beneath the arch of the antechamber wore threadbare black, the skirts of his robe girded up above tightly bound leather boots suitable for traipsing the Waste. He was tall for a city dweller, taller than Khat even, and broad in the shoulders, though the hair under his dark headcloth was whitened by the sun and by age. Condemned criminals were made to wear black, and it wasn't odd to see robes of that color out in the Waste, but a painrod hung from his wide leather belt, so he must be a Warder. Khat decided he must be more off-balance than he had first thought, to have missed this apparition waiting with the other Warders outside.

Then he met the man's eyes, pale, amused, and utterly mad.

Khat started to fold up the book automatically, without any thought but that it was better out of the scuffle that was sure to occur.

Sonet Riathen followed his gaze, and the reaction was amazing. Kythen Seul came to his feet, snapping the painrod off his own belt. One of the lictors brought his air rifle up as if to fire, but the other Warder grabbed the barrel to stop him.

Riathen held up one hand to restrain them. Theatrical, Khat

thought, and saw that thought reflected in the eyes of the intruder. Only Elen hadn't moved, sitting where she was bolt upright on the edge of the cistern.

Riathen's face was grim, as if he faced a threat too much for even a Master Warder. Softly, he said, "What do you want here, Constans?"

"I wanted to see what you wanted here. Surely you didn't think your exodus would go unnoticed?"

Khat recognized that voice. *But you were here long before the First Tier delegation arrived.* The man's size seemed right, from what little he had been able to guess last night. Khat tucked the folded book carefully back into its case, keeping his eyes on it, trying to look like no one of particular importance.

"To carry the tale back to your master?" It would have been a sneer, if Riathen hadn't been too well bred for such things.

"Our master." The answer was gentle mockery.

"How did you get past my men below?"

"Easily. They're all dead."

Khat looked up, startled. The others were held immobile in an instant of shock. Then he saw the faint smile, and the man Riathen had called Constans said, "No, I left them alive, unfortunately, to plot more treason."

Riathen's brows drew together. "Nothing I do here is treason."

"I prefer not to debate the point. You know politics has no interest for me." Constans looked down at Khat, who was still holding the book and felt he had failed in his attempt to remain inconspicuous. "That must be the brilliant addition to your collection that I have heard so much about. Or was it meant to be a secret?"

Khat said nothing under that calm, amused gaze, thinking, *He knows that was me last night, that I know he followed Elen out here, and not Riathen.* He felt himself being drawn into a conspiracy he wanted no part of.

Riathen's lips thinned. "No secret," he said, with a smile that acknowledged the lie even as he spoke it. "My students wished to study the past. I brought it out here so they could see it in its context."

Not in context, Khat thought, irritated. There was no evidence that the Survivors ever took shelter in the Remnants.

"Then there would be no objection to my examining the book," Constans said, all sweet reason.

"It is far too valuable to allow casual handling."

One of the lictors leapt forward suddenly, raising his rifle like a club. He was less than a step away from Constans when he staggered backward as if he had been struck a heavy blow. The rifle clattered to the stone floor, and the lictor's face turned pale, then past fear-pale to death-pale. He collapsed with a sickening thump, and everyone started back. Everyone except Riathen, Elen, who dug fingers into the well's rim, and Constans, who regarded Riathen without rancor or apology and explained, "He startled me."

The Master Warder didn't answer, but his eyes were furious.

The lictor's corpse looked as if it had been sun-dried three days, the skin of the face as stiff and brittle as old parchment, and the others stared down at it in shock. Khat felt the warm stone of the well's basin grate against his back and realized he was still pressing against it in an effort to put as much distance between himself and Constans as possible. He made himself relax, thinking, *Warder magic, and he's mad already, so he's not reluctant to use it.* No knotted cords, no arcane engines, just a moment of thought and a man lay dead on the Remnant's ancient stone. Khat realized he was still the one holding the damn book.

Riathen found his voice. "If you have no better control than that . . ." he began bitterly.

Riathen's anger seemed to annoy Constans more than the lictor's attack had. He said, "I'm running out of patience, Sonet, and can stay no longer to admire your first adventure into subtlety. Give me the book."

The Master Warder hesitated, then looked down at the fragile leather case in Khat's hands. Khat had made an agreement with the Master Warder, so in a way he had already chosen sides. He stood as if he meant to hand it to Riathen, then leaned back on the cistern's edge and held the book over the water. "Come and take it," he said, his voice even.

The old ink would dissolve, the paper turn into a sodden lump. Elen was staring at him with wild hope. He saw why she hadn't moved. She still held the colored crystal relic, and had simply flipped a corner of her mantle over it where it lay in her lap.

Into the silence the mad Warder asked, "Would you really do that, to an item worth how many thousands of Imperial coins?" He seemed more curious than anything else, those pale eyes thoughtful and confident.

"It's not my book," Khat answered. He would rather have dropped himself off the top of the Remnant. Destroying any relic went against all his instincts, and the thought of destroying an original Survivor text of this quality was like a crime against nature. But he was holding it out over the water at an awkward angle, and if the man struck him dead, or even leapt at him, he could hardly help but drop it.

"Stalemate, then. For the moment," Constans said, looking to Riathen. He seemed more amused than angry now, but Khat didn't feel that was a particularly encouraging sign.

"For the moment," Riathen agreed, nodding cautiously.

Constans turned back to the ramp down to the central chamber, seeming almost to meld with the shadows there, and vanished.

After a moment of tense silence, Riathen said, "Follow him, Gandin. But not too closely. Only make certain he is really gone."

The other Warder nodded an acknowledgment and slipped after Constans, and Khat hugged the book to his chest. His arm had been getting tired. Seul went to kneel at the side of the dead lictor.

"It was my fault," Elen said miserably, watching him. "I called attention to us by coming here."

"No, he knew enough already." Riathen shook his head, absolving her of responsibility. "You merely gave him an opportunity to force a confrontation. And he has told us something else." He nodded at Khat, who was still leaning on the edge of the cistern. "He could have forced you to destroy it, but he did not. He wants it intact, for himself."

Shaking his head, Seul rose and muttered, "I didn't realize how powerful he was."

Gandin came back up the ramp and reported breathlessly, "He's gone, as far as I can tell. I lost him at the door of the Remnant. And none of the others were harmed. They didn't even know he was here." He was a young man under his loose veil, and the hair escaping from his headcloth was as blond as Elen's.

Seul glanced at Khat, then asked Riathen, "If he had dropped the book, what would have happened?"

Riathen rubbed his forehead, looking like any other old man who had had a trying day. Khat almost liked him for a moment. The Master Warder said, "Constans might have simply bowed to the inevitable and left, or . . ."

He hesitated and Khat supplied, "Or killed all of us in a fit of pique."

"There was that possibility," Riathen admitted ruefully. "You've fallen in with dangerous companions, I'm afraid."

Khat handed him the book, thinking of all the things Riathen didn't know. "Well," he told him, "so have you."

The sun flooded the Waste with red light, the dust in the evening air adding the colors of gold, orange, and amber, as the Warders' large steamwagon rattled and clanked and shook its way back to Charisat. Watching the sunset, Khat thought of the cult in Kenniliar Free City that worshiped the sun's nightly descent as a ritual death by wearing red mourning robes and holding an elaborate funeral every evening. He supposed he could understand their need to somehow mark the passage of beauty, and it did give them something to do.

Elen leaned next to him on the railing of the wagon's back platform, the lictors ranged around, watchful for pirates and other dangers in the fading light. Seul and the other Warders were up at the front or on top of the housing, except for Gandin, who stood against the railing near Khat and Elen. The body of the dead lictor had been wrapped in its own mantle and laid inside the housing. It had surprised Khat a little that they had bothered. He hadn't expected either Patricians or Warders to have so much care for the corpses of their servants. But no one had spoken of the man who had killed him. "Who is Constans, Elen?" he asked, just loud enough to be heard over the wagon's rattle.

The wind whipped her man's robes around her, and her lips were set grimly. "A madman," she said.

"Besides that."

"His name is Aristai Constans." Riathen's voice answered from the vicinity of the housing behind them, and Khat managed not to start too obviously; he hadn't known the old man was back there. Riathen continued, "There have always been Warders who press their abilities past their learning, despite the danger. Perhaps because of the danger. He is one of them."

"When he killed Esar, the lictor . . . that act alone would have been enough to drive any one of us over the edge," Elen added, and shivered.

Khat waited until Riathen moved away toward the front of the wagon. The old man had been stalking back and forth as if he expected trouble. Gandin moved a little closer, watchful. Probably he had been set to guard the unwilling guest. Ignoring him, Khat said, "Tell me about Constans."

Elen glanced at him, frowning, perhaps puzzled by his persistence, but she said, "He was with Riathen from the time he was a boy. He came from Alsea, near the coast. Riathen brought him back when he went there on an embassy. Everything I know is hearsay, of course." She shrugged uneasily. "He was always powerful, always Riathen's best student. He became friends with the Elector, and I suppose Riathen was glad." She lowered her voice. "Riathen never has gotten on with the Elector, as far as I can tell. That's not very good. The Elector's safety is the Master Warder's most important duty.

"But when Constans was my age, he went too far. The way I heard it, he was only doing a future-seeing—"

"Is that different from fortune-telling?"

"No, it's just a different term for it," Elen explained, a little exasperated. "But he must have pressed his power too far, because he went mad. He killed another young Warder." She shook her head. "The Elector wouldn't let Riathen put him to death. He didn't understand what had happened to Constans, I suppose. Or he wanted to use him for his own ends."

Or he didn't want to see a friend die, Khat thought. But maybe they didn't have that kind of loyalty on the upper tiers. "Is that who Riathen and Constans meant, when they talked about their 'master'? The Elector?"

She nodded. "Now it pleases him to pit Constans against Riathen. I suppose he thinks the Master Warder is too powerful. Perhaps he's right. It's a game to him. It's life and death to us." She stared back at the glowing rock of the Waste, turned to dying coals by the sun's departure. "Riathen thinks the relics, the one we have now and the other two in the book, provide the key to the Ancients' power. That if we could find them, learn their secrets, perhaps even use the knowledge they give us to build an arcane engine, we would know why our magic drives us mad, and perhaps how to stop it from happening. The Elector doesn't want to take that chance. The free use of our skills would make us all as powerful as Constans, and the Elector would have to give us equal weight in his councils."

"And everybody would be happy," Khat said, in an attitude of mild skepticism. His thoughts were more serious. For a group that was supposed to do the Elector's will without question, the Warders' relationship with him seemed downright adversarial. He wondered if it was that way in all the Warder households on the First Tier, or just the Master Warder's.

"You don't believe it, of course," Elen said, irritated at his tone.

Khat's head still hurt, and he was weary from tension. "Elen, I've heard this story a hundred times. Maybe not this variation with Warders, but it was this story just the same. The only arcane engines ever found that still work and aren't in a hundred-hundred pieces are the painrods, and the only magical relic is the Miracle, but you'd know more about it than me, because it's kept up on the First Tier where nobody can see it."

"That's not my fault."

"Did I say it was?" He noticed Gandin was moving closer to them along the railing, perhaps to make sure Khat didn't savage Elen in the course of the argument. Khat said, "The point is, if you're waiting for somebody to dig up an arcane engine to solve your problems, you have a few dozen long decades ahead of you."

Elen glared at him. "I am not waiting for any arcane engine to solve my problems for me. I am perfectly capable . . ." she began, then ran out of steam.

"Of . . ." Khat prompted, tired enough to be more malicious than usual.

At that point, Gandin chuckled.

Elen leaned around Khat to stare coldly at her fellow Warder, until he wisely retreated back to the corner of the platform. She returned to her position at the railing and glared out at the steadily fading glow on the rock. Finally she said, "You certainly aren't being much of a help."

"No, I'm not. So let me go."

Elen's sigh had an air of long suffering to it. "You are not a prisoner."

He looked at her. "Really?"

"Really."

In an instant he was perched up on the railing, ready to go over, off the back of the wagon and into the endless maze of the Waste.

A startled Gandin took a step forward, and there was a rattle as the nearest lictor swung his rifle up to aim, but Elen held up her hand. Unlike Riathen's confrontation with Constans, there was more irritation at the unwarranted interference than theatricality in the gesture. The lictors hovered uncertainly, and Gandin stared at her as if she had gone mad, but she didn't take her eyes off Khat.

He looked down at her. Her face was calm. The hot evening wind ruffled his hair, and tore at her ridiculously frayed cap, but she didn't move. Then Khat slipped off the railing to casually lean on it again. The lictors gradually relaxed, and even Gandin backed away.

This time Elen's sigh was from relief. She said, "I had to trust you. Can't you at least try to trust me?"

Khat looked away, not answering her. His ribs were aching from the too-quick movement, and she didn't know what she was asking.

It was full dark by the time the wagon rolled into the docks at the base of Charisat.

Made strange by lamplight, the wagon docks were labyrinthine, crowded, and extensive, as befit their status as trade gateway to all the cities stubborn enough to exist on the Fringe of the Waste. Piled stone piers extended out into the sand for the loading of the tall steamwagons. Metal scaffolds stretched overhead so the handcarts that were used to transport goods could pass over the confusion below to the multistoried warehouses that clung precariously to the rocky faces of the crags. The piers were crowded with workers, crew, and beggars, even at this time of night, and the whole was watched over by the towering colossus of the First Elector, its upper half lost in shadow as it loomed over a hundred feet above the docks. During the day it would be visible as a masked figure carrying a torch, cast entirely of black iron. It had been painted and gilded once, but windborne sand had scoured the colors away.

From here you could also see the high-walled corridor that started from the top level of the wagon docks and went winding up around the tiers until it reached all the way to the First. The corridor had once been used only by handcarts and human labor; recently a new type of steamwagon that ran on two metal rails had been installed. It hauled more weight, moved faster, and rumor said that almost a hundred hand-carters had been driven to beggary because of it. It also carried Patrician passengers who needed to go to the wagon docks but wanted to avoid traipsing through the lower tiers with everybody else. All Khat knew about it was that it made a lot of noise, and if the vigils caught you jumping from the wall down to its top deck, they shot at you.

Their wagon chugged toward one of the middle piers, releasing a long blast of steam as it slowed, and the others automatically moved up to the front. As Elen turned to follow, Khat went over the railing and landed lightly on the packed dirt below.

He circled behind the wagon, out of the reach of the lamps. Tying the skirts of his robe around his waist, he went past the hard-packed wagon tracks down to the lesser-used piers near the end of the docks. The day's heat was starting to break, and this section of the docks was cooler, having been under the shadow of the crags above for much of the day.

There was a group of beggars perched on the pilings of the last pier. The docks were usually the last refuge of those so poor they could no longer afford even the Eighth Tier slums and were about to be forced out of the city altogether, where they would either join a pirate band or feed one. Most of this lot were already showing signs of heat sickness and sun poisoning, and would probably suffer the latter fate.

The Fringe Cities forced their poor out into the Waste, to become pirates; the kris killed the pirates to keep them from raiding the Enclave and the trade roads. *The Elector should take care of his own dirty work,* Khat thought. As he came within range of the torches and lamps, the sight of a man slogging through the deep sand drew curious stares from the beggars. Most city dwellers were wary of walking on loose sand, even though Waste predators never ventured this close to the city.

Khat climbed the pilings and stood on the pier, looking down to where the Master Warder's steamwagon was coming in to dock. Recognizing he was kris, the beggars drew away a little, making superstitious signs against ghosts and the evil eye. There had been other kris in Charisat when Khat had first come here; all had been loners or exiles, and most had moved on or died since then. He might be the only one left in the city now.

The Warders didn't seem to be raising an alarm, and Khat hadn't thought they would. They hadn't seemed anxious to let anyone know their business, and wouldn't want to draw that kind of attention. And if he was really going to work for Sonet Riathen, a show of independence at this juncture couldn't hurt. If he was really going to work for Riathen. *As if I had a choice.* Disgusted with himself, Khat shook his head and started down the pier.

Khat dropped down onto the cracked sandy brick of his home roof from a projecting ledge on the next house. He had hoped to make an inconspicuous return, but Ris was climbing up the ladder through the roof trap and immediately called down one of the vents, "It's Khat, and he's been beaten up again."

Ignoring him, the krismen found a pile of old matting and flopped down onto it. He didn't want to go down into the house until exposure to the city deadened his sense of smell again. His own odor was bad enough, but the nearest bathhouse was several courts away, and he didn't feel like walking that far, even to get rid of the dried blood.

Ris came over and peered curiously down at him, taking care not to come too close. "What happened?"

An arm flung over his eyes, Khat said, "Go away," in a tone that didn't invite argument.

The ladder rattled, and Sagai's voice seconded him. "Go home, Ris."

Khat lowered his arm to look up at his partner, who winced at the damage. He was lucky Sagai was not the kind of person who said "I told you so."

Disregarding Khat's protests and threats, Sagai examined the knot on the back of his head. "Not so bad," he pronounced finally. "Better than usual, I think."

"What's wrong down there?" an irritated neighbor asked suddenly from the overhanging window of the next house.

"Nothing," Sagai called back, a growl in his voice. "The day's excitement is over. Go to bed."

The neighbor withdrew, grumbling.

"Now," Sagai said in a softer tone. "What happened?"

Khat sat up on one elbow and told him all of it, leaving out nothing except his first encounter with Constans. He wanted to think about that a bit more before he talked about it, and told himself he would mention it to Sagai later.

Sagai was far more interested in relics than in Warders, anyway. "A new Survivor text in Ancient Script? Intact?" he asked, his eyes gleaming with the light of discovery. Finally someone was giving the find the attention it deserved. Relics weren't a trade, they were a passion. *It makes us unique,* Khat thought. Did peddlers get passionate over pots? Sagai said, "What I would give to see it, to handle it . . . You read much of it? What was it called?"

"*On the Motion of Thestinti.* I read bits and pieces. It was confusing; I couldn't follow what it was trying to say. And I didn't want Riathen to realize I could read it." He wished his partner had been with him, for that at least. Sagai, who had studied Ancient Script in the Scholars' Guild in Kenniliar, was better at deciphering the intricacies of it than Khat. "What does *thestinti* mean?"

"That's a difficult one. I don't suppose you remember the intonation markers?"

"No, I was a little distracted at the time."

"Hmm. It could mean walls, barriers . . ."

"I don't think it was about architecture," Khat said. "I could read the words, but they didn't make sense to me. Something about 'to enter and leave by the western doors of the sky' and 'to know the souls of the Inhabitants of the West.' "

"And there was no dynastical seal, I assume?"

"No, not one of the Recognizable Seven, anyway. I wasn't looking for one of the Hundred Hypothetical." Amateurs were always claiming to find new dynastical seals; the Academia kept a register of them, and some scholars worked their whole lives to verify them, though none had been added to the Recognizable list in decades.

"Perhaps it's a philosophical work. You said the Warders believed it related to their power. The Walls of the Mind, maybe. The Academia would be interested. Thousands of coins' worth interested. An intact text of Ancient Script and a piece of an arcane engine that can actually be associated with a Remnant. Why, it might lead to a proof of Robelin's theory about the Remnants' housing arcane engines. Treasures beyond price! I can hardly believe it."

Khat didn't want to dampen his partner's excitement by pointing out how unlikely it was that either of them would ever have another chance to closely examine the text or the engine relic again. "I doubt Riathen wants to sell them."

"No." Sagai sighed, and looked away over the dirty rooftops to the east, past the low clusters of mud-brick houses to where the tier's rim dropped away and the Fringe desert and the Waste stretched out forever, the black rock featureless in the distance. The breeze was up, and the night that was never quiet inside Charisat was at least calm, with the rumble of handcarts from the streets and the shouting and scuffling from the more combative denizens of the nearby courts seeming far away. "He will hide them, and fight for them, and worship them, perhaps. And never think to sell them to the Academia, where the scholars could glean far more knowledge from them than he ever could."

Khat yawned, and discovered one of his back teeth was loose. Another souvenir from the Warders. He would have to pull it out later, so the new one would grow in straight. "You think there's anything to that story about the relics helping them find an arcane engine that's going to unlock all the secrets of the Ancients?"

Sagai smiled down at him. "Unlocking all the secrets of the Ancients" was a stock phrase, something used to overwhelm inexperienced buyers. "I don't know everything. But what I do know tells me to doubt it."

Khat nodded, hearing his own belief confirmed.

After a moment, Sagai asked, "But will you help them?"

"I have to, don't I? That or leave the city."

Chapter Six

ELEN KNELT ON the floor of her room, facing the doorway into the small fountain court. The sun hadn't risen high enough to top the bulk of the house, so the muted predawn light turned the bright colors of the tile to gray and dulled the sparkle of the water. The early morning heat sent sweat trickling down her back and between her breasts, and the tickle of it was enough to disrupt her meditation. She gave up, wearily rubbing the back of her neck. The Discipline of Calm and Silence had always helped her make up for lost sleep before, but now it refused to have any effect on her. The fault was doubtless with her and not the exercise.

A soft step in the doorway behind her, and Lithe, the servant woman who took care of her rooms, said, "Elen, the Master Warder wants to see you now."

"All right." Elen stood and stretched. Riathen never slept. He and the older Warders had learned to use the Disciplines to entirely take the place of physical sleep. *Maybe that's why we go mad,* Elen thought, then winced at her own sour mood.

She pulled a mantle on over her kaftan and padded barefoot down the corridor to the wide sweep of the central stairs. The episode with the spider bite had left a mark on her leg that looked much worse than it felt now. She was hardly limping at all. Of course, explaining to the household physician what had been used to puncture the wound so the poison could drain away had been an exercise in bland-faced innocence she would not like to repeat.

Last night Ellen had also convinced Riathen that she would be the best one to go down to the lower-tier maze today and make sure Khat meant to fulfill his part of their bargain. The krismen's disappearance last night had badly worried him. Elen had been a bit worried, but hardly surprised.

None of the other Warders in the household possessed more than common knowledge about the kris, which made Elen the current authority on the subject. She wished she had time to locate a book with a history of the Enclave's contact with the cities, or at least a monograph that would tell her how to interpret the changes in eye color. She knew that a lightening to gray was for anger, darkening was for pain or distress, and rapid shifts between green, blue, and brown seemed the rule otherwise—*if* that was the rule, and not a sign of instability in this particular individual.

Riathen's rooms were on the top floor, at the head of the stairs. At the landing she paused, looking at the door that led into the Master Warder's chambers. If anyone had asked her a year ago if she had Riathen's trust, Elen would have firmly said yes. Now he still hadn't told her why he was so certain the relics were part of an arcane engine, or what sort of engine it could be that would help them discover the lost secrets of their power. She touched the new painrod at her waist, a little uncomfortably. It was proof that some of the Ancients' arcane engines could be dangerous indeed.

She shook her head, telling herself not to follow where those thoughts led. She had pushed Riathen far enough by taking the plaque out to the Remnant without his permission. *And can I blame him?* Jaq's death, and to some extent Esar's, were on her head. She didn't deserve trust.

Elen went on into the main chamber, which ran the whole length of this quarter of the house. The large windows in the inward wall looked down into the central court four stories below, where guests were often sent to wait under the shade of the stone gallery for an audience with the Master Warder.

Lamps were still lit in wall niches, casting warm light on the shelves packed with Riathen's books and his astronomical instruments. The Master Warder was sitting on one of the cushioned stools at a low stone table inlaid with jet and turquoise, serving tea to Kythen Seul, who looked as fresh and rested as if he hadn't been nearly killed by pirates or walked for miles along the trade road in the past two days. In the privacy of the house, neither man was veiled.

Riathen looked up at Elen's entrance and smiled a welcome. Elen smiled back, and nodded to Seul, though she wasn't terribly happy with him. Last night he had lectured her all the long way up from the docks to the First Tier about Khat. Seul seemed to think she was a trusting fool. She hadn't told him that she had tried to use her power to protect herself and that the working had failed.

"I've spoken to Kythen," Riathen said, setting aside the silver-veined quartz tea decanter and spooning a few mint leaves into his cup. "And he assures me the blame for your 'excursion' to the Remnant was all his, and that he was the one who persuaded you to 'borrow' the plaque and tear off into the Waste like a pair of mad children."

Seul frowned. Elen correctly guessed that the wording of the charge was all Riathen's and not the younger Warder's. It was hard to tell what either one of them was feeling. The air in the room didn't seem tense, but ever since Constans had gone mad all Warders habitually protected themselves against soul reading, and both Riathen and Seul were particularly good at it. She said calmly, "But all the blame isn't his. I agreed with him completely. If I hadn't, I would have told you what he meant to do."

Seul sighed, as if she had spoken foolishly, and made an "I tried" gesture to her. To Riathen he said, "If the pirates hadn't attacked the wagon, everything would have gone well, and you wouldn't have had to make the journey yourself."

Elen managed to keep silent. She supposed Seul meant well, but Riathen had been her guardian since she was a child, since she had first shown Warder talent. He had rebuked her before, and she supposed he would again; she didn't need anyone's protection from him.

The Master Warder raised an eyebrow at Seul, and added, "And Constans would not have discovered you, and nearly taken the text, and two of our lictors would not be dead?"

Seul said quietly, "I apologize, Master."

"You will accompany me when I go to inform their families today, and repeat your apology to them." He looked at Elen. "You're ready to go down to the Sixth Tier today?"

"Yes. I was waiting for sunrise before I left." She had wanted to speak to Jaq's family herself, and was startled Riathen hadn't required it of her. Perhaps he considered her mission too important. Well, she would go anyway, as soon as she could.

"Good. It will leave myself and the others free to try to find the source of that painrod the pirates had. I suppose it could've come from a cache in another city, but still . . . Constans must have supplied it to them somehow, and he must be prevented from obtaining more."

Elen agreed. She was lucky Riathen had replaced her lost painrod and not made her go without one as punishment. If the number of Warders hadn't been lower than usual this decade, there would have been none to replace it with at all. Her old rod had had no sentimental value; before her it had belonged to a student of the old Warder who had been Riathen's master, but it annoyed her no end that she had been so careless as to lose it. If Khat hadn't taken it, it must still be somewhere in the Waste. She supposed the pirates had found it by now.

Riathen's expression was serious. "Seul suggested that it was not Constans who arranged the pirate attack, but our relic dealer. Do you believe that possible?"

Elen snorted. "Hardly. They tried to kill him just as hard as they tried to kill me. And he could have taken the relic at any time and left me stranded there." *He took care of me, and I certainly gave him no reason to,* she wanted to add, and found herself holding back. Seul was watching her so intently.

Riathen nodded, satisfied. "Then I want you to find out everything you can about him. When he came to Charisat, and why. As much as you can."

She frowned. "What does that have to do with recovering the relics?"

"Are you sure it's wise to send Elen?" Seul countered. "She was alone with that creature for almost two days, and we're only lucky nothing . . . that nothing happened. Sending her down there might be . . . dangerous for her."

Elen didn't look at him, didn't allow herself to react to the note of possessive disapproval in his voice. She suspected her cheeks were reddening with embarrassment and anger, and she hated herself for it. She said, "I'm perfectly safe. He doesn't find me attractive. And I have good reason to know."

Seul almost spilled his tea. Riathen pretended the interruption had not occurred. "It has nothing to do with recovering the relics," he answered Elen, his expression grave. "But I've looked forward, and the results have not been as clear as I would like. Of course, they never are. I need more information."

Elen nodded. "I understand." She didn't understand. She merely wanted out. "I had better go now."

Riathen nodded permission, and she made for the door, not bothering to take leave of Seul.

Halfway down the main stair she realized she hadn't changed her clothing yet; the plain kaftan, cap, and an old battered pair of sandals that she needed to meld into a lower-tier crowd were waiting for her on her bed cushions. *What am I doing,* she asked herself, *bolting out of the house like an angry child?* She went through the arch into the garden court, intent on taking the back way to her rooms. She shouldn't let Seul shake her confidence like that. Elen knew herself to be a skilled infighter, especially for someone her size, and that her knowledge of the Elector's court and the emissaries sent there from the other Fringe Cities, as well as the dangers they represented, could not be faulted. She had even acted as bodyguard for foreign ladies on high state visits, and spied on them when necessary, missions that would have been difficult if not impossible for a male Warder. It was only her power that failed her.

That oh-so-dangerous and unnatural Ancient magic that fled her grasp like shadows under the noon sun.

The garden court was small, filled with delicate green plants brought from the shores of the Last Sea, screened from much of the sun's harshness by a netting of fine white gauze stretching high overhead, and quiet except for the soft music of water running in the stone basins. Someone called her name as she sped down the path, and she stopped, startled, and looked back.

It was Kythen Seul.

She considered continuing on down the path and ignoring his summons, but he was too close already, and she refused to run away.

He caught up with her and said, "Elen, take care."

She faced him, her mouth grim. "Seul, I told you, I—"

He held up his hands, asking for a truce. "I'm sorry."

Elen sighed. There were a number of things about him she found frustrating. He had come to them from the household of another elder Warder, and Riathen had embraced him like a son. Everyone believed he would be the Master Warder's successor, and it was clear what Seul thought the relationship between himself and the woman Warder who had been raised as Riathen's daughter should be. "Really, there isn't anything for you to worry about."

"I know," Seul said, looking down at her uneasily. "But take care, anyway."

After a moment, she managed to say, "Thank you."

He nodded and walked away.

Khat slept on the roof until the predawn light woke him. It took long moments of staring at the glowing horizon and the gradually fading stars to remember what had happened, why he was so sore and stiff. Then he remembered what he had agreed to do and whom he had obligated himself to, and winced at the depth of his own greed and stupidity.

He stretched carefully and came to the reluctant conclusion that he was going to live, then sat up on one elbow. The court below was still quiet, and the city's never-ending thunder was only a dull background roar of handcart wheels creaking, voices calling, the distant puffing of the rail wagon, the ceaseless movement of goods up and down the ramps connecting the tiers. Simply rolling over and going back to sleep was impossible, at least up here. This section of the Sixth Tier was fully exposed to the merciless rise of the morning sun.

The Inhabitants of the West, Khat thought, remembering the Survivor text. There were no living cities further west than Charisat, so if the Inhabitants of the West had lived in one it lay buried under Waste rock. If they had even been real at all, and not a symbol for some forgotten philosophical ideal.

Khat went down the ladder into the crowded house, making it out into the empty court without waking anyone, and headed for the nearest bathhouse.

When he came back an hour or so later Elen was sitting on the edge of the fountain basin, watching the old keeper counting his tally sticks. She wore a plain undyed kaftan, a cap decorated by cheap beads, and sandals of lacquered wicker. *It's started already,* he thought. The Warders could have at least allowed him a day or so to regroup.

Khat went to Sagai first, who was leaning in their house's door-

way and smoking a clay pipe, thoughtfully watching the young
Warder. As Khat joined him Sagai asked, "Is that your Elen?"

"That's her. How long has she been here?"

"A little after full light."

"That long? We are anxious, aren't we?"

Sagai gave him worried look and said, "Go carefully."

Khat walked over to lean against the wall near the fountain. The
sewer stink had faded, and the morning air was almost fresh. The
smell of grain boiling somewhere nearby couldn't disguise the rare
promise of one of the infrequent rains that fell this time of year. A
few of their neighbors were already out, gossiping over tea or ready-
ing bundles to carry to the markets. No one looked at Elen with anything more than mild curiosity. Dressed as she was, she wouldn't get
a second look anywhere on the Sixth Tier, a thought Khat was none
too comfortable with.

He glared at the fountain keeper until the old man got the message, gathered his sticks, and retired in huffy silence to the other end
of the court.

Without looking up at Khat, Elen said, "Riathen is worried. You
left rather abruptly."

"I didn't think I needed his permission," Khat said, and thought,
First they try to hire you, then they try to own you.

"You don't." Elen shifted uneasily on the rough stone of the
basin's rim. "It was just a little disconcerting. He wants to speak to
you again. I think he just wants to make sure that you will try to find
the relics."

Curious to see how she would react, Khat made no comment. As
if needing to make conversation, Elen looked up at Sagai, still watching from the doorway, and asked, "What did you tell your partner?"

"Everything." She finally met his eyes then, worried, and he said,
"If you think I can do this without his help, you're wrong."

Elen hesitated, then nodded reluctantly. "I can understand that."
She looked at Khat more carefully and added, "You look awful."

He narrowed his eyes at her. "Is that what you came down here to
tell me?" He knew he didn't look that bad. The swelling had gone
down, leaving the livid bruise on his jaw the most visible damage.

"No." She took a deep breath. "Riathen wants me to work with
you."

Wants you to spy on me, Khat thought. "I can't do this with a
Warder hanging around my neck."

The stubborn line between her brows appeared. "He wanted to send Seul, or one of the others. I convinced him I would be a better choice."

"Then maybe he should find someone else to run his errands. I may have to talk to some dealers on the Silent Market. I'm not going to do that in front of a Warder."

Her voice rose. "You think I'll report them? I don't care what the Silent Market does. I'm not a Trade Inspector. I don't even like Trade Inspectors. Can't you get that through your thick head?"

It was a treat to make Elen lose her temper. He said, "No."

She fumed silently. They were still drawing no undue attention from the neighbors. A man and a woman arguing, especially this early in the morning, wouldn't produce a flicker of interest unless someone drew a weapon. Finally Elen said, "You could take me as your apprentice."

Khat hadn't been prepared for this line of attack. "My what?"

"Dealers take apprentices too, don't they? That way anything I saw would be a secret between master and student, and I'd be breaking the trade law if I repeated it to anyone."

"Since when does trade law apply to the upper tiers?"

Elen jumped to her feet. "You either trust me or you don't. Should I go and tell Riathen to look for someone else?" She threw up her hands, exasperated. "I know you don't believe these relics will be what Riathen thinks they are, but you said they were rare. Don't you want to find them just on that count?"

It was Khat's turn to look away. Yesterday, surrounded by hostile Warders, the decision had been easy. Valuable relics were thin on the ground, and that Sonet Riathen had special knowledge of their location and was willing to pay tokens to see them found was a powerful motivation. But the fact remained that dealing with Warders was dangerous. The Elector's patronage gave them authority even over the Trade Inspectors, and the situation today was really no different from yesterday. He glanced back toward the doorway where Sagai still waited, and raised his voice to ask him, "Well, should I take an apprentice?"

Sagai came forward to eye Elen critically. "She's a little small. I suppose she isn't afraid of hard work?"

"No," Elen said firmly. "And I want to learn."

"Good." Sagai nodded to Khat. "I accept her. I hope she is as wealthy as you think."

"What?" Elen asked, startled.

"Relic dealing is a trade, and you know that trade apprentices have to support their masters during the time of their teaching," Khat reminded her.

Elen eyed them both warily. "No, I didn't know that."

"Support to the best of their ability, of course," Sagai explained. "If you were a potter's daughter, we would not expect you to contribute much. But you are not a potter's daughter, and our household has many children."

Walking with his new apprentice down the winding narrow streets of the Sixth Tier, Khat rubbed his face tiredly. "Why is Riathen so sure those relics are in Charisat?" Sagai had gone on to the Arcade to keep up business and make a few inquiries of his own. Too many absences from their regular trading spot would cause excitement among the other relic dealers, all of whom would decide that it meant that Khat and Sagai were on the track of some important deal. They could find themselves badgered constantly. But Khat had often pursued other business while Sagai kept up their usual trading; holding to that system as much as possible would keep the other dealers from nosing around.

"He found the crystal-inlaid plaque here in Charisat. And he's seen one of the others," Elen replied. She was none too happy with the financial burden her apprenticeship represented, and not satisfied by Khat's answer that it was her own fault for being so rich. "The small one, with the winged figure carved into it. He saw it last year, in the house of a Patrician on the Second Tier. He loaned Riathen the Survivor book, and said there was much there to interest the Master Warder. He'd studied the book himself, and traveled everywhere in search of the kinds of relics mentioned in it."

Habitually cautious, Khat scanned the street, the narrow alleys that led into back courts, the balconies, and the edges of rooftops even as he was turning over Elen's story. Now he knew why Riathen was so sure the relics pictured in the text existed; the original owner had done all the footwork. "Did he say where the text came from?"

"No. And Riathen didn't ask, of course, since he didn't know then what it was. The Patrician showed Riathen the relic with the winged figure on it, and the drawing of it in the book. Then a day or so later he died, and thieves entered the house and stole most of his collection. Fortunately, Riathen still had the book." She looked down at her feet, already darkened by the black dust of the roadway. "The old man was probably poisoned, but we never discovered who was responsible. Riathen searched for the relics that were in his collection, and he finally found the crystal plaque in the home of a man . . . Well, he was a High Justice of the Trade Inspectors."

Khat looked at her sharply.

"You don't have to glare at me like that. I don't socialize with the man. Anyway, he told Riathen that he bought the plaque legally, of course, but Riathen knew he must have gotten it from the thieves, or whoever they originally sold it to. The High Justice gave it to Riathen as a gift. Or, really, I suppose as a bribe, so Riathen wouldn't say a High Justice of the Trade Inspectors was a buyer of stolen relics." She looked up at him. "Will you go up to see Riathen with me sometime today?"

"Maybe." Khat was reluctant to put himself in the Master Warder's hands again, though he supposed if he were really going to go through with all this he would have to. But it would do Elen good to wait and wonder. "Does he know how many stolen relics leave the city every day?"

"He looked into the future through the burning bones and saw both the relics still in Charisat."

"Saw them where?" Hopefully Warder fortune-telling was more accurate than the common street variety. Sonet Riathen was undoubtedly wealthy enough to afford krismen bones, sold into the city by pirates who raided the kris Enclave. The practice wasn't smiled on by the First Tier, since there were agreements going back almost to the Survivor Time with the kris to keep the trade roads clear of pirates, but no one ever did anything to stop it.

"That isn't so easy. He saw that both relics will be in his possession, and that he will obtain them from somewhere in Charisat, but as to where they are now, and how they will get to him . . ." She shrugged.

For many, the day was well advanced, and people were everywhere, arguing with water keepers, baking bread in the small ovens outside the doors of their houses, hanging clothes out to air from the balconies and rooftops, and hurrying on errands. Everything taken into account, Khat hadn't found the Sixth Tier a bad place to live. If you learned to survive the smell, the crowding, and the low quality of the water, it was paradise. The Seventh Tier was between it and the Eighth, so for the others the fear of dropping a tier and being forced out was less, and the danger from the bonetakers who haunted the alleys and closed courts on the levels below was not quite so immediate. There was a comfortable mix of foreigners, many from outside the Fringe Cities, so few objected to Sagai and Miram for the minor crime of being from Kenniliar.

And even Khat was well accepted in the general area of their court. There were thieves who preyed even on houses as poor as these, and others who preyed on the people who lived in them, knowing the vigils seldom bothered to patrol here. Both these types of predators now tended to avoid the area after discovering that the resident kris slept lightly and often prowled the surrounding courts at unpredictable times during the night.

Khat said, "If they're still in the city, stolen relics will be easier to find. I don't know about the block. If something that unusual hasn't turned up yet, it's not likely to."

"A stolen relic is easier to find?"

"Unless a relic is offered for sale, or is in the Academia, it sits on a shelf in someone's house and gathers dust, and no one ever sees it. If it's stolen, it's handled by a dozen people at least and goes on the Silent Market. Much easier to get word of it."

They turned a corner, and abruptly the narrow street opened into a broad square housing the Sixth Tier marketplace.

"We're going to hear of it in this place?" Elen asked in disbelief.

The market was noisy chaos to untrained eyes. Portable awnings of sun-faded colors sheltered tinsmiths, rope makers, basket weavers, coppersmiths, tailors, and cap makers, all vying for the crowd's attention, their barkers shrieking at the tops of their lungs. The poorest vendors squatted in the sun in the winding alleyways off the forum, their goods laid out on the dirty paving stones. But the alcoves carved into the alley walls were where the real business took place, where the wagonloads of coal and grain brought down the trade roads changed hands.

"This place," Khat said, and led Elen to a seat on a low wall between a group of women selling lengths of used cloth and braid and a rope maker's pavilion. She reluctantly settled next to him. The market lay in the open area where the inside edge of the Sixth Tier met the base of the Fifth. Laws enforced by Trade Inspectors kept peddlers from building stalls up against the tier wall itself, so the area just at the base was occupied only by someone's goat herd grazing on the garbage tossed down from above and the ungainly structure of a crane. It was a sheer leg tripod, towering above the black stone of the tier wall, lifting huge bales of goods up for the Fifth Tier markets by a complicated system of pulleys at the top, its heavy ropes drawn by a treadmill that was at least three times the height of the men who worked to turn it.

Khat said, "Anyone with real business comes here eventually."

"They sell valuable relics here?"

He snorted with mild contempt. "No, nobody sells valuable relics here. They deal relics. It would be crass to produce the merchandise in public."

Elen shaded her eyes and, not happily, surveyed the growing crowd, the rising dust, and the heat shimmers already bending the air above the pavement in the distance. "Seul still doesn't trust you," she said, with a hint of reproach.

"That sounds like his problem." Khat wondered if Seul's distrust could have led him to follow Elen, and if it would be wise to try to contact a Silent Market dealer while he was possibly under the other Warder's observation. But no tokens would change hands today, and there should be nothing to tell anyone that the man was anything other than a market idler. Silent Market dealers were thorough professionals, or they were dead at the hands of the Trade Inspectors: there was no margin for error. "I don't think much of Seul either. Somebody had to tell the pirates what wagon you and your relic were on." And those same pirates had supposedly not only left the unconscious Warder for dead, but failed to return later for the body—not a mistake hungry pirates often made.

"That wasn't Seul; he would never betray us like that." Elen dismissed the whole idea of Seul as a traitor with an unconcerned shrug. "Surely it's no mystery. It must have been Constans. He could have burned bones to see where the relic was going to be, and he gave the pirates that painrod in payment for their services."

Khat thought she was relying a bit too much on fortune-telling, but he knew Constans hadn't sent the pirates or given them the painrod. The Elector's mad Warder had been out there that night killing pirates long before Khat had thought of it. And the only reason to kill the pirates was to distract them from the Remnant. But why hadn't

Constans entered the Remnant himself during the night and just taken the relic? *He could have been waiting for Riathen to bring the book,* Khat told himself. *If he's so all-powerful, he would know Riathen would have it with him.*

"But Seul is just too . . . protective," Elen was saying. "I'm not Riathen's pet, or his child. If I wasn't competent he would never have made me a Warder and given me duties and responsibilities." She shook her head. "Who are we waiting to talk to?"

"Someone who knows something about relics."

"Do we look for him?"

"No. If I wait here long enough, he'll find me." Seeing she had another question primed, he relented and explained, "He's a dealer for people who don't want their names known. You can't just walk up to somebody like that; you have to coax him out. If Riathen's right, and the pieces were stolen and sold on the Silent Market inside Charisat, he'll know about it."

The Silent Market had a presence in every civilized city. It dealt in a variety of goods, from air rifles, which were prohibited to noncitizens in Charisat, and mirage oil, a fragrant essence that gave the wearer the most wonderful waking dreams and with protracted use caused madness, to harmless textiles and incenses from the Ilacre Cities in the Low Desert, which had no agreements with the Fringe Cities and were banned from trade. But in Charisat the main commodity was relics.

The wait wasn't uneventful. Khat was well known in this area, and people brought him relics to value for the bargain market price of a few copper bits. Some were fragments they had found in rubbish heaps or under the foundations of crumbling buildings on the Seventh or Eighth Tiers; some were treasures handed down through families for generations. In the time they waited, he identified four unworked chunks of *mythenin,* a tile fragment inlaid with a flower, and pointed out to one elderly man that the "Ancient wooden scribe's palette" he possessed was only about a year old at the most and that he should sell it immediately before the price of teakwood dropped with the return of the Low Season caravans. Then he found one treasure.

The woman was Elen's age, barefoot and dressed in an undyed kaftan that had turned gray with age, and had two small children in tow. She held out a glittering fragment and Khat took it with reverence. It was only an inch or two long, of a heavy, smoky glass.

"Some kind of bird?" Elen asked, leaning over it and getting in Khat's light.

He moved her out of the way with his elbow. "No, a water creature. Those winglike things and the big triangular tail are for moving through water. See, they're smooth, no feathers."

"Oh, I've read about those. There are some in the Last Sea."

The woman was looking hopeful. Khat said, "This broke off something, maybe a bowl. It's the only piece you have?"

"Yes." She wet her lips nervously, and he wondered how close she was to dropping a tier. If she was already on the Eighth and close to being forced out she would look far more desperate than this. "How much . . ."

He handed it back to her. "Take it to the Academia. Ask for fifty days, but don't take less than forty. That's fair. It's the material that makes the value. You don't find much of this glass anymore."

"Forty?" She tucked the bauble away carefully, astonished. "That much?"

"It's fair. They won't argue that. But ask for fifty, just in case."

Watching the woman collect her children and disappear into the crowd, Elen said, "If it's that rare, why didn't you trade for it?"

"I couldn't give her that price. She couldn't afford to take less."

"But you set the price."

Sometimes Elen was too obtuse. He gave her a withering look. "There's some people I don't mind cheating. She isn't one of them. How long do you think she'd last in the Waste, or even on the Eighth Tier?"

After a moment's thought, Elen shook her head and didn't answer.

Then Khat spotted his quarry. The Silent Market dealer was taking a casual path toward them, stopping to admire the stalls along the way. Khat affected an absorbing interest in the activity at the nearby coppersmith's pavilion as the man drew near. The dealer was eating roasted beans out of a cheap sun-hardened clay bowl, and had the doleful, unreadable face and flat expressionless eyes of a hardened gambler. His name was Caster, and he might not look as if he was just here to enjoy the ambience of the marketplace, but it would be impossible for the untutored to guess what he was here for.

"Seeing much business today?" Caster asked as he came up to them.

Khat shrugged one shoulder. "Not much. It's been terrible lately. Nothing but junk on the market."

"It's a misery," Caster agreed, and sighed heavily. Dealers, even Silent Market dealers, never admitted that business was good. The market was always terrible, the relics available were always junk or forgeries or as common as dust. Cautiously, he nodded to Elen. "Who's this?"

"My apprentice."

"You took an apprentice?" His interest quickened, Caster looked almost animated. "Tagri Isoda will go mad. He wanted you to take his son."

"His son's an idiot."

Caster nodded agreeably. "But you can't tell him that. Oh, I know you told him, but he doesn't listen. I'm not taking the boy on either, that's a sure one." He looked at Elen with new interest. "Sagai going to teach her too?"

"He hasn't decided yet. Probably." Khat thought Caster was almost ready to deal, but he wanted the other man to initiate the discussion.

Caster gazed thoughtfully at the nearby pavilions. "Looking for anything today, or just showing her the trade?"

Khat shook his head regretfully. "I've got a buyer looking for a good trade, but I can't find anything special for him. And his tokens are upper-tier, too."

"Really? That's too bad." Caster offered the bowl to Elen, who took one of the beans and bit into it cautiously. "Anything certain in mind? Maybe I can turn something up for you."

"A *mythenin* oval, faceted, maybe about so big, with a carved figure, winged, in the center, like this." Lightly, in the dust on the wall, he sketched the shape of the figure. "The other one . . ." Khat felt like a fool even describing it, the thing was so unlikely as a relic. If he hadn't seen it pictured in an authentic Survivor text he would never have believed in its existence. "It's a large square block, about four by two, with incised line patterns."

Caster's eyebrows went up, but he didn't comment on the dubious possibility of coming across such a relic. He was silent for what Khat thought was a longer time than necessary. Finally he asked, "How particular is your buyer?"

"Very particular." To Elen, Khat explained, "He was asking me if the buyer would take a forgery."

"Oh," she said, startled.

"Got to ask," Caster explained to her helpfully. "Skilled craftsmen need to make their living too." He asked Khat, "Is this a recovery?"

Some collectors hired dealers to "recover" stolen pieces, whether from their own collections, someone else's, or the Academia. Khat knew he was in luck now. He said, "Call it a rediscovery, instead."

"I know the oval piece, or one close enough to it to be its twin, but it's not on the market anymore."

"The offer could go high."

"I would if I could, but it's not a deal I could arrange. Really. Tell him to look for something else."

"A private collector?"

Caster shrugged.

"We might pay for a name."

Caster looked away, disinterested. "I'll ask, but don't count on anything." Khat knew that for a good sign.

The dealer's eyes narrowed suddenly. "Huh. What company we're keeping."

A litter had appeared at the edge of the market, a gaudily expensive one with colorful silk curtains and much ornate golden brightwork. It was Lushan's litter.

Caster faded into the crowd, and Khat wished he could follow him. He still had a headache and was in no mood for an encounter with Lushan.

A man in a stained and threadbare robe had been hovering nearby, politely out of earshot. He had the distinctive look and smell of the gleaners who made their living unblocking the sewage outlets down on the Eighth Tier. Now he came forward eagerly, upending at their feet a damp sack of somewhat sticky junk, probably collected out of the sewer flow. Elen gripped the edge of the wall and rocked back at the aroma.

Khat leaned over to look at the pieces. At least the smell would blot out the odor of Lushan's perfume. "Relics," the man said, grinning up at him toothlessly.

"Does this happen often?" Elen managed to gasp. She did look sick.

"You can find some interesting things this way," he told her. He separated out some pieces of broken clock innards, which the unsophisticated were always mistaking for bits of Ancient arcane engines.

"That's not a relic, and that's not a relic." Out of the corner of his eye he was watching Lushan, who had struggled out of the litter and was lurching toward them. He wore a gold silk overmantle that gleamed in the harsh light, and one servant cleared the way for him while another held a tasseled shade over his head, as if it were possible for the sun to penetrate all the elaborate layers of veiling. Two muscular enforcers were loitering with the litter bearers. Lushan came to all the different markets in turn, to oversee the dealers who worked for him and to frighten his competitors. It was Khat's bad luck he chose today to come to this market.

Lushan reached them as Khat finished sorting out the few fragments of *mythenin* from the gleaner's pile. "I see you have a new boy to help you," the broker said. "Is the trade in sewer leavings so brisk, then?"

Elen blinked at being mistaken for a boy without her disguise, but wisely said nothing. The gleaner peered up at her, confused. Flies and gnats were gathering, attracted by the stains on the man's robe.

"Am I taking business away from you, then? Isn't this how you started out?" Khat said. The rumor was that Lushan had been born on the Eighth Tier, and fought his way up. The broker hated to hear it repeated.

The veils trembled in irritation, the only reaction visible. "You'll beg to work for me again, krismen. They always do." Lushan gestured angrily at his servants, and the whole procession moved off.

That's nice, Khat thought, watching the bulky figure depart, *but you're the least of my worries.* Elen owed him enough to pay his debt now, and Lushan was too easy to bait.

"That awful person thought I was a boy," Elen said, sounding indignant.

"That was Lushan. He's blind in one eye," Khat told her. "And it's probably just as well he thought you were a boy." Lushan's reputation among the women relic dealers was anything but lovely.

"Is a girl," the puzzled gleaner said, pointing at Elen.

"We know," Khat assured him. "Eight copper bits for this lot."

"Done!"

As the man took his copper bits and his sack and hurried off, Elen asked, "Why did that Lushan want you to work for him?"

"He's a greedy bastard, and nobody's told him no before." Khat squinted up at the sky. He had felt the rain coming out of the east since early this morning, and now a few dark gray clouds dotted the brilliant blue. All around the marketplace, people were beginning to regard the clouds hopefully, to wipe off pots and bowls and set them out just in case.

"Well, what Caster said was promising," Elen commented, wiping brick dust off her hands onto the skirts of her kaftan. "Do you think he knows something?"

"No, but I think he'll find out something before too long."

Abruptly the rain started. The clouds were sparse, so the sunlight was still bright, and though the raindrops were big they were far apart. All commerce stopped in the general scramble to get outside, to catch the meager fall of water in pots and basins or on bodies. Khat leaned back on the wall to absorb as much of it as he could.

The downpour stopped as abruptly as it had started, and activity resumed in the central square. The frenetic mood of the market had lightened considerably, though this probably hadn't been enough rain to drop the price of water today.

Elen used her dampened scarf to scrub the dust off her face. "Can we go see Riathen now?"

She had sat through her first lesson patiently, for the most part, Khat decided. Time to play by her rules, for a while, anyway. He smiled at her. "After you buy me breakfast."

On the way up the ramp to the Third Tier, Khat fell in behind a party of respectable Fifth Tier tradesmen who were probably going to a Patrician's home for a private showing of their wares. The gate-vigils passed Elen and him without comment.

The tier gates were all built along the same design. A ramp climbed the tier wall, zigzagging back and forth so the incline wasn't too steep for handcarts, and bridged the top of the rail wagon's corridor to reach the level of the next tier. At the top two massive pylons supported the iron frames of the gates.

"I thought we might have trouble," Elen confided when they were several yards past the gate and on the central street of the Third Tier. "Patricians' homes on this tier have been entered by thieves during the past few tendays." The Third Tier allowed entrance during the day, but closed at sundown to anyone but Patricians and their retinues. The gate from the wagon docks into the Eighth Tier was the only lower-tier gate with guards, and even it had stood open so long the metal had rusted into place.

Khat shrugged, too interested in looking around to make a reply.

His previous forays onto this tier had been after dark, when entrance from the lower tiers was forbidden, and the necessity of making those trips only during moonless nights had kept him from seeing much of it.

The Third Tier didn't seem too different from the better residential areas of the Fourth. The shops were smaller and sold little else besides luxury goods. There were sellers of mint and rare herbs, book dealers, and weavers who spun precious metal into thread, all industries that catered only to the wealthy. There were few peddlers and fortune-tellers, and no crowding of loiterers in the alleys. The artisans that took the imported raw materials and gave Charisat its trade goods worked mainly below the Fourth Tier.

The lower Patricians had their homes here, large manses set back from the cleanly swept streets, with high walls and gates enclosing private courts. Every house boasted wind towers, tall narrow chambers projecting above the roof that caught the wind in slatted vents and drew it down into the structure. Through the few gates that stood open for visitors Khat caught glimpses of fluted columns, fountains, and potted flowers.

"Why do you need a partner?" Elen asked him suddenly. "Doesn't that just mean splitting up the profits more?"

Khat snorted, thinking, *Profits? You're an optimist, Elen.* "Sagai studied in the Scholars' Guild in Kenniliar. He should be at the Academia, but they won't allow foreign-born scholars."

Surprised, Elen considered that. "Then why does he need you?"

"The other dealers look at him and see gray hair, and they think, here's an old man who's an easy target. He's harder to take than he looks, but he was always having to prove it. He doesn't like to hurt people." He looked down at her. "I don't mind it as much as he does."

"I'm trembling," she assured him, straight-faced. "Is everyone afraid of you?"

"Everybody needs someone to watch their back." He shrugged uncomfortably. "I was jumped by bonetakers down on the Eighth Tier once. Sagai found me just as they were about to cut my throat. He was almost too late. I've still got the scar."

Bonetakers would take anybody and say they were kris, or an executed murderer, or a child with a caul. They operated mainly on the Eighth Tier, where poverty was intense and, if they took a child, the family was more likely to feel guilty relief than to pursue them with a howling pack of relatives and neighbors. Many takers sold lizard or rat bones as human, or stole already dead bodies from charnel houses before they could be burned. But they all knew where the real profit was.

The takers who had trapped Khat hadn't killed him immediately because they knew they could get more from their buyer by proving he was really kris, and they had disagreed over whether this was best done when he was alive or dead. He had come back to consciousness facedown on the blood-soaked floor of a charnel house, head pounding and sick, bound too tightly to move and choking on a gag. The one who thought he could be shown off just as well dead had just won the argument. He had lifted Khat's head by a handful of hair and put the point of the hooked skinning knife at a corner of his throat when Sagai had come crashing down through the overhead trapdoor. Neither of the takers had survived the experience, and since then Khat and Sagai had had no more trouble when venturing down onto the Eighth Tier.

"Oh," Elen said, uncomfortable herself now. She asked finally, "How can you stay here with that hanging over your head?"

"The best relics are here," he said as if it were self-evident, which it was. "Besides, you can die anywhere."

At the upward gate to the Second Tier, under the shadow of the gate pylons, he waited for Elen to handle it, wondering how she was going to get herself, let alone him, past the well-guarded portal.

Elen simply produced an engraved seal about the size of a trade token and showed it to the vigil. He bowed to her and waved hurriedly for the others to open the embossed-metal gate.

"If relics are so valuable, why aren't you and Sagai rich?" she asked as they went up a wide street that was entirely free of sewer stink. High walls enclosing private courts lined it, the buildings behind them huge structures with domes, glittering spires, or narrow towers topped by gilded tiles. Everything was faced with limestone or marble, and even the street walls were set with inlay of semiprecious stone or mosaics of enamel and glass. It was nearly midday, and few people were out: some servants on errands, who stared curiously at them, and a few Patricians, veiled, their attendants shielding them from the sun with white parasols. Sweating bearers carrying an overelaborate litter with diaphanous silk curtains and gold sunburst ornaments on the poles trotted by.

"Neither of us can get a trade license to handle Imperial minted gold, so if by some miracle we run across a rare piece, we can't sell it outright to a collector," Khat told her. They had only come a short distance from the gate, and the street was already making him nervous. It was too clean, too quiet, too closely watched, and he was drawing attention simply by being there. On the Third Tier there had been more activity, tradesmen, street sweepers, and he hadn't felt so conspicuous. "We can only deal the pieces that are cheap enough to be sold for trade tokens, and take commissions on valuations or sales we help someone else with, if the seller doesn't cheat us out of it. And Sagai gives good deals to people he feels sorry for."

"Sagai does that." Elen sounded amused, for some reason.

"He does. Besides, for the Sixth Tier, we're comfortably well off. As far as the Seventh and Eighth are concerned, we are rich."

Several passersby gave them wide berth, one old woman ostentatiously snatching her robes away, as if she feared contamination. Elen ignored them as thoroughly as Khat did.

They went further up the street, until Elen took a pebbled path that led off through what was apparently a public garden, with stone tubs holding swift-blooming desert flowers and stunted, thorny acacia trees. They came to a high gate shaped into vines and leaves, and as Elen reached for the latch it was opened from the inside by a white-robed lictor, an air gun slung over one shoulder.

Khat stopped where he was.

Elen looked back at him from the gate. "Come on. It's a private way up to the First Tier. It's much quicker than going around to the tier gate."

Khat hesitated. He had known this would probably involve going into places where there would be men with guns between himself and the way out, but it hadn't really hit home until this moment exactly how far into enemy territory this venture would take him. Elen was beginning to look puzzled. *It's too late to back out now,* he told himself, and followed her through the gate.

The lictor watched them both with unreadable eyes.

Chapter Seven

T HE WAY LED deeper into the garden, Patricians' manses rising up on either side, the black stone wall that was the base of the First Tier looming ahead. Khat noticed the area between the tubs of flowers and trees was covered with silversword, a tiny plant with narrow leaves like white spires and shiny hairs that reflected the sunlight and made the ground a glowing carpet. He wondered if the Patricians of this tier knew it was a plant that thrived in the sand pockets of the deep Waste. If they learned that, they would probably have their servants burn it out.

They reached the tier wall before he saw the passage Elen had said was there. An alcove was cut into the wall with narrow steps leading up. Anyone climbing them would be sheltered from view by a fold of rocky, uneven wall, and the cut would be all but impossible to spot from the street outside the garden.

"This goes right up to Riathen's house," Elen explained, climbing the steps that were almost as steep as a ladder. "You mustn't tell anyone about it, of course." He didn't answer, and she added, "And I must say, you're containing your enthusiasm at seeing the First Tier very well."

She reached the top, where the steps gave onto a courtyard paved with blue and gold tiles, surrounded on the other three sides by the polished limestone walls of what was undoubtedly a very large and very fine house. Khat followed her more slowly, and said, "On the way down, I'll be enthusiastic for you."

Elen stopped to scrutinize him seriously. "You really aren't enjoying this, are you?"

There was a wide porch set back into the inner wall opposite them, guarded by another gate with two more imperturbable air gun–armed lictors on the other side. It was only a sensible precaution. Anyone forcing their way up the stairs would find themselves in a trap. The narrow slits of windows that looked down from the second floor were probably more for firing from cover than for ventilation, as well. Khat was beginning to feel like a goat invited cordially into the slaughterhouse. He said, "Of course I am."

These lictors recognized Elen too, opening the gate for them without comment and locking it again behind them. The inside of the porch was tiled with all different shades of blue, giving an illusion of coolness, and a three-level fountain played at the base of a wide stair leading up into the house.

They went up past landings with carved arches opening into other rooms. Netta's house would've fit easily into the stairwell, roof and all. The walls that weren't tiled were faced with polished marble, and it actually felt cooler inside than it had out in the court. There was, of course, no sewer stink, and no odor of unwashed people; the only scent was the lightest fragrance of sandalwood incense.

But the oddest thing was the quiet. No noise from the street, or leaking through cracks in the walls from other houses, or from the noisy inhabitants of this one. It was a kind of stillness Khat had thought was possible only in the open Waste. Despite it, or perhaps because of it, his shoulders kept hunching in anticipation of an attack from behind.

At the next landing a large door curtained by sheets of gauze led into an interior court open to the sky, and Khat stopped to look out, intrigued in spite of himself. On the sun-warmed gray stone of the court were ten people, all Elen's age if not younger, moving through the steps of what looked like a formalized ritual dance. Khat recognized it as one of the first preparations for learning infighting, the only Ancient Art to be passed down almost entirely intact. The magic of the Warders was an Ancient Art too, but it was unnatural, like the rise of the Waste was unnatural, and perhaps that was why most of the Survivors had abandoned it.

The dance the students in the court moved slowly through was exercise only, teaching the muscles to move in certain ways. The dances that taught the more graceful—and deadly—moves came later. *So this is where Elen learned to kill pirates,* he thought.

Elen came up beside him to look and said, "So few of them. Fewer initiates each year, Riathen says."

Khat didn't comment. In his opinion there were far too many of them already.

There were footsteps above them coming down the tiled stairs, and without thinking Khat shifted to put his back against the wall.

It was Gandin, the young and excessively earnest young Warder who had accompanied Riathen and Seul yesterday, and he was followed by an armed lictor. Gandin was dressed in Warder white, and in the privacy of the house his veil had carelessly slipped down around his neck. "Elen, you're finally here. Riathen was called to speak to the Heir. He wants you to join him."

"I'll wait for you outside," Khat told her, relieved. Outside on the Third Tier, if he could get past the gates.

"No," Gandin said. "He wants you there too."

"Me?"

Elen glanced down at herself and bit her lip. "I'll have to change. They wouldn't let me past the first portals dressed like this." She looked at Khat. "And you too. There would be too much curiosity about who you were and why you were here, otherwise."

"Me?"

Before he could form a more articulate protest, the lictor had his arm and was urging him away down the passage in the opposite direction.

The room he was not quite shoved into was high-ceilinged and cool, with a round shallow pool in the center and lit by an open air shaft overhead. An expensive expanse of mirror was set in one wall. Khat freed his arm with an annoyed jerk, and found himself facing Gandin, who said, "First, hand over your weapons."

If Khat had had any weapons he would have used them by now, rather than be trapped in a little room with a Warder. "I don't have any."

Perhaps naturally skeptical of this statement, Gandin said, "You had a knife out on the Waste yesterday."

"Your lictors stole it. And a flea glass. Tiny glass lenses must be very dangerous where they come from." That glass and the amber bead in his knife hilt had cost him months of honest work, but he doubted that would mean anything to the Warders.

"I don't believe that," Gandin said flatly. "Search him."

The lictor stepped forward, and Khat dropped his robe and lifted his arms obligingly. The search was thorough but not rough, and Khat put up with it, knowing there wasn't anything for them to find. He kept his eyes locked on Gandin's, and was rewarded by seeing the younger man's cheeks flush. Finally the lictor stepped back and said, "Nothing. Not even a fruit knife."

"We don't have fruit on the Sixth Tier," Khat said, folding his arms.

Gandin was flustered by being proved wrong and determined not to show it. Another lictor entered, carrying a bundle of clothes. Gandin took the bundle and shoved it at Khat, saying brusquely, "Put those on."

Khat found himself holding a stretch of bleached cotton, soft as silk, a veil of spiderweb-fine gauze, and a wide belt made of silver beads and a higher grade of leather than he had ever touched before. And it was probably their second best, if that. "Say please."

Neither of the lictors laughed. Either they were well disciplined or Khat would have to revise his estimate of Gandin's status. Gandin gritted his teeth and said, "Now."

"All right. Get out."

Gandin was startled. It was a commonly held belief of the upper tiers that servants, noncitizens, and other nonpersons did not have the right to or desire for privacy that the Patricians guarded so jealously. It was part of the reason Gandin and the other male Warders let their veils slip in front of Khat without embarrassment. Since he wasn't a person, it hardly mattered if he saw them unveiled. Recovering, Gandin said, "I don't have time for—"

"Oh, are we in a hurry?" Khat interrupted. Bodily modesty didn't matter much to him, especially since he had been using the public bathhouses on the lower tiers, but he knew it mattered to them, and he was determined to push the issue.

"Fine," Gandin snapped, beaten and knowing it. "Just be quick about it." He gestured the lictors ahead of him and followed them out. Khat wasn't fooled; he knew a retreat when he saw one.

He hurried, because apparently there really was some urgency in the proceedings, but mainly because the sooner this was over with the better. He stripped, got the underrobe and the mantle on, and belted and kilted them correctly so he wouldn't trip over the skirts. He kept his own boots, because he wasn't accustomed to sandals and they would interfere with his ability to run, then caught a look at himself in the mirror and lost all squeamishness about putting on the veil and headcloth. Without them, he looked like an upper-tier working boy.

Gandin came back in then, and this time he had his own veil properly in place. The Warder watched Khat's fumbling attempts to wind the veil, then said grudgingly, "Let me do that."

Khat hesitated. There were only a few people that he didn't mind coming that close to him, and all of them lived in Netta's house down on the Sixth Tier. Exasperated, he reminded himself that this whole business was because his presence was urgently required somewhere else, and if Gandin had wanted to kill him he could have done it just as well in front of his lictors as not. Still, it took self-control to turn his back on the young Warder long enough to let him adjust the veil.

Out in the cool passage Elen was waiting, dressed in a kaftan and mantle of white silk, with a cloisonné cap. A narrow silver chain held her painrod at her waist. "What took so long?" she demanded.

"Nothing," Gandin told her. "Let's go."

"Wait," Khat interrupted, determined not to be dragged along any faster than was absolutely necessary. "One thing first."

"What?" Elen asked, a worried frown creasing her brow. Gandin was ready to explode.

"The tokens you still owe me."

"Oh, that." She looked relieved. She had probably been expecting him to refuse to go altogether. "You want them now?"

"No, I want you to send someone to deliver them to the house of a relic broker. It's on the Fourth Tier, the biggest house in the third court off the Theater Way." There was no need to mention Lushan's name; he was the only relic broker in that court.

Puzzled, Elen called a lictor over and gave instructions, ignoring Gandin's fuming impatience.

After that, Khat followed them. The filmy soft veil was trying to climb down his throat, and he felt horridly out of place. They went down more cool empty halls, past two more locked and guarded gates, then outside into an open rectangular court, larger even than the public forum on the Fourth Tier. It was paved with slabs of dark marble and encircled by a colonnade of red onyx. Khat gave up estimating the cost of things.

"This is where the new Electors are acclaimed by the Patricians," Elen explained as they crossed the court. She pointed to the immense structure now visible over the top of the colonnade. "And that's the palace. It's a model of the city."

It rose in eight concentric levels like Charisat, but the outside walls were layered with polished limestone so it glowed in the sunlight, the creamy surface broken by balconies and open terraces.

"Does that mean the bottom five tiers have bad water?" Khat asked her.

Gandin glanced at him sharply, but Elen replied equably, "It's not an exact model."

Other buildings were visible over the top of the colonnade, their domes and pinnacles catching the sunlight with gemlike reflections—except for one. Its dome was pitch black against the hard blue of the sky, and it might have been carved entirely out of obsidian or onyx. Khat had to ask, "What's that?"

Elen shaded her eyes to look, and her expression went grim. "That's the Citadel of the Winds. It was a prison for . . . well, for Warders who used their power unwisely and lost their sanity. It belongs to Aristai Constans now. The Elector gave it to him."

Khat had heard the place mentioned before, usually by fakirs invoking it as some sort of place of power, like the Dead Lands or the Mountains of the Sun; he had thought it just as mythical as those places. "Didn't they use to kill the Warders who went mad?" Elen had said something about being "sent away" if she went mad, but he had thought it a polite euphemism.

"They did. But they needed somewhere to hold them before the Justices could meet. Now they still send them there, but only to serve Constans." She glanced up at Khat. "Everyone says the last Mages built the Citadel in the Survivor Time."

"It doesn't look Survivor," Khat said, always skeptical of such claims. The only authentic Survivor Time structures in Charisat were several bare, cavernous stone buildings in the dock area, still in use as warehouses. The Survivors, Mages or not, hadn't had the resources to build fancy palaces.

"How can you possibly tell from here?" Gandin demanded.

Khat didn't bother to answer.

The square gave on to a wide avenue lined on either side with a double-tiered arcade for viewing ceremonial processions. They were passing more people now, Patricians in lavish robes with gold and silver beadwork and embroidery, sumptuous litters so large they were carried by six or eight bearers, court officials with gold skullcaps, trailing entourages of servants and archivists. Khat fought the irrational feeling that everyone was staring at him, knowing that if they were staring, it was because they thought he was a Warder, not because of some preternatural ability to tell that he didn't belong here.

The arcade ended in another forum, and then they were in the shadow of the palace. A wide sweep of steps led up to a triple arch that gave entrance to the first level, and the glare of the white surface of the walls was almost blinding.

The lictors at the arches wore the heavy gold chain of Imperial service. Gandin stopped them at the base of the steps and turned away to tell his own men to wait for them out here.

"Private guardsmen aren't allowed in the palace or the Elector's presence," Elen explained. She looked over Khat critically. "With the veil, no one's going to notice your teeth. But don't smile, just in case."

"I don't think that's going to be a problem."

"Hmm. I hope they don't notice your eyes."

"There's a trick of not looking at someone directly," he admitted, looking away partly to demonstrate and partly to marvel at how many Imperial lictors were stationed around the plaza before the palace's entrance. Apparently the Elector was expecting an armed uprising at any moment. "Not many people are that observant."

"Well, there are some very observant people in there," Gandin said as he came back to them, his voice grim.

"Then why don't you wait outside?" Khat asked him. He was nervous enough without a doomsayer at his elbow.

Gandin bristled, but Elen said, "Riathen will be waiting. Come on."

Up the stairs and past the lictors. Khat was sweating, despite the fact that the fabric of the robe and overmantle was lighter than it looked.

The hall past the arches was high-ceilinged and vast, the walls stretching up to a flattened dome overhead. All surfaces seemed dressed in dark colors of marble, and long hallways led off in all directions. A few dozen paces away, near one wall of the huge chamber, was a little domed pavilion of soft gray stone. Narrow doorways at regular intervals gave entrance to it. As Khat watched, the inside of the little place lit up with a pure white light that was just as abruptly extinguished.

With a shock Khat realized what that small pavilion must contain. The Miracle was a legend among relic dealers and collectors. It was a true arcane relic, as well as one of the handful of relics that actually had some function other than decoration. Not that anyone knew what that function was.

Elen tugged on his sleeve, and Khat realized he was staring like an idiot.

"The steward of the hall will ask us our business," she whispered.

The figure approaching them was short and squat and wearing a slitted mantle heavy with gold embroidery and brocade, earrings of heavy gold beads, granulated gold on his skullcap—enough gold to feed the Eighth Tier for a month.

"We are Warders," Elen announced formally, and unnecessarily, Khat thought, but apparently stating the obvious was called for. "We have been sent to attend the Master Warder."

The steward's hennaed brows went up in surprise, perhaps at being addressed by a female Warder. But he bowed smoothly and said, "Of course. Master Riathen apprised us of your arrival. He wished for those called Elen son Dia'riaden and Gandin Riat to attend him at once, and for the other to wait."

"Thank you." Elen bowed in return. As the steward withdrew, she said quietly to Khat, "Wait here."

Khat watched them leave, then looked around the hall, seeing Patricians and servants go back and forth and turning over the implications of Riathen wanting a private conversation with his Warders while he was trapped out here.

But the Miracle pulsed again, its light spilling out of the chamber built to contain it. Two Patrician women walked up to one of the doorways and peered in, until another pulse of light startled them. They turned away and went toward the outer arches, talking animatedly.

It isn't guarded, Khat thought. No more so than the palace itself was guarded. His heart was pounding, and not from fear. He had heard of the Miracle for years, seen drawings of it, but he had never expected to be this close.

No one was watching him, and nothing seemed to bar the way through any of the little pavilion's doors. *Go carefully*, Sagai had said this morning, and this was probably no time to sightsee. But it was a chance he was unlikely to have again.

He went to one of the doorways. Inside the pavilion, the Miracle sat atop a pedestal of plain brick. It was a stone of pyramidal shape, as tall as a man, of a material that was dark charcoal gray, with a sheen like steel and somehow also like dark marble. Light burst from it suddenly, and Khat winced away. A fire that brilliant should permanently scar the domed chamber's unadorned walls, not to mention kill anyone in its range, but the Miracle's light was apparently without heat.

He forced himself to look at it again. The dazzling illumination seemed to emanate directly out of the dark surface. It came in bursts, like a heartbeat, and the silence of it was uncanny; each pulse of light was so brilliant it should have been accompanied by an explosion, at least.

A waist-high barrier had been constructed around the pedestal. Without consciously making the decision to enter the chamber, Khat found himself standing at that barrier. The stone silently exploded again, dazzling his eyes and temporarily blinding him.

Then someone said, "A legend made reality. A magical relic." The slight pause seemed to hold a wealth of unvoiced irony. "Before they knew what it was, they kept it in the Elector's Garden."

Khat knew the voice immediately, and felt a sensation of cold that started at his skin and proceeded right down into his bone marrow. His vision returned gradually, and the next burst showed him Aristai Constans standing beside him. Khat's throat had suddenly gone dry, but he managed to say, "You turn up in the strangest places."

"Oh, I'm here a great deal." Constans leaned casually on the brick barrier, chatty and unconcerned and as dangerous as a sharp drop off a cliff. "I was here, in fact, twenty years ago on the day the Miracle first chose to call attention to itself. I remember it very well. It was the day I went mad."

The Miracle pulsed once more in the pause, blinding Khat again. "Why did you go mad?" he heard himself asking. It surprised him that he really wanted to know, even though instinct and common sense were both saying *Run.*

"What a pity someone else has never thought to ask that question."

"You mean Sonet Riathen." Silence. *Is he breathing?* Khat wondered. It should have been audible in the stillness in the little chamber, but maybe the pounding of his own blood was masking the sound. He said, "But what's the answer?"

"It was the best of several bad alternatives." From his voice, Khat thought Constans had turned away from the Miracle and toward him. The Warder asked, "Why are you here?"

"I didn't have a choice." Khat made his voice sound light instead of bitter. There was something he should be noticing about the Miracle, and he kept his eyes on it despite the near possibility of being killed by the Elector's mad friend.

"Oh, I think you did. Everyone has a choice."

"Are you going to call the lictors?" He sensed Constans moving behind him and didn't react. "There's probably a law against a krismen profaning the sacred halls where the Elector walks."

"Don't be ridiculous," Constans said from his other side. "The Elector never ventures down here."

The Miracle pulsed again, a heartbeat of living, heatless light. This time Khat had been looking directly at it during the pulse, and the image of it was burned into his memory. If he were to describe the Miracle he would call it a large pyramidal stone etched with a fading web of lines, and if Riathen's second lost relic, the unlovely square block, wasn't its twin brother, it was at least its second cousin.

"Besides, that is not the tone I want to set for our relationship," Constans was saying.

"We don't have a relationship," Khat said, irritated despite the danger.

"Didn't you chastise someone recently for claiming to know everything?"

Someone spoke sharply out in the central chamber, and without thinking Khat turned his head toward the noise. He realized his mistake when Constans grabbed him by the back of the neck. That voice hissed in his ear, "Riathen knows nothing. They don't know what we are, what happened to us, what the danger is. My advice is to agree with everything they say and don't let them bring you here again."

The shove sent him stumbling, and Khat caught his balance against the edge of the doorway and turned back. An abrupt burst of light from the Miracle showed him an empty chamber.

Outside in the entrance hall Elen was looking for him, peering at the robed figures clustered at the opposite end. Khat managed to be right next to her when she turned, and she started. "Where were you?"

"I was right here. Didn't you see me?"

Elen's expression was skeptical, but obviously she had no time to pursue the issue. "Never mind. This way."

They went down long halls, up wide staircases, past more lictors. The twistings and turnings might have been meant to confuse, but Khat knew which direction was north with the same certainty that he knew up from down, and to him the way was simple. The difficulty was in not thinking about Aristai Constans.

Elen took what might be a shortcut through a curving corridor, its walls inset with squares of somber indigo stone. Every few feet was a waist-high pillar plated with gold electrum, each supporting a jar of the most delicate ceramic. The lids were sculpted into detailed busts of different people. They were crematory jars, and Khat had heard of this hallway. Each jar held the ashes of some dead Elector.

Elen stopped abruptly, and Khat just managed not to walk into her. Some distance ahead a young man moved across the corridor. His robes and veil were black, melding into the dark stone lining the walls. In a low voice, Elen explained, "That was Asan Siamis of the Warder household of Gian, who is Riathen's cousin. I grew up with Asan. He went to Constans only a few months ago."

Black was the color condemned criminals were forced to wear. If all the mad Warders who followed Constans affected it, it said odd things about their status, even though the Elector was supposed to support Constans completely. Curious, Khat asked, "Would you rather see him dead?"

Elen pressed her lips together, and didn't answer.

After a few more turnings of the corridor they came to a long room filled with the sound and smell of running water. The inside wall had a gentle curve and wide windows looking down on an interior court a level or so below that was filled with a noisy gathering of people. Servants disappeared unobtrusively as Elen led Khat through, and the opulence was incredible. The carved marble of the high ceiling was touched with gold leaf, the painted tiles on walls and floor glistened, and drapes of light silk and gauze framed the windows. When they passed the source of the water Khat involuntarily stopped to stare. One wall was set at a slight angle, and water from some invisible source within a recess in the ceiling ran down it over a slab of multihued jasper. The water was collected in a shallow trough at the bottom of the wall, running away out of sight again.

Elen caught his sleeve and pulled until he recollected himself and followed her. They came to another arch guarded by a servant who bowed as he opened one of the tall doors of copper mesh for them.

"It's not going well," Elen whispered to Khat, and moved on before he could ask why. *Everyone has a choice*, Constans had said. *Everyone but me*, Khat thought, and followed her.

The Heir to the Elector's throne was reclining on a low couch, looking up at Sonet Riathen with an attentive smile that still seemed to convey a gentle skepticism. Khat hadn't expected her to be as beautiful as the portraits on the minted coins implied. Everyone knew the Elector was short and fat, and singularly unprepossessing, though his image on the coins left out those defects; it followed that the Heir's portraits would be altered as well. But her features were finely formed, her eyes large and dark and knowing, without benefit of kohl or malachite or any other powder. Her skin was the warm color of cinnamon, and her kaftan and mantle were wisps of gold and amber silks, with strings of gold and amber drops draping her lithe form and decorating her cap.

Riathen, wearing the white robes of office, a headcloth with gold chains twisted through it, and the brief veil his age and station allowed him, was pacing in front of her silk-draped couch, saying, "The two relics that are still missing are the keys to unlock the knowledge we need to survive." He had glanced up as Elen and Khat entered, but didn't stop to acknowledge them. Gandin was waiting for them near one of the windows, and exchanged a nod with Elen. "Without it," the Master Warder continued, "we are no better than the street fakirs."

There was a long waist-high table made of what looked to be cedar, another shocking extravagance, and near one of the wide windows was a large bronze armillary sphere, an astronomical instrument that was forbidden to private citizens. The chairs were cedar and ebony, with gold and ivory inlay, delicate as flowers.

Khat particularly noticed a large cabinet of glass reinforced by bronze that held gorgeous floral tiles of all the different sizes. There was also an Ancient bowl of thick milky glass etched with a pattern of flowing waves perhaps meant to symbolize the water that had once surrounded Charisat, a score of *mythenin* ornaments and vessels set with gems and precious stones, carnelian intaglios, etched fragments of polished silver mirrors, and rarest of all, there were jewelry, mirrors, and boxes all set with the soft, round white stones that were said to be the hardened excrement of some long-dead sea animal. *The Heir owns enough relics to set up in business on the Fourth Tier,* Khat thought in bone-deep envy.

The Heir idly smoothed the brocaded fabric covering the couch cushions. Her attitude of indolence was very much at odds with Riathen's worried pacing, and Khat felt sure the old man was the one getting the worst of the dispute. She looked up at Riathen now and said, "When you say 'we,' I assume you mean the Warders, Sonet." Her voice was deep but rasped agreeably on the ears, like rough silk.

Next to Khat, Elen shifted uneasily. Riathen's pacing had taken him to the cedar table, and he leaned on it wearily. His hands, resting lightly on the polished surface, were trembling. Khat looked up at him, startled, but the Master Warder was staring into space. He said, "You will simply have to trust me, Great Lady."

"I do trust you, Riathen. It's Constans that worries me." She stood, the silk of her robes flowing like water, and went to one of the broad windows to look at the crowd below. "His support is growing." Her mouth thinned with distaste. "My beloved father the Elector is surrounded by his lackeys. That's one of them now."

The court was decorated as a garden, with trees and flowers in marble tubs and a carved stream in the stone floor which wandered through shallow pools with fountain jets. Finely robed courtiers gathered there, talking over the music of the water and the spirit bells tied in the stunted trees. Moving through the elegant throng in the court below was a tall woman, dressed in black flowing garments with her head covered only by a hood so loose the sun glinted off her light hair. The crowd parted for her with a shade too much alacrity for courtesy. "That's Shiskan son Karadon, the daughter of the Judge of the Elector's court. It's bad enough that Constans and his ilk forswear Patrician customs, but to corrupt the daughter of a Judge . . ."

When the Heir had spoken her name, the woman below had

stopped, and now her head tilted deliberately up toward the window, as if she had heard the other woman thirty yards away and over the noise of the gathering.

"Careful," Riathen murmured. Moving to the window, he drew the Heir gently away. "Don't speak her name again." Meeting her puzzled stare, he only said, "I'm aware of her . . . conversion. I had offered her a Warder's robes last year, offered to make her one of my personal apprentices even, and she refused me. I was not surprised when I learned she had sworn herself to Constans. Do you know how many others there are? Men and women with the spark of the Old Knowledge in them who could have taken their places as Warders? And some do not declare themselves as openly as she."

They don't know what we are, what happened to us, Constans had said. The woman below moved on, cutting a path through the crowd.

Frowning, Riathen said, "She isn't wearing a painrod, at least. I have reason to suspect Constans has found a cache of them, though I thought I knew of all the rods left intact in the city. He is evidently using them for the lowest purposes, even as bribes for pirates. Where has he gotten them?"

The Heir shook her head, her mouth set in a grim line. "Perhaps my beloved father the Elector procured them for him, somehow. Would that surprise you? Do you think my father would refuse him anything?"

No one answered this rhetorical question aloud. Khat wondered if the Heir realized that whenever she said "My beloved father the Elector" the venom in her voice was so intense she might be in danger of poisoning herself with her own saliva. Once they were out of here he should probably tell Riathen about his meetings with Constans, or at least the first encounter out in the Waste. Aristai Constans was mad, all right, but not mad enough to bribe pirates with rare painrods and then hunt them down through the Waste. Or at least Khat didn't think so.

The Heir turned back to Riathen. "If you find these relics, you will support me when the time comes for my acclamation?"

"I have sworn it." If Riathen had repeated that as many times now as Khat thought he might have, the old man didn't show it.

The Heir's dark eyes regarded the Master Warder intently, and Khat was sure she was on the verge of giving him whatever permission or blessing he needed from her and they would all be able to go.

But then she shook her head and said, "How can I know you will find these relics after they have been missing so long? And have you not tried to look for them before?"

Riathen nodded to Khat, who felt the lowering of doom. "I have other resources now. This man has experience with the lower-tier relic markets, which have previously been closed to my inquiries."

"Really." The Heir turned her intent stare on Khat. Normally that kind of concentrated attention from such a beautiful woman would have been gratifying, but Khat suddenly realized he didn't like her much. Then she said, "Lower the veil."

Khat hesitated, and hated himself for it. Veils were uncomfortable and unnatural, he had never had one on before today, and now suddenly he was reluctant to remove it. And simply knowing what it meant as a symbol in Charisat's bizarre social scale had nothing to do with it. It was the way the Heir had said it: possessively.

In a way she did own Khat and everyone else in Charisat, or she would when she was Elector, since having absolute power over something was equal to ownership. But usually there were buffers between someone in Khat's lowly position and that ownership; powerful Patricians, Trade Inspectors, even Warders, all had to be gotten over or around or through before the word of command actually got down to noncitizen krismen relic dealers on the Sixth Tier. Hearing it so plainly now, so personally, was like feeling the tug of a leash.

Uneasy that his slight hesitation had revealed his thoughts, Khat jerked his veil down. The Heir studied him, her slight smile never wavering. If she was hoping to see Khat blush from self-consciousness, she would be disappointed. Even if he did it would probably be impossible to detect past brown skin and yesterday's bruises, and anyway Elen, waiting forgotten against the wall like a piece of furniture, was doing enough blushing for both of them.

Over her shoulder to Riathen, the Heir observed, "He's krismen. How extraordinary."

Of course she could tell. He had met her eyes. He could have kicked Gandin for being right. After another long, warm stare, she asked, "And who are you?"

He couldn't tell if she was asking for his name or his importance in Riathen's quest. He said, "Nobody important."

"Oh?" One perfect brow lifted at the challenge.

Gandin started to speak, perhaps to answer the Heir's question, but Riathen silenced him with a look. *So that's how it is,* Khat thought. *Let the lady play with the new toy without interference.*

The Heir asked, "And you are certain you can find these mythical relics?"

"No," Khat said. He shifted the ball back to the Master Warder without compunction. "He is."

But Riathen smiled as the Heir turned to him. He said, "I suggest a test."

She hesitated a beat. "Very well." She raised a finger, and a robed female servant materialized from a curtained doorway and, after a low-voiced instruction from the Heir vanished back through it. The Heir turned an amused gaze on Riathen. "It isn't a good idea to wager against me, you know. I'm a noted gamester."

If it was an attempt to lighten the heavy air of tension in the room, it didn't succeed. But Riathen bowed, smiling self-deprecatingly. "As am I, Great Lady."

These people smile too much, Khat thought. All this teeth-showing would not be reckoned polite where he came from, not that the Master Warder and the Heir meant it to be taken for courtesy anyway. At best, they were uneasy allies. He made the mistake of glancing at Elen, who communicated her feelings on the matter by allowing her eyes to glaze over and cross, as if the courtly sniping was causing her to drift into catatonia. Khat looked away quickly. It would take less effort to maintain the proper paranoia toward Warders if it wasn't so easy to like Elen.

The servant entered again, this time carrying a lacquered paper tray with a scattered collection of relics on it.

All were worked *mythenin* fragments. Some were rounded lumps incised with leaves or the long-dead fauna that had once inhabited the Waste; some were formed into the shapes of birds, strange human faces, fish and other sea creatures, not unlike the one the woman in the marketplace had shown them. They might be jewelry, gaming tokens, ornaments.

The Heir said, "One of these is not a relic but a clever fake. Choose it."

A careful and dedicated forger could do just about anything, even hide an unlicensed forge equipped to attain the high, even heat necessary to form an unworked lump of *mythenin* into a more valuable relic. The servant placed the tray on a low table of jade, and Khat knelt next to it and picked up each relic, rubbing it gently between his fingers and trying not to think. Whoever kept that unlicensed forge in operation would be very clever indeed, but there was a place where knowledge and guile left off and instinct took over. When he came to the one that didn't feel right, a flat, round piece with a delicate carving of a flowing fountain, he set it aside, not thinking twice about it. "That one."

He sensed Riathen shift position; undoubtedly the Master Warder was smiling his carefully respectful triumph at the Heir again. Still, Khat checked the remaining three pieces and found the catch: the last one, a bird with a loop for a chain to be run through, felt wrong as well. "And this one."

He held it up to the Heir, and she took the graceful piece and turned it over in her fingers. "Very good," she said, looking down at him. "Those are excellent forgeries. Not one relic expert in the shops of long and august reputation on the Fourth Tier could have made the choice. Where did you come by your knowledge?"

At the moment, Khat didn't care whether she actually wanted to know or was merely sparring again. He had decided some time ago not to tell her anything. "Not on the Fourth Tier."

Her lips twitched in amusement. Of course, she would enjoy an occasional rebuff; it happened so seldom. And she would especially enjoy it from someone as effectively helpless as he was. When it became apparent that that was all the answer she was going to get, she turned back to Riathen, and said, "Very mysterious. I suppose you knew this business would pique my curiosity? Well, I agree to give you the time you need. I will keep my beloved father the Elector from naming Constans Master Warder in your place, at least until you can produce these relics. Then you must fend for yourself, because I will need all my resources to defend my own position. Will that suit?"

"It will suit most excellently, Great Lady."

She nodded in dismissal, already moving away to the window. Riathen had bowed and turned for the door, and Khat had had time for the first breath of relief, when she said suddenly, "One thing more. I would like to speak to your relic expert in private. Perhaps you could leave him here."

Riathen turned to regard his relic expert thoughtfully, and Khat felt something lodge in his throat. It was panic. In a low whisper he said to the old Warder, "You leave me here and you can make plans to burn my bones to tell fortunes, because that's the last help you'll get from me."

"You are overreacting," Riathen said, and took a step nearer, his voice cautiously low.

Probably. Even Khat didn't know what he was afraid of. He raised his voice just a trifle. "You heard me. Do you want her to hear me?"

Riathen turned back to the Heir, unruffled. "I'm afraid that isn't possible now. Time is too precious to us. You understand."

The Heir didn't answer, leaning against the stone window casement, all languid ease. Then she said, "I suppose I do. Very well, you may go."

Khat held his peace until they were outside the palace and between the high double-tiered arcades of the processional avenue. Then he asked Riathen, "What was that about?"

Gandin hissed at him to lower his voice, glancing worriedly at the passersby.

"The Heir is an avid collector of relics," Riathen replied, imperturbable.

"I think she collects other things, too."

Riathen glanced at him briefly, eyes measuring. "Even if she had refused to allow you to leave with us, no harm would have come to you. Surely your own experience would tell you so."

Khat couldn't argue with that, low blow though it was. He couldn't even explain to himself why he had panicked.

That long direct stare would have meant only one thing if it had come from a woman on the street. Riathen had thought so too, obviously, and so had Elen, if her blush had been any indication. The Heir knew he was kris, and she undoubtedly knew the traditional use Patrician women had for krismen men; she could have simply wanted a lover for the long afternoon whom she could use and throw away without having to worry over consequences. The using part was all right, but in her case he couldn't be sure that she really would throw him away afterward instead of having him killed to stop him telling anyone that she had age tracks at the corners of her eyes.

Maybe her request wouldn't have worried him so much if Constans hadn't warned him first—as if Constans wasn't a liar and mad as well.

But Riathen had been willing to use him as a bribe, maybe trusting to Khat's stubbornness to avoid any of the Heir's difficult questions about the search for the relics. And really, he knew nothing that could hurt Riathen. Maybe the old man had wanted the Heir to question him, wanted him to tell her all he knew.

"She also dislikes, and fears, her father," Riathen added. "Which is a great help to me."

"Really?" Khat said, putting a little acid in his voice. "I would never have guessed, except for the bit of foam at her mouth whenever she mentioned him."

"She thinks he killed her mother," Elen informed him reprovingly.

Riathen frowned down at her. "That is hearsay, and not to be repeated. The primary cause of their disagreement is that she believes he favors the three children of his second wife. The poor woman died only last year, and the Elector's preference for her children may be merely sentimental. But the Heir feels it greatly, and was disturbed when her father sent them out of the city to their mother's family in Kirace."

Khat remembered the funeral rites for the Elector's last wife. They had gone on and on for days, far longer than custom required. In his wife's honor, the Elector had free grain and cakes distributed on the lower tiers, and there had been a release of waste water from the First Tier into the sewers, greatly relieving the usual problems of blockages and sickening stench. He winced, suddenly imagining how Sagai would feel if Miram died. He grumbled, "Can't they talk? Why doesn't she just go and ask him if he still wants her to be his heir?"

Gandin snorted derisively, and even Elen lifted an eyebrow at him.

Riathen said, "There will be no more discussion of this. He is still the Elector."

The Master Warder didn't add "for the moment" aloud, but Khat wondered if the thought had crossed his mind.

"Khat, nothing is going to happen to you. I swear it," Elen said patiently.

The afternoon sun was hot in the blue and gold court with its stair down to the Second Tier, and Khat was back in his own clothes and very ready to leave. She added, "And Riathen would not have left you there."

She was saying it to convince herself. "It didn't seem that way from where I was standing."

"You're always thinking things like that." Elen's patience evaporated rapidly, possibly due to her recent overexposure to the lower tiers, but more likely to her fear that he was right. "You think everyone is after you for some reason. You're as mad as Constans."

And speaking of Constans . . . But the words didn't come. The Elector's mad Warder had him in a very neat trap. Telling Elen about Constans's presence in the Miracle's chamber would lead to difficult questions about their prior meeting out in the Waste, and perhaps even more difficult questions from Riathen about Elen's missing painrod and why he hadn't spoken up before. And besides, he was too angry to hand out free information.

He looked up at a squeak from the house's gate and saw Gandin coming toward them across the court. Khat watched his approach without enthusiasm; the young Warder had not been a bringer of good news.

Gandin stopped and nodded briskly to Elen, then held out something wrapped in cheap cloth to Khat. The krismen hesitated and Elen, her eyes round and ingenuous, asked, "Do you think it will explode?"

Gandin frowned at her, puzzled. Khat gave her a sour look and took the package.

It was his knife and flea glass that the Warders' lictors had taken the day before.

"One of my men took them. That was poor discipline," Gandin said. It was an apology.

Khat said nothing, not having anything to say and knowing a direct stare was a good substitute for a verbal rejoinder when your mind was blank. Gandin hesitated, then turned and went back across the court.

Softly, Elen said, "Well, we're not all bad, are we?"

Are you? Khat thought. "Come at dawn again tomorrow," he told her. "We'll get an early start."

Back down on the Sixth Tier, Khat went again to the street market, hoping to see Caster there. He talked to a few other Silent Market dealers he knew, and gave up on seeing Caster again that day when twilight fell.

No matter how hard Sonet Riathen pressed, no matter how ready Khat was to be rid of the whole thing, all would have to happen in its own time.

It was near full dark when he made his way toward home, through the narrow streets past the fading dinner smells of bread and corn gruel. He was tired, tense, and still angry at Riathen, and worse, Constans's warning kept flitting through his thoughts.

Much as he might like to, he couldn't dismiss that warning as gibberish. Constans wasn't mad in that way. Possibly he was trying to earn Khat's trust so he could trick him into betraying the Master Warder. *Earn my trust,* Khat thought. *That's funny.*

When he turned down the alley that led to his court, caution slowed his steps; there was more noise than usual for this time of night coming from the cluster of houses.

He stopped at the end of the alley. There was a small crowd around Netta's house and the one immediately next door on the right, where Ris and his family lived. The doors were open, and the bottom levels glowed with lamplight, a bad sign. Lamps were never used inside at night on the lower tiers unless there was some emergency. They wasted oil and overheated rooms that would have to be used for sleeping. There was just enough light to show him that it was their neighbors gathered there and that Netta was coming out of Ris's house with a bowl of darkly stained cloth.

In another moment Khat was shoving his way through the crowd. He almost ran down Senace at the door. "What happened?"

"It's Ris. Someone beat him. He looks awful . . ." The young man stepped aside for Khat to enter. The house Ris's large family inhabited was smaller than Netta's and crowded with a near-hysterical collection of relatives and siblings of all ages. Ris lay on the floor on a matting pad, with his father Raka holding the boy's head still while Miram wiped the blood away from his face. "Why so much blood?" Raka asked, anguished.

"It's mostly from his nose, I think," Miram said calmly. Ris stirred a little, moaning, and she said, "I know it hurts, pet, but I have to find the cuts."

"What happened?" Khat asked again.

Netta shouldered him aside, bringing Miram a bowl of clean cloths, muttering, "Street thugs. No one's safe."

Sagai had followed her in, and answered Khat in a low voice.

"Two men caught him when he was coming back from the Garden Market. He had nothing to steal, and they wanted nothing from him but to beat him as if they meant to teach him a lesson. Or teach someone a lesson."

Sagai was looking at him speculatively, but at the moment Khat didn't care. "Did he recognize them?"

"Oh yes. It was Harim and Akai."

Two thugs who hired out to Fourth and Fifth Tier debt collectors, but Khat knew that Lushan really paid most of their water money. The broker had been paid his tokens by one of Elen's lictors early this afternoon, long before Ris must have been attacked. Khat was certain about that. Elen had checked for him when they had returned to Riathen's house.

The anger was startling, burning cold right down to his bones: the same anger he had felt when he found out that the idlers in the court were habitually rude to Netta's daughter, and thought themselves safe because she had no male relatives to defend her. He had disabused them of that notion quickly enough.

Maybe everything the city dwellers said was true, and at heart kris were just territorial animals. But Harim and Akai should have been sent after Khat, if Lushan was still so angry. *All Ris does is carry messages,* he thought. *The vindictive bastard knows that.*

It was suddenly too crowded, too noisy in the room, with the family carrying on, the boy's moans, Miram's and Netta's reassurances. Khat pushed his way out to stand in the still hot air of the court.

Sagai followed him, and after a moment asked, "You know why the boy was attacked?"

"No," Khat answered honestly. *But I'll find out. After I cripple Harim just a bit.*

Sagai accepted the answer without comment. They stood in the relative calm as the neighbors began to drift back to their own homes and all the lamps except those Miram still needed were extinguished, one by one.

Sagai started suddenly. "Ah, in all the confusion I almost forgot. Caster came by the Arcade. He said he would have a name for you tomorrow, if you still wanted it."

Khat closed his eyes in relief. "I don't want it, but I need it."

Sagai shook his head. "The sooner this Warder business is over with the better. You take care. You can't trust those people. They're different."

"I'm different," Khat reminded him.

Sagai gestured that away. "You know what I mean."

Chapter Eight

KHAT LEANED BACK against the pillar. "Remember to tell her about the greater weight with the rougher texture."

Sagai was showing Elen how to judge the difference between various lumps of Ancient worked metals and modern trash. He stopped his lesson to fix his partner with a deadly eye. "Are you doing this or am I?"

Khat shrugged and looked away. He had to admit Sagai was the better teacher; Khat got testy if he had to explain anything more than once.

They were at the Fifth Tier Arcade in their customary trading spot, a nook formed by two massive broken columns long ago scavenged out of the remains of some Ancient structure. The columns were covered with little faded human figures in stylized poses—dancing, fighting, lovemaking—that were too shallow and crumbled to make good rubbings from, and too common to bother cutting out and carrying away.

The Arcade itself was a maze of overhung galleries and twisty covered walkways more than five floors high in some places, supported more by the buildings around it than by its own buttresses. The spot Khat and Sagai had long claimed for their own was near the edge of the open central well on the third floor. Two floors above them the sun came slanting down through the holes and old air shafts in the aging roof, and occasionally a stone dislodged from one of the walkways above would drop and crack against the busy gallery below.

Loud talk from the merchants and artisans at work echoed off the cracked and chipped stone facings, complemented by the constant banging from the coppersmiths' alley on the bottommost level. The mat makers worked on the floor just above them where the light was better, and further down the row were the olive oil millers, candle makers, charcoal sellers, and the dealers in henna, malachite powders, eyeblack, and agents to purify the blood. All spent most of the working day complaining about the other inhabitants of the Arcade.

Business had been sparse today. A few other dealers had come sniffing around, and some scavengers from the Seventh Tier had shown up with a basket of junk for them to sift through—Sagai was using the results of that labor for Elen's lesson. No shady dealers with valuable and mysterious relics from unspecified sources had appeared. Khat let his head loll back against the stone in boredom and scratched his pouch, wishing, as he always wished when the eternal waiting-for-something-to-happen became too much to bear, that he had taken up some other occupation.

Sonet Riathen's Survivor text: now there was a mysterious relic, with all its talk of the souls of the people of the west, and the western doors of the sky. An intriguing relic, and not at all like the only other Ancient Script text he had been able to read in the original, which was the one kept in the archive of the krismen Enclave, said to be the only existing record of the Ancient Mage-Philosophers who had created the krismen during the formation of the Waste. It told little about the Mages themselves, and spoke mainly of how there had been many nervous days spent in preparation of the magical essences that were needed to make the transformation and long hours of work on the gigantic arcane engine that would distill them.

Khat knew some of that text was accurate, because he had seen the engine, or at least what was left of it—hulks of dead *mythenin* metal, covered with indecipherable Ancient script and still-beautiful scrolling, the silver and gold brightwork in melted lumps or tarnished past saving, the whole surrounded by heavy shards of Ancient glass. The remains were scattered throughout most of the caves and passages of the deepest level of the Enclave. The text had said the arcane engine had destroyed itself in the completion of the last essence, killing many of the Ancient Mages in the process. The Survivors who had agreed to test the essence hadn't really believed it would work—until their children were born.

After that the text had turned dull as dust, going on forever about breeding lines and the importance of continuing the Ancient Mages' work, and how their magic couldn't govern all, it was up to the descendants of those first newborn kris children to finish their work, and on and on and on. The writer had become obsessive on the subject, but that should be no surprise, Khat decided, considering the poor bastard had been trapped in the Enclave as the Waste spewed fire outside, with no one for company but terrified Survivor parents, mewling infants, and a pack of muttering Mage-Philosophers who probably thought of themselves as gods.

Sagai's voice called him back to the present. His partner was ending Elen's lesson, saying, "That is all I can show you from this poor collection." He pushed the scraps over to Khat, who started to separate out the raw *mythenin* lumps again, which could be sold to certain individuals on the Sixth Tier who claimed to be collectors but who in actuality made the same type of fakes the Elector's Heir owned.

Elen leaned back against the rock, looking hot and dust-covered. No sweepers worked here, so the dust formed choking clouds above the better-traveled walkways. After only a short time she had broken down and bought a small jar of water from a passing water seller. There were no fountains selling drinking water in the Arcade, though on the bottom level a trench had been cut into the rock floor, and possibly it had originally been meant to provide running water for the inhabitants. It was dry now, and served only as a latrine. Elen checked the edges of her plain cap to make sure her close-cropped hair was safely tucked within, then said idly, "Did you know the krismen Enclave has sent an embassy to the Elector?"

Khat realized he hadn't answered her, that she was watching him curiously, when the edge of the dull shard of Ancient glass he was holding broke the skin on his palm. He said, "No, I didn't know that."

"Really? Have they been here long?" Sagai said, regaining Elen's attention while Khat put the piece of glass down and thoughtfully licked the blood off his hand.

"A few days," Elen said. She picked up one of the *mythenin* fragments and rolled it between her fingers, probably trying to duplicate Sagai's ability to detect the minute differences in texture which could reveal what type of relic the piece had come from. "There are going to be at least three meetings with the Elector, which is rare. The embassies from the other Fringe Cities are allowed only one. I think they're going to talk about the trade roads that run through the deep Waste, and the pirate attacks."

Khat asked, "Which lineage are they from?"

"I don't know. I didn't know there were any." Elen looked surprised, then thoughtful. Too thoughtful. "I can find out."

Alarmed, Khat shrugged and looked away. "It doesn't matter."

Sagai coughed to get their attention, and Khat glanced up to see Caster coming down the walkway, passing the mosaic makers and idly inspecting the examples of their art they had set out to draw trade.

The Silent Market dealer reached them and sat down next to Khat, nodding courteously to Sagai and Elen. "Well?" Khat asked him, feigning more interest in the bits of *mythenin* and Ancient glass the scavengers had brought. It was important not to appear too anxious. He needed the information Caster had very badly, but he had no intention of being overcharged for it.

Caster considered the question thoughtfully, his opaque eyes going from Khat to Sagai. "Ten days," he said.

Sagai laughed indulgently and shook his head. Elen drew breath to speak, but Khat kicked her foot, and said, "Ten days! For what?"

"I had to use a favor from someone high up in the Market to get this name," Caster protested. "Ten days is the least—"

"Five," Khat said.

"Nine."

"Six."

"Seven."

Khat exchanged a look with Sagai, then said, "Not seven."

Elen bit her lip and looked desperate. Fortunately Caster was studying his sandaled feet at the moment, considering. Finally the dealer shrugged, and said, "Six it is. A small faceted oval *mythenin* piece with a winged figure in the center was bought a year ago by a man named Radu, who lives on the Fourth Tier in a house in the Court of Painted Glass in the ghostcallers' quarter."

Sagai rummaged in his robe for trade tokens and counted them into Caster's palm, frowning at the unfamiliar name. "He's not a collector?"

Caster shook his head. "He buys, though not as much as he used to. He's a foreseer."

"A fortune-teller?" Khat asked, startled.

"A very upper-tier fortune-teller, for Patricians. They even come to him sometimes. He claims to have an oracle."

"Who sold the relic to him?" Elen asked.

Khat gave her an annoyed look, but Caster considered the question, then shrugged. "You don't want to buy those names. There were three of them, but they're all dead men now."

Since the dealer was giving out free information, Khat asked, "How did they die?"

"Trade Inspectors, how else? Some High Justice went after them." Caster got to his feet. "There it is, for all the good it does you." Then he hesitated and said, "I heard about the boy, Ris . . ."

There was little that went on in the lives of those who practiced the relic trade, or who were even only peripherally involved in it, that Caster did not know. Khat looked up to meet his eyes, cool and deliberate. "Who?"

Caster grinned suddenly, and said, "That's how I thought it was." He nodded farewell to the others and walked away, humming to himself.

"Why did you bargain with him?" Elen demanded, as soon as the Silent Market dealer was out of earshot. "I had more than enough tokens. He could have refused to tell you the name at all."

"There's no point in wasting money," Sagai told her, his expression stern. "And besides, if we didn't bargain he would have been suspicious, and he would have sold his suspicious thoughts to one of our competitors, just the way he sold us Radu's name."

"Which Radu must have wanted kept secret, or what's the point in selling it?" Khat pointed out thoughtfully.

"But if he buys relics . . ." Elen began.

"When Caster said 'he buys,' he meant from the Silent Market dealers," Khat corrected her. "Not from the shops on the Fourth Tier, or from independent dealers like us who have to stay on the legitimate side of the Trade Inspectors if they want to sell to the Academia."

She frowned. "Is that odd, that he should only buy relics from the illegal market?"

"A little." Sagai shrugged. "A genuine collector will buy from whatever source he can find. He may be buying the relics to sell again at a profit, which is a chancy proposition if he doesn't have the right trade license." When Sagai had first come to the city he hadn't much liked the less than legal aspect of the relic business, the necessity for dealing with the Silent Market on occasion, but he had grown accustomed to it. Khat suspected he had come to enjoy it, even.

"I see. But perhaps it's better that he's not a genuine collector," Elen said. "A collector wouldn't want to sell anything to us, would he?"

"Do we have to buy it?" Khat asked her in turn. "Can't Riathen go up to Radu's gate, bang on it, and tell him to hand the piece over now or else?"

"I think that would tend to draw unwanted attention." Elen's voice was dry.

"Then I'll go and see if I can speak to this Radu, and discover if he is perhaps willing to sell some of his less important pieces," Sagai said thoughtfully. Glancing at Elen, he added, "Without mentioning a *mythenin* oval with a winged figure. You never tell them what you really want."

"Especially if they're amateurs," Khat said, rolling the *mythenin* pieces around in his palm. "I'll walk up to the Fourth Tier with you. I have some ideas about that second piece."

"The big ugly block?"

"Maybe big, but maybe not so ugly."

"I'll go with you," Elen said.

"No, somebody has to stay here and play trade as usual. Especially since Caster came by. If we all three run off, we could have every dealer on this tier trailing us."

"And what is more natural than leaving our new apprentice to mind things while we take care of other business," Sagai said.

"You just don't want me to come along. You don't trust me," she accused.

"You did mention something about promising to behave as an ordinary apprentice," Sagai reminded her, smiling. "And really, there is nothing else for you to do."

Truly, Elen did a good job of pretending not to be a Patrician. She didn't complain about the heat or the stench in the Arcade, and she was adept at avoiding casual physical contact without seeming to do so. "Oh, all right," she said, giving in. "But what am I going to do if someone wants to sell me something?"

"Examine it carefully, using the methods I've shown you," Sagai told her, getting to his feet. "Then look thoughtful and say you can't make an offer without consulting one of us, and that we'll be back later."

"That won't be suspicious?"

"It's what everyone else's apprentice does," Khat said. "Good luck."

They went along the walkway to the wide, cracked stone stair leading down, and Sagai said suddenly, "It's a large city, and the kris embassy may spend their entire stay on the First Tier. There's no reason to panic."

"Panic?" Khat looked at him in disgust. "What makes you think I'm panicking?"

Sagai shrugged one shoulder. "You could always go and talk to them. See for yourself which lineage they come from. Unless you think they are going to drag you back to the Enclave against your will."

Khat fixed his eyes on the glittering swirl of dust in a shaft of sunlight. "They might."

"I'm not giving advice, I'm only stating facts."

"Bad advice, bad facts, what's the difference?"

Sagai snorted, but said no more. He didn't have to. Khat had already thought of the reply that facts had to be faced whether they were bad or not.

They didn't really speak again until they reached the Fourth Tier, and found the turning into the ghostcallers' quarter that Sagai needed to take to reach the fortune-teller's house. "You think you're going to have any luck?" Khat asked his partner as they paused there.

"If I see the piece we want and hear whether he is willing to sell it or not, I'll count myself lucky. But I doubt it will go so far."

"The best thing about this is that the price doesn't matter. It's all Riathen's coin, anyway."

"Yes, there is something oddly satisfying about that. You really think to find a trace of our big ugly block here?" Sagai's gesture took in the shops lining the wide Fourth Tier street, with their expensive bleached white awnings and upper-tier goods.

"No," Khat admitted. "There's something else I have to take care of. But I have got an idea about that block. I'll tell you later."

They parted, and Khat went down through the maze of streets where the relic shops clustered.

The shops here were better quality than the cavelike affairs like Arnot's on the lower tiers. Curtains of sheer gauze suspended from the awnings let in moving air, deflected dust, and screened the wealthy and the Patricians who shopped here from casual view. Under the awnings there would be piles of colored matting and inlaid stools, desert flowers in copper pots, and servants to exhibit the relics to interested customers and serve them watered date wine and honey melons. Dealers from the lower tiers, though they supplied the relics that brought in all this wealth, would enter through the back alley doors, if at all.

But it wasn't relics Khat was looking for today.

If the ugly block was going to be found at all, it was not going to be found in the upper-tier relic shops of the Fourth Tier. The scholars of the Academia regularly combed those shops searching for rare pieces overlooked by dealers, and those scholars would all have had a chance to view the Miracle, and would immediately recognize the similarity. Sonet Riathen, with his interest in the Ancients, had undoubtedly seen the Miracle, but he might not have recognized the block for what it was because he had never been taught to categorize relics into groups, to explore their differences by finding the similarities to better-known relics. Or he had recognized it, and said nothing, for some reason of his own.

Khat took a position up one of the alleys, winding his way past the usual crowd of peddlers, gamblers, and fortune-tellers. He found a shady spot along the wall where he could watch the door of one shop in particular.

He sat on his heels there, so settled and quiet that within a short time the busy inhabitants of the alley forgot about him.

The back entrance he was watching belonged to Lushan, as did the shop it was attached to, though Lushan himself had nothing to do with the day-to-day running of the business and was unlikely to be there.

A squabble broke out among the peddlers, a cloud of gnats moved down the alley, the faded brown curtain on the door swayed occasionally as someone within the shop passed close to it, and time crept slowly by. Khat turned over the various aspects of his current difficulties, but he didn't find this kind of waiting onerous. This wasn't waiting, really; this was hunting.

Finally a figure in red pants and shirt with a dingy brown over-mantle came down the alley and entered the back door as if it owned the place. Khat had recognized Harim immediately, from seeing him standing guard at Lushan's back when the broker held court. He had greasy dark hair and smelled worse than most city dwellers, and seemed to enjoy his job of beating people when Lushan told him to. He hadn't seen Khat, immobile as a statue against the shaded part of the wall.

Khat knew Harim came down to this shop of Lushan's every day in the afternoon, to deliver messages or threats as needed, and he knew today would be no different. Harim was too stupid to expect the expected.

It was not long before Harim emerged from the shop. He passed the krismen again without seeing him, and Khat stood up, stretched, and followed him.

Up the alley, away from the crowded streets, into a nearby resi-dential quarter where many of the shop workers lived. The Fourth Tier was not a good place to do this. Many of the inhabitants were well off, so their houses were better kept, better watched. Khat was unwilling to wait until a more opportune moment on a lower tier; retaliation had to be immediate or the point of the lesson would be lost. And next time instead of Ris it could be one of Sagai's children, or Netta's.

They reached a street that was quiet, still. Bright paint and carv-ing decorated the overhung balconies. Khat closed the distance be-tween them, and Harim turned, perhaps warned by some ponderous sense of approaching doom.

But Harim watched the krismen walk up the street toward him with amusement, not alarm. He was thick-set, solid, and tall for a lower-tier city dweller, with a head rumored to be as hard as a rock. His eyes were on a level with Khat's. With a grimace that was proba-bly supposed to be a sneer, he asked, "What do you want?"

Khat stopped just out of easy reach, casually aggressive, his hands on his hips. He was wearing his knife at his back, where his shirt and the drape of his robe hid it, because Harim would know that he nor-mally kept it in a boot sheath. "Lushan was paid. Why did he send you after the boy?"

"Just sending you a message. You'll work for him until he tells you to stop. That's all." Harim grinned, glad to tell the news.

There was a scar on the right side of his face that ran along the cheekbone up to his ear. Khat decided that whoever had put it there had had the right idea. He stepped forward so Harim couldn't possibly mistake his intent, his right hand coming up in a fist for a swing.

Harim jerked his head back so Khat's blow would barely graze him, braced to instantly retaliate. He didn't see that Khat was holding his knife, the pommel in his fist and the blade pointing down and held tight against his forearm, didn't feel it until the line of pain opened across his face just below the old scar. Harim staggered back, mouth open in shock, dripping blood onto the dusty stone and showing bone in the gaping cut.

Khat stepped back. Harim usually depended on his not inconsiderable muscle and a club; another knife fighter would never have let him come so close. "This message is for you," he told him. "The next time somebody wants to teach me a lesson, don't help."

Harim sat down hard, his hand pressed to his face, still in shock. Shutters swung open somewhere above, and there was a cry of alarm from up the street. Khat walked unhurriedly away.

The dust and heat were harder to ignore in the mostly enclosed space of the Arcade than in the open street, but Elen was still enjoying herself. There were people to watch in plenty, an amazing variety of them. Some men wore veils, but most didn't bother. The tradition of Patrician men wearing veils went back to the Survivor Time, when they had needed the extra protection from the sun's glare and the harmful airs hanging over the new Waste rock when they went out to forage for food. When Charisat had been only a city and not the capital of the Fringe Trade Empire, the veil had been only a sign that one came from an old family. Now it was a rigid symbol of status. Status was also why Patrician women still followed the old custom of close-cropping their hair; something that had once been a measure against the heat was now a strict rule. Lower-tier women seldom bothered with it.

But in many ways, living on a lower tier meant far more freedom for a woman, Elen knew. Lower-tier women might do everything from becoming street entertainers to running market stalls or traveling with caravans, and no one thought anything of it. If Elen had never been selected by the Warders, she would be married by now to as high-ranking a Patrician as her mother could secure for her, to es-

tablish an advantageous family connection. And she would be bored
to distraction. By custom Patrician ladies couldn't seek employment,
even with their family trading interests. A daughter of a wealthy
Fourth Tier merchant family had it better; she at least would be expected to involve herself in her family's business matters up to the
elbows.

Time passed quickly, and no one tried to sell Elen anything,
much to her disappointment, though several people of disreputable
appearance came by and eyed her warily. She had just begun to settle
down for a long dull wait when she saw Sagai returning along the
walkway.

"You haven't been gone very long. No good news?" she asked
him as he sat down across from her.

"He wouldn't see me. The servant I spoke to said he occasionally
sells relics, but he 'does not deal with intermediaries,' and by that I
suppose he means the fortune-teller only sells to his Patrician clients." Sagai regarded Elen thoughtfully. "I have an idea how we
might get around that. We'll discuss it when Khat returns."

Elen nodded, willing to wait. Sagai seemed lost in thought, but
whatever those thoughts were, she wasn't able to sense them. Sometimes Sagai was almost as hard to read as another Warder. She hadn't
forgotten Riathen's order to find out more about Khat, and this
seemed a good opportunity. Though she didn't think she would ever
discover anything that would be of any importance to the Master
Warder. But Khat had been oddly unwilling to talk about the kris
embassy; that bore looking into.

She knew Sagai wasn't the sort to be fooled by any attempt at approaching the subject obliquely, and Elen suspected it would ruin
any chance she had to speak freely with him. She asked, "Where did
Khat live before he came to Charisat? Was it at the krismen Enclave?"

Sagai eyed her for what began to seem a long moment, then said,
"Is this Elen the Warder who asks the question, or is it Elen the
young woman?"

"I'm not so young. I have friends younger than I who have had
their third child." Elen smiled, knowing he was trying to lead her off
the subject.

"Yes, that's the way of it in Charisat. In Kenniliar early marriage
is considered improper. But Kenniliar doesn't have Patricians, and
doesn't force out its beggars, and has too many people as it is. But I

wouldn't like my own daughters to marry so young anyway. They have no sense now, and I don't expect that to change for some years." He shrugged. "Or perhaps I don't want them to marry in Charisat."

Elen had heard that food and water were much cheaper in Kenniliar Free City, which had its own trade route directly to the coast. "But if you don't like it here, why did you leave Kenniliar?"

"My uncle is an artisan there, one among many. When the Fringe Cities closed the trade routes to crafted goods coming from Kenniliar, he found himself hard-put to support all of us. There was no work for me, and though I had been educated in the Scholars' Guild, I could not afford the fee to buy a position there. The only other trade I was fit for was the relic trade, and Kenniliar has few relics in the market, and they are far more expensive to buy. Charisat seemed the best opportunity, especially as the relic trade is one of the few I could engage in without buying citizenship."

So Sagai would discuss his past as much as she liked, but he wouldn't talk about Khat's. Elen tried to come at the problem from a different direction. "And did you meet Khat here in Charisat?"

Sagai's gaze could be as penetrating as Sonet Riathen's, but it was still kinder. "No," he said finally, and for a moment she thought that was all he meant to say. "We met on the trade road, when I was bringing my family here.

"This was seven years ago. The trade roads we had to travel were more dangerous then, and the wagons we had in the caravan were powered only by our own sweat and labor. Steamwagons were still too expensive for ordinary folk. It was slow going, and some miles outside the Fringe Cities boundary we were attacked by pirates. They were a small band, though of course we didn't know that at the time. They knew they were too few to take the caravan, which was seventeen wagons strong, but they meant to take some of the defenders.

"I was one of those sent to flush the pirates out of the loose rock at the edges of the road, after we had turned back the first attack. I carried a borrowed rifle, and I thought I had hit one of them. I made my way through the rocks, ignorant enough to think I was stalking him, when something struck me from behind and I was unconscious.

"I woke with a bloody scalp and the feeling that my head had been split open. When I saw where I was I wished that it had been.

"The pirates had made camp in a narrow gorge with a rocky floor. I was tied securely out of the sun on a ledge in the wall of it, and the ropes were attached to an iron stake driven into the rock. I counted twenty of the creatures, as if knowing their number did me any good in my present situation. They were filthy and stunk like beggars, and I thought two were women, though that was difficult to tell. They spoke such a guttural pidgin of Tradetongue that I could hardly understand them, as if the Waste had worn away at their minds the way it had worn away at their bodies.

"They had taken two others from the caravan with me. One was dead, and they had built a fire down in the gorge and begun to butcher his body. I had known what pirates did to captives, of course, but seeing it . . . My other companion was trussed up as I was on the same ledge, but he was badly wounded, stabbed in the belly, and he was dying. Later in the day they took him down to the floor of the gorge and amused themselves with him, then killed him and did as they had with the first man.

"I knew I had been left to last because I was the least wounded, and I cursed myself for condemning Miram to care for our small children alone in a city completely strange to her, all by my stupidity in allowing myself to be caught.

"But nightfall came, and I still lived. There was a gap in the wall of the gorge above my ledge, but the stake prevented me from trying to reach it. And I had worked all day to loosen my bonds, without success. The pirates slept on the floor of the gorge, and I saw they had posted at least one sentry on the top level. I was sure it was hopeless.

"Then suddenly I did not see the sentry anymore. I thought perhaps I had dozed off, but I watched and he did not reappear.

"Then I heard the faint sound of shifting rock from the tunnel behind me, and something tugged at my bonds. I held still, afraid to alert the pirates. The ropes fell away, and I looked. I saw a crouching figure in desert robe wrapped around dusty clothes. I wondered if he was sent by the caravan—perhaps someone had seen us taken and followed—but I was too grateful to ask questions.

"I followed him down the tunnel away into the midlevel, saw the body there of the sentry I had missed.

"Then something alerted the pirates, and they shot at us from the top of the gorge when a gap in the Waste rock revealed us. The bullet struck Khat, and he fell. I dragged him along, not knowing if he was dying or not, but the last thing I wanted was to leave anyone to the pirates. I went in the direction he had followed, and I was lucky I didn't manage to tumble both of us down a sinkhole into the bottom level.

"The pirates didn't try to track us. Later I learned that Khat had been following them for some days, picking them off one at a time by night. They didn't know how many kris were following them, and they didn't want to find out.

"When we reached the shelter of rock overhead again, I could see that he had been shot in the thigh, or at least that's where the blood was. I was surprised to see he was younger than I. I had to wait until he passed out before I could look at his wound, and see that the pellet had passed through without damaging the bone, and bind it up with torn strips of my shirt. Before that he had fought me off as if I was after his virtue."

Sagai shook his head, smiling faintly at the memory. "We did not have an easy time together. It was two days before Khat stopped pretending he couldn't speak any recognizable language. He was willing to risk his life to free me simply because I was a prisoner of the pirate band he had chosen to harry, but he wanted nothing to do with me once I was liberated, and he wanted my help least of all. I think almost that he would have been perfectly happy to bleed to death in the Waste if only he could have done it in private, without an ignorant city dweller pestering him.

"I knew enough about the Waste to stay in the midlevel. At first all he would do was point me in the direction of the trade road. I quickly discovered the way to make him show me which midlevel plants held pulp water was by choosing the one that I felt was least likely to contain it and hacking away at it. Then exasperation would overcome his reluctance to have anything to do with me, and he would show me the correct one."

"That was clever," Elen said. "I can just see that. Why did he pretend not to speak Tradetongue?"

"To annoy me, to make me think him nothing more than a krismen savage, to make me abandon him. It was impossible for him to trust me then, for him to seriously consider the notion that I might really want to return kindness for kindness, and not treachery.

"It took me until the second day to realize what he was doing. I started to talk to him, and he was only able to hold out for one more day before he had to reply." Sagai smiled again. "By coincidence, I spoke to him of the subject I had spent much of my life studying."

Elen understood suddenly. "Relics, and the Ancients," she said.

"Exactly. It took us four days to reach the caravan, and when we came within sight of it, he didn't like the idea of it at all. I suppose he had grown used to me, but the thought of being trapped, wounded and helpless, among so many of us, was too much. Fortunately by that time he was very weak—I was no good at hunting the Waste predators, and we had had little to eat—and I was able to carry him without being too badly hurt." Sagai chuckled. "It was another month before he told me his name."

"What was he afraid of?" Elen asked, frowning.

"City people. If kris are caught as children, especially in the cities further east, they're sold to brothels. Their bones are a commodity on the Silent Market. In many places they're confused with pirates and killed on sight. He takes a risk whenever he deals with the Silent Market, but he takes a risk living here, and you can't deal relics in Charisat without dealing with the Silent Market."

Elen drew a meaningless pattern on the dusty stone. Khat had told her something of this before, and it had certainly put their commerce with Caster in a new light. "And when the caravan reached the city you went into the relic trade together?" she asked finally.

"No," Sagai corrected. "It was more than a year after reaching Charisat that we began to work together, though I saw him off and on during that time."

"So when he came to Charisat with your caravan it was the first time he had been to one of the Fringe Cities."

"I didn't say that. In fact, he is far better traveled than I. But about that you'll have to ask him." His gaze was thoughtful. "Now I've told you my tale, and you owe me yours. When you're willing to tell it."

"All right." She found herself smiling. "When I'm willing to tell it."

Once Khat returned, they decided that the best course would be for Elen to go to Radu's house, not as a Warder but just as a Patrician woman, and ask to buy from the fortune-teller's relic collection.

"Tell him you want his relics because they've been in his home, the home of a powerful mystic," Khat instructed her. "You know that this increases their spiritual power."

Elen was shocked. "I can't say that. He'll think I'm mad."

"Believe us," Sagai said grimly. "It is not nearly as odd as some things we hear from buyers."

Khat went early to the Court of Painted Glass so he could meet Elen outside Radu's house and not seem too closely allied with her. He sat in the shade to one side of the octagonal court, which was bordered by houses that were either empty or whose inhabitants were mad for privacy; all the shutters were tightly closed, and there were no signs of life in the tiny courtyards visible through the locked gates. The painted glass for which the court was named was colored fragments set into the walls of the houses, glittering in the late afternoon sunlight.

We should've waited until morning, Khat told himself, then shrugged off his misgivings. The quarter where the ghostcallers lived and worked was an exclusive neighborhood, but for all the wrong reasons. The fortune-teller had probably chosen this spot for his residence with care, picking a place that would give Patrician clients all the thrills of venturing into the dangerous squalor of the lower tiers without ever having to leave the vigil-patrolled safety of the Fourth. On his way down here along the narrow alleys, Khat had seen many doorsteps where shallow copper bowls stained with the grimy residue of blood had been set out, put there to attract wandering ghosts. Balconies and ledges overhung the passage badly, blotting out much of the harsh afternoon light and making it a perfect spot for ambush. If we ever make enough tokens to afford Fourth Tier water payments, we can always move up here, he had thought grimly. There would be plenty of room, especially after the ghosts carried off a few of the children. This was the only place in all of Charisat where otherwise sound houses stood empty.

Now there was not much sign of activity at Radu's house either, though its gates and outer door stood open, and only a curtain and a dusty door servant squatting motionless in the courtyard guarded the entrance.

Khat looked up as Elen's litter appeared at the head of the alley. It was a modest litter, with bronze rings for the yards of billowy gauze curtains instead of gold and translucent silk. Elen's appearance was modeled after that of a Third Tier Patrician daughter. Her kaftan and mantle of blue silk, the gold jewelry weighting her ears and neck, and the application of rouge and malachite eye powder helped her look the part.

The two bearers adjusted their holds on the padded handgrips of the ornate metal poles and looked bleak, knowing that if she dawdled too long they would be forced to make the trip back through the ghostcallers' courts in the gathering darkness. Conscripted by Elen as an attendant, Gandin walked beside the litter, wearing the plain robe of a family guard and carrying an air rifle. He was veilless, so the expression of distaste he was also wearing was clearly visible. Nonetheless, Khat didn't think there was anything about him or Elen to make Radu instantly leap to the conclusion that they were Warders in disguise, unless the man was a better fortune-teller than everyone seemed to think.

Gandin eyed the court in evident dissatisfaction, greeted Khat with a wary nod, then went back and held a brief whispered colloquy with Elen. Khat got to his feet unhurriedly, dusted off the back of his pants, and ambled over to join them.

Elen's mouth was set in a firm line. *A wild guess says Gandin's been making objections,* Khat thought. Low-voiced, he said, "Let's not wait too long and give anything away." Elen had told him the bearers would come from Riathen's household and were professionally deaf, but there was no point in taking chances.

"Yes," she whispered to the other Warder. "Go on."

"I hope you know what you're doing," Gandin told her, turning to go up to the gate to Radu's house.

"That's the last time I ask for your help," Elen muttered to herself as soon as he was out of earshot.

Khat asked her, "Do you get this much trouble all the time, or is it just lately?" He was wondering if it was his presence that bothered Gandin or if the other Warders just put roadblocks in Elen's path out of habit.

Still fuming, but keeping her voice low, she said, "Yes. I know my power isn't reliable, but I have a great deal of experience at this sort of thing. I caught a spy from Rowan-ly in the Elector's court only two months ago. I don't know why they . . . Oh, never mind."

Gandin reached the stone-flagged courtyard and asked the grimy door servant for entrance with a peremptory gesture. The servant leaned around him to eye the litter, then vanished through the curtained doorway.

Gandin waited, air rifle slung back on his shoulder, but scanning the front of the house alertly. Khat developed an itch between his shoulder blades, as if someone was taking a bead on him. He didn't know why he should feel so alert for ambush; all this trickery was so Radu wouldn't realize it was Sonet Riathen who wanted one of his relics, not because they suspected attack from a jumped-up fortune-teller who catered to crazy Patricians.

The curtain was swept aside by a grander servant in a brown mantle and copper skullcap. He held the curtain open in welcome. Elen slipped out of the litter, the bearers hardly adjusting it at all to compensate for the shift of her light weight. She caught up the train of her mantle over one arm and crossed the courtyard. Following her, Khat marveled at her performance.

Her normal walk was a determined stride, as if she meant to go through anything in her way. Now she didn't quite mince, but managed to give the impression that she didn't do much of her own walking and didn't quite know how to go about it. Khat wondered how he could ever have been fooled into thinking that Elen would be a poor liar.

The short entrance hall was lit only by stubs of candles floating in shallow silver bowls of scented oil, one on either side of a round still pool set in the center of the room. This would be to reassure the Patrician clients, who would expect some display of ornamental water as a sign of the fortune-teller's wealth and status. The dim light revealed little, only smoke-stained walls with mosaics depicting passable imitations of Ancient designs. Khat found himself holding his breath against the suffocating cloud of incense that was wafting into the entrance hall from the interior of the house. It wasn't the light, expensive scent of sandalwood that had hung in the air of Riathen's home, but a sweet, sickening stench with some sour odor beneath it.

The impressive servant bowed profoundly to Elen, straightened, and noticed Khat with a slight tightening of a face well schooled to blandness. But Elen's face was well schooled to impervious Patrician reserve, and the servant didn't quite dare to ask any questions.

They went up a short flight of stairs past a door curtain of dust-heavy cotton and into a large, high-ceilinged room. Khat stopped just inside the threshold. Something hidden was moving and breathing somewhere, something that made the short hair on the back of his neck prickle.

The place seemed empty. A wall of high arches suggested an interior court lay just beyond, but the openings were screened off from air and light by rolls of matting and dark curtains, and the room was lit by hundreds of small candles set in niches, pot lamps, and bowls everywhere. Their flames flickered in the breeze from half a dozen clockwork fans moving slowly back and forth overhead, sluggishly stirring the hot, scented air. There was another mosaic on the floor, but only glimpses of bright colors were visible through the covering of matting and cushions.

A sense of movement somewhere near the ceiling drew Khat's gaze up into the shadowy dead air between the fans. Then his eyes adjusted to the light, and he saw it was not a shadow but something draped in black cloth suspended from the highest arch of the ceiling. Then the drape moved suddenly, as if whatever was under it had plucked at it.

Elen had stopped with Khat, and now she followed his gaze to the hanging thing above. "What's that?" she whispered. Standing next to her, Gandin shifted his grip on the rifle's polished stock.

"Only the oracle, Honored," the impressive servant said, startling all three of them. Khat had completely forgotten about him. "It is well caged, and cannot harm you. Please be at ease." He bowed and retired back through a door barely visible in the far wall.

Elen gestured imperiously for Gandin to wait in the entrance hall, and he grimaced and went as reluctantly as a real vigil would. The only furniture was a low table of pure alabaster, its edges set with green and blue polished stones. Elen sat at one of the matching stools near it, carefully arranging the folds of her mantle.

Khat sat down on the floor even though he hadn't been invited to, and tried to ignore the stealthy motion of the oracle in its cage overhead. There was something vaguely familiar about the place, something disquieting, but he couldn't quite pin it down. The slow waving of the fans sent shadows jumping in corners and caused the drapes that covered the windows and doors to gently stir, giving the nerve-racking impression that the room was filled with surreptitious motion.

The door curtain moved in earnest then, sweeping aside to reveal a tall thin man dressed only in plain gray robes, no cloth-of-gold, no silk, imitation or otherwise, no bright colors. His skin was pale, as if he never ventured out, and the eyes above the formal veil were startlingly dark.

He bowed. "Honored, I am at your service. What do you wish?"

Radu might not have the appearance of a showman, but he had the smooth polished voice of a man who made his living catering to upper-tier whims.

Elen smiled up at him in perfect confidence and said, "The benefit of your spiritual guidance, of course. And to make a request."

Radu came further into the room. "The guidance, of course, is yours. The best my poor skill can offer. But the request?"

"I have heard from . . . certain agents in the marketplace . . ." She hesitated delicately, as if debating whether or not to reveal the origin of her information. Khat couldn't have thought of a better way to plant the idea in Radu's mind that she also bought from the Silent Market. She continued, ". . . that you are a collector of relics and treasures of the Ancients, as I am, and I wondered if there might be any in your collection you were willing to part with."

Radu took a seat at the low alabaster table opposite her. "Ah. You sent a servant earlier?"

"A dealer in the trade of relics. This man's partner."

Radu followed her gesture, and his critical gaze came to Khat. His black eyes were hard to read, even though Khat had learned years ago to interpret emotions from eyes that never altered color unless by a trick of the light. He saw the man's brows lift as he realized the lower-tier relic dealer his Patrician client had brought with her was kris, saw his eyes turn sly as he looked back to Elen and came to the obvious conclusion. Khat almost smiled; the suspicion that she was a Warder or Trade Inspector in disguise would never enter Radu's mind now.

Apparently oblivious, Elen finished, "He said I would have to come to see you myself."

The impressive servant reappeared with a tray of wine cups and honey date cakes, and served Elen. Khat looked away and willed his stomach not to growl.

"I see." Radu began to take out the implements for augury from under the table: copper plates charted with diagrams for interpreting the ash patterns after the bones were burnt, something only the more expensive brand of fortune-teller bothered with, and a shallow metal bowl. The servant brought over a brazier filled with coals, set it on a wicker pad to protect the table, and withdrew again. A low mutter rose and fell from the draped cage hanging above the fortune-teller's head. Giving no indication he was aware of it, Radu asked, "And are you interested in any particular piece?"

Remembering how eager for Caster's news Elen had been in the Arcade, Khat tensed, waiting for her to fall into that trap. But she was wary now, and said only, "No. My own collection is not extensive, though I flatter myself that I have bought wisely. But there is one thing . . . I wondered if your collection might contain . . ."

Radu watched her attentively, betraying nothing, and she leaned forward, lowering her voice earnestly. ". . . some relics rumored to possess . . . arcane powers?"

Radu didn't do anything so blatant as to nod to himself in satisfaction, but Khat sensed that he was smiling under the veil. "Yes," Radu said, his voice grave. "It does help one of my craft to own relics of the Ancients, particularly mystic ones. But before we continue . . ."

He lifted a hand, and the drape was swept away from the suspended cage. Not by magic; the impressive servant was in the corner, pulling on a dark-colored rope that was almost invisible against the indigo ceiling tile.

The cage was round, of ornate ironwork, and the oracle crouched in the bottom, peering down through the bars. Some of the filth-matted hair seemed to be on its face, so it was presumably male. Clad in rags, with burning mad eyes, it glared down at Radu and snarled inarticulately. It was small, but it was impossible to tell if it was young or old.

The fortune-teller said, "Perhaps my oracle will prophesy for you, lady. Did you have any type of relic in particular in mind? Something large, something small?"

He's trying to rattle her, Khat thought. He felt a little rattled himself. Elen managed to tear her eyes away from the cage, her hands playing nervously with the silk fringe on her mantle; Elen, who was as fluttery as a rock when nervous. Smiling uncertainly, she said, "Something small—I wish to carry it with me."

"I have many small pieces of great beauty, and some of mystic import."

The oracle shrieked suddenly, and Elen winced, probably the first genuine reaction she had betrayed so far. She said, "Another foreseer told me that winged images are symbolic of my soul."

Khat rubbed the bridge of his nose to hide any reaction he might have had, thinking, *Careful, careful.* Now that the drape was removed the source of the stench that the incense was meant to mask was obvious.

But Radu didn't seem suspicious. "A winged image? Not a bird? The lady has seen the drawings of birds from the Last Sea cities, of course?"

"Of course. But this foreseer was very particular. A winged image."

"Relics with winged figures are very rare, very . . ." Radu hesitated. Khat suspected he was veering away from the word "expensive." "Very dear. I reluctantly parted with the only one I had."

"Oh. Could you tell me who has it now?"

Khat held his breath, and not because of the stench.

Maybe Elen was reading Radu's thoughts, or else she was a genius at reading faces, even veiled ones. She added brightly, "After I look over your collection and make my other choices, of course."

Radu bowed his head, playing the grateful servant, but she had him now. "Of course. But first I will burn the bones for you."

Khat felt weak with relief. He let his attention wander as Radu got on with the fortune-telling business. Maybe Elen would be able to buy the thing outright, fulfilling the first part of their commission without a single trade law being broken, though that thought would be more comforting if he didn't think the second part of their commission was hopeless.

The oracle was quiet in its cage, all its mad attention focused on its master. A slight movement drew Khat's eye to yet another heavily draped door, and a flicker of candlelight revealed half a shadowed face peering out: the impressive servant, watching from another room. Not liking to betray too much intelligent interest in his surroundings, Khat looked back to Radu's performance.

The fortune-teller had taken out a silk bag that gleamed in the light, and now carefully shook out a bare handful of bone fragments. All the while Elen kept up a lively babble about arcane relics, mixing together so much truth, half-truth, rumor, and outright fabrication that Radu grew more and more complacent, and was probably already counting the coins he was going to have off her. Khat thought of the kris embassy up on the First Tier and found himself wondering if Radu was wealthy enough to afford the best in foreseeing materials, or if he used lizard bones like the street fortune-tellers.

Elen paused for breath, and Radu held up a hand, saying, "Now concentrate, Honored, while I look into the shadows of time."

Elen was obediently silent, watching him attentively. Yellowed bone fragments trickled from Radu's pale hands into the coals. The wisps of smoke rose up, but the fortune-teller started back, suddenly on his feet, knocking over the heavy alabaster stool.

Elen stared up at him in blank surprise. Khat half uncoiled from the floor, almost going for his knife before sense caught up to him. Gandin thrust the curtain aside from the entrance hall, glaring around the shadowed room suspiciously.

Radu was looking from Elen to Khat, his eyes wide with fear. Elen gasped, "What is it? What's wrong?"

The oracle started to screech, rocking back and forth, slamming itself against the bars of its cage. Its shrieks turned to gasping cries. Its voice became human suddenly, and remarkably like a young man's. "Hear the voices," it choked out, as if every word ripped its throat. "They failed, and died, the great work left undone. Death is the path. The voices . . ." The last word turned into a raw screech, and it was an animal again, grinding its filthy head against the bars.

In the stunned silence, Radu bowed choppily. "Forgive me, Honored, I have . . . You will have to leave."

Elen opened her mouth, but nothing glib came out. To play for time, Khat interrupted, "I came here to value relics, not watch a future-telling. Is somebody going to pay me for my time?"

Radu didn't deign to notice the distraction. "Forgive me, Honored," he said again. "You must come back another time." He bowed to her again and almost bolted for the inner doorway.

The impressive servant appeared, embarrassed and almost as flustered as his master, to show Elen out. She glanced at Khat, who shook his head, as puzzled as she was.

In moments they were outside in the court. Sunset streaked the sky red, and it was nearly dark. Two red pot lamps had been lit in Radu's courtyard, but the bearers looked uncommonly happy to see Elen, leaping to their feet to ready the litter.

"That's that, apparently," Elen said, frustrated. She handed Khat a honey cake she had palmed from the tray and hidden in her sleeve.

Gandin shrugged helplessly. "I could hear you from the entrance hall. It sounded as if it was going well."

Elen ignored him. "Did I do something wrong?" she asked Khat. "Was that a performance just to get rid of me?"

He shook his head. "No. No, it was almost as if he . . ." He couldn't quite make himself say it.

Elen said it for him. "Saw something when he burned the bones. You said he was a charlatan."

"I said he was probably a charlatan. And what do I know about it?"

"I wouldn't have thought he had true sight. Anyone who would keep an oracle . . ." She hugged herself, as if feeling a chill despite the ever-present heat. "Poor demented thing."

The bearers were almost bouncing with impatience to be out of the area before full night. Gandin said, "We'd better go. He might be watching."

He moved away, and Elen reluctantly turned to follow.

Khat made his decision on impulse. He caught the sleeve of her mantle, remembering at the last moment not to touch her arm, and whispered, "Meet me on the Odeon's steps, second night hour."

She nodded without hesitation, then went to climb obediently into the litter like a good Patrician lady.

Chapter Nine

T HE ODEON'S PALISADE was lit by torches and blood lights and crowded with milling theater patrons, idlers, and those whose business it was to profit from them. A pair of tumblers threw each other into the air as if they were weightless, the light sparking off their dark, sweat-slick skin. A fire-eater drew a larger circle, but one that was careful to keep a respectful distance around her. Gamblers had staked out small territories for dice or tables, and a storyteller had taken a place at the base of the furthest pillar on the steps, an island of quiet amid all the noise and laughter.

At this time of night the crowd was mostly lower-tier, except for the few Patricians who lingered to be shocked at the tumblers' display of so much bare skin. Khat leaned against one of the pillars out of the way of the open double doors, watching everything with a cynical eye.

He hadn't been there long when Ivan Sata materialized out of the shadows and stood grinning up at him, as if he thought his presence would be welcome. Sata pretended to be a relic dealer, but so much of his trade was with the Silent Market that the Academia had banned him. The fact that he hadn't been executed by the Trade Inspectors yet caused many to speculate that Sata informed for them. Khat had offered to throw him off the Sixth Tier wall several times himself, but this probably happened so often to Sata that he didn't see it as a deterrent. "Lushan's looking for you," he said helpfully. Most of his teeth were missing, and he looked as if he belonged under an Eighth Tier sewer outlet.

Sata was short, even for a lower-tier city dweller, so Khat continued to survey the crowd over his head. "Is he," he said, without much interest.

"He's not happy, either. You must have made him very angry," Sata persisted.

Khat shrugged. "I'm competition."

Sata chuckled. "Competition, hah. With the ladies, maybe. Now I'm wondering what he thinks . . ."

"Do you want something?" Irritated into looking directly down at the much smaller man, Khat leaned forward, and Sata backpedaled.

"Just giving you a friendly word," he said, grinning nervously as he melded back into the crowd.

Watching him go, Khat caught sight of Akai going up the steps into the Odeon, probably to meet with Lushan. Akai was gaunt, his dust-colored robes hanging limply on his lean frame. He was a knife-fighter too, and would be whipcord strong, and dangerous. Really too dangerous for Lushan to waste his talents giving out beatings to boys like Ris, but Khat had always known Lushan to be wasteful by nature. He also thought he would probably have to kill Akai.

Elen appeared at the edge of the crowd around the fire-eater. Khat pushed away from the pillar and went down the steps toward her.

She had had time to get rid of her jewelry and smudge dust on her cheeks in place of the cosmetic powders, and she wore a cheap dark-colored kaftan and cap—a lower-tier street urchin.

He stood beside her for several moments to give her time to notice him, then started away down the street. She followed and caught up to him after they were through the First Forum and past much of the crowd.

"We're going back to Radu's house?" she asked. In this quieter area the lamps were farther apart and passersby walked with more haste.

"He never answered your last question," Khat said. "Very impolite of him."

"Fatally impolite?"

He stopped abruptly and turned to stare down at her. "What?"

"I was just asking," she said, looking up at him defensively. "I just want to know what we're doing."

"We're going to poke around the outside of the house, see if we can look through any windows on the upper floor." This was something of an understatement, but he wanted to make a point. "And try to find out where he sold off our relic. 'Fatally impolite.'" Khat shook his head, disgusted. "You listen to too many stories, Elen."

"We're going to do this by looking in the windows?" she asked, skeptical.

"Do you want to help, or do you want to hear about it in the morning?"

"I want to help, of course."

He started down the street again, and she hurried to catch up.

Khat took the turn down into the ghostcallers' quarter. It was not any more attractive at night than it had been in the long shadows of late afternoon. A few lamps glowed behind shuttered windows, and there were no reassuring blood lights or neighbors taking advantage of the less suffocating night air to sit outside and gossip.

In the first lighted court they passed, a ghostcaller was performing. Khat skirted the silent circle of rapt watchers, stopping at a gap where he could see what was happening.

Elen, who had apparently been craning her neck to see too, bumped into him from behind and muttered, "Sorry."

The ghostcaller was bare of anything but dabs of white and blue paint and smeared blood from the self-inflicted wounds in his fingers. His face and body were a young man's, but his long mane of hair was gray; ghostcallers tended to age before their time. He had made a circle of blood drops in the dust of the street, and now stood at its center, head flung back, swaying and crooning nonsense words to the cloudless night sky.

The circle of blood was supposed to confine the ghosts, keep them from attacking any spectators, but Khat wouldn't have bet his life on it. The ghostcallers who performed in the open-air forums were mostly fakes: crowds paid to see skin and a great deal of gratuitous thrashing about, and to feel a thrill of danger without ever actually experiencing any. This performance in the ghostcaller's home court put on for a few of the faithful could too easily be real.

"Come on," Khat said softly, and Elen willingly followed him out of the dimly lit court.

The moon was in quarter, limning the crumbling edges of walls and disused balconies with silvery light. With no lamps to night-blind you it was almost enough to see by, Khat decided. The rock-cut houses looming overhead cut off any wayward sound of revelry or trade traffic from the rest of the tier. They might have been in a city of the dead.

They reached the court behind Radu's, which was small and ramshackle. Only two of the narrow houses had the tightly closed shutters that betrayed possible occupation; the rest had windows that gaped open into empty blackness. Khat could just see the darker shape of Radu's house where it towered in rock-cut splendor over its less wealthy mud-brick neighbors.

Elen stopped suddenly, whispering, "There's somebody up there." She was looking up at the roof of the fortune-teller's house, three stories above the court and lost in shadow.

"Where?"

"Up on the roof. Someone crouching over."

That he hadn't expected. Khat ducked inside the empty house that leaned against the back wall of the fortune-teller's home. Something fled across the floor, skittering, at their approach—more confirmation the place was deserted. It was nearly blind dark except for the moonlight coming through the windows, but the house was so small it scarcely mattered, just two boxlike rooms one atop the other. Khat took the narrow, crumbling steps three at a time, Elen scrambling after him.

The trapdoor to the roof was missing, and Khat peeked out cautiously before risking more of his head. The roof was a flat landscape, featureless in the moonlight. Radu's house towered about six feet above it, the smaller dwelling swaying drunkenly into the larger.

Khat drew himself up onto the roof, keeping to a crouch. The other rooftops made an angular sea around them, cut through by the pitch-dark chasms of alleys, empty and silent until it reached the lighted boundaries of the more ordinary quarters. Elen climbed out of the trapdoor and sat on the edge, fishing under her robes. Before he could ask, she pulled out a painrod and attached it to the loop at her belt, murmuring, "Just in case."

Khat stood, caught the edge of the higher roof, and pulled himself up onto it. Radu's house had four wind towers and several piles of broken brick rubble decorating the open expanse of its flat roof: more than adequate cover for any number of intruders. He waited for Elen to find toeholds in the wall below, watching carefully for movement. Nothing stirred, but remembering that her Warder eyes were considerably better in the dark than his, he didn't find himself much inclined to doubt her.

Elen hauled herself up next to him, and he asked her in a low whisper, "See anything?"

She shook her head.

He gestured for her to circle around to the left, and took the right side himself, drawing his knife. If these were local thieves who had unluckily decided to turn Radu's house tonight, they would far rather run like hell than risk confrontation. At least, when Khat had turned houses on the Third Tier, that's what he had always done. He reached the first wind tower and found no one crouching behind it, moved silently on to the next.

If they were thieves.

Just before he reached the second wind tower something exploded from behind it. He had half expected that whoever it was would try to rush Elen, who was obviously the smaller opponent, and be unpleasantly surprised by a painrod in the hands of a trained infighter and trapped until Khat could get to them across the roof. It was the best tactic someone in this situation could adopt, but this person obviously cared nothing for tactics.

He had time for one knife thrust, but the point hit his attacker's collarbone, and the weapon was jolted out of his hand. Suddenly he was locked in a struggle with someone his height and almost too quick. Then one of his feet was hooked out from under him, and he was on his back on the warm stone of the roof, trying to keep a painrod away from his head. The weight on top of him was heavy, but definitely female. He was holding her forearm, trying to keep her from bringing it down on his throat, and the texture of her skin was like silk over solid rock. He twisted her wrist, and she dropped the painrod but smashed her elbow down on his chin with enough force to shock him into losing his grip.

She surged to her feet, hood torn away, and the dim moonlight showed him a profile and glittered off loose, colorless hair. *I know who this is,* he thought, confused. He couldn't see if she was bleeding from the knife wound or not. It hadn't seemed to slow her down at all. Then two other dark figures bolted from cover, leaping down to the next roof, and as she grabbed up her painrod and turned to follow them he kicked her in the back of the knee, knocking her flat.

She hit the roof hard, but rolled to her feet again as if the fall and the blow had been negligible.

She hesitated, but as he struggled to stand she bolted after her companions, easily making the leap to the roof below.

Elen was beside him suddenly. The fight had only taken moments. "Did you see who that was? Shiskan son Karadon. We saw her at the palace..It means Constans is here."

"Was here. I don't know if you noticed, but they were in a hurry to leave." Khat rubbed his sore jaw, remembering the Judge's daughter who was Constans's disciple, looking up as the Heir spoke her name from a window that was obviously too far away for the sound to carry. He hadn't seen her very clearly tonight either, but that had little effect on his reaction to her.

He got to his feet, and after a moment's search found his knife where it had fallen and thoughtfully ran his fingers along the blade's flat. They came away darkened by Shiskan son Karadon's blood. He had gotten her, all right, but she had simply ignored it, the way Constans had ignored the blow from Elen's painrod in the Waste.

"They must have followed us the first time we came here." Elen pounded her knee with her fist in frustration. "If they found out where Radu sold the relic . . ."

"Can't hurt to look, anyway." Maybe it would keep his mind off what it would be like to make love with the woman who had just tried to kill him. "Come on."

Set into the roof was a light copper hatch reinforced by iron bars at some point in its past. This hadn't helped it when the lock had been smashed off.

Inside, a narrow flight of steps led down to a small shaft with two doorways, one that opened into a disused pantry and the other curtained with heavy cotton. Khat lifted the curtain and saw it led directly into Radu's fortune-telling room. This was the door from which the impressive servant had watched them this afternoon.

Most of the candles had guttered, and the clockwork that drove the fans had wound down, making the large chamber silent, still, and dark as a cave. Something like a robed body lay on the alabaster table; a step forward and Khat saw that it was actually the cover of the oracle's cage.

He looked up and saw the cage was empty, its door torn open and hanging on broken hinges. He hesitated, listening hard, but the room felt empty. There was no noise, no sign of life from Radu or his servants, but Khat hadn't expected any after a visit from Constans or one of his minions. The entire house felt empty.

But no use taking chances. "Elen." He pointed up at the cage. "Be careful."

She glanced up at the empty cage and made a face. "Oh, how lovely. But if I was that thing I'd run right out of here and keep running until I got to the edge of the tier." She looked around the room, biting her lip thoughtfully. "He had some drawers, or compartments or something, under that table."

"You check those, and I'll do the rest of the rooms down here."

There seemed to be nothing on the ground floor. No sign of the impressive servant, though Khat found the cubby where he probably slept, off the room where the water, oil, and grain were stored. The open court in the center was bare of anything except an unadorned fountain that served the pantry and a domed bread oven. The windows of the upstairs rooms that looked down into it were bricked up to hamper thieves; only sensible in this half-deserted quarter. If Radu kept anything valuable, it would be upstairs.

Khat stopped to scoop a handful of water from the fountain for a drink. At least the bricked-up windows couldn't stare down at him accusingly. *Radu's dead in this house somewhere*, he thought. The odd thing was that there was no reason he and Elen shouldn't be dead up on the roof now. *I should have made a better deal with Riathen*. Relic dealing wasn't the safest business in the world, but it wasn't normally this dangerous, either.

A breeze moved over the roof, stirring dust and loose bits of brick and plaster, and Khat stepped back against the wall. Nothing else moved, and he reminded himself not to let his imagination get the better of him. Even in the Waste, ghosts and air spirits were rare.

He went back into the main room, where Elen had emptied the contents of the hidden compartments onto the table. "Nothing in here but junk—props, I suppose, for fortune-telling," she reported. "Seeing what he has here, I'm beginning to doubt whether that was a true vision he had or just a trick to get rid of me."

"Maybe it was," Khat admitted. "But it's funny, then, that he didn't make you pay for his time."

The curtained door at the back of the room hid the interior stairwell that led to the house's upper rooms. Khat took one of the candle bowls from its niche and started up.

The fortune-teller's sleeping room was at the top. He had one of the cheaper upper-tier styles of bed: a bronze frame set up a few inches off the floor and piled with cushions. And there was Radu.

He lay half on the bed, his arms stretched across it and his legs sprawled on the matting-covered floor. He was still dressed in the gray robes he had worn for Elen's fortune-telling. He probably hadn't been awakened, but had run into this room in blind panic and been caught when he tripped on the bed. There was no blood that Khat could see or smell, and Radu's eyes were still open, staring fixedly at the far wall.

"It must have been Constans," Elen whispered. "Or Shiskan son Karadon."

"Can she kill somebody just by looking at him, like he did at the Remnant?" Khat asked. He realized with some irritation that he was whispering too.

"I wouldn't think so. It takes many years to acquire that kind of power." She leaned over the body, peering at the head. "I suppose this might have been done with a painrod. It looks like he died of fright."

There was nothing for them here. Khat went through the small door that opened off the bedroom and made a pleasant discovery. Shelves had been carved out of the walls in the long room to hold Radu's collection of relics.

He went down the room, looking, pausing occasionally to pick something up. Radu had only a few glazed tiles, two in very poor condition with cracks that made their designs difficult to make out. There were some *mythenin* ornaments, several set with rather nice stones of Ancient cut, and many of the more unusual type of relic: *mythenin*, glass, or stone shaped into animals, stylized faces, or sea creatures. Suspicious, Khat picked up the best of the stylized faces, and rubbed it thoughtfully. The weight was a little wrong, and there was something funny about the texture. A *fake*, he thought. None of the relics looked disturbed by the night's intruders.

In the corner was a metal box, the brocaded cloth that must have covered it pulled to one side. In the candlelight Khat examined the front cautiously. There was no sign that it had been opened. Elen came in from Radu's sleeping room. "Found anything?" she asked, looking over the collection speculatively.

"This." The box was covered with scrollwork and incised figures of dancing skeletons—a warning to potential robbers. He handed Elen the lamp and said, "Don't get too close. It's a trick-lock box. There are poisoned needles in the catches. I've seen this a hundred times."

Since there was no need to worry obsessively about noise, he used the hilt of his knife to thump each catch, then to break off the tip of the needle that protruded at the pressure of the blow. The first time he had opened a box like this he had caught his hand on the needles. The poison, which had probably been harvested from a Waste predator, had made him a little ill the next day, but that had been the only effect. It was possible to poison a krismen; it just wasn't easy.

The compartment within contained a small amount of minted gold and silver bits, probably fees from Patrician clients, and what looked like an empty cloth bag. Khat lifted it out, and the remaining contents clinked. From the size of it and the strain on the seams, it must have once been full to bursting. *If this was all minted gold, why is he living in this quarter?* He opened the sack and emptied it onto the matting.

"Trade tokens," Elen said, frowning.

There was a handful of trade tokens, each worth about five days of artisan's labor. Khat smiled to himself. "Because he was telling you the truth about our relic. He did sell it. And now we know where."

He held up one of the tokens for her, and she peered at it. It was stamped with the Imperial symbol of the sun, but centered on it was a loose spiral, the Survivor symbol for a book.

"The Academia," Elen gasped in sudden understanding. "These tokens were stamped in the Academia."

"Exactly. He must have had debts to pay, so he sold his best relic to the Academia. The Silent Market loves to get their tokens—they look so nice and legal, nobody ever questions them." He scooped the tokens back into the sack and handed it to her. "Now let's get out of here."

Elen was so excited by their find that she didn't even notice he had lifted one of the better tiles and a *mythenin* mirror frame on the way out.

They reached the foyer with its shallow pool and its copies of Ancient mosaics. The outer door stood open as well as the front gate, and the candles in the red pot lamps burned low. This wasn't surprising; they hadn't found the bodies of either of Radu's servants, who must have taken the sensible course and run away in the confusion, most likely followed by the oracle. *An oracle loose in the ghostcallers' quarter,* Khat thought. *But it's probably not so bad as some other things that are loose in this place.* He wondered how it had gotten free of its cage. Possibly Shiskan and her friends had released it out of sheer perversity.

The court was empty, the other houses quiet. Khat started forward, but Elen caught his arm suddenly, hissing, "Stop. There's something out there."

He froze, studying the open gate, the empty expanse of the court beyond. If it had startled her into overcoming her Patrician training and grabbing his arm, he was willing to believe it was dangerous. "Where?"

"It's very close, right around here." She slipped in front of him, holding out one hand as if she could sense something in the hot night air. "I don't know what it is . . ."

Then he felt the cold, sudden as a slap on the face, bone-chilling, lung-crushing cold.

He grabbed Elen's arm and dragged her toward the gate. She stumbled against him but managed to stay upright. Freezing mist enveloped them, and he realized the thing had shifted to block the gate. Momentum carried them through it before the cold could stop their breath, and they bolted across the empty court and down the first alley. He didn't let her stop until they had crossed two more courts and put several clusters of buildings between themselves and Radu's ill-fated house.

He let Elen go, and she leaned back against the dirty wall of an empty house. She was breathing hard, but not from the run.

"You all right?" he asked her. He couldn't see her expression in the dim moonlight. He had only felt the very edge of the thing, but by stepping in front of him she must have been completely enveloped in it.

Elen nodded, cleared her throat, and said, "Yes. I couldn't breathe. Was that a ghost?"

"It was," he told her, relieved. If she could still talk, then it hadn't had time to work much damage on her. "Think you'll know that if you run into one again?"

"Oh yes, I think so." She looked back down the narrow alleyway. "What would have happened if we hadn't run?"

"If it caught us?" He slid down the wall to sit on the crumbling edge of its foundation, arms resting on his knees. After the sepulchral cold of the ghost, the leftover warmth of the day's heat radiating from the stone felt strange on his skin. Elen sat next to him. He said, "Ghosts take your breath, and make your skin turn blue and then white, and it feels funny, not like skin anymore, but like wax. At least that's what the bodies look like after you find them. It's never happened to me personally."

"That's horrible." Elen rubbed her arms briskly, as if trying to warm herself.

"It happens to people who are lost in the Waste and make the mistake of falling asleep on the top level at night. Sometimes it's ghosts roaming the surface, sometimes it's air spirits that come down from the wind and fall on them."

From here they could hear more street noise from the theater area and the forums. It was a reassuring counterpoint to the quiet of the quarter and the looming darkness of the houses around them. Footsteps crossed the court at the alley's end, and after they had faded away Elen said, "Maybe that's why Shiskan son Karadon and her people left in such a hurry. But . . ." She shook her head. "I really can't see them running, even from a ghost."

"Neither can I. I think that they were in a hurry because they'd done what they came to do. They made Radu tell them who he sold the winged relic to at the Academia. That's where we're stuck. We can't find that out in a hurry."

Thoughtfully, Elen said, "Not necessarily. The Academia must keep records of the relics it buys, and what scholar buys them, how much he pays. We could look at those records and see which scholar recently paid a huge amount of tokens for only one relic. There can't be that many of them."

"We can do that?" It was a novel idea.

"Of course. Or Riathen can. I could probably get the records released to me on my own authority as a Warder; I just don't know who I go to for them. We can do it tomorrow morning. I wish we could do it tonight, but Riathen is attending the Elector in the palace, and it would cause trouble to disturb him."

Khat was glad she saw the need for haste. An Academia scholar wouldn't be as easily disposed of as Radu the fortune-teller, but sooner or later one of them was sure to get a visit from Aristai Constans.

* * *

Miram opened the door as Khat fumbled with it and said, "Finally. We were worried."

"Why?"

"Running all over the ghostcallers' quarter? At night?" Netta's voice answered from somewhere across the darkened room. "Wait, I'll light a lamp."

"Only one," Miram cautioned as she shut the door behind them. "Or we'll have all the neighbors over here again."

A flame bloomed in the small room, in the clay bowl of an oil lamp. Netta set it down on the shelf, and in its light she and Miram stared expectantly at Elen, who hovered uncertainly by the door.

"That's Elen, that's Miram, that's Netta," Khat said. "Is there anything left from dinner?"

"Hello," Elen said, tentatively.

The other two women nodded a greeting, then exchanged a look that held a wealth of silent communication. Miram said, "There's a little bread. Sagai's waiting for you on the roof. I'll bring it up."

"Up there," Khat told Elen, pointing her toward the narrow steps that led up to the top level and the roof ladder. "Don't step on Libra and Senace." The two street entertainers were sleeping next to the wall, curled up together like children.

Elen stepped over the pair carefully and went up the steps, one hand on the clay-patched wall to steady herself.

Before Khat could follow her, Miram caught his robe and yanked on it, nearly strangling him. He grabbed the wall to keep from being pulled off-balance and almost stepped on Senace himself. "Hey!"

"That's not a Warder," Miram hissed at him. "That's somebody's daughter!"

"So?"

"So be careful with her." She punctuated this with another yank, then let him go.

When he climbed up through the vent Elen was already telling Sagai about Radu's house and what they had found there. Khat took a seat near the edge of the roof that looked down into the court. The encounter with Shiskan son Karadon had made him restless in the worst way, and he considered going out to look for company. There were two sisters he knew who kept a street food stall a couple of courts over, who would just be closing up about now . . . No, best to stay here. If he left he would only worry that someone or something had followed them from the Fourth Tier. He slumped down against the crumbling pediment, unaccountably depressed.

Sagai sat tailor-fashion, listening to Elen's account thoughtfully, his clay pipe slowly going out. When Elen had finished he said, "This Shiskan and her companions could have easily killed you both, if they had the same unnatural powers that Constans demonstrated for you at the Remnant."

"Why should they bother?" Khat shrugged one shoulder and looked out toward the edge of the tier, not bothering to conceal the bitterness in his voice. "We led them to Radu, right where they needed to go. And now they're ahead of us."

"That was no one's fault," Elen said quietly.

Sagai smiled at her, but said, "Yes, we must find the scholar Radu dealt with as quickly as possible. And once we find him we must take the winged relic to Riathen as fast as we value our lives, because if we are caught by these people with it there is no doubt what will happen." He looked to Khat again, and asked, "What of our big ugly block? You said you had thought of something concerning it?"

Khat had wanted to consider his idea more carefully, but the day and a half since he had seen the thing hadn't changed his mind. "Have you seen the Miracle?" he asked Elen.

"In the palace? Well, yes, I've stepped in to look at it once or twice, out of curiosity . . ." She looked from Khat to Sagai and back again. "What?"

Sagai sighed. "She has one of the few truly arcane relics ever found intact at her fingertips, and steps in to glance at it once or twice, out of curiosity."

"Yes, well . . ."

Khat shook his head over Elen's single-mindedness, then said, "I think it's part of an arcane engine."

Sagai's eyebrows lifted in surprise and speculation.

"But it can't be," Elen protested. "The arcane engines were made of metal with glass balls and crystals and pipes carrying quicksilver. They looked like giant orreries."

"And that's why they're found only in painrods, or in pieces," Khat told her, exasperated. Leave it to a Warder to think she knew what every arcane engine ever made looked like. "But the Miracle is part of an arcane engine, just like the crystal plaque."

"You said you thought it was probably just decorative," Elen accused.

"That was when I still thought I could talk you into selling it to the Academia, before I knew what fanatics you people are."

"I am not a—"

Sagai leaned forward, cutting her off. "Explain this theory of yours. Why do you think the Miracle is part of an arcane engine?"

"Riathen's Survivor text. The engraving of the three relics. It says they're pieces of arcane engines, doesn't it?" Khat looked at Elen. "That's why he's so sure finding them will make the Warders more powerful."

"I don't know. I can't read Ancient script. And Riathen never discussed the particulars with me. He just told me his hopes of what it will lead to."

Khat turned back to Sagai. "The Miracle is bigger than our big ugly block, and shaped differently, but there is definitely a family resemblance."

Under Sagai's questions he described both pieces carefully, and finally his partner nodded agreement. "I'd like to see for myself, of course," Sagai said. "But it is certainly a valid point to work from."

Elen frowned. "You only saw the picture in the book once. Are you sure you're remembering it accurately?"

Before Khat could answer, a preoccupied Sagai said, "His memory is very good. Too good for his own good, in fact. If you think the plaque and the block are both bits of an arcane engine, where does the small inlaid piece fit in? It is no different from the decorative relics, except for the rareness of the winged figure."

"I don't know." Khat shrugged, looking away toward the Waste. His memory was too good for his own good, but somehow Sagai saying it was a little like a quick stab in the heart, and he wasn't sure why.

They sat quietly. In the distance Khat could hear the steamwagon that ran on rails, its engine panting as it painfully negotiated the steep incline from the Sixth Tier to the Fifth. Then a mournful voice from the overhanging window of the next house said, "I couldn't live next to a couple of peddlers who'd sit up on their roof all night under my window and talk about women. No, I have to live next to a couple of whatever-you-people-are who sit up on your roof all night and talk about *history*."

Elen gaped, shocked that they had been overhead. Sagai told their neighbor, "Then go and live somewhere else."

The ladder rattled as Miram climbed up through the vent. Taking a seat next to Sagai, she handed Khat a hunk of bread and asked, "Did the search go well today?"

Elen looked shocked again. *She's going to have to get over that,* Khat thought. Whom did she think Miram was going to tell, the Elector, maybe? Khat was the only one who was on speaking terms with their enemies.

Sagai said, "It becomes clearer, but I don't entirely like some of the things we are discovering."

Khat expected Miram to ask more questions, but she seemed preoccupied. The first time Khat had met her had been on the caravan to Charisat, where Sagai had taken him after Khat had been shot by the pirates. He had woken up with Miram leaning over him, trying to tend his wound. He had shown his teeth at her, and she had delivered an open-handed blow to the side of his head that had almost knocked him unconscious. After that they had had no trouble getting along. Miram was small and a city woman but fierce and not to be trifled with. She turned to Khat and said suddenly, "Someone came here looking for you today. It was Akai, one of the men who beat Ris."

Khat almost choked on a mouthful of bread, swallowed with difficulty, and said, "He came here?"

"Yes. He said he had seen the message you left with Harim, and wished to discuss it with you personally." Miram demanded, "Did you kill this Harim?"

"No!" Khat's wounded outrage was tempered by the thought that Harim might very well have died of blood poisoning in the meantime. At least, he would have if Khat's luck held. He certainly meant to kill Akai now for daring to come to the house. But it seemed his message had been received; now Lushan's men would concentrate on avenging themselves on him and no one else.

"Did you hurt him?" she persisted. It was a lucky thing for lower-tier malefactors that as a foreigner Miram could never become a questioner for the Vigils' Undercourt.

"Well, yes."

She turned on Sagai, who had been conspicuously silent. "You knew about this."

"I did not," he said with dignity. "I suspected that Harim and Akai might suffer accidents in the near future, but I didn't know exactly when it would happen or what form it would take."

Miram threw up her hands. "Men and children, they're all the same. The two of you together have no sense of . . . no sense of . . ." She searched for the right word in vain, and finally finished, "No sense at all." She turned to Elen in appeal. "Don't you think so?"

"Well, Sagai isn't as bad as Khat," Elen said, giving the question serious consideration. "But that's not saying much."

"Sagai is a scholar who sees a relic and goes mad," Miram corrected. "I'm not complaining. We live better than anyone in our court, and my husband does not come home half dead from hard labor." She looked at Khat, her eyes fierce. "And before you came here, Netta was afraid to send her daughter to the market alone because all the idlers there knew she had no father to defend her. Now she can send her daughter anywhere in the quarter, and no one dares look twice at her. And I don't worry so much now that Sagai has someone to watch his back when he goes among those relic thieves in the Silent Market." She stopped to take a deep breath. Instinctive self-preservation kept Sagai and Khat silent, and Elen was too fascinated to speak. Miram continued, "All I am saying is that I want you to be careful." She glared at Khat. "Both of you." She stood abruptly and went to the ladder to climb back down into the house.

They sat in silence until finally Khat asked, "Was she angry or not?"

"My wife is a very passionate woman," Sagai explained. "But she doesn't often tell people what she thinks of them, even people she cares for. It made courting her a great trial."

Chapter Ten

IN THE HOUR before dawn Khat walked Elen back up the tiers to Riathen's house.

He had meant to leave her at the Third Tier, but after they had passed the bored gate vigils, he saw how dark and quiet the streets up there were, and thought of Constans, and decided it couldn't hurt to stay with her.

On the Second Tier they were stopped three times by patrolling vigils, who were much inclined to throw Khat off the tier wall, but finally passed them both on after examining Elen's token. Finally they reached the small garden, which was strange with shadow shapes under the darkened sky, lit only by the lamps hanging on the walls of the nearby houses. Khat stopped at the gate, and Elen asked, "Aren't you coming up with me? Riathen could have questions for you. What if there's a delay, because you're not there?"

Khat leaned against the garden wall. "Elen, no offense, but I don't like it up there."

"It's early, and there won't be anyone about but Warders," she pointed out. He was sure it sounded reasonable to her. She gestured down the street, where the swing of a ghostlamp marked another patrolling vigil. "The lictor is posted at the top of the wall during the night, and you can't stay down here alone. They could take you into custody."

He felt trapped, and he didn't like that, and she was right, and he didn't like that either.

They went up the alcove's rock-cut steps; past the lictor at the top, who recognized Elen and let them by without comment; through the empty court and up the wide stair, which was lit by wax candles and lamps burning lightly scented oil. There were few people about, though Khat heard voices off the first landing. Then on the second landing they met a brown-robed servant woman, who got a good look at Elen's companion and almost dropped a tray of dirty crockery.

After she beat a hasty retreat, Khat said, "That's it, Elen. I'm not going any further."

"All right. Hmm. This way." She led him through an archway and a little maze of connecting courts, each with a bubbling fountain and plants stirred by the warm night breeze, and out onto a broad open terrace. Beyond it was a great empty space, and past that an occasional lighted window showed that it was surrounded by other expansive houses. The top few levels of the Elector's palace were visible above the dark shapes of the surrounding buildings, and they were lit like the Odeon on a festival night, with flaring torches and mirror-backed lamps on open balconies reflecting off the limestone walls.

Elen said, "You can't see it now, but there's a garden out there, and the homes of some of the high officials in the court have their back terraces giving on to it." She hesitated, then added, "There's a little pavilion out there too, where the embassies from the other Fringe Cities are quartered sometimes. The embassy from the krismen Enclave is there now. They're here for another day at least."

Khat looked down at her sharply, but her expression was bland. Still he dropped down onto the nearest stone bench and looked up at her expectantly, not betraying any interest in what the view would be in daylight.

Elen, who didn't betray any interest in his lack of reaction, said, "I'll be back as soon as I can," and went away.

Khat settled in to wait, not happily.

Elen went up the main stair toward Riathen's rooms. After the lower tiers in general and the ghostcallers' quarter in particular, the slow waking quiet of the Master Warder's house was like another world. Polished stone under her battered sandals instead of crumbling mud brick, the scent of sandalwood and cool water instead of sweat and sewer stink. She supposed that you became accustomed to such things, after a time. She supposed that Khat and Sagai and the others had become accustomed to it. She couldn't imagine how. But she remembered the first time she had brought Khat up here and the way he had completely ignored the passersby who were all but spitting on the dirt at his feet. And at her, because she was with him. She supposed it was possible to become accustomed to anything.

When Elen was a child she had thought the lower tiers were all filth and degradation; living on the First Tier had given her no experience with hardworking poverty, and no idea that there were noncitizens and outsiders who were not criminals. Without the benefit of a Warder's experience and senses, most Patricians undoubtedly still thought that.

On the third landing Seul stepped in front of her suddenly, almost startling her off the top step. His voice low, he said, "You didn't come back last night."

Elen blinked up at him, astonished. "I know." She was still not really fully awake, though sleeping on the roof of Netta's house on scraps of matting judged too old and ragged for the rooms below had not been as uncomfortable as she would have thought. She had been bone-weary, and perhaps the encounter with the ghost had taken more out of her than she knew. Both her power and her ability to Look Within were weak, but even she had felt the pull the thing had exerted on her soul. It was something Warders should know of. Maybe, when this was over, she would give a lesson for the apprentices about her experience.

None of this was an answer for Seul, who was still staring down at her, his expression growing even more stony. "Where were you?" he demanded.

This time she understood him, and felt her face go hot.

In growing anger, she considered the indignity of explaining to Seul, who was glaring at her with a wrath more suitable for a father or a betrayed husband, that while she had spent the night in Khat's company, they had been more than adequately chaperoned, that Sagai was a fatherly sort of person, that Miram and Netta were perfectly respectable women, that their children had been everywhere, that she didn't see how intimacy was possible at all in the crowded warren of their court. That in the predawn stillness she had woken with someone's small child sleeping under her arm. That the thought of any impropriety had never occurred to her. Until now, and that impropriety concerned telling Seul to perform an unnatural act on himself.

Her voice shaking, she began, "You have no right—"

He wasn't even attempting to soul-read her, and mistook the quiver in her voice for embarrassment. "I know you went back to the lower tiers last night. Gandin told me. You don't know what you're getting yourself into with this krismen. If you've already gone that far . . ." He shook his head regretfully. "I know you're young, and you must be curious. But you can't trust him, and it's dangerous to associate yourself too closely with—"

Elen was too angry to think. "We've almost found one of the relics!" she shouted, not caring if she brought everyone in the house running. "Everyone said it was impossible, and now we've almost found one! Doesn't that count for anything?"

Evidently it did not, but at least this time he heard the rage in her voice. "Elen, you have to put your feelings aside and listen to me . . ." he began.

She was in no mood to hear out any speech that didn't start with "I apologize." She stepped around him. He grabbed her arm, and she shook him off with such violence that he drew back and let her pass.

Elen went up the stairs in a blind fury. When she reached the top floor, one of the apprentices told her Riathen had only just returned from the palace, and she had to cool her heels in his anteroom, muttering angrily to herself while the shadows gave way to pearly dawn light. Finally the door servant held the curtain aside for her, and Elen entered the quiet room and saw with relief that Riathen was alone, seated at the low table, the Ancient Survivor book unfolded before him. He looked up and smiled at her approach. "You have news."

"Yes, there's been progress." Firmly putting Seul out of her mind, she took a seat on a stool and began to tell him what they had discovered. She reached the part about Radu's death, and Khat's conclusion about the Academia, and Riathen stopped her and called for one of his archivists.

When the man had taken down his instructions on a wax tablet and hurried away, the Master Warder said, "It will take them a short time to persuade the record keepers at the Academia to open their books so early, and some time for them to go through the lists, but he should have news for you this morning."

"Good."

Riathen's eyes lifted to meet hers then, opaque and difficult to read. "And did you discover anything about our mysterious relic dealer?"

This wasn't a question Elen was quite prepared for. She thought of what Sagai had told her, but that seemed more his story than it was Khat's, and she couldn't see how Riathen would be interested in the fact that Khat was single-mindedly bent on killing pirates. The other things that she had learned about him seemed too commonplace for the Master Warder's interest. She said, "Nothing, really. He's been in the city for some time." She gestured helplessly. "He's exactly what he appears to be."

"I don't doubt that." Riathen began to fold up the book, using exquisite care with its fragile creases. "The krismen embassy has made inquiries about the possibility of any of their kind living in Charisat. It is thought by some in the court they are searching for one person in particular. And I have yet to hear of any other krismen in Charisat at this time except Khat." His eyes rested on her thoughtfully. "Bear this in mind."

She felt a qualm, wondering if he was seeing past the guards she had carefully set about her soul. She had pointed out the embassy pavilion to Khat, and thought herself idly casting out a lure for information. "What do you mean?"

"They are leaving the city tomorrow. I have been given to understand that the Elector was not entirely satisfied with the progress of his meetings with them. He has no hold over them, you see, and they virtually control the Waste trade roads. He, or the Heir, could greatly benefit from having something they wanted, as a bargaining point." He tucked the book carefully back into its case, and got to his feet, shaking out his mantle. "If you could find out if Khat is the man they are looking for, it might further our cause."

"I see," she said, carefully neutral.

He smiled down at her, suddenly warm. "I know you do. You are the best of my students, Elen."

If only your power was stronger, he might have added, she thought. But he would never say that.

Elen took her leave and started down the stairs, feeling her anger building again. It was unfair of Riathen to ask her to betray someone who had saved her life twice, who had so casually become her friend, just as it was unfair of Seul to take such a proprietary interest in where she spent her nights.

She would have to be careful now about what questions she asked. She would have to be careful not to ask the right one, because as cautious as Khat was, he might answer her. Despite this resolution, she felt like a traitor anyway.

Night gave way to false dawn, and the garden became a large rambling oasis filled with artfully arranged stands of acacia, tamarisk, persea, and fig. Khat watched a gardener lift a shadoof from a pool thick with lotus, and pour the water into the stone gutters that irrigated the greenery. The houses surrounding it were small palaces themselves.

The "little" pavilion Elen had spoken of was a good three stories high, round with columned terraces on each level, faced with a white marble that caught the early light.

Khat heard people approaching, and a group of twenty or so young men dressed for some athletic pursuit in loose trousers and singlets swarmed onto the far end of the terrace. An older man in formal white Warder robes formed them into lines and started them off on one of the beginning defensive exercises of infighting. Khat debated retreating back into the house or one of the sheltered courts off the terrace, then decided it was safe to stay where he was, as long as he didn't draw any attention to himself.

After a while, the older Warder left, and Khat studied the practicing infighters critically. Their motions were smooth and fluid, though maybe too fluid, too much like dance and not enough like combat. The result of much practice and little real experience. Their style was different from the one he had learned in the kris Enclave, but then it had to be. The center of body on a kris male was a little lower than the center of body of a Survivor-descended male, either city dweller or pirate, which changed everything about the way you balanced. Oddly enough, the center of body was the same for kris women and Survivor-descended women. The city dwellers, even those who studied infighting, probably didn't know these interesting facts, but then so few exchanges took place between the Enclave and the cities.

Except for the kris embassy, here for another day at least by Elen's reckoning.

Khat shook that uncomfortable thought away. He hoped Riathen could be persuaded to hurry; someone in the Academia needed to be warned. If Khat hadn't been barred from the inner courts after Robelin died, he could have found the scholar in question simply by going in and asking. It was mildly ironic. The Academia had made it more than clear that it wanted nothing to do with him except through the trade entrance, and he was risking all to protect one of its members from a visit from Constans. *But I've always been an idiot that way,* he thought.

"What are you doing here?"

Startled, Khat dug his fingers into the rough stone at the edge of the bench and just managed not to jump. He had forgotten how good Warders could be at sneaking up on people. He looked up at Kythen Seul. "I came with Elen."

Seul had put his veil aside. His expression was all cool contempt, though his eyes were angry.

There were two other men with him, both young Warders, one blond and so fair-skinned he was reddening under the morning sun, the other dark. Both were dressed in the fine, formal overmantles and robes of the court, their veils pulled aside. The dark one was smiling. He said, "So this is Elen's pet kris?"

Khat waited for Seul to answer, since the question had apparently been addressed to him. Instead, his voice soft and dangerous, Seul said, "Don't you know to stand for your betters?"

Khat looked down at the scuffed pavement, then back up at Seul. *You asked for this,* he told himself. *You came here.* He said, "Probably not."

The blond one frowned. His long features were classically Patrician, though the lightness of his skin and hair indicated a lower family. "You heard him. Stand."

Khat ignored him, keeping his eyes on Seul, who was smiling now. The scene had caught the interest of the other young Warders out on the terrace, and some had stopped their practice, stumbling awkwardly to a halt in the midst of the exercise.

The dark one glanced at Seul. "It's true, isn't it? They don't have souls. I can't read him at all."

"Can't do what?" Khat said, startled into an honest question.

Seul said, mildly, "Of course it's true. They aren't any more human than rock demons."

The blond one was tiresomely persistent. "I said stand up."

This time Khat did, almost in the young Warder's face.

Seul didn't react, but the other two had been expecting him to be about the height of a lower-tier city dweller, and were startled to suddenly be eye-to-eye with him.

Recovering, the blond one said, "It's none of our business if Elen wants to keep pets, but she shouldn't bring them up here."

The other young Warders were drawing up to watch and listen, and it was already too late to retreat. Khat said, "Why don't you tell Elen that?"

Seul stepped back, still smiling, and turned away. Permission for the other Warders to do whatever they wanted was implicit. Khat felt he could hardly claim to be surprised. He had known Seul was a bastard before this. He was trapped against the wall, any retreat into the house blocked and not a friendly face in sight.

Someone in the group was saying, "Gandin said he's supposed to be some kind of an infighter. He started a fight with a couple of our lictors, but they didn't have much trouble with him."

"Oh, a fighter," the dark one said with a grin, glancing back at the speaker. "That's not what I thought they were known for."

The blond one had to elaborate on this theme. "Maybe he showed the lictors how well he did that, too."

The humor was about the same level as that demonstrated by lower-tier thugs who roamed the streets looking for people to harass. Too bad Khat couldn't handle this group in the same fashion, and simply put a knife in the leader's guts and leave. He said, "Maybe so. Why, is it usually your job?"

More laughter greeted this, but this time at the blond one's expense. Even his companion grinned derisively, saying "Is it, Therat?"

Therat ignored him, and with an edge in his voice said, "I think we should teach him a lesson."

"I think we should throw him off the tier," someone else suggested helpfully.

A few of the apprentice Warders were drifting back to their practice, out of boredom or an excess of common sense. Still, there was a murmur of agreement, uncomfortably loud despite the defections, and Khat felt a prickle of unease go down his spine. He had his knife, but he might as well use it to cut his own throat, because that would certainly be the long-term outcome anyway. Even striking a Patrician could earn him a messy public execution, if Riathen for his own reasons chose not to intervene. And they were only upper-tier bravos; it wasn't as if they could do anything to him that somebody else hadn't already done.

But he didn't want to be beaten up again.

"We'd get our hands dirty," Therat's friend objected. He was bored with the game and ready to leave. "Therat, why don't we go? We're expected and—"

The painrod appeared out of a fold in Therat's robes, was too close to avoid almost before Khat realized he had seen it. He threw himself backward, fell against the wall behind him, and the rod brushed his midsection.

His legs gave way, and he hit the edge of the bench with bruising force, then collapsed on the pavement, twitching helplessly, unable to take a breath. All sensation was intense, the smooth pavement unbearably grainy under his hands, the weight of his own body almost too much to bear. The effect was different from that of the painrod the pirate had used on him in the Waste; maybe they were all a little different, each individual little arcane engine producing a slightly different brand of pain. Maybe the difference was in the person who wielded it. Then the wave of agony faded under a wave of rage, and his vision cleared. He lifted his head.

To the other apprentices, Therat was saying, "I have it. If he fights one of us and wins, maybe we should let him go back to the lower tiers." He looked down, smiling. "What about that?"

"All right," Khat said. He came awkwardly to his feet, no longer thinking of consequences. No longer thinking at all. "I pick you."

The painrod went flying one way, and Therat went the other. Another Warder swung at him, and Khat caught his arm, shifting his weight and slinging him into someone else. Therat had time to roll to his feet and now ran at him again.

In the next moment of coherent thought Khat had Therat facedown on the pavement, his arm twisted into an easily breakable position. Two of the other apprentices lay unmoving a short distance away. The others were scattered.

Elen was standing over him, saying mildly, "I'd really rather you didn't do that."

He looked up at her. For an instant, her eyes widened in fear. That startled him, because he had never been interested in frightening Elen, only in irritating her as much as she irritated him. He let the boy go, standing up. His right knee gave a twinge, and ribs still tender from the beating at the Remnant ached again.

Gandin stood behind Elen, and now he looked around at the other young Warders, and shook his head in disgust. Elen started away, and Khat followed her through the arch and into another smaller court. She turned to face him, and now she looked angry. "You could have killed him."

Khat couldn't answer. The fear and anger were so mixed up his thoughts wouldn't come straight. He remembered the fight only in bits and pieces; most of it was blotted out by rage. The apprentices had been trained well, but none of them had ever had to apply that training to the lower-tier streets of Charisat, and none of them had ever fought for their lives. He had remembered not to use his knife, at least. He looked away.

"Say something," she demanded.

The Warders had provoked him, but the truth was that if Khat started a fight every time he was provoked to it he wouldn't have time for anything else. He looked down at her, sneering. "Me? An inferior creature from the Waste, kill a Warder? Are you joking?"

Elen threw up her hands in disgust. "Oh, don't start that. I can't listen to it now."

She turned away, weary, and suddenly he thought he owed it to her. "Elen."

She stopped, waiting. Elen always seemed to listen when people wanted to talk to her; it probably caused her a great deal of grief.

He said, "When I lived at the Enclave . . ." She turned back to look at him then, and he avoided her eyes. "Pirates attacked the caves my lineage held, and they killed most of us and took prisoners, including me. They had us for three days, but I don't remember much of it. When the others came after us everyone was dead but me.

"What's-his-name said that they would leave me alone if I fought one of them. I think one of the pirates said that to me then. But that's not what happened afterward." It had been more than that. Perhaps he had been disoriented from the painrod, but for a moment he had been back there again.

Elen came toward him, stopping near the fountain. She rubbed her palms on her kaftan, uncomfortable. "Is that why you don't live in the Enclave?"

Somehow it didn't sound like much of an explanation, or any kind of excuse. He didn't know why it had seemed so important to tell her. "If they killed everyone except me, there must have been some reason for it. Or that's what the other lineages thought." She drew breath to answer, and he interrupted her. "What did you find out from Riathen?"

She hesitated. "He's sending someone for the records." It was Elen's turn to look away now. "I want to tell you something. Please listen, and don't ask me any questions I can't answer. There's a good chance the kris embassy is here looking for you. If you can settle that with them, it would . . . make things easier for both of us." She hunted distractedly in her kaftan, and produced the token she had shown the vigils and used to pass into the upper tiers. She handed it to him. "I have to wait for Riathen's clerks to find the right scholar for us, and I'll take care of the trouble with the apprentices. Perhaps you should go and get Sagai, and we could meet at the Academia."

Khat turned the token over thoughtfully, with no idea how to react. It was solid and coin-shaped, still warm from her body heat and embossed with the crossed sun symbol of the Elector's court. He liked Elen, and thought her honest in her own Warder way, but he hadn't expected her to return the regard enough to betray Riathen. And everything in her face, the way she stood, said this was a betrayal.

He glanced up and saw Kythen Seul watching them from the terrace side entrance to the court.

Khat caught Elen by the shoulders, half lifted her, and kissed her on the lips. He was gone before she or Seul could react, out through the archway on the near side of the court and away.

Elen sat down on the edge of the fountain. The heat in her face told her she was turning a lovely shade of red. She was surprised she wasn't turning blue from shock.

As Seul bore down on her from one direction, the training master and Gandin entered the court. Gandin sat next to her. He was grinning. She wanted to slap that expression off his face, but just managed to contain herself. It was Seul she really wanted to strike.

Gandin said, "Did you see what he did to Therat?"

Seul stood over her now, glaring down. She ignored both of them and said to the training master, "I'm sorry that happened. It shouldn't have."

"Therat asked for it," Gandin pointed out.

"I know that," Elen snapped, impatient at the interruption.

The training master nodded. She had known him at least as long as she had known Sonet Riathen. He had given her the infighting skills that had saved her life more than once, when court intrigue had turned deadly. He said, "They're young fools, most of them. I'll make sure there's no trouble over it." He lifted an eyebrow. "If I have to, I'll say I arranged it, as a test."

"Thank you." Elen looked up at him, surprised and gratified. She had expected to have to stand bond for Khat when Therat charged him and to try to find a way to keep him from having to appear before the High Justices. Noncitizens couldn't testify except under torture, even when they were only witnesses.

"It was a lesson they needed to learn," the training master continued. "Now they know that just because an opponent is an inferior doesn't mean he can't beat you into the ground in an open fight."

"Oh." Elen remembered what Khat had said when she had accused him of nearly killing Therat. She rubbed the bridge of her nose. *I think I'll save my coins and move to Kenniliar, the way Sagai wants to. No Warders there. I could take up some occupation that doesn't require me to think.*

Gandin was frowning at Seul. "What's the matter with you?"

"Nothing," the older Warder said, his voice tight.

Elen looked up at Seul, put as much cold iron into her voice as she could, and wished she dared put what little of her power there was into it as well. "Don't you have somewhere to go? Some task to perform?"

Seul's eyes narrowed, but Elen was too angry to be stared down. He retreated finally, striding off across the court.

"What's the matter with him?" Gandin demanded again.

Elen shook her head, with no intention of answering.

The training master grunted noncommittally. "Thinks too much of himself," he said. "Friends in high places."

"What?" Elen asked, curious at the disapproval in his voice.

He shrugged. "Gossip."

The training master left the court to return to his apprentices, and Elen ignored Gandin's attempts at conversation until he went away. She had a great deal of thinking to do.

Khat had to show the token only once, at Riathen's gate. News of the fight hadn't found its way there yet, and the lictors were beginning to regard him as a commonplace if not entirely welcome visitor.

The streets that led off from the central avenues and wandered between the manses were little more than paved, shaded paths, almost as narrow as lower-tier alleys. Khat finally realized it was because there was no need for handcarts. Street space had been given over to trees and plants instead. Few people were out, even now, and it was ridiculously easy to climb the garden wall without being seen.

Khat avoided the pebbled paths, making his way through the fragrant groves toward the pavilion, trying not to tread on the moon flowers. There were two Imperial lictors at the copper screened doors on the first terrace floor, an honor guard, only. The pillars were twined with carved snakes, as easy to climb as a ladder. Khat circled around to the back of the building and started up one of the columns.

Reaching the second level, he hauled himself over the balustrade. There were open arches every ten paces, set into the marble-faced walls. The pavilion would catch every available breeze, and the roofed terraces would keep the sun at a distance until it sank past the surrounding houses. He went around the outer terrace, moving quietly from archway to archway. The rooms he could see had mosaics on floors and walls, colored pebble scenes of Charisat: the Elector's palace, the Porta Major and other old buildings in the Academia, the First Forum down on the Fourth Tier. The colors were too bright, lacking the soft glow of Ancient work, and he couldn't admit to liking the modern style.

He paused at the side of one arch, hearing soft voices. They were speaking Old Menian—though he couldn't make out the words—speaking it the way it was meant to be spoken, not the corrupted version that had become Tradetongue. Time blurred for a moment, and it almost seemed as if one of the voices was familiar. He could tell they were arguing, and that was familiar too.

It gave Khat an uneasy coldness down his spine, as if he were alone out in the Waste, hearing the piping voices of air spirits on the wind. That was ridiculous. He had been around the Warders too long; they were enough to make anyone crazy.

He edged forward just enough to get a poor view of the far side of the room, but still couldn't see anyone. He didn't dare move further in; these were his own people, not half-blind city dwellers, and extra caution was called for.

The voices faded as the speakers left the room. Khat waited, then stepped around the side of the arch—and was staring at his cousin Rhan, not ten paces away.

Rhan was hardly less startled than Khat. He came forward, and Khat backed away, out onto the terrace again. Rhan stopped just inside the archway, as if he realized this wasn't going to be a joyous reunion. "How did you get here?" he asked.

There were a dozen not-so-clever answers to that. Khat asked only, "Did you come here looking for me?"

Rhan was his age, his height, dressed as if he had just come from the desert but without the dust, in robe and boots and loose trousers. In the years since Khat had seen him last, he had also become a shaman-healer. His forehead was tattooed with a blue circle, meant to represent the third eye that saw past the natural world into the realm of the unnatural. Khat and Rhan had used to look somewhat alike, but Khat couldn't see himself in his cousin's even features anymore.

"No," Rhan answered now. At Khat's expression he grimaced, and added, "It's only part of the reason. We had business to settle about the trade roads. But we heard from a trader in the High Season caravan that you were in Charisat. It was the first we'd heard since Leslan saw you in Dunsaru. We came—"

"What trader?" Khat interrupted. He noticed he was speaking the pure Old Menian of the Enclave now too; it was a wonder that he remembered it.

Rhan looked confused, as if he couldn't see how it mattered. "A city man named Biaktu."

Khat swore. He could have guessed that. Biaktu would talk to anybody.

Impatient, Rhan said, "We want you to come back to the Enclave with us." He took a step forward, and Khat took a step back against the balustrade. Rhan stopped, startled again. He said slowly, "You've changed."

Maybe that was true. Khat was finding it almost impossible to meet his cousin's eyes, for fear of seeing what he felt, and for fear of revealing himself. He didn't know why he had come here. Curiosity, maybe. The kind that led you to poke at half-healed wounds and make the blood flow again. He said, "So you want me back. Tell me why." His uncle, Rhan's father, was probably the most influential man in the Enclave councils now. That was certainly the way things had been heading when Khat had left.

"Leslan told you . . ."

"I want to hear it from you."

Rhan took a breath. "You're one of the last of the Amaher lineage. If you don't come back, if you never leave us children, the Enclave could lose that line entirely. That's why my father wants you back. The rest of us just . . . want you back."

Khat had known when he left the Enclave his lineage was near to dying out; it wasn't his problem anymore. "He should have thought of that before he told me to leave."

"He didn't tell you to leave."

Suddenly Khat had no trouble meeting Rhan's eyes. He said, "No. He told me I should have died with the others. He wondered what I'd done for the pirates to keep them from killing me. He was sorry they couldn't think up anything quicker than putting a knife through my leg and leaving me staked out to bleed to death, and he was sorry you and the others got there before I'd quite finished doing it—and at the time, I was sorry about it too. If that's not telling me to leave, I don't know what is."

Rhan shook his head, but he was the one who wouldn't make eye contact now, and it hadn't been so long that Khat couldn't recognize the significance of that gesture from another kris. Rhan said, "He was wrong, and now the rest of the family is condemning him for driving you away. He needs you. He sent me here to find you. Isn't that revenge enough?" Rhan gestured out toward the city, suddenly angry. "How can you live in this place? They're ignorant and dirty, the city reeks, they turn their own people into pirates . . ."

"Yes," Khat said softly. "We're much better than they are. We only turn our own relatives into pirates. Or try."

Rhan's eyes darkened. "I know you don't believe me, but that's not what my father intended."

"You're right, I don't believe you."

That was two deadly insults in the space of as many breaths, and the way the words were spoken in Old Menian left no doubt of the intent. But Rhan only looked away again, and said, "We're leaving tomorrow. Whatever you've done here, you can still leave with us, part of the embassy and under their Elector's protection until you're out of Charisat."

Khat looked out over the garden, smiling grimly. The assumption that he had done something terrible here, that it would take the Elector's protection simply to get out of the city safely, was almost flattering. And it was strange that the belief that a kris living in a Fringe City must be a criminal was shared even by other kris. But he knew the offer was genuine, whatever he thought of the intentions behind it.

Khat wasn't fool enough to feel any affection for Charisat itself, but he liked living here. He liked the relics, the access to books, the food, even some of the people, occasionally. But he could leave this place behind him now, leave Riathen to deal with the Elector's nasty Heir, leave mad Aristai Constans unable to find him. Sagai and Miram need never find out that he had ever stolen for Lushan, leaving all well on that score, as long as he didn't think about the fact that he would never see them again. He could do that. He was used to leaving friends. Elen . . . Elen could get the scholar's name and continue the fool's quest on her own.

Except that Constans didn't think it was a fool's quest, or he wouldn't have sent Shiskan to kill Radu the fortune-teller. So maybe it wasn't a fool's quest.

He couldn't decide if he was being a fool or a coward, or both. He looked back to Rhan. "No."

"What . . . ?"

"No, it's not revenge enough," he said, and swung over the balustrade before Rhan could move to stop him.

Khat hesitated at the edge of a grove. There was movement in the greenery off to his right, a flash of bronze from a vigil's robe. Someone must have seen him pass through the garden. He still had Elen's token, but explanations would be difficult, if not impossible. Khat bolted through the trees, heading for the garden wall.

The gardeners had been piling loose brush here, and Khat crashed into it. He had no idea how loud dry wood could be when it cracked. The vigils were after him in an instant.

Khat came to an open space where the ground was covered by silversword and a small fountain built into the garden wall trickled water into a low gutter at its base. He turned at bay—they would be on him in moments.

But the two vigils didn't break through the flowering bushes after him. He could see them—they stumbled, pointed in different directions, called conflicting orders to each other, and finally veered off out of the grove entirely.

Khat watched them, amazed and thinking, *Drunk this early?* Well, it was the First Tier.

"I told you not to come back here."

Khat spun and scaled the wall as if he had springs in his legs. Only when he was perched on top did he look for Constans.

The mad Warder leaned against a fig tree as if he owned the place—which, for all Khat knew, he might. He still wore the dusty black mantle, with no veil. He said, "I told you it would do you no good. Was I wrong?"

"I didn't know you came out in daylight," Khat said. That was only partly a taunt. Constans didn't look quite real under the morning sun. With his height and sun-faded hair and light eyes he could have been kris, somebody's crazy old granduncle. Except somebody's crazy old granduncle couldn't make two men lose themselves in broad daylight simply by wanting it.

"Was I wrong?" Constans was gently persistent.

Khat dug his fingers into the stone to keep his balance and glanced around. There was a walkway on the other side of the wall, with a shaded colonnade to one side with tiled benches for passersby. No sign of anyone. He said, "This wasn't what you meant."

"True," Constans admitted. "But I wasn't wrong."

An errant breeze ruffled Khat's hair, and through a gap in the trees he saw the vigils halfway across the garden by the lotus pool, arguing. He didn't know how much longer he dared stay here. "Why did Shiskan kill Radu and not me?"

Constans shook his head, mildly exasperated. "If you don't know what happened there, you still know nothing."

He's not wrong about that, either. Khat snorted. "Then why bother with me?"

"And how long can you run from everything?" Constans countered, sounding as if he really wanted to hear the answer.

In this city where Khat's dead body was worth more than he was alive, not long. And the Waste was nowhere to run to. The person Rhan thought he and the others wanted back was long gone, had died years ago when the pirates had shown him just what helplessness was. If he ever went back to the Waste to live for good, it would be with the ghosts. Constans saw far more of that than was safe, and any answer that even approached the truth was dangerous. Khat asked again, "Why bother with me?"

"Has Riathen burned the bones for you lately?" Constans started forward, moving unhurriedly. "You should let me do it for you. I don't let my preconceptions cloud my vision."

Khat thought, *That's enough of this*, and fell back off the wall, landing on his feet. He ran down the walkway, not looking back.

Chapter Eleven

E LEN IS A sweet girl, and to be searching for relics of strange re-
pute is wonderfully interesting," Sagai said thoughtfully. "But I wish
there was some way we could bow out of this game."

"I shouldn't have dragged you into this," Khat said. He had told
Sagai about his most recent adventure, leaving out only Aristai Constans's part in it.

"I invited myself in, and if anyone is going to be assigned blame it
should be this Riathen, who sounds like a very unpleasant sort of
man."

Khat couldn't argue with that. They stood at the wall of the Academia, under the shade of one of the double row of colonnades that
ran along it. This was as much as most people ever saw of the place,
and here the students and lesser scholars taught classes for those who
could afford to pay. Reading and writing Tradetongue for archivists,
numbers and sums for clerks, and an occasional wild-eyed and
threadbare scholar who told stories of the Ancients for copper bits.
This was also where scholars bought relics from lower-tier dealers,
and there were a few such transactions going on now. Khat saw Danil
and another dealer he knew displaying a collection of tile or ceramic
fragments for an eager young scholar, and he hoped Elen would get
here before they finished and came over to pump Sagai and him for
information.

Across the street a gaggle of peddlers sold anything the scholars might want, from scraps of paper and ink cakes to the backings for wax tablets. The Academia had been founded by the Seventh Elector as a small school for the study of the Ancients. As Charisat had grown in power and relics had grown in value in the markets, the Academia had grown in size and influence. It now taught everything from medicine to philosophy, and had one of the largest archives of Survivor texts in the Fringe Cities.

Elen appeared out of the crowd and came up to them. She nodded a greeting to Sagai, then said stiffly to Khat, "I was going to apologize to you, but after what you did to me, I don't think I will."

"Did Seul die of apoplexy?" he asked her.

Elen's lips twitched as she suffered through some internal struggle. Then in a more normal voice she said, "No, but he's going to die of something else if he keeps behaving the way he has been."

"Do you have the name?" Sagai asked her.

Elen held up a scrap of paper. "Yes. I came as soon as the clerks found it. It's a scholar named Arad-edelk."

"Never heard of him before," Khat said. He had been hoping it would turn out to be someone he had done work for, someone who might be inclined to believe their warning, but at least it wasn't one of the more prominent scholars, who were notoriously contemptuous of relic dealers. Maybe this Arad would be easier to talk to.

Armed with the clerk's scrap of paper, Elen went up to the gate vigil. "We need to speak with the scholar Arad-edelk." As she spoke, she twitched her plain brown mantle aside to show the painrod hanging at her waist.

The confused vigil looked at Elen's lower-tier robes, at her painrod, at Khat and Sagai, then unlocked the gate.

They came through into a small court, where blue and white tiled archways led off through a gray stone gatehouse. An old scholar hastily trying to arrange his veil came toward them. "Warder, there is some problem?"

"We must speak with the scholar Arad-edelk. That's all." Elen's smile was meant to be reassuring, but the man looked askance at her.

"I see. He has very important work, but perhaps ..."

Just then another scholar came striding up toward them as if he thought they were there to storm the place. His mantle and robes were richer, and he wore the *mythenin* chain of office the ranking scholars affected. Khat recognized him with a mental grimace. It was Ecazar, who had held the position of Master Scholar for the past ten years. The Academia might have other fields of study, but Ecazar was first and always a relic scholar. Despite this he and old Robelin had never agreed on anything.

Ecazar looked Khat over as if he suspected him of something disgusting, then asked Elen, "What is the meaning of this?"

Elen gave up on smiling. With an edge in her voice, she said, "I'm a Warder, of Master Riathen's house. I would simply like a few moments of Scholar Arad-edelk's time, if it's not too much trouble."

Ecazar struggled to think of a way he could refuse, then gave in with poor grace. "Hmm. This way." He strode off across the court, the older scholar who had greeted them trailing him like an obedient servant. Ecazar had always harbored a resentment against the Warders, since the Academia was answerable only to the Elector and the Warders were the only court officials who could conceivably question the Master Scholar's authority inside its walls. That Elen appeared here with Khat didn't help.

Elen and the scholars drew a little ahead, and as they followed, Sagai asked Khat, "What did you do to Elen?"

"Nothing," he told him. "She's making it up."

Sagai didn't appear to find this believable.

Ecazar led them through an archway, up a short flight of broad steps, and through another series of courts. The buildings were all rambling and stone-built, their arches and doors framed by tile or colored pebbles. The fountains were shaped into tortoise shells or abstract suns, and most had two or three tiers, showing they were more for looking at than for drinking or washing, but the Academia got its water money straight from the Elector's court anyway. They also passed the little plaza with the clock tower, almost as old as the Academia itself. The clock rang a bell for each hour, and outside of each of its five galleries a procession of bronze and gold suns, moons, and other astronomical symbols rotated at the appropriate times. The three-story escapement was supposed to be the finest precision instrument of its kind in all the Fringe, and the clock also told phases of the moon, the annual movement of the sun, and predicted the first days of the High and Low Seasons every year, but these were of use only to scholars.

Students talking or reading in the shade of the little courts stopped to stare curiously at them. There were veiled Patrician boys and young Patrician women in jewelry and fine kaftans, but most were humbler sorts from the trading families of the Fourth Tier.

It's been a long time, Khat thought. Once he had been such a common sight here few had stared. He noticed his partner's preoccupied look. This was the life Sagai should have had, as a member of the Scholars' Guild in Kenniliar. Sagai had managed to do some work for the Academia when he had first come to Charisat, but most of the tasks that could be given to noncitizens went to one of the many apprentice scholars instead, and he hadn't been able to support a family on so few commissions. Khat asked, "Do you miss it?"

"Occasionally," Sagai admitted. "After the excitement of the relic trade, I might find it dull."

Not likely, Khat thought. *Not likely.* He missed it himself, especially the free access to the Academia's libraries. Books were occasionally sold in the Fifth Tier markets, but these were always cheap pamphlets filled with wild tales of adventurous caravaneers and traders in foreign cities. Miram saved her tokens and bought a few every so often, read them aloud to Netta and the children until the pages threatened to split, then sold them to dealers on the Sixth Tier. There were booksellers on the Fourth Tier who regularly obtained copies of scholars' notes from the Academia and would lend them for relatively modest fees, but none were happy catering to noncitizens, and none would even let Khat in the door. Even Sagai at his most persuasive was only allowed to take out one volume at a time; he called trips to the booksellers tests of humility, and said it was the only place in the city where one paid for the privilege of being reminded that one was a foreigner and a resident of a lower tier, instead of getting it for free from strangers on the street.

They came to a low building with a pillared portico, set all by itself in a roomy court. As they went up a broad flight of steps and into its cool, bare entranceway, Ecazar told Elen, "This is where Arad resides. It's been set aside for his work."

Sagai raised an eyebrow at Khat, who shrugged one shoulder. If Arad had an entire house to himself in the crowded Academia, he must be important indeed.

They passed down a short hall, quiet and bare, and into a large central room with several obliquely angled ceiling louvers letting in the daylight. The walls were unadorned, but in the past someone had scribbled figures and notes on them that a scrubbing hadn't completely erased.

"Wait here, and don't touch anything," Ecazar said. "I'll summon Arad."

As he left, the older scholar took up a position at one of the doorways, watching them as if he was on guard.

"Of course," Elen muttered, and glanced around. "Why do you think they're so nervous?" she asked quietly, but Khat and Sagai didn't hear her.

Their attention had been firmly captured by what was obviously Arad-edelk's current project and the reason he had been allotted such spacious quarters.

On the floor in the far corner of the room was a splash of soft, glowing color. It was an Ancient mural reconstructed from cracked tile pieces. The central portion was at least seven feet long and ten wide. The edges were uneven still, and some sections had gaping holes, showing the job was far from finished. Sagai gasped, and Khat felt weak in the knees himself.

"Oh," Elen said, noticing it. "Look at that."

Many of the surviving murals were views of the sea, but this was a landscape, and different from anything seen before. It seemed to show a place of limitless horizon, of low rolling hills covered by high grass, dotted by flowers of red, yellow, even purple. In the foreground was a stand of trees of unrecognizable types. Some might be acacia, but a taller, leafier form of acacia than Khat had seen even in the garden up on the First Tier. In the shade of the trees sat a woman.

Her skin was a warm brown, and her hair was long and heavy and dark, hanging down to her waist and braided with strands that glittered with crystals or glass mixed in with a silvery pigment. Her features were too blunt for Patrician standards of beauty, but the smile on her face and in her dark eyes put those standards to the lie. She wore a brief light-colored shift with a net of beads or tiny gemstones over it, and it was evident that her figure was generous, though her waist was as small as a child's. She sat on a stool and was leaning down, offering her hand to the creature that played at her feet.

"What is that?" Sagai muttered to himself.

Khat realized that he was sitting on his heels by the mural, though not close enough to risk disarranging the precious pieces, and that Sagai was beside him. "A very ugly baby?" he suggested.

The creature looked like a diminutive, emaciated old man, covered with short ginger-brown hair and with a weird snakelike tail. It was grinning up at the woman with a look of idiotic pleasure, but Khat felt that if he had been in its position he would've had much the same expression on his face.

"I don't think it's a person," Elen said from behind them. "It only has four fingers. It's some mythical creature, or maybe an animal."

A few of the pieces lay to one side, waiting to be edged back into place. Others were stored nearby, laid out on low racks of light wood, probably fresh from being cleaned of whatever dust or muck had collected on them over the years.

"At a guess," Sagai said, still talking to himself, "five thousand, five hundred days."

"Six thousand, maybe seven," Khat corrected. "Look at that blue." The sky was a pure and valuable cerulean blue, dotted with the white lace of clouds. Modern tiles tended to lose their color over time, but these were as brilliant as the day they were made. Little details said this work had been finely crafted: not only had the blue kept its luster, but the red had stayed red and not faded to rust-brown as sometimes occurred on otherwise well-preserved Ancient tiles.

"Ah, yes. You're right. Six or seven thousand. At least. I'm not sure I could put a value on this."

He was probably right. Allowing for whatever changes time had wrought on the tiles, they were looking at the sky the way the Ancients had seen it, before the Waste had burned the clouds away and melted the blue into the brighter color it was today.

"It was found on the Eighth Tier, under the rubble of a collapsed warehouse," a quiet voice said.

Elen straightened, stepping back self-consciously. Sagai barely glanced up. "How long has this taken you?" he asked.

"A year. It goes more quickly now."

"And where does it go when you finish?" Khat looked up at the newcomer for the first time.

Arad-edelk was short, and the eyes above his veil were dark, narrow with weary suspicion, the brown skin around them lined with worry. The hyphenated second name was an old custom from the Survivor Time. In most cities it had died out, and it was really only prevalent on the lower tiers of Charisat. Arad-edelk might come from an old family, but not one whose members often made it past the Fifth Tier. He eyed Elen warily, and answered, "The palace."

Khat and Sagai both looked up at her. Elen glared down at them. "How fortunate there's an Imperial representative handy for vilification."

"We didn't say anything," Khat pointed out tightly. "Do you think you need vilifying?"

"You might as well have said it."

Ecazar was waiting in the doorway behind Arad, watching them all suspiciously, and Arad was looking at Elen as if he thought she was mad. Seeing her not only speak to lower-tier dealers but argue with them was probably all the proof he needed. Elen seemed to realize it and composed herself. She smiled at him. "I'm sorry. It's been a long day. Perhaps we could speak to you in private?"

Uncertain, Arad turned back to the other scholars. Ecazar snorted derisively and walked out. The older scholar gave Elen a stiff-backed little bow and followed.

"You are the scholar Arad-edelk?" she asked him.

"Yes." This was admitted with great reluctance.

"You recently bought a relic from a fortune-teller named Radu?"

"No."

Arad had looked her right in the eyes when he lied, too. *The little bastard,* Khat thought.

Elen studied the scholar thoughtfully. She said, "It isn't illegal to buy a relic. There isn't even any shame in it. But what you bought is a very dangerous relic to own."

Arad was stubborn. "I don't buy relics from the Fourth Tier. I buy from gleaners."

Elen hadn't said anything about Radu living on the Fourth Tier. Khat cleared his throat, hoping she would notice the slip. She glared horribly at him again, so he supposed she had.

Sagai hadn't appeared to be listening; he was studying the mural as if he meant to memorize every inch, but now he glanced up at Arad and in a tone of polite disbelief said, "You bought this wonder from Eighth Tier gleaners?"

Arad's eyes narrowed, and he didn't answer.

"Radu's dead," Elen added quietly. "He was killed because of the relic he sold you."

"That means nothing to me. You must have the wrong scholar. I ask you to leave, so I can return to my work."

"You have to listen to us," Elen persisted. "You could be in great danger."

"You have the wrong man," Arad repeated stubbornly. "You must leave."

Khat stood. "It's not doing any good," he told her. "Let's go."

Arad eyed them both with that same wary caution.

Ecazar didn't deign to reappear, but the older scholar returned as they left the building and conducted them back to the gate in silence.

"He wasn't surprised," Elen said quietly, once they were outside the Academia's walls. "But why did he deny it?"

"If he bought relics from Radu with Academia tokens, but concealed them from the other scholars, he could suffer for it," Sagai said. He shrugged. "It's a common enough practice, but it can be used to oust scholars who become unpopular with their superiors. The question is, did he already know the relic was dangerous to own?"

Elen shook her head, unable to answer.

The sun was almost directly overhead now, and few people were out. Most of the scholars and students had vanished from the colonnade, and the peddlers had retired under robes tented up to provide shade. Khat and Sagai turned by habit into the narrow street that led back into the area of the relic shops.

"He's got it in there with him, somewhere," Khat said. "We have to go back tonight and find it."

Elen stared. "You mean, enter by stealth?"

Even Sagai was startled.

"If we pound on the front gate, I don't think it'll do much good," Khat said.

"I don't like it," Elen protested. "If we're caught, Riathen would have to intervene for us and everything would come out. That is, if he intervened for us. He couldn't risk the Heir's part in this being revealed."

Khat glanced down at her skeptically. Riathen would intervene for her, he was sure of it. He doubted the Master Warder would lift a finger for Sagai or himself, unless he thought he still needed them. That was why he meant to arrange things so Sagai would wait outside the Academia.

"I'm not happy with it either," Sagai said, "but I can't see any other course." He glanced over at Khat. "How are you so sure we can get inside?"

That question would take some answering. As Khat was considering how much to say, a hooded figure stepped out of the alley they were passing and brushed past him.

A familiar hooded figure.

Khat turned and ducked his head, seeing nothing of the knife but the sun's flash on steel, the slash that should have opened his throat missing by inches. Off balance, he fell against the alley wall, shoved away from it in time to miss the return stroke aimed for his eyes.

Sagai had pulled Elen out of the way, and now he started toward their attacker. Akai shook his hood back. His hard eyes were angry, but his lean face revealed only rapt concentration. He said, "Stay out of this, dealer. Lushan isn't interested in you."

Khat motioned Sagai back. He didn't want him involved in this, but his partner had bought him time to draw his knife. He eased forward, and Akai circled leftward so he could keep Sagai in sight. Out of the corner of his eye Khat saw Elen backed up against the wall of the alley. From the way she was standing he knew she was thinking about trying to use her painrod. He hoped she stayed out of it. Akai was too fast, too vicious for one of those cumbersome weapons.

The smartest thing to do at this point in a knife fight was run away. But neither of them had any intention of doing that.

Akai feinted and came in high, going for the neck again. Khat stepped in under the blow, and then they were on the ground. Akai's knife was trapped against his side; Khat felt it biting into his ribs. He drove his own blade home, and Akai screamed.

Khat rolled away from him. There was blood all over the ground, and it took him a moment to realize little of it was his. Akai was scrabbling in the dust, gasping for air. Khat's blade had caught him in the upper thigh, where the big artery ran close to the skin. He was trying to stanch the wound, but every beat of his heart was forcing out more blood.

Elen was leaning over Khat anxiously. "Are you badly hurt?"

The blade had torn his shirt and drawn a long shallow cut along his ribs. Khat shook his head. Akai had lost the fight when he failed to kill him with the first attack.

"We have to go," Sagai was saying. "Trade Inspectors could be here any moment."

A death fight on the Fourth Tier, this close to the shops, would be considered an impeding of trade. Khat struggled to his feet. He had had two fights today, one for his pride and one for his life, and he wasn't looking for a third.

They went down the alley, crossed a second, and down another. Sagai stopped at a fountain in a quiet court where most of the inhabitants seemed to be either away or asleep. Elen threw some copper bits at the old fountain keeper before he could even stir off his bench and dipped her scarf in the water. She handed it to Khat, who used it to scrape off a little of the dust and blood. "Who was that man?" she demanded. "Why did he want to kill you?"

"That was Akai. He works for Lushan," Khat told her. "I was expecting him to turn up sooner or later."

Elen was still confused. "The man Miram said came to your house?"

"Yes." Sagai was looking down at Khat with a determined expression. "And there is something I want you to explain."

Khat shifted uneasily. It was too late to avoid this by pretending to be more injured than he actually was.

Sagai said, "I thought Lushan sent his bullies after Ris to make you work for him, and that you were reluctant to admit it. Is this true, or is it because he wants you to work for him *again?*"

Khat looked into the fountain. "When I first came here, I did a lot of things I don't do now." Since he was being truthful, he added, "And I enjoyed them, too."

"Stealing for Lushan?" Sagai was grim.

"That was one of them."

"Then why did you stop?" The question came from Elen.

"I didn't like it." There was no sport to taking things when the owners were asleep or absent, too much danger for little return when they weren't. It was easier by far to find relics of your own under ruined buildings or in sewer outlets and middens. But Khat had had more sense than to try to explain this viewpoint to Lushan.

Elen looked skeptical. "Is that all?"

"No," Khat admitted, in the interest of telling the whole truth. "I got caught." He looked up at them. "I was in a Patrician house on the Third Tier. Lushan knew there were some fine relics there, and he especially wanted the *mythenin* incense urn they were supposed to have. I didn't expect it to amount to much. Those are almost never found intact, unless they've been repaired with lousy Survivor-work metal. But when I found it . . . intact, openwork lid, gold inlay with a floral design." He saw Sagai struggling not to seem interested. "They had it in a cabinet with a bunch of Survivor pots and fake crematory jars." He turned to Elen. "In the Enclave you can't own relics. They belong to everybody. Nobody can take one away and hide it and say no one else can look at it."

Sagai folded his arms. "Khat. You read three languages. You've been to most of the Fringe Cities. You have the Trade Articles of Charisat memorized, and you've forgotten more about the Ancients than half the supposed relic scholars in the Academia will ever know. Don't try to tell me that you didn't understand what you were doing."

"Well, no, I knew what I was doing," Khat admitted. "Their vigils were more alert than I thought, and I got out of the house, but I couldn't get down off the roof. I went over a couple of houses; then they took a shot at me and I had to duck in through a window. There was a man sitting on the floor, writing by lamplight. It was Scholar Robelin."

"Ah," Sagai said. "I wondered how you had met him."

"The vigils came to the door, but he wouldn't let them in, and he said he hadn't seen anybody. Told them shooting at windows in the dark was a poor way to insure the safety of honest citizens. They left, and he gave me a lecture on why I shouldn't be up on the Third Tier stealing. I'd read what he was writing by that time, and it was a treatise on relics found near the Remnants, so I showed him the urn, and we had an argument about whether the designs on it were related to the Battai murals. They weren't. The background design is in a similar style, but it's coincidence."

"What makes you say that?" Sagai asked, then caught himself and shook his head. "Never mind, go on."

"He said he wanted me to come to the Academia and help him work on the Remnants. That was the first time I'd had any chance of getting in there." Khat shrugged. "He didn't have to help me. So I gave him the urn."

"Wait," Elen said. She was still confused. "He lectured you about stealing, but he accepted the stolen urn?"

Sagai frowned at her. "An intact *mythenin* incense urn? Of course. He would have to be mad to refuse." He turned his attention back to Khat. "And Lushan, I suppose, wanted you to pay him its value."

"He's crazy. It wasn't his. I could give it to whoever I wanted. But he never got over it. Sometimes, to make him leave me alone, I'd take something for him. I haven't done it for a long time, though, because we were so busy. I paid him finally, but it just made him madder. That's crazy for you."

"Let me make sure I understand this," Elen said carefully. "While we are searching for these relics that could make the difference in life or death for all the Warders living now and all the generations of Warders to come, you are carrying on a private war with this . . . this . . . jumped-up Fourth Tier thief?"

"What did you expect me to do, drop everything because of your business?" Khat asked her, exasperated. "And I told Riathen at the time he shouldn't have hired me."

Elen buried her face in her hands, apparently fighting for calm. "I understand perfectly," she said finally. "Did you ever consider that perhaps Lushan didn't go crazy until after he met you?"

Khat ignored her. He was watching Sagai carefully. "Still partners?" he asked.

After a moment, Sagai sighed. "Who else would have you?"

Chapter Twelve

KHAT TOLD ELEN and Sagai that they couldn't possibly consider entering the Academia until after the fourth hour of the night. This was true.

It also gave him time to make his next move in what Elen called his private war with that jumped-up Fourth Tier relic thief.

The loss of Harim and Akai would cause an upset in Lushan's household arrangements, and the broker had never been particularly cautious anyway, relying on fear of retaliation to keep thieves away. Now the time was right, Khat decided, for one or two enterprising young professionals to try their luck on Lushan's vast store of relics. Especially if they had advice from someone who had been in the rooms the collection was kept in, and could describe the house to them. And Caster would be just the one to arrange it all.

Khat found him in the Arcade, just as it was closing down for the night. They retreated to one of the highest levels, dangerous from weakened supports and holes in the flooring and always deserted, while Khat laid out his plan and drew the different rooms of Lushan's house in the dust.

While Caster was figuring everyone's percentage from the possible take, Khat looked across the Arcade, shadowy from the gathering darkness outside and growing quiet as the noise from below faded. He hadn't heard anything. He might have seen something, just at the corner of his eye. "Did you see anything?" he asked Caster.

"No." The Silent Market dealer scanned the area suspiciously. "Did you?"

"No." Khat shrugged it off. Lushan had more enemies than any other broker in Charisat; it wasn't likely he would suspect Khat of planning this, and he would hardly be able to report the theft to the Trade Inspectors—too many of the relics in his house were stolen, and bribes would only protect him so far.

"I heard Radu the fortune-teller is dead."

Khat glanced over at the dealer thoughtfully. The statement had been as noncommittal as possible. Caster would have known about the death and the house's contents as soon as the local street thieves had built up the courage to enter the deserted building. The dealer probably thought Khat had killed Radu.

Without looking up, Caster added, "Not that he had long for the world, anyway. Rumor said the Trade Inspectors were after him."

"Trade Inspectors are after everybody," Khat said, to have something to say, then wondered at it. From Radu's money chest, it had looked as though he only sold relics for tokens. The minted coins there had been small amounts, probably fees for fortune-telling. "Do you know why they were after him?"

"A woman Radu knew said he had a High Justice interested in him." Caster shrugged one shoulder. "Told him a bad fortune, maybe."

Khat frowned down at the ants crawling out of a crack in the floor. Elen had told him how Riathen had taken the crystal plaque from a High Justice. How very odd that a High Justice should be interested in Radu the fortune-teller, when there weren't that many Justices in Charisat. And he could be just imagining connections and conspiracies where there weren't any. He said, "Did she say anything else about it?"

Caster shook his head.

They finished working out the details of the arrangement, and Caster said, "The best time to do it is tonight. I'll come to your court sometime tomorrow night after I make the deals." He got to his feet, and looked down at Khat. "Watch yourself."

As Caster went toward one of the rickety walkways, Khat thought, *Silent Market dealers are telling me to be careful.* Well, he knew this wasn't the wisest thing he had ever done. But it was, just possibly, the most satisfying.

* * *

Khat had chosen the spot carefully.

People were not allowed to build up against the Academia's wall any more than they were allowed to build up against the tier walls, but in the Academia's case the obligatory twenty paces of empty pavement between the wall and the nearest dwelling was not strictly enforced. Khat had long ago found places where crowding on the Fourth Tier had caused mud-brick houses to grow sometimes as close as six or seven paces to the wall. Vigils would be on the lookout for thieves trying to jump from the roofs to the wall top or to lower a rope, but they couldn't be everywhere at once, and the houses safely screened anyone scaling the wall itself.

He found Sagai and Elen already waiting where he had told them to, in a narrow alley between the rock wall and the mud-brick bulk of a row of illegal houses. "Where were you?" Sagai asked in an almost voiceless whisper. Now was not the time to be overheard by anyone, and people might be sleeping just on the other side of the crumbling walls.

"Had to take care of something," Khat whispered back. The moon was barely a sliver in the sky, and he could hardly see the others except as crouching forms. He took the rope from under his robe, making a looser coil of it so he could sling it over one shoulder. It was thin and strong, made of braided hair, and so dark it would be invisible against the wall. Sand grated under his boots. Obviously the street sweepers didn't bother with this stretch of alley, and the inhabitants would hardly complain for fear someone official might notice and make them move their homes.

"Remember, you're staying here as lookout," Khat whispered to Sagai. They had had that discussion earlier. His partner nodded, and Khat started up the wall.

Reaching the top, he struggled up onto the narrow ledge. There were a few pieces of cut glass still stuck into it, but most had broken away. The buildings of the Academia stretched away on the other side, a maze of stone and tile, quiet and all but pitch dark. There were a few lighted windows, and ghostlamps glowed in the more frequented courts further away. Only the scholars, students, and servants who were without families would live inside, and only the most dedicated would be up this late working in lamplight. Directly below was a long narrow court, little more than an outdoor connecting passage between a few silent structures.

Khat paused to uncoil half the rope, drop it down for Elen, and work it into a gap between the stones, where it couldn't pull loose and sever itself on the glass. Then he dropped down to the court below.

He waited, crouched on the pavement, but the only response was the skittering of a few startled lizards.

He felt the rope jerk behind him as Elen scrambled over the top and started down. In another moment she was beside him. He stood up to pull the rope down, and suddenly Sagai was coming over the top. Cursing under his breath, Khat stepped back to give him room.

"You were supposed to be the lookout," he hissed as Sagai dropped down beside him.

"We don't need a lookout," Sagai whispered calmly, jerking the rope to free it and drawing it back down the wall. "It would be suspicious if someone saw me."

Khat had the idea he was being paid back for not telling anyone about his little problem with Lushan sooner; Sagai had certainly picked a moment when it was difficult if not impossible for him to retaliate. Disgruntled, he took the rope away from Sagai, coiled it again, and put it away under his robe.

They made their way silently, Khat relying on Elen's night sight to help guide them. He knew what direction to go to reach Arad's place, but he didn't know which of the narrow little courts led into other courts and which ones dead-ended. They heard voices at times, and the footsteps of restless scholars or servants, and once they had to huddle in a doorway as two vigils passed not twenty paces away, talking idly and swinging their ghostlamps.

Finally they reached the court where Arad's house lay. It looked deserted and silent from the outside, but a glow from somewhere along the gently pitched roof meant that lamps were still lit in the large chamber with the louvers. Watching it from the shelter of a gap between two other buildings, Khat didn't know whether he was relieved or worried by the lack of lights and vigils. "Shouldn't it be guarded?" Elen whispered. "That valuable mural . . ."

"Yes, it should be," Sagai answered her. "But careful guarding of otherwise innocuous places often attracts thieves, and the Academia cannot afford all the vigils it needs. And Scholar Arad may have discouraged the posting of guards, if he has something to hide."

"If he doesn't, this is a wasted trip," Khat muttered. He led them across the square at a walk, knowing that if they were seen at a distance there was nothing to show they didn't belong here. Once up the steps and under the porch of the building Khat felt less exposed, but he was experienced enough to know any feeling of security in this situation was deceptive.

There were no vigils lying in wait in the foyer, and from here Khat could see the glow of lamplight from the rooms deeper within. He motioned for Sagai and Elen to stay back, and went quietly down the little hallway. He could sense someone breathing in one of the rooms ahead.

Khat reached a point where he could see through the arch that led into the central chamber, and his first thought was that he had somehow picked the wrong house.

Awash in lamplight the room looked larger than it had before, and there was an extra door, this one leading not into another hallway but into a small chamber that seemed packed with wooden racks and shelves. But there was the tile mural, a pool of glowing color under the flickering light, and there was Arad, sitting on the floor with a book folded out before him, examining some small object that glittered with the characteristic luster *mythenin* took on in firelight.

Khat stepped out into the room, and Arad looked up, startled and guilty. He was wearing a pair of reading lenses, held on by cords looped over his ears, and they made his eyes look larger. When he saw who was standing over him, the guilt changed to fear.

Khat said, "Never deal with the Fourth Tier, do you?"

Then Elen came barreling in behind him. She snatched the small object out of Arad's hand and shook it under his nose. "You had it all along! Do you know how much danger you put yourself in, and us, with your lies?"

Arad was scooting backward. "What do you want here? Are you thieves after all?"

Sagai said, "Stop waving it about, Elen." He took the little relic away from her and added, "And don't shout at the man. It's not doing any good."

He held the relic where Khat and he could both see it. It was a tiny oval of *mythenin*, faceted along the edges, with the figure of a faceless man with wings spread out behind his body delicately engraved in the center. It was smaller than Khat had expected from the description in the book, about the size of an overlarge coin. It didn't even cover the center of Sagai's palm. Khat said, "It's smaller than the book said it was."

"Yes," Arad said, perhaps seizing on the one thing he had heard that made sense to him. "The figures in the book were wrong." Then the scholar blinked. "But how did you know that?"

Khat and Sagai exchanged a look. Mystified, Elen said slowly, "Because we've seen the book. How did you know what it said?"

Arad gestured. "But I have it here. When did you see it?"

They looked down. The text that lay unfolded on the floor had brown, weathered paper, faded ink. Khat saw a page with a colored engraving on it, and swore under his breath. He sat on his heels to look more closely, gently unfolded a few pages. Arad watched, worried, but didn't object. "This is the book, Elen," Khat said.

"You mean that's it, the Survivor text?" Sagai knelt to examine the book eagerly.

"It's a copy," Khat corrected. "Maybe made at the same time as Riathen's, maybe a little earlier." One side of the cover was sun-faded, and some of the pages were torn.

Sagai unfolded the section with the colored engravings, studying them in wonder.

Elen was staring at Arad, as if something was finally starting to make sense to her. "The old man had two copies," she said. "Of course. That's why he gave one to Riathen so casually."

"He gave him the one that was easier to read," Khat said, sitting back to let Sagai examine the text. If the old Patrician had wanted the Master Warder's opinion on the contents, that only made sense. "This one isn't nearly as well preserved, and the ink is faded on some of these pages."

"Two copies?" Arad was even more confused. "I got this from Radu, the Fourth Tier fortune-teller. I thought you must know all about that."

Elen sat down on the floor and rested her head in her hands. She said, "A copy of this book, and that relic with the winged image, were originally owned by a Patrician on the Second Tier. He gave the book to Sonet Riathen, the Master Warder, and then the old Patrician was murdered, his home broken into and all the relics stolen. Riathen found one of the relics, a sort of *mythenin* plate with crystal pieces, in the hands of a High Justice . . ."

So far Arad had shown no inclination to shout for help. He turned eagerly to the page of the book with the colored engraving that Riathen had put such emphasis on. "This *mythenin* plate?"

"Yes," Elen nodded. "That one."

It didn't appear the relics had gone far afield at all. "Funny that Radu should have two relics from the same theft," Khat said, looking over at Elen.

"Funny indeed," Sagai agreed. "Perhaps Radu arranged the theft himself."

Khat shrugged. It was a possibility, but Radu hadn't brokered or dealt relics in a large enough fashion to be much noticed by the Silent Market. Khat didn't find it too likely that he would have arranged the theft himself. "Or he just bought them, knowing they were stolen."

"I can't say I would be surprised to hear that Radu was in league with any number of thieves," Arad said. "I tried to find out his source for such unusual relics, and all I could get out of him was mystic nonsense. By the way . . ." He peered at them curiously. "Who are you?"

There seemed little point in keeping it a secret. "That's Sagai and I'm Khat. We're relic dealers from the Sixth Tier, and Elen really is a Warder."

"It was too much to hope that she wasn't." Arad sighed. "I hoped to solve this mystery on my own, but you seem to know everything else." He shook his head in defeat. "Let me show you."

He climbed awkwardly to his feet, taking one of the lamps and going toward the opening of the little room that had somehow been tacked on to the larger chamber since this afternoon. Khat followed him, and saw that it was little more than a large cupboard. It seemed to be normally sealed off by a stone slab several inches thick that was lowered and pushed forward to sit flush with the outer wall by a system of counterweights high in the ceiling of the concealed space. The slab even had false seams carved into it to match the blocks the rest of the room was constructed with. "Did you make this yourself?" Khat asked Arad.

"It has been here many years. I discovered it by accident," the scholar explained.

The hidden relics were neatly stored, glass objects to one side, metal and *mythenin* to the other, with tile and other ceramic fragments in the center. Most were sitting on top of folded squares of paper, which would contain notes on how the individual relic had been found and any interesting features about it that Arad had observed. This was a method Robelin had used as well.

Arad pointed to the dusty area beneath the racks and said, "That is something else you've been looking for, isn't it?"

On the floor was a solid block of some shiny black stone. The book had been wrong about it, too. It was two feet in height but closer to three feet long and three feet wide, not four as the caption had said. It also clearly wasn't made of *mythenin.*

"I bought it from Radu last year, at the same time I bought the book," Arad said. "His price was ridiculously low. He seemed anxious to be rid of it."

Khat sat on his heels to run a hand over the block's surface. "That's why no one ever heard of it before. It went from the thieves to Radu and then to you. It was never on the Silent Market." The feel of the stone was cold, with the silky texture of the inner walls of the Remnant. He couldn't make sense of the lines etched into it; like the carvings on the Miracle, they seemed to be nothing more than abstract designs, spirals and whirls, mingling, crossing, melting into each other. Trying to follow the pattern with your eyes was oddly hypnotic. Khat shook off the effect and looked up at Arad-edelk. "What is it?"

The scholar shook his head and adjusted his lenses. "I don't know. That is one of the mysteries I hoped to solve. I wanted to complete a full translation of this text, which I hope will explain the importance of the relics which are so prominently featured in the engravings. I meant to present the whole to the Academia when I was finished . . . The resemblance this block has to the Miracle can't be coincidence, but there is no magical effect. That I've observed, at least."

"The Miracle didn't do anything for years either. They kept it in the Elector's garden until it started to make light," Khat said, then wondered if anybody was going to ask him how he knew that. Sagai gave him an odd look as he knelt to examine the strange stone block, but the others seemed to take his knowledge for granted.

Arad was watching them warily. Now he asked, "Will you take it away tonight?"

Elen started to answer and stopped, then made another attempt, and those words didn't make it out either. She wasn't high-handed by nature, and taking prized relics away from this little scholar who was standing before her so helplessly wasn't something she had bargained on.

Getting to his feet, Sagai said, "No one will take anything tonight. Perhaps we should talk this over."

* * *

While Arad warmed tea over a brazier on the other side of the room, Khat watched Elen, who was biting her lip and turning over the little plaque with the winged figure as if she suspected it of concealing something. "What's the matter with you?" he asked her. "We found them, just like you said we would."

"There's something I don't like about this. The theft, Radu's death, Constans's involvement," she said. "Did Radu arrange the original theft or was it only a coincidence?"

Sagai had been examining the Survivor text, and now he glanced up and said, "It's possible. It's also possible the thieves betrayed the one who ordered the theft, and dispersed the relics for more coin."

Elen didn't look up at him, still studying the winged relic intently, and her voice was grave. "But who wanted the relics stolen in the first place? Constans?"

It must be Constans, Khat thought. Except that Constans had the skills to perform the theft himself, and had no need to trust to lower-tier hirelings. And somehow he had gotten the impression that Constans had become interested in the relics only after Sonet Riathen had started his search.

Arad came back to them and took a seat on one of the low stools. He had closed the secret cubbyhole again, and even now that Khat knew its location it was difficult to trace its outline in the wall. Considering the care Arad took with it, he wondered if the other scholars knew of its existence at all. Arad asked Khat, "Didn't you work with Scholar Robelin at one time?"

"For a while."

"I thought your name was familiar. Ecazar still speaks of you."

Before Khat could ask what that worthy had to say about him after all this time, Elen leaned forward and said, "Scholar Arad, can you tell us what you know of the book and the relics?"

Watching her closely, Arad asked, "Your Master Warder will take them, won't he?"

She nodded seriously. "Yes, but he will pay you for them."

Arad gestured toward the mural. "I'll be paid for my work on that, but I'll never see it again."

Elen seemed to debate with herself, then said, "Please, I know you have no reason to want to help us, but can you tell me what you've learned from the book so far? I think it's important."

"Very well." Arad took off his lenses and rubbed his eyes wearily. "It talks of magic, of an invasion—"

"Invasion?" Khat interrupted, ignoring Elen's frustrated glare. "From across the Last Sea?"

Sagai handed Arad back the text, but the scholar held it on his lap without opening it. "No, not from there. It says 'They came down through the Western Doors of the sky, from the land of the dead . . .' "

"But the land of the dead is said to be under the earth," Sagai said, puzzled.

Arad tapped the cover of the folded book. "Not according to this scribe."

"But who are 'they'?" Elen asked.

"The people of the West?" Khat said, remembering the fragments he had read of Riathen's copy.

"The Inhabitants of the West," Arad corrected. "The distinction is important. It never calls them people." He unfolded the text, idly running his fingers over the delicate pages. "It speaks of destruction, of men and women seized and taken away through these Western Doors, of fire . . ."

"The formation of the Waste, perhaps?" Sagai said.

"I believe so." Arad shrugged. "But it speaks of it in such a cryptic fashion, with so many double meanings and such deliberate obfuscation, that it has taken me a great deal of time to extract even that much sense out of it. That some pages are partly illegible doesn't help either."

"Does it speak of arcane engines?" Elen asked urgently. "Of how to build them?"

Sagai looked up and caught Khat's eye. It was what they had been saying to each other all along. Arad was right; the block's resemblance to the Miracle was no coincidence. *What exactly does Riathen think this arcane engine will do, once he puts it together?* Khat wondered. The Master Warder had told Elen he meant to unlock the secrets of the Ancients' magic with these relics, and Khat, though he was all for rediscovering the past, found himself wondering if some of those secrets should be unlocked.

"Something of the sort," Arad answered. "But I've only just scratched the surface of that section. The actual history of the events seems far more important." He picked up the coin-shaped plaque with the winged figure. "But I learned enough to know that this seems to be a part of some greater—I don't know if engine would be the proper word . . ."

Khat stretched out on the floor, propping himself up on one elbow. "That crystal plaque in the engraving fits into one of the shapes on the anteroom wall of the Tersalten Flat Remnant," he told him. "Does it say that?"

"No." Arad looked incredulous. "Truly? Robelin's theory that the Remnants housed arcane engines . . . This is the first real support."

Khat nodded, smiling faintly at the scholar's growing excitement.

"Why, before this is over you could discover more evidence that would conclusively prove it!" Arad finished.

Khat looked away, brought back abruptly to reality again. If he proved Robelin's theory, there was no chance of his taking the credit for it as far as the Academia was concerned. Any scholarly documentation of the discovery would excise his part in it completely. He saw Elen watching him curiously, and avoided her eyes.

Arad hadn't noticed. He was saying thoughtfully, "This is fascinating. The text mentions the Remnants a great deal . . ."

"It does?" Sagai looked even more intrigued, if that was possible. "But in the other existent texts, the Remnants are mentioned only in passing, if at all," he said.

Arad smiled faintly. "Yes, this is the text scholars have hoped to find for decades, praying that it existed somewhere other than their imaginations. It may provide a clue as to why the Remnants were built." He looked seriously at Sagai. "Think of it. The Waste rock was rising, the seas had drained, the cities were dying. In the mountains that became the krismen Enclave a group of Mages must have already begun their great experiment, to create a people who could survive what our world was in the process of becoming. Yet other Mages devoted what must have been a great expenditure of their power, and a great toll in human life, to build the Remnants. Why?" He glanced down at the book again. "One fact I have been able to discern is that the presence of these 'doors of the sky' was how they chose the locations of the Remnants." He shook his head. "It's still a mystery. But when I finish my translation and present it to the other Scholars . . ."

"Wait," Khat said, sitting bolt upright. He had heard something, from the passage that led to the outside door. He stood and went to the archway. Behind him he heard Sagai whisper, "Just in case, fold the book back up and put this . . ."

Khat remembered the louvers. He looked up, taking a step back, just as the first dark form dropped through.

Someone shouted, and Khat fell back against the wall, bracing himself. One man hit the stone floor not two feet from him, taking the twenty-foot drop easily. They were dressed in black and indigo to meld with the shadows, veiled and featureless. The nearest recovered and came at him all in one smooth motion. But Khat had already drawn his knife, and only excellent reflexes saved the intruder from a messy disembowelment. The man flung up an arm to shield his eyes against the return stroke, and Khat stepped in close for a kill. Then something smashed him down from behind.

For an instant he was stunned, pinned to the floor by something heavy. The stone felt gritty against his cheek, and his head hurt. He could see Elen had her painrod out and was backed against the far wall. She had used the Ancient weapon; one of the invaders was huddled on the floor in front of her. Somehow she had ended up with the book, and was hugging the folded text tightly to her chest. Arad had been knocked back against the opposite wall, and Sagai stood in front of him, two of their opponents at bay. Khat wondered why nobody was moving, then thought it was probably because someone was bracing a knee on his back and holding a knife to the big vein in his neck, just below the scar where the bonetaker had almost killed him.

Shiskan son Karadon said, "You know what we want."

The floor was hard, and she was heavy. It was the first time he had heard her voice. It was soft and husky. She sounded entirely calm. *Probably does this every day,* Khat thought. There was a scraping sound off to his left; then he saw the man he had cut standing, hugging a bloody arm.

Elen looked at Sagai, and he said evenly, "Give it to them, Elen."

He hadn't put any undue emphasis on the word "it," but Khat understood. The winged relic lay in the dust against the wall near Elen, gleaming faintly in the lamplight; the secret cubby was safely shut with the big ugly block inside. It depended on how long Shiskan and the others had been crouched on the roof, listening.

Shiskan said, "Ardan, get the book."

The veiled man confronting Elen took a step toward her, and

suddenly she moved, her painrod missing him by a hairsbreadth as he leapt out of reach.

Elen stepped back. Shiskan cursed under her breath at the near miss. Still shoved back against the wall, Arad-edelk looked up at Sagai worriedly, and Sagai watched Elen, who might have been a statue frozen motionless in marble.

Not loud enough to be heard by the others, Khat said to Shiskan, "Can you move your knee?" It was pressing into his back in a particularly painful place; it was also in the optimum position to keep him from breaking her hold and rolling over, if he didn't mind the chance of her cutting his throat.

Softly, she answered, "Afraid not."

Worried, Sagai said, "Elen . . ."

Khat wondered where in hell the Academia's vigils were. This commotion should draw them, if anything could. He wondered what Elen would do.

The moment of decision came without warning. Alive again, Elen lifted the book. She said, "Let him go first."

Khat couldn't believe that she was going to do it; he would've bet anything that she wouldn't. "Elen, don't give it to them."

Shiskan nudged him reprovingly. "Let her alone, and all this can be over in a few moments."

That's what I'm afraid of, he thought. *A distraction, please, Sagai . . .* There were five of them to worry about: one facing Elen, one still incapacitated by her painrod, two watching Sagai and Arad, and the one he had wounded, who was leaning against the wall and panting. And that was without Shiskan son Karadon, which was discounting quite a bit. He could see Sagai's eyes shift from the two men confronting him to Shiskan and back. To anyone else he might have looked nervous, but Khat knew his partner was thinking. Arad hadn't moved, except to look up at Sagai once. He was watching everything, not without fear but nowhere close to panic. He could probably be counted on to do something in a moment of crisis, even if it wasn't something terribly effective.

One of the men watching Sagai shifted, coming dangerously near the edge of the incomplete mural, and Khat said, "Tell your friend to get his big feet away from those tiles."

Shiskan said, "Lyan, careful."

The man glanced down and moved a step away.

To Elen, Shiskan said, "Give us the book, and I'll let him go."

"Let him go first," Elen insisted stubbornly.

"I can't, he'll kill me," Shiskan pointed out reasonably.

"You're going to confuse each other," Khat told her.

"Hush," she said. Her voice hardened as she spoke to Elen again. "Give us the book."

"Elen, please, you must," Sagai said, taking a step toward her with his hands open. The next instant he was locked in a struggle with the man nearest him. Arad was moving, flinging himself forward to trip the other.

Shiskan moved, shifting her weight and balance, and the knife point came away from his neck. Before she could realize her mistake Khat caught her wrist and pushed himself up, dumping her off him. The one he had wounded earlier made an awkward attempt to rush him, and Khat stepped out of his path and tripped him. The man sprawled helplessly, and Shiskan was gaining her feet again. Khat grabbed his knife from where it had fallen, and looked up to see another dark form coming down through the louver.

Sagai shouted, "Run!" and everyone seemed to bolt for a different doorway at once.

Khat saw Elen vanish down the hall toward the outer door and darted after her. She still had the book, and the pursuit would concentrate on her. He hoped Sagai or Arad would remember to get the winged relic, and he hoped more that Shiskan and the others would not bother to chase them.

One of their pursuers had followed Elen already. Khat overtook him at the outer doorway, spun him around, and smashed him into the wall. Knowing the others were right behind him, he leapt down the steps without pausing to finish him off.

He caught up with Elen midway across the square and dragged her toward one of the arches leading off from it. The night air was hot and heavy, stagnant in his lungs. He stopped in the shelter of a roofed arbor, looking back at the darkened square. It was empty and suspiciously quiet.

"Did the others get out?" she asked, her voice a breathless whisper.

"I think so; it's that book they're after."

"I know that." She was still clutching it tightly to her chest. "What are we going to do?"

Khat heard a careless step on the arbor roof above them, and whispered, "Run."

They ran down the narrow court, emerged into an almost equally narrow garden, crossed it into another sheltered colonnade. He was glad again for her night sight, even if it was a Warder trick; she avoided potted flowers and low pools and found steps that would have left him staggering at this pace. At the end of the colonnade he stopped her again to listen, and she whispered, "I meant, when you followed me out here, didn't you have some sort of plan of action?"

Somewhere back the way they had come he could hear shouting. Shiskan's people would hardly need to shout; it was probably the Academia's vigils, finally awake to the notion that something odd was happening. "Didn't you have a plan of action when you ran out here?" he asked her.

"I see your point."

"They shouldn't have been able to take that drop from the ceiling without breaking legs; is flying another Warder talent you forgot to mention?"

"There are Disciplines, mental exercises, that allow the human body to overcome pain, to be physically stronger for a short time. Riathen said Constans was always very good at Disciplines."

"Very good" is something of an understatement, Khat thought. He wanted to work his way to the outer wall, where once over it they would have the whole city to hide in. His worst fear was of getting cornered down one of these blind courts. He tugged her sleeve and led the way down the colonnade, at a slower pace so he could hear their pursuers.

"I know," Elen whispered suddenly. "Why don't we leave the book somewhere, toss it through someone's window, then lead them away from it?"

Khat had considered that, but it didn't alter the fact that if they were caught with the book or without it, they were dead. And once he had his hands on a relic, he didn't like to let go until it was absolutely necessary. Especially a relic like this.

He started to answer her, but she halted abruptly and he stumbled into her instead. Before he could protest he saw the darkness just in front of them move. Something was there, shapeless but alarmingly solid, as if a piece of one of the dark walls had stepped forward to challenge them. Elen grabbed his arm, and together they backed away, instinctively slowly, though Khat couldn't have said where the conviction that quick motion would antagonize it came from.

It passed out from under the colonnade and into the moonlight, and for an instant lines of dim red light shot through it, revealing something vaguely human-shaped, but with a rounded crest spread out behind its head and an oddly formed body. The hackles on the back of Khat's neck itched.

It hovered, as if uncertain. "I don't think it knows we're here," Elen whispered, almost soundlessly.

Suddenly it moved like lightning, darting first away from them, and then directly toward them, coming so close the smothering cold of it forced Khat back a step.

It stopped, then drifted toward them again, slowly and deliberately.

"It knows we're here now," Khat said grimly, pulling Elen back with him.

It was moving them toward the dark opening to a court. Khat tried to step past it, and it moved quicker than thought, blocking escape and herding them again toward the court. *Because it can trap us in there*, Khat thought, desperate.

"Is it a ghost?" Elen said. "Like the one at Radu's house?"

"I was hoping you knew."

"My education didn't cover this area. It's getting stronger, or something. Can you feel it?"

He could. The air was turning chill around them, forcing them back under the arch of the entrance to the court. It acted like a ghost, it felt like a ghost, it would probably kill them like a ghost, but he had never heard of a ghost you could see as a blot of darkness. They were only visible if they stirred dust or knocked things over. *Maybe everyone who ever saw one like this is dead*, Khat thought, which was a theory they might be about to prove.

They were trapped. The court was small, with high windowless buildings to either side and a wall behind.

Abruptly the chill in the air was gone, and the thing seemed to be swirling about, caught in some internal struggle. Then it shrank in on itself until only a point of red light remained.

And Aristai Constans was standing behind it, blocking the exit from the court.

Elen took a deep breath, muttered, "Oh, no."

Constans gestured, and the last of the red ghost light winked out. He came toward them unhurriedly, and said, "Well, I think we know what I'm here for."

Khat was moving forward, no real plan in mind except to distract him so Elen could perhaps run out past him. The next moment he was on the ground, the breath knocked out of his lungs, his legs numb and unable to move.

Constans said, "Stay out of this for a moment, Khat, if you can."

"Leave him alone," Elen said. She held out one hand, eyes narrowed in concentration. The air between them seemed to thicken, shadows taking substance, growing heavy with the presence of power. Constans stepped through it, and the delicate structure was swept away, scattered like straw in a sandstorm. He said, "I haven't time for games, Elen. Give me the book. Riathen was a fool to let it out of his keeping. Don't add to his foolishness by opposing me."

He thinks it's Riathen's copy, Khat thought, startled, then tried not to think at all.

Elen shook her head, wisely not sparing breath to answer or correct his mistake. She flexed her hand, trying something else, something that made the air around them grow brighter, brought out the muted color in the tiles in the court's pavement, then turned them gray with its intensity. Khat wanted badly to look away but didn't dare. The feeling was coming back into his legs, and he cautiously levered himself up off the pavement a little. It hadn't hurt as much as being hit with a painrod, but he was willing to rank it high on the list of the most frightening things that had ever happened to him. He remembered the lictor Constans had killed so easily out at the Remnant and supposed he should feel lucky.

Elen's face looked terrible in the unnatural light, pale as death and tense with pain. No wonder she hated to use her power, and never did anything but small simples that often as not refused to work.

Constans stopped, regarding her thoughtfully. He took another step toward them, this with more effort, but said, "I see Riathen's teaching hasn't improved with time. You didn't even realize Shiskan and the others were on the roof, Elen. Is your skill at soul-reading still so poor?" Abruptly Elen's wall of light was scattered, caught in some invisible wind that trapped it in a miniature dust devil and sent it swirling away into the night sky.

There was lamplight from behind the wall suddenly, and someone shouted, "Look, over there!"

Constans swore and started forward.

Elen was faster. She flung the delicate text up and back, over her head and over the wall and down to whoever had shouted.

Elen fell back, and Khat managed to catch her, dragging her out of Constans's reach, but they were both still trapped against the wall. Suddenly a large group of vigils, air guns ready, appeared in a blaze of lamplight at the end of the court. Constans flung himself to the right, at the steep wall of the house, scaling it as if it were a ladder. Khat heard the crack of pellets striking stone and slumped back to the ground, pulling Elen down with him. The firing stopped abruptly, and he risked a look.

Constans had vanished. The vigils filled the little court, pointing and shouting directions to each other, lamps swinging.

Elen sat up, holding her head in both hands as if it hurt too much to move. She was breathing hard and trembling. "Are you all right?" Khat asked her, trying to see if she had been hit.

"I think so." She rubbed her eyes. "Where's the book?"

A rifle barrel came down between them suddenly, lamplight glinting off the chased silver arabesques along it, and Khat looked up at a grim-faced man with a subcaptain's chain of office. "Your friend won't get far," the vigil said. "Tell us who he is."

"You don't want to know," Khat said. Anyone chasing Constans at this point would be lucky indeed not to catch up with him.

Elen said, "I'm a Warder. Which one of you has our book?"

The subcaptain sneered. "You're a thief. When I—"

She was on her feet before he could react, her painrod just lifting his chin. He was a head taller than she, but it didn't seem to matter much. Her voice low and shaking, she said, "I'm not going to tell you again. Give me the book."

Khat stood, slowly so as not to distract her, wondering if the others would try to shoot her and what he could do about it if they did.

But the subcaptain said, "Your pardon, Honored."

After a tense moment, Elen stepped back. One of the other vigils gingerly held out the leather-cased text to her. She tucked it under one arm, and said to Khat, "We've got the book. Are you all right? We should go find the others now."

He nodded. The physical effect of what Constans had done had disappeared completely, though he would certainly remember it for a long time. The vigils were blocking the front of the court, most of them staring as if they were at a theater. "Make them get out of the way," Khat suggested helpfully.

There was a muted scramble in the ranks to clear a path, except for the subcaptain, who stepped out of their way slowly and gave Khat a look that should have melted bone as they went past.

Elen was heading determinedly for Arad's house, and Khat was glad, not knowing if he could talk her out of it if she stormed off somewhere he didn't want to go. They needed to find Sagai again, and if anyone could help them brazen this all out it was going to be Arad-edelk. Because he was curious, and to see if she was in her right mind again, he asked, "Did he set that ghost after us or did he send it away?"

Elen frowned. "I don't know." She sounded more like her normal self, at least. "It did look like he sent it away, didn't it?"

There were now vigils guarding the doorway of Arad's house, and as they went up the steps Khat could hear Scholar Ecazar's voice, the sarcasm in it discernible even at this distance. The vigil subcaptain motioned for the others to clear a path, and moved in front of them to lead the way, though he was careful not to jostle Elen.

There were more vigils in Arad's workroom, and Scholar Ecazar was pacing back and forth, saying, "At the very least you have jeopardized your work. This mural is the most important commission given to any scholar this year, and if you are mixed up in any illegal dealings . . ."

Sagai stood nearby, composed and watching Ecazar thoughtfully. Arad-edelk was shaking with rage at being accused. Neither looked any the worse for wear for their experience.

When Ecazar paused for breath, Arad said, "Your accusations are ridiculous. I was attacked, in my house, by . . ." He gestured angrily, obviously buying time. "By . . ."

"By thieves," Sagai murmured.

"By thieves, and was only saved from death by the presence of my friends here, who came to consult with me on another matter."

"Friends." Ecazar was contemptuous. "You hadn't seen them before today, you said so yourself this afternoon. And what about this?" He shook something under the smaller scholar's nose, and Khat realized with a sinking feeling that it was the little winged plaque that had gone unnoticed by Shiskan and the others. "They accused you of purchasing it from some Fourth Tier thief—"

"Not an accusation, merely a question," Sagai objected.

Ecazar saw Khat and Elen, and shook the plaque in their direction. "I might have known you would have something to do with this when I saw you here again today." It was the first time he had spoken directly to Khat since he had ordered him out of the Academia after Robelin's death. "And you, Warder, what are you scheming with this kris relic thief?"

Elen stalked forward, still clutching the book. "I am on Warder's business, and that is all you need to know."

"What is that book?" Ecazar asked, distracted and frowning. He might be a scornful old pedagogue, but he knew a Survivor text when he saw one. "Where did you get it?" the scholar demanded.

"They had it when we caught them trying to escape," the subcaptain said, watching them carefully. "Tried to get rid of it by throwing it over a wall."

"I was trying to save it from the thieves, who were chasing us," Elen said, looking unconcerned. "Your vigils frightened them away. Better late than never, I suppose," she added, and the subcaptain winced.

Ecazar turned back to Arad. "Did she get this book from you? What is it?"

Arad took a deep breath, obviously at a loss, and Elen said, "It's my book."

"Yes," Sagai said, unruffled. "She brought it to show Scholar Arad, on the Master Warder's orders. It had to be done tonight."

"Exactly what I was about to tell you," Arad added, folding his arms triumphantly.

Ecazar's brows drew together in frustration, and he stared around at them all suspiciously. Khat kept his mouth shut; they had muddied the well enough without his help.

"And what about this?" Ecazar asked finally, holding out the winged relic. "Where did this come from?"

Elen drew breath to claim it, stopped at a warning cough from Sagai. Ecazar smiled. "Of course it can't be yours, Warder. You asked Arad-edelk if he had it today. And Arad denied it."

"I did . . ." Arad began. "I did deny it, because . . ."

"Because the thieves dropped it in their search," Sagai finished for him. "That's how it came here, Master Scholar. Obviously it was stolen from someone else earlier tonight. An astonishing coincidence, since we had looked for it all the day. Better give it to Elen, so the Warders can take it to its rightful owner."

"Yes," Elen agreed. "That would be best."

" 'Best,' " Ecazar sneered. "You're lying. Tell me the truth, Arad. These people broke in here to steal relics from you, relics you bought from some illegal source and were concealing from your brother scholars, and you were interrupted by another group of thieves."

Khat couldn't help himself. "Getting a little complicated, isn't it? Every thief in the city, here on the same night?"

Ecazar's glare was sulfurous.

Arad shook his head stubbornly. "These people are friends, here to consult with me on a matter of importance. The thieves have escaped. That is all I will say."

"If you maintain that lie, then on your head be it. I'll see you lose your charter over this, Arad." Ecazar turned to go.

Elen blocked his path, holding out her hand. "The relic."

"Oh, I think not," Ecazar said, looking down at her. "If it was dropped here by thieves, then indeed it must be stolen, and should be returned to the Trade Inspectors. And you, there is no reason for you to be within our gates, and . . ." He hesitated, and Khat knew he wanted to order Elen to leave, but he had no real authority over her, and she didn't look inclined to forget the fact that she was a Warder simply because he shouted at her. Finally he said, "I suggest you take yourself off, Honored Warder, and be more careful about the company you choose." He glanced at the vigil subcaptain. "Continue the search. And post guards on this house to make sure no more thieves visit here tonight."

He strode for the door, and the vigils trailed out after him, the subcaptain last.

"Impossible man," Arad fumed when they were gone. "Because I was born on the Sixth Tier, he thinks he can get away with this. He's dying with envy because of my mural, that's what it is."

Sagai said softly, "Trade Inspectors. That's all we need now."

"We have to hurry," Khat agreed. "Constans was here himself. That's why Elen threw the book at those vigils." He went to Arad, who was still seething with indignation, muttering to himself about overbearing pedants. "Arad, where is Ecazar taking that relic?" He kept his voice low so as not to be heard by any vigils who might be lingering in the hall.

"I don't know." The scholar shrugged helplessly. "To the Trade Inspectors . . . ?"

"No. If he does that, it's over."

"Khat, it's over *now*," Sagai pointed out reasonably.

"No," Elen said suddenly, her eyes alive again. "He'll want to examine it first, and he'll have to send a servant to bring the Trade Inspectors."

"To his rooms in the Porta Major, that's where he'll take it," Arad said, perking up. "You're not thinking—"

"If we go there now, I can get inside and steal the relic back before Ecazar even knows what's happened." Khat nodded to himself. "It's a good thing they missed the block; we'd never get that back without help."

"I always knew he was mad, and now I have proof," Sagai muttered.

"We can do this," Khat insisted.

"That's what frightens me the most."

Elen turned toward Sagai. "Please . . ."

"Is it worth our lives, Elen?" Sagai asked her, his voice harsh. "The Trade Inspectors will be involved now. You know more than you've told us, and I think the time for secrets is past. Is it worth our lives?"

"I don't really know more," she insisted, and gestured helplessly. "It's only speculation, but it's worth *my* life, and I'm going, even if I have to go alone."

Sagai cursed, shook his head, and said, "Fine, then, let's hurry off to be killed."

Arad caught up a lamp and led the way out of his workroom and down the steps to the empty square. Two vigils watching the doorway looked up in surprise at their appearance, and one called, "Scholar, where are you going?"

Arad drew himself up, a picture of abused dignity. "I am conducting these people to the gate. I assumed that is what Scholar Ecazar wanted. Why? Am I a prisoner in my own chambers?"

The vigil waved them on, and they heard him mutter to his companion, "I was only asking."

They crossed the empty square, Arad leading them down one of the courts that would take them to the main gate but also to the Porta Major. Down the narrow byways they could see the lamps of the vigils, searching in vain for more thieves. Khat wondered if he was acting the fool, risking everything for no good reason. But whatever he might say to Elen, he knew she wouldn't exaggerate out of hysteria; if she thought the return of the relic was worth her life, then she really believed it to be true.

Behind him, Elen was anxiously asking Sagai, "You didn't tell Miram that we were coming here, did you? Not where anyone could overhear?"

"Am I mad? To tell my wife I was breaking into the Academia? Of course not." Still piqued at having to act against his better judgment, Sagai was making up for it by being as difficult about the whole thing as possible.

"We didn't tell anybody," Khat told her impatiently. "What are you getting at?"

"I told Riathen."

Khat stopped so abruptly Sagai ran into him. They both stared at Elen. Khat said, "You didn't."

Elen stopped too, and nodded. "I did."

Arad-edelk noticed they weren't following and hurried back to them, asking anxiously, "What's wrong?"

Elen motioned at him to wait. She said, "I told him because I wanted protection for us. If we were caught, they might let me go, but they would never . . . And if you both could say you did it with the Master Warder's knowledge . . . But that doesn't matter now. I told Riathen everything. Almost everything. I told him we went to see Radu, before we went back that night, I mean. Don't you see?" She gestured agitatedly. "Constans didn't follow us to Radu's house, no more than he followed us to the Academia. Someone told him. Someone overheard Riathen and me, or Riathen told someone else, someone close to him and trusted, and that person betrayed him to Constans."

Sagai clapped a hand to his forehead. "Oh, that's a relief. We may live after all."

"What?" Past her agitation, Elen looked annoyed that her revelation hadn't been granted more fanfare.

"Stop telling Riathen everything we do, Elen. Dammit, what goes through your mind?" Khat didn't wait for an answer. He stalked off, Arad catching up with him to lead the way.

Following, Sagai said in a low voice, "This is much better. I didn't want to say anything, but I thought this Constans was spying on us with his powers, seeing all our actions in the bones, or some such."

"I did too," Khat agreed, quietly. And he had far more reason to believe that than Sagai did. It would be wonderful if Constans's ability to follow him came only from a spy within Riathen's camp.

Elen caught up with them, fuming. "You don't understand what this could mean to Riathen."

"Who cares?" Khat said, setting off Elen's temper and ending all discussion for the moment.

Chapter Thirteen

THEY REACHED THE turning where one long passage led to the Academia's outer gate and the other led deeper within the jumbled maze of buildings to the Porta Major. The vigils were still searching the outlying areas, and none were here in the quiet center. Khat stopped Arad when he would have followed them, telling him, "You're in enough trouble with Ecazar as it is."

"But I could be of some use," the little scholar protested. "I could keep watch, or perhaps there would be something where my skills—"

"No, you'd just be risking yourself for no reason." Someone had to stay and protect the block relic, and someone had to finish that mural, and it was better done by Arad than some fumble-fingered crony of Ecazar's.

Elen said, "Yes. If we're caught, go to the Master Warder and tell him everything that happened, everything we said."

"About the traitor in his house," Arad said gravely. "Will he believe me?"

"Just tell him what I said; he'll know you're speaking the truth. Please," she added more softly. "I can't do this with a clear conscience unless I know you'll tell the Master Warder what happened."

"Why is a clear conscience necessary?" Sagai asked, not helpfully. "All it takes is a confused sense of duty and a disregard for personal survival."

"Elen will enjoy herself more with a clear conscience," Khat told him. He asked her, "Are you done? Can we hurry?"

"Just be quiet," Elen snapped. "You two are worse than Gandin, Seul, and Riathen all put together. This is a nightmare." She turned back to Arad. "Will you tell the Master Warder for me?"

"I will, Honored. Have no doubts. But I won't have to, because I'm sure all will go well."

Khat wished he was as sure of that. He let Elen get a little ahead as they went down the long empty passage between the closed, sleeping houses and the open galleries of the teaching forums, and said quietly to Sagai, "Shiskan son Karadon didn't want to kill us."

"I noticed," he answered, frowning. "I wagered my life, and yours, on that supposition at one point. Odd, isn't it? Why such forbearance?"

"They killed Radu, and he didn't even have anything they wanted anymore," Khat pointed out.

"Did they kill Radu?"

"They were there. But so was I, and Elen."

"A point to consider."

"What are you saying?" Elen whispered, pausing to wait for them.

"Nothing."

They came to the open square at the center of the Academia, and paused in the shelter of a columned portico. The Porta Major had been the entrance to the Academia decades ago, when it had been only a small collection of buildings and a tiny garden. The two arches one could pass through into that garden, now an elaborate confection of fountains and rare plants instead of simply a shaded place for teaching, were still there. Above them were two levels of rooms, with a scrollwork parapet on top. To each side was a round tower, one four stories high, the other three, both topped with an onion-shaped dome and a gold spire, with wide arched windows and arcaded passageways on the upper floors open to the evening breeze. The bottom levels were also ornamented with columns and arches, but they had been left walled shut with stone for defense. The remains of the old walls to either side had long since been incorporated into new houses for scholars.

The doors had been shut tightly for the night, except for one at the base of the shorter tower, open and guarded by a circle of lit ghostlamps, ready for the vigils to catch up as they ran out. As Khat watched, one came to the door and looked out, an air gun slung casually over his shoulder, then turned back inside.

The Master Scholar's quarters were on the second level above the arches, between the two towers. As Khat watched, a lamp was lit behind one of the windows. Yes, Ecazar had returned, given his orders, and taken his find up to his rooms to gloat over in private.

"Are we going to climb up the outside?" Elen whispered.

Khat would have to go up this side to reach Ecazar's room, but the square was too well lit, the Porta's face too exposed. "No, I'm going in through the door. You and Sagai are going to create a diversion."

"Create a diversion?" Sagai objected. "If I'm going to be a criminal, I want to be in the thick of things, not waiting outside. It'll be a fine thing when we're brought before the High Justices and all I can say is 'I created a diversion.' I might as well be at home."

"I wish you were," Khat said. Sneaking into Arad's quarters had been enough of a risk as it was, and they were lucky the scholar had decided to throw in his lot with them. If they were caught now, after Ecazar had ordered them out, it was thievery pure and simple, and no lie of Arad's or political pull from Sonet Riathen would help them. "If you do this right we won't be brought before the High Justices."

Elen asked doubtfully, "What kind of diversion?"

That was a good question. Khat hesitated. The things he could think of—Elen demanding to speak to Ecazar again, Sagai pretending to be a scholar and calling out that there were thieves somewhere—all seemed to be inadequate or to end with it being completely obvious who had taken the relic. And there was the gate problem.

Ecazar had ordered them to leave, and it was only in deference to Elen's standing that he hadn't ordered the vigils to throw them out. Now either Elen and Sagai had to go through the outer gate without him, which would be suspicious to everyone but a simpleton, or all three of them would go out after a long, equally suspicious interval, or they could bypass the gate entirely and go over the wall the way they came in, making the truth still more obvious. And Ecazar was probably waiting, even now, for news that the gate vigil had let them out. It was like the puzzle of the man trying to cross the canyon with the goats and the grain sack. He explained the problem to the others.

Sagai pursed his lips. "It's difficult. We are already under suspicion." That he couldn't see a way around it either was worrisome; he was far better at logic than Khat, who tended to think on the run.

"Well, fine, then," Elen said, sounding tired. "There's something I can do. I can go out the gate alone, and make the vigil think you and Sagai are with me. Then Sagai can shout that there are thieves, distracting the men here and letting you slip in. Then both of you can go out over the wall with the rope."

She didn't sound very confident, or enthusiastic. Khat had seen her use more unnatural magic tonight than ever before, something she had been afraid to do even when they were trapped in the Remnant. He asked, "You can't do that with a simple, can you? You have to use Ancient magic."

"Yes. Are you afraid I'll go mad?" she challenged.

"No, are you?"

"No. At least, not very," she admitted, after a moment. "I don't feel as if I'm close to going mad. I feel tired and frustrated and angry with Ecazar for stopping us when we're so close. But I suppose I wouldn't feel it until it happened."

"You aren't engendering confidence in us, Elen," Sagai pointed out. "What we want to know is, are you sure you want to do this?"

"Yes, I'm sure. Drawing a veil over the sight is the least difficult of all the workings to do. At night, it's almost as easy as a simple." She hesitated, perhaps remembering that sometimes her simples failed too. "There won't be anyone here to see through it, unless Constans turns up again."

Khat had been thinking about Constans. He knew Warders were supposed to be able to read thoughts, or at least the loudest thoughts, on the surface of the soul. But Constans had been standing only a few steps away, taunting Elen about not "soul-reading" well enough to know Shiskan and the others were there, yet he hadn't realized there were two copies of the text, even though that had certainly been the uppermost thought in Khat's mind. And Khat remembered where else he had heard that term today. "Elen, today at Riathen's house they said they couldn't soul-read me, so that proved I didn't have a soul. What did they mean?"

Elen rubbed her eyes. "Soul-reading is like a sense you have of a person's presence, sometimes their intentions, or the thing that's most on their mind at the moment. And it's not always possible for

Warders to soul-read at all. For instance, most of the time I can't read Sagai, but at the moment I can sense that he thinks that you shouldn't be bringing this up now." Sagai looked startled. She added, "And we guard against being read by each other. But no Warder can soul-read a kris. I know I certainly can't, though I wouldn't judge it by me, because apparently I'm no good at it." She took a deep breath. "They were just being rude." She turned away, going alone toward the gate, being careful to stay in the shadows.

Sagai asked softly, "You think she's all right?"

Khat shrugged, not wanting to closely consider the possibility that she wasn't. He had never taken Elen's fears too seriously before; she was too careful, and the last person one would expect to misuse her power and fall into madness. Now he hoped these relics were as important as Riathen and Constans thought they were, at least for her sake.

They waited, giving her time to reach the gate and work her trick, and for the Porta's residents to settle down after the earlier alarms. They couldn't afford to wait nearly as long as Khat would have liked; there wasn't that much of the night left, and the vigils who were searching the grounds might come back. He noticed the lamp in Ecazar's window stayed lit.

Sagai meant to start his diversion further back in the courts, to give himself better opportunity for slipping away from the vigils. Before he went to look for a likely place Khat gave him charge of the rope; if he was caught inside the Porta there was no reason to trap them both here.

After giving him enough time to get in place, Khat made his way around the edges of the open square before the Porta. He reached the tower with the ghostlamps set out by its door, and just before their light would reveal him he stepped into the deep shadow at the base of one of the ornamental columns.

There was a hoarse shout somewhere down one of the courts leading into the main way—Sagai, not sounding very much like himself, doing a good imitation of an aging scholar rudely awakened. "Help! Thieves! Thieves in my rooms! Help, vigils!"

Two vigils burst out of the open tower door, catching up a lamp from the stoop and racing to the rescue. An old door servant came out after them to the edge of the lamplight, stumbling as if he had just awakened, and peered shortsightedly into the dark. Khat slipped along the wall and through the door, easily.

This was evidently a guard room for the night vigils. It was bare and swept clean, with empty lamps stored on shelves above heavy water jars, and the scattered counters of an interrupted game of tables in a corner. Two doorways led off to more rooms, and one to a narrow stair, curving up into the floors overhead. Someone called out from the next room, wondering loudly what had happened. Khat was up the steps, past the first turn and out of sight before the door servant stumbled wearily back in to answer.

Pausing on the stair and trying to hear if there was anyone moving above him, Khat swore softly. The Academia obviously didn't see this kind of excitement every night, and there were more people still awake than he had counted on. There was no help for it; he had to get the relic back tonight, before Constans or the Trade Inspectors got their hands on it.

No footsteps or voices sounded from above. He went up to the next landing, which led into the first floor of the section that bridged the two towers. It was lit by hanging oil lamps, and one wall was lined with windows looking down on the great dark space of the garden behind the Porta, the other with curtained doorways. The back of his neck prickled with the thought of someone stepping out suddenly.

Behind him he heard someone coming down the stairs from the upper floors of the tower. He stepped back against the wall and eased the first door curtain aside. A little light from an uncurtained window fell on the doors of a bronze cabinet and a low table with a clerk's pens and ink bottles abandoned on it. He stepped inside and pulled the curtain to just as whoever it was reached the landing and came down the passage.

Footsteps from the other direction, then from the hall a woman's voice asked softly, "What was that shouting about?"

He didn't stay to hear the muttered answer, making his way silently across the room to the window. Obviously the Porta was still too awake to chance making his way up through the inside. He would have to risk climbing up to the floor above from the outside, and simply hope no returning vigils crossing the square looked up.

Outside the window the ledge was broad, its edge an entablature that ran the length of the facade. He climbed out and stood cautiously, leaning back on the wall to get his bearings. The scrollwork around the windows was of fine stone that didn't crumble. He hauled himself slowly up to the next floor and sat on the ledge there to rest.

In the square below, the two vigils Sagai had decoyed were returning, shaking their heads, lifting lamps high to peer into dark cubbies and alleyways, but never looking up at the face of the Porta. Some more vigils appeared out of another alley, and they all consulted, pointing in different directions and arguing, then broke up and disappeared down various courts for more searching. Khat took this as a good sign; if they had caught Sagai, they would have appeared considerably more elated. He began to make his way down the ledge toward Ecazar's window.

He crouched in the shadow just to one side of it, where the gauze curtains didn't do much to impede his view but hid him from anyone casually glancing out. The room was large but not luxurious. The matting was sun-faded, and much of the wall space was taken up by bronze cabinets holding books and the notes and journals of past scholars.

Near the center of the room, Ecazar sat before a low table piled high with bound folios. He held the winged relic in one hand, unfolding the pages of one of the books with the other. Squinting, Khat saw that he looked through pages of scribbled notes, diagrams, drawings.

He's recognized something about it, Khat thought. The scholar was obviously searching for some information about the relic. *He wouldn't do that if he thought it was just another decorative plaque.* Well, Ecazar wasn't the Master Scholar for nothing. Khat would have given a great deal to know what he thought of the winged design.

Time passed; Khat was too interested in the outcome of Ecazar's search to be too bored, though he found himself having to suppress yawns from time to time. Finally Ecazar shut the book with an irritated frown, and got to his feet, massaging the back of his neck. He carried the little relic over to one of the cabinets, placed it in a small compartment, and locked it carefully away, pocketing the key. Picking up one of the candle bowls and blowing out the others on his way, he went out through the doorway at the far end of the room.

After his eyes adjusted to the room's darkness Khat eased himself off the ledge and over the sill. He crossed the room to the cabinet and felt for the compartment, examining the lock hole by touch. He took out his knife to break the mechanism, feeling a pang of guilt. He had never stolen from the Academia before. He snapped the lock and took out the relic, scrupulously ignoring the other contents. The *mythenin* was still warm from Ecazar's hand.

Then, just at the edge of his vision, something moved. Darkness solidifying, a faint trace of red light. Instinct made him freeze.

Whether by accident or design it had cut him off from the door. *This,* Khat thought, nerves jumping from the nearness of the thing, *is no coincidence.* First trapping them when they were escaping from Constans, and now following him here. Khat eyed the nearest window and knew he wouldn't make it. It could move fast when it wanted to, and the ledge wasn't nearly wide enough to run on.

It was fully formed now, drifting in front of the doorway, as if trying to make up its mind. Ecazar had sat here fondling the relic for more than an hour, and it hadn't bothered him. Arad hadn't mentioned being haunted either. But Khat remembered the ghost that had appeared so suddenly in Radu's court. It hadn't seemed odd at the time—a ghost in the ghostcallers' quarter—but now . . . And the ghostlamps in the court had still been lit, perhaps preventing them from seeing the telltale traces of red light that he could see now just at the corners of his eyes. Comforting to know just how ineffective ghostlamps really were . . .

It shifted sideways, drifting nearer to him, still not leaving a clear path to the door. Perhaps this was what Radu had seen in the bones when he sent Elen away. Perhaps this was what had killed him. Khat hoped so. Because the other explanation was that it hadn't bothered Ecazar or Arad because it was following him, just as Constans had . . . Whether Khat's presence helped it find the relic or the relic helped it find him, the outcome was depressingly the same. *Look at this logically,* he told himself. It could see you when you moved; it had tracked Elen and him easily in the court near Arad's house. It couldn't seem to see him now, when he was frozen still. If he moved very slowly, could it follow him?

It was worth a try. Slowly and with utmost care he moved, one foot an inch or so toward the window. It didn't veer toward him, still drifting vaguely toward the cabinet that had held the winged relic. One more deadly slow, careful step, and no reaction. He was about ten paces from the nearest window.

Suddenly the door curtain was flung aside, and lamplight filled the room, the telltale traces of the ghost vanishing in its intensity. Khat nearly jumped out of his skin and swung around.

Red robes, Trade Inspectors. One filling the doorway, others behind him.

Khat dove for the window, tearing through the gauze curtains and scrambling out onto the ledge.

Bullets struck the stone near him, and he didn't bother to look for the marksman in the courtyard, swinging down and dropping to the ledge of the level below. He clawed at the wall to keep his balance, and fell through the nearest window.

The room was dark, but as he jumped to the floor, someone squawked in alarm, obviously startled out of sleep. He darted out the door and into the oil-lamp-lit passage again. Shouting from the stairs. He went to one of the windows overlooking the garden, but ducked back from it immediately. Lamps lit the normally quiet area below. The Trade Inspectors must be surrounding the place. *Did Ecazar tell them we were making off with the whole Academia?* he wondered desperately. Footsteps pounded from the other end of the passage, and he dived into another room.

It was dark and blessedly, temporarily empty. Khat paused, leaning against the wall near the door, breathing hard with exertion and fear. They had him trapped, and there was no way out. He knew what he had to do: trust Elen, and worse, trust Riathen to buy him out. But if the Trade Inspectors found the stolen relic on him, even the Master Warder might not be able to get him out of their hands. He couldn't hide it here; he knew Trade Inspectors, and knew they would tear the place apart searching for it.

There was one hiding place where they might not find it. If they did . . . He would worry about that later. Khat lifted his shirt and felt for the pouch lip on his lower stomach, pressing gently on just the right spot and . . . nothing happened. He swore, and tried to calm himself, to ignore the blood pounding in his ears. He pressed again and felt a brief, unfocused surge of sexual desire that made him catch his breath; then the lip parted, and he slipped the relic inside. The resulting sting of pain, as the metal slid against the delicate tissues, cleared his head nicely. He hastily tucked his shirt in again and pushed away from the wall, making for the window. They might have left the square unguarded, concentrated all their men on the house, and he didn't intend to be caught unless it was unavoidable. He had just clambered up on the sill when the first red-robed Trade Inspector burst in through the door curtain.

* * *

Moving with care, Khat rubbed his face against the inside of his arm, trying to keep the sweat from burning his eyes. His hands were chained over his head to a hook suspended from the rocky ceiling, just high enough that he could barely support his weight.

The Trade Inspectors' prison had been roughly gouged out of the tier's bedrock beneath the High Trade Authority, the dark walls mostly smooth now from the years of sweat on human hands. The place where he was being held was not so much a cell but a landing on a wide stairwell, lit by smoky oil lamps in wall niches, with one set of stone-cut steps going up to the passages above and the other curving away down, leading to someplace where someone had screamed for an hour late last night.

Khat had discovered early on that the chain was set so solidly into the bedrock overhead that even putting all his weight on it and swinging back and forth was insufficient to pull it loose. Now the strain had begun to tell, and he didn't have the strength to try that anymore. His hands and arms were mostly numb; it was his shoulders that hurt the worst. Lately he was so exhausted that he kept losing consciousness, only to be jerked awake when his weight came down on his much-abused muscles. His back ached for other reasons.

Khat had remembered not to fight when they took him prisoner, but in the suffocating confines of the prison that resolution had fled, and he had fought like a madman all the way down to this level. Wondering when he would be taken further down had occupied a good deal of his time, but he was at the point now where he felt fairly sure they meant to let him die right here.

Khat tried to shift his wrists in the manacles, and winced at the result. There was no air moving at all, and the heat was like the inside of a bread oven; sweat that had that special scent of fear was stinging in the cuts and sticking what was left of his shirt to his chest and back. It didn't help that behind the nearest wall he could hear rushing water, which could be from one of the city sewers. This theory was supported by the fact that in the greasy light of the oil lamps he could see moisture of a thick and unhealthy consistency beading on that particular wall. The rest of the place seemed to be bone dry, just like his throat.

Even after all these long hours, panic was still close, so close he could almost smell it over the choking smoke of the lamps. *Elen will get you out of here,* he kept telling himself, *Elen just fucking better get you out of here, or you'll come back as a ghost that will make that thing following you look like a dust devil,* and never mind that in the cosmology of the Fringe Cities kris had no souls and couldn't return as ghosts.

These thoughts had been close companions all night. Then he would think that the reason Elen hadn't come yet was that her trick at the gate had failed, and the vigils had shot her. He pushed that specter away again. If Elen wasn't coming then that was it. Even if Sagai had escaped, there was simply no way his partner could come after him in here. And Sonet Riathen would certainly not bother to lift a finger.

He tried to shake the hair out of his eyes, and lines of fire went down his shoulder blades. Gritting his teeth at the pain, he tried to make himself relax. And what if he had badly misjudged Elen? She knew where the ugly block relic was now, with the added bonus of Arad's copy of Riathen's book. The Trade Inspectors would tell her that no relic had been found on him; she might think it still in the Academia somewhere, that she could search for it without him . . . *No, not that either,* he told himself, again. *Think about something else.*

If the Trade Inspectors did find out where he had hidden the little relic, their method of removing it would be fatal at best. The flap of skin that formed the outer layer of his pouch was not very thick; if anyone pressed down on his abdomen, the small, hard lump of the relic was there to be felt. The Trade Inspectors had searched him thoroughly, but they had been certain he had hidden it somewhere in the Porta. And the city dwellers mentally associated kris pouches with babies, and therefore with women, and never thought of men having them too. He just hoped no one punched him in the stomach.

The relic was an unspecific ache in his abdomen, like something caught in a tooth that you couldn't quite get out. A minor discomfort compared to all the others, but its presence probably wasn't doing him any good. He remembered one of his maternal-line aunts practically beating him into the ground for doing something like this as a boy, even though it was a common enough trick among kris children. Well, he had never meant to help perpetuate his proud but fatally foolhardy lineage anyway.

Not that that was an option anymore. It was one small consolation that no one would find the relic until after his body had been rendered down.

There was a sharp crack from overhead, and Khat flinched, unable to help himself. Two Trade Inspectors in dull red robes were coming down the steps, the second one tapping his rod of office against the stone. It was a long staff of rare hardwood, banded with copper and iron. The two vigils following them were lower-tier, and they both looked uncomfortable with their surroundings. The Trade Inspectors could conscript lower-tier vigils at will, and not all of the conscripts were pleased by this fact.

The Trade Inspectors stopped within a pace of Khat, who had to fight to keep from trying to draw back, his spine prickling in anticipation of pain. Before this night he had never seen them in their full formal attire; the ones that patrolled the streets usually dressed as ordinary folk. Both these men had the heavy bronze breastplates over their robes, but instead of a veil and headcloth one man wore a bronze half-mask covering his eyes and nose, its brows sculpted into a beetled shape better suited to a rock demon than a human, and a gold skullcap. Khat racked his memory for his carefully acquired knowledge of Charisat's bureaucratic hierarchy and realized this was a High Justice.

The lesser Trade Inspector said, "A krismen Waste rat, as you can see. It has refused to tell us anything so far."

That one had come before; Khat recognized his voice and mannerisms. The other was an unpleasant novelty.

The High Justice's eyes, dark through the sculpted holes of the mask, were intent on him. He leaned on his rod of office, and nodded to the other Trade Inspector. That one moved behind Khat, who forced himself not to try to turn his head to follow him.

The High Justice nodded again, and with no more warning than that the other's rod of office snapped across Khat's back. He gasped, feeling another line of fire open across his flesh. His knees went weak, and he held on to the chain, supporting himself on it. That had been a surprise; usually they asked the questions first.

In a voice sounding rusty with disuse, the High Justice said, "Where is the relic?"

Usually the one behind him wielding the rod did the asking, but they had been through this over and over again, the same questions, the same penalty for unsatisfactory answers, all through the night.

Sometimes Khat wondered if they knew what relic they meant at all, if these were the same questions they asked everyone. Still breathless from the suddenness of the blow, he said, "I don't know what you want. I didn't steal anything." He tried not to listen for the one waiting behind him with the rod. He didn't know why they wanted an admission of guilt so badly. He wasn't so naive as to think that they couldn't make him tell them; the screaming from the lower levels would have convinced him thoroughly if he hadn't already known it. For some reason they had held off on the more serious torture. Possibly this waiting was part of it, though why they didn't simply get down to business was beyond him.

This High Justice was shorter than Khat, but stocky and strong. Despite all the gold finery, the shoulders of his robe were stained from contact with the greasy walls. Now the man's thin lips twisted in a sneer, half disgust, half irritation. If he gave some kind of a signal this time, Khat didn't see it, but the rod of office snapped across his back again, sharp as fire on muscles already strained to the breaking point. He cried out, not making any attempt to restrain it. ("Yell loud," an old relic dealer had once advised him, years ago. "They like that.") Again he felt the skin break. One of the vigils, waiting back against the wall, actually winced.

"You've hidden it," the High Justice said. "Where?"

Khat let his head fall back wearily, feeling the blood trickle down his back. They hadn't even bothered to ask why he had been in the Academia, what he had been doing in the Porta. Perhaps they had questioned Ecazar; perhaps they just didn't care. "I didn't have anything, I didn't steal anything."

"What is your connection with the Master Warder?"

That was new, and far more important. Knowing he was risking another blow, Khat tried to focus; his mind was starting to drift, trying to distance itself from his body. How to answer? His choices were limited, but which would help him more, lies or truth? Knowing he was running out of time, he said, "Ask him."

The Justice shook his head and turned away. "Take him down."

This hadn't happened before. The one behind him grabbed a handful of his hair, jerking his head back. Khat tensed helplessly—it was the preferred method of attack for street throat-slitters—but the man only unlocked the manacles from the ceiling chain, and with the sudden release of his own weight Khat's legs collapsed.

He lay in a heap on the stone floor. His wrists were still manacled tightly together, but he was too dizzy and sick to move anyway. Blood began to flow back into his deadened arms, and sensation returned with a thousand pinpricks. The two vigils pulled him up, giving him a little time to get his feet under him before hauling him toward the stairs.

They were taking him back to the upper levels. He couldn't believe it. The stairs came up into a short hall, low-ceilinged and smoky, and they went down it, pausing only for one of the Trade Inspectors to unlock an iron grille barring a doorway. He got barely a glimpse of the room beyond it before the rod of office cracked against the back of his knees and he was knocked sprawling. He landed on a carpet that was dust-covered and smelled of blood and urine, and dug his fingers into it, trying to find the strength to get up, or at least struggle. The rod came down between his shoulder blades, pinning him down.

Then Elen's voice, grim and determined, said, "Let him up."

Khat twisted his head, squinting to see her. She was standing across the room, still wearing the threadbare brown robe from last night.

"What concerns you with this thief, Honored son Dia'riaden?" That was the High Justice with the handy rod of office. He would know that voice from now on.

"You have the word of the Master Warder. Release him."

"Without explanation?"

"I wasn't aware the Master Warder owed you an explanation. Must he come here himself, or do I merely need to send for my lictors?"

Khat suspected that if Elen was in a position to make Riathen come here, or to send for her lictors, she would have already done so by now. Possibly the High Justice did too. Amusement in his harsh voice, he said, "Hardly necessary."

The bruising pressure from the rod eased, and Khat tried to lever himself up. He was thumped to the ground again, effortlessly. "But I am not in the habit of releasing street trash to young women without some excuse."

Elen came forward. She said, "I am a Warder, warranted by the Elector, under the hand of Sonet Riathen, Master Warder, and I have given you his order. I will not ask for your obedience again." Her hands came up, palms outward, as if she were preparing to use her power.

Khat felt a sudden easing in the pressure, almost a flinch; then the rod was removed.

"Very well. Take him." The voice didn't betray anything, but that flinch had spoken volumes. This High Justice might try to find Elen amusing, but he feared her power.

Khat struggled to stand, hoping his legs wouldn't give way again. If Elen had to help him . . . there was simply no way she could lift his deadweight, and he hated the thought of making her look ridiculous in front of these men. He made it to his knees, then caught hold of the rough stone of the wall and managed to haul himself up. His legs shook, and he clung to the wall, helpless for a moment.

The High Justice was watching, his cold eyes derisive. Then he bowed his head mockingly to Elen and turned away. She gestured sharply to the vigils who remained, and one hastened over with the key to the manacles.

Khat met Elen's eyes, and noticed she looked awful. Pale under her sun-browned skin as if she was ill, and white around the lips from rage. He would have to tell her so as soon as they got outside.

The manacles dropped away, and the vigil withdrew. Khat worked his hands, trying to get some feeling back, wincing at how hard it was to move his fingers.

Elen whispered, "Come on."

He followed her down another low, short passage, up more stairs. He kept bumping into walls, but no one tried to stop them. He dimly remembered seeing these places on the way down last night, but now they were going up, and that was all that mattered.

They came out into a large, sandy-floored chamber filled with staring vigils; then they were through a doorway and out into the dusty street. The brilliance of the sun was like a blow, and he staggered under it.

Elen took his arm, steered him out of the way of a handcart and across the street to where a public fountain played under an awning. He sat down on the cracked tile basin, weaving back and forth while she fumbled in her robe for copper bits and the keeper brought her a battered tin cup without being asked. From here they could see the graceless, heavy stone pile of the High Trade Authority. This was the Fourth Tier, near the downward gate, and from the shadows he could tell it was still early morning.

She waited until he finished three cups of water and poured the fourth over his head, then asked, "How are you?"

"I'm better than I was." His wrists were badly bruised and lacerated from the manacles, and he didn't think his arms and shoulders would ever stop hurting. His back alternated between aching and stinging as the sweat got to the newest cuts. But the air smelled fresher than Fourth Tier air ever had before, and after the prison it felt almost cool.

She sat next to him and used the dusty hem of her robe to wipe the sweat off her face, oblivious to the long dirty streaks she was leaving on her nose and brow, saying with weary relief, "I've been trying to make them release you all night."

He was still too stunned to know how lucky he was, Khat decided. And recalling how he had suspected her of every perfidy under the great bowl of the sky during that night, he said, "Thank you."

She snorted. "What was I supposed to do, leave you there?"

He was glad it was a rhetorical question. "Where's Sagai?"

"Waiting with Arad-edelk, at the Academia. It's all right, he was never caught. I convinced him not to come with me because I thought it better if the Trade Inspectors didn't see him. Oh, here. They gave me back these, before they brought you out." She was handing him a dusty brown bundle: his battered robe wrapped around his knife and the Warder's token she had given him yesterday morning.

Having the knife back didn't make him feel any less vulnerable. Maybe it was sitting here in sight of the place, but he doubted it. Khat put the knife away and tried to give her back the token. "Don't you need this?"

"No. I have others." She hesitated. "I think it's what saved you. It was proof that you were working for a Warder, and I knew you had it. That High Justice couldn't simply dismiss it, the way he did everything else I said."

The High Justice. There was something that that should tell him, but he couldn't think. He wanted to fall over backward into the fountain, but it would probably pollute the water terribly.

Elen was looking down at her dirty sandaled feet, distracted. "Last night I waited outside the Academia, until I saw the Trade Inspectors go in through the main gate. I threatened and bullied my way back inside, and saw the lights and confusion around the

Porta . . ." She looked up and frowned. "Your back is still bleeding. How bad is it?"

He tried to look, which was a mistake.

They were attracting an audience. The fountain keeper was still standing nearby, and a few beggars, a date peddler, and a water seller who had been resting under the awning were staring, fascinated. Some street vendors had put down their handcarts and gathered round, discussing the matter in low voices.

Elen glared around at them all. "This isn't a show. Everyone move along, please."

Whether it was the dirt on her face or the fact that she didn't look anything like a Warder and they didn't recognize her painrod for what it was, the bystanders shifted a little self-consciously, or backed up, but nobody went away.

Looking at her, Khat said, "They never saw anyone come out before."

Elen's expression was bleak. She rubbed her face again, and said, "We're just lucky you didn't have it. If they had found you with it . . ."

Khat's mind wasn't working too swiftly at the moment. He dumped another cup of water on his head to help him get his thoughts in order, and asked, "With what?"

"You know—*it,*" she said, glaring around at the onlookers. The last few edged back out of earshot, but she lowered her voice cautiously anyway. "I told Riathen that I was sure you had it with you. A bad lie, I know, but I wasn't thinking properly, and that was all that would come to mind. I wanted to make sure he would . . ." She was turning red under her dirt. "Well, keep up his obligations to you. But Ecazar told the Trade Inspectors he didn't have it, and they searched the Porta down to its foundation, so I suppose Constans must have gotten to it before you did. We're stuck now. I don't know what we're going to do."

"Oh. That it. No, I know where it is."

"But how can you? I was sure Constans had it." She whispered, "Where is it?"

It was his turn to eye the onlookers. "I'll tell you later."

They stopped at a Fourth Tier bathhouse, which was as different from the lower-tier places where Khat usually went as Riathen's house was from Netta's. It had unheard-of amenities, and though Elen refused to go any further in than the cool shadows of the portico, she paid for a private room for him. He thought the fee for it shocking, but it was the only way the steward would allow him in the place, and the way he looked and smelled at the moment, Khat almost didn't blame the man.

Elen also paid for the services of a physician who worked in a tiled chamber off the vestibule. Khat was more doubtful about that; he didn't think he could stand to be touched by anyone, no matter how badly he hurt. But the physician turned out to be a little old woman in a clean white kaftan who clucked her tongue at him but didn't ask any questions. She also didn't make him nervous, which was something of an achievement at the moment.

He had never been treated by a city physician before, because the prices were usually so exorbitant, but it wasn't much different from having Miram do it. The salve this woman used was considerably stronger, burning like salt on his flesh but taking much of the pain away after, so it was probably worth the coin. Elen had also bought him a shirt to replace the one that was in bloody pieces, and hired one of the bathhouse's messenger boys to run ahead to Arad's house in the Academia and tell Sagai that both of them were on their way. Not much of a message, but enough to keep him from worrying until they got there.

Khat hoped Riathen was paying her back for all this. After getting the stink of the prison off his body, he was almost thinking again. Elen had lied to Riathen to save him. Or at least she thought she had lied, not knowing he really did have the winged relic with him. She hadn't trusted Riathen enough to believe the old man would keep his implicit promises to support them in their search. At the beginning of this he would have said Elen trusted Riathen with her life. Well, maybe she still did. It was only other people's lives she didn't trust him with . . .

When Khat finally emerged, Elen was pacing in the shade of the columned portico, and now she looked worse than he did, though she had washed her face. She had probably spent the night in the High Trade Authority too, though hopefully in less uncomfortable circumstances.

There were basins on the portico for passersby who just wanted to wash their feet or hands, but it was empty at the moment, and the two young attendants were lounging on the steps at the far end, talking. He handed her the winged relic. She stared at it, turning it over and feeling the raised design as if she couldn't believe it was real, and said, "I thought you were hallucinating."

"I thought you had confidence in me, Elen. That's why you hired me, isn't it?"

She tucked the little relic away. "It's over. I can't believe we really did it. You did it." She frowned up at him. "How did you do it?"

"Just before they caught me, I put it in my pouch." Khat started down the steps and into the street, toward the Academia, so she would perforce follow him. He wanted to see Sagai. And, considering the need for secrecy Constans had demonstrated earlier, he didn't think their favorite mad Warder would try to come after them in such a public place, but still . . . His muscles were still trembling from fatigue, and he felt as if he had been run through a grain grinder. Elen was hardly in the shape for any magic, unnatural or otherwise. She looked hopelessly confused now, so he explained, "The one I was born with."

"Oh." She turned red instantly, as if from an abrupt attack of sun poisoning. "I forgot about that."

"Most people do." He eyed one of the street dumpling vendors, knowing he should eat something, but his stomach felt like a lead weight, and even the thought of bread made him ill.

Elen shook her head, still baffled, still red. "I didn't know it was possible."

"Neither did they."

"But how . . . No, umm, I don't want to know. But it doesn't sound safe."

"It was better than being caught with the damn thing." He glared down at her, exasperated. "What did you want me to do?"

"Well, I certainly don't know. Still . . ."

They reached the gates of the Academia without incident, and seeing the vigils waiting there made Khat a little uneasy. But Elen said, "I went in and out several times last night. Ecazar never made an issue of it." She hesitated. "I only spoke to him for a moment, but he almost seemed sorry about what happened."

"Sorry?" He looked down at her. "That bastard sent for them."

Elen nodded, biting her lip. "Yes, he must have. He said he was going to. But something isn't right. I need to think about this."

Khat didn't see it as a mystery. Someone had sent for the Trade

Inspectors, and that someone had to be Ecazar. Both Riathen and Constans, much as he would like to blame either one, had a need to conceal their actions from each other that superseded even their desire for the relics.

The gate vigils stared curiously but let them in without trouble, and no one tried to stop them on the way to Arad's quarters. Servants did peer at them from windows and doorways, and scholars and students tended to stop and talk behind their hands. News apparently traveled swiftly in the closed community of the Academia.

Sagai was waiting for them on the square in front of Arad's quarters. Khat was surprised at how his partner looked. Surely Sagai hadn't been this gray and tired, or this old, yesterday.

For his part, Sagai knew better than to ask a lot of questions. "Well?" he said softly.

Khat started to shrug and thought better of it. "Nothing permanent."

They went up the steps into the house, and the two vigils still on guard there watched them suspiciously. *Only two*, Khat thought, surprised by the lack of caution on Elen's part, if not Ecazar's, then saw the other pair standing inside the hall.

"I feel the need to apologize again, Elen," Sagai was saying.

"I wish you wouldn't," she answered. "I'm still not sure you were wrong."

"What are you talking about?" Khat asked.

Sagai smiled, a little ruefully. "Not having anything else constructive to do last night, I blamed Elen for all our troubles. We shouted at each other quite loudly, and shocked Arad. It was disgraceful."

Elen shook her head. "It was nothing."

In the main chamber Gandin was waiting with Arad-edelk, another wise precaution. Khat glanced up and saw that there were some vigils on the roof, peering down through the louvers at them.

Arad greeted him like a long-lost son, leading him over to where he had the Survivor text spread out on the floor amid a welter of scribbled notes. "Sagai has been showing me a different translation method, one used by the scholars in Kenniliar, and together we've made some progress," the scholar said eagerly. "But I wanted your opinion on—"

Gandin came to his feet suddenly, giving Khat's already strained nerves a jolt, and said, "Riathen's here."

Dismayed, Arad looked up at the doorway. Khat heard the voices from the outer hall, but he supposed Gandin had been warned by some other sense. Elen was watching the doorway too, looking a little unnerved herself. He wondered just what she had said to Riathen last night. Arad's gaze went back to the text.

"Just fold it up," Khat said, low-voiced and starting that process already. "And don't mention it."

The scholar's expression was grim. "Will that do any good?"

"It might." Khat met his eyes. "It's a dangerous thing to own. You saw that last night. Even if Constans thought it was Riathen's copy, they might come back, just to make sure."

"And that is a safe thing to own?" Arad asked, jerking his head toward the mural, but carefully folding the text's pages anyway. "Worth so many thousands of coins, with so many people in the city desperate and starving? All relics are dangerous. With this one"—he slid the book back into its cover—"the danger is just of a more obvious nature."

He was right, Khat decided, and there wasn't much else to say.

Then Sonet Riathen was striding into the room, and there was no time for anything else.

He hadn't changed much from the last time Khat had seen him, except that he wore plain Warder's robes and no gold. There were lictors with him, armed and wary, and at least two other Warders, anonymous under their veils. Master Scholar Ecazar followed them in, probably here to watch Arad and defend the Academia's interests.

The Master Warder looked around at all of them, then turned benign eyes on Elen.

Khat decided to stay where he was on the floor; getting up seemed a difficult process at the moment. Riathen hadn't remarked on Sagai's presence, at least not that Khat could tell, and he didn't know whether Elen had told him about his partner's involvement or not. Sagai was standing back against the wall, quiet and scholarly, and except for the lack of a veil might easily be taken for another member of the Academia. Arad was a noted scholar, and his robes were almost as threadbare as theirs.

Elen was holding out the winged relic, and Riathen took it, examining it carefully in a shaft of sunlight from the louvers overhead. The *mythenin* gleamed, and Khat felt a qualm; all that effort to find the thing, and he had hardly had a chance for a close look at it.

Ecazar gasped when he recognized the relic, and turned a harsh glare on Khat. Riathen noticed, and caught the Master Scholar's eyes, one brow raised inquiringly and somehow managing to convey that any comment at this point would not be well received. Ecazar fumed, but said nothing.

"You've done well," Riathen told Elen. He looked down at Khat. "And you also, of course. I hope your experience with the Trade Inspectors was not too difficult."

"Oh, no," Khat said. "Happens all the time." At any other moment he would have paid good coin to see Ecazar squelched so firmly, but he still couldn't muster any charitable feelings towards Riathen.

"I don't suppose you would care to tell me how they failed to find this during the time they held you."

"It's a trick of the trade."

Riathen waited until he could see that was all the answer he was going to get, then turned back to Elen. "And the other piece is . . . ?"

Elen cleared her throat, and indicated Arad, who was standing nearby. "This is Scholar Arad-edelk. He had obtained the piece for his studies, and had no knowledge of the fact that it was stolen until we told him last night."

Riathen nodded to Arad. "You will be compensated for your expense, of course, Scholar."

"No compensation is necessary," Arad said, stiffly. Turning to the panel that closed the hidden room and pressing the catch, he spared a moment to glare defiantly at Ecazar. "I kept it in here, for safety."

Rigid with indignation, Ecazar turned away.

The panel lifted, and Riathen ordered two of his lictors to drag out the block. When it had been pulled out into the better light the old man knelt by it and ran a hand over the carvings, marveling at the texture.

It was the first time Khat had seen the Master Warder react to a relic as other collectors, scholars, or dealers did; the first time he had shown any kind of emotion in response to one. Khat asked, "What are you going to do with them?"

Riathen looked at him sharply. Elen shifted a little uneasily, and he could sense Sagai holding his breath. *Yes,* Khat thought, *I remember what Elen told me. That's her theory. I want to hear it from him.* "You don't have enough there to build an arcane engine," he elaborated. "If you want them to be studied, isn't that best done here?"

Both Ecazar and Arad were watching intently. Riathen said, "I wish to pursue my own studies. I will be sure to apprise the Academia of my results."

And looking into those guarded eyes, Khat felt a faint chill, as if a ghost had drifted somewhere nearby. Riathen stood, and gestured to one of the other Warders, who drew a bulging leather coin purse out of his robes. "In light of your efforts on my behalf, I've added significantly to the fee we agreed on."

For an instant it was in Khat's mind to refuse the tokens, to refuse to have anything more to do with any Warders or upper-tier plots, but he knew Sagai would feel a completely justifiable desire to strangle him, and he was in no condition to defend himself. He said nothing.

The other Warder put the purse on the floor, and Riathen turned away. There was a moment of bustle as the lictors wrapped the block in heavy cotton batting and prepared to wrestle it onto a sledge hauled in for the purpose. Ecazar and Arad both forgot their enmity long enough to move to defend the mural against any careless feet, and Riathen and the other Warders went back down the entrance hall. Only Gandin stayed to help the lictors, and Elen, who stood in the middle of the room looking as if she didn't know quite what to do with herself.

Khat called her name softly, and she glanced at him, startled, and flushed self-consciously.

Riathen might think it was over, but there were too many unanswered questions, and Khat had paid too dearly for those relics. But the one thing that had been niggling at him all morning had finally become clear, and when she came near enough he said, "Elen, you said that Riathen got the first relic, the one you took out to the Remnant, from a High Justice of the Trade Inspectors."

She nodded, surprised. "Yes, and we speculated that the Justice had received the relic as a bribe, from the original thieves, and—"

"And Caster told me there was a High Justice after Radu. Was that the same High Justice who questioned me?"

Elen froze, mouth open. A variety of expressions crossed her face. She whispered, "I'll find out."

Chapter Fourteen

ON THE WAY back to the Sixth Tier, Khat had to stop and rest. It was getting on toward late afternoon, the heat in the streets was at its worst, and he was feeling it as he never had before.

Sagai watched him with worried eyes as they stopped again in a shaded alley near the entrance to their court. He said, "You look as if you have heat sickness."

"I can't get heat sickness." Khat supported himself against the mud-brick wall. He was light-headed and sick, and his skin was oddly sensitive. Even his clothes hurt.

"Are you sure?" Sagai put the back of his hand against Khat's forehead. "You're far too hot."

He shook off the light touch. "I've just had a hard day."

When they entered their court it was empty, quiet under a fine coating of dust. Most of their neighbors would be at work in the markets or dozing in their houses in the afternoon heat. But Miram flung the door open as soon as they drew near, and said, "There was a man here, asking questions. What happened?"

Sagai ushered Khat in past her. "What sort of questions?"

The house was relatively calm. Netta and her daughter would be at the market at this time of day, probably with Sagai's oldest daughter. Khat could hear the two younger girls upstairs, engaged either in an argument or a loud game. Netta's youngest was asleep in the corner, and the baby was playing under the table.

"He wanted to know about any relics you bought recently," Miram answered.

They both stopped and stared at her, momentarily paralyzed. She smiled faintly. "I said, of course, that you had bought nothing, not having the proper licenses to handle coins."

Khat sank down onto the narrow stone bench, too relieved to comment. Sagai caught Miram's shoulders and kissed her, saying, "Clever wife. I think I'll keep you."

Miram wouldn't be distracted. "I also told him the things you had traded for were small trinkets of *mythenin*, and there seemed few relics on the market, and so on." She frowned down at Khat. "You look terrible. When Sagai sent word that you were both to be working at the Academia all night, I thought it was good fortune." She eyed her husband suspiciously. "Tell me what really happened."

While Sagai broke the news, Khat eased down to sit on the floor, pulling the pouch of tokens Riathen had given him out of his robe. He upended it on the table, then stared down at the contents, unable to believe his eyes. The baby crawled into his lap, bumping his head against Khat's chin, and he remembered to breathe. "Sagai," he said, "these are all hundred-day tokens."

"No." Sagai stared, then knelt to run a hand through the glittering little pile. "Not all, surely. A few, but . . ."

Khat turned the last ones up so the numbers were visible, each a heavy little oval of bronze-coated lead, all with the Academia's spiral and a hundred-day marker. The baby selected one carefully and tried to eat it, grimacing at the taste, and Khat took it away from him, dropping it back into the pile. It was enough to buy Arad-edelk's Ancient mural. It was more than enough.

Miram leaned over Sagai's shoulder. "I've never seen that much . . . I've never even seen a hundred-day token. What does this mean?"

Sagai was biting his lip, his stunned expression turning to worry. "Academia tokens, not First Tier . . ."

Khat closed his eyes, and felt the room shift around him, an effect of the fever. He said, "More 'convenient' for us. And no one can trace them back to him."

"Does he think we're fools, or is he one?" Sagai growled.

Miram thumped Sagai on the back, startling him. "What does it mean?" she demanded again.

"The Master Warder didn't promise to pay anywhere near this much." Sagai's mouth twisted in distaste. "He is buying us off."

She was still confused. Khat edged more of the tokens out of the determined baby's reach, and explained, "It implies that he needs to buy our silence."

Sagai rested his head in his hands, looking his age. "And why should he buy our silence when all he has to do is send the Trade Inspectors? We disappear beneath the High Trade Authority, as you almost did, and he's rid of us forever."

Miram sat next to her husband; she understood now, and it frightened her. "He wouldn't just be . . . grateful?"

They both looked at her, and she sighed. "Sorry."

Sagai lifted one of the tokens, watching it glint in the late afternoon light. "There is no guarantee the Trade Inspectors or our friend Constans will leave us alone, or that Riathen will protect us, even if we do keep silent about these events."

"He won't trust us to keep silent. He could, but he won't." Khat knew Sagai was watching him steadily, and he met his partner's eyes.

"There is only one thing to do," Sagai said softly.

"I know."

"Leave the city."

Miram's jaw dropped. "Back to Kenniliar? All of us?"

"All of us." Sagai stirred the pile of tokens. "There's more than enough here to buy a house in the quarter where my uncle lives, to buy two places in the Scholars' Guild."

"You don't know that they would let me in," Khat interrupted.

"I don't know that they wouldn't," Sagai said firmly. "And it would be worth a try. Kenniliar is, in many ways, a kinder place than Charisat. Especially if one has money, and since the exchange rates are weighted in Charisat's favor now, these would be worth even more there."

Miram was rapidly adjusting to the idea and considering the practicalities. "The trade road is better patrolled now, isn't it? And we could take a caravan with steamwagons."

If Sagai had been keeping up with the exchange rates between Charisat's trade tokens and Kenniliar's state currency, then he had been seriously considering this option for longer than just today. Well, Khat had always known Sagai had come to Charisat only to make his fortune, that he would far rather raise his family in Kenniliar. And if Khat badly missed the brief involvement with the Academia that his association with Scholar Robelin had allowed him, he knew how Sagai must feel about the Scholars' Guild.

"A nice house, near your uncle's, maybe," Miram was saying to herself. She looked up at Khat then, her dark eyes concerned, and apparently read his mind. "But you must come with us. It's too dangerous here."

Khat had already discounted the possibility that the Scholars' Guild would allow him admission; it was simply too rare a chance to count on. His share of these tokens would be enough for a stake in Kenniliar's far more expensive relic trade, but it would mean starting all over again, not knowing any of the other dealers, who was honest and legal and who sold for the Silent Market. His head ached, and it wasn't something he could face now. "I'll go, I'll go," he agreed. "But I can't come right away. I've got something to do first. I'll find you on the road."

Sagai's brows went up, and Khat knew he had given in too soon, but his partner only said, "It takes less than four days to reach Kenniliar now, by steamwagon."

"I'll be able to leave tomorrow night. If I don't catch up, I'll come to your uncle's house in Kenniliar."

Sagai wasn't entirely convinced. He gestured to the glittering pile on the table. "Half of these tokens are yours," he said mildly. "By rights, all should be yours. If you don't come, you'll make a thief out of me."

Khat rubbed the bridge of his nose, trying to look beaten and knowing he would have to be very convincing to fool Sagai. "I know I have to leave here. I don't want anything else to do with crazy Warders and stalking ghosts." He had forgotten to tell Elen about the reappearance of the ghost in Ecazar's quarters, forgotten it almost until this moment. That was odd. He must be more ill than he thought. "I'm not saying I won't ever come back here again, but I'll come after you as soon as I can. If not on the trade road, then in Kenniliar."

Sagai was frowning, reluctant to believe him and equally reluctant to call him a liar. But Miram firmly ended the discussion by declaring that Khat needed rest, and he obediently dragged himself up the steps to the upper room to collapse.

The roof would have been cooler, even at this time of day, but Khat was feeling the urge to be somewhere quiet, dark, and enclosed.

He slept for some time, and woke from a dream where he was telling Elen that something didn't make sense. The dream thoughts faded rapidly, and he couldn't recall what the something was. He lay there a while longer, dozing and listening to the muted sobbing from the rooms below.

From what he could hear, Netta had come back from the market, heard the decision, and gone into strong hysterics. Sagai and Miram had made no plans that hadn't included her; Netta had all but given them her home, and had always been able to pull her own weight and take care of her children too, and they meant to take her with them wherever they went. They had set about persuading her, and he could hear their voices, sometimes taking turns at it, sometimes talking at the same time, with Netta weeping in the background and the voices of her daughter and the other children occasionally chiming in. It only made sense; she would have a home with Miram and Sagai as long as she wanted it, and, since there was no prejudice against widows or abandoned wives in Kenniliar as there was in Charisat, she would probably be able to marry again if she wanted. Netta was only balking at the idea of leaving the city she had been born in, and it was difficult for her to believe that Kenniliar would hold a better life for her. Or maybe, Khat decided, she was used to being left behind, and it was difficult for her to accept that this time she wasn't.

He knew it was settled when Netta's daughter came upstairs, humming happily under her breath, and started to pack the spare clothes, even though Netta herself still wept downstairs.

Khat went to sleep again after that, sprawled facedown on a pile of matting, and didn't wake until he sensed Miram leaning over him. "I can't understand why you feel so hot," she was muttering, half to herself. "The cuts aren't taking on badly."

Khat sat up, running a hand through his hair and remembering in time not to lean back against the wall. It was night now; he could tell that from his inner sense of the sun's passage, even though this room had no windows and light seldom made it down from the vents and roof traps in the room above. He felt better, or clear-headed at least, and his skin wasn't so oddly sensitive. Miram was watching him thoughtfully, and he told her, "It's nothing. Did you get Netta settled?"

"Finally, yes. It took her a little while to get used to the idea, but some of that crying was for joy." She sighed. "We're giving the house to Ris's family. They can cut holes in the wall and combine it with theirs. Libra and Senace are going to stay and live with them."

"You didn't tell them where we're going, did you?"

"Sagai told them we were going to Denatra, towards the coast. So if anyone asks they have an answer to give." She frowned. "You are coming with us, aren't you?"

"I told you I was."

"Kenniliar really is a better city than this. We would never have left except that it takes so much money to live there, and to buy places in the guilds, and Sagai didn't want to be a burden on his uncle."

He looked away, consciously avoiding her eyes. "I've been there. It was all right." Kenniliar didn't have the high foreign population of Charisat, or the larger city's limited experience with kris. He had drawn far too much attention there simply walking down the street.

"It will be better, having people there, and a home. A real house, I mean, with its own fountain." Miram looked around at the familiar room, visible in the wan light from a single candle bowl. The wicker chests that were normally pushed back into a corner had been pulled out for packing, the piles of matting shoved aside, the children's battered rag-and-bead dolls collected in a heap. "Sagai went down to the docks before dark and bought our passage on a caravan leaving in the morning."

"He didn't use his own name . . ."

"No, he is Athram-selwa, a trader in beads and dyestuffs, moving his wife and sister and children to Kenniliar." Her eyes came back from faraway as she stopped thinking about the journey and concentrated on him. "Are you worried about Elen?"

Khat lifted one shoulder in a careful shrug. "A little. There's some things I should have told her at the Academia, before she left."

"She is a Warder," Miram said, considering it carefully. "Even though she looks so young. She should be able to take care of herself."

"I should be able to take care of myself, and you're treating me like one of your babies."

Miram smiled, getting to her feet, and slapped him lightly on the cheek. "Now I know you're feeling better."

Once they reached the First Tier, Riathen had the relics carried up to his chamber, then locked himself away without a word to anyone. At the moment, this suited Elen perfectly. She avoided Gandin's questions by avoiding him, and slipped down to her rooms to change her dusty and sweat-soaked kaftan for a fresh one and to put on her white Warder's mantle. Then she escaped the house.

On the way back she had asked Riathen about the High Justice from whom he had taken the crystal plaque, and, too preoccupied with his success to wonder at the question, he had told her the man's name was Vien'ten Rasan.

Custom allowed High Justices of the Trade Inspectors to conceal their names as well as their faces when doing their duties on the lower tiers, but Elen was sure she would recognize the man she had encountered in the prison. *And if it is him, well then,* she thought. There were only twelve High Justices in Charisat, and she supposed coincidence was possible. But she was simply in no mood to believe in coincidence.

She knew this would be her last part in this. If their suspicions were correct and Riathen did want the relics to use as pieces of some arcane engine he was constructing, the rest would be a matter for Warders of power. *And perhaps that's for the best,* Elen thought. She had stretched her power as she never had before in the past few days; she knew she couldn't take much more.

Justice Rasan's house was across the tier from Riathen's and a long walk in the afternoon heat. Approaching it, she thought it quite in character for a Trade Inspector: the place was blocky and designed as if for defense, with thick limestone-faced walls concealing everything but the very top of a central dome, and narrow gates guarded by wary private vigils.

The door servant unlocked the gate for her without argument, and she walked in through a low arch. There was a long court to one side, with a square fountain and two ranks of potted fig trees, and a trellised veranda with tiled benches to the other. A second gate and another pair of vigils barred entry into the rest of the house, which towered over the entrance courts, heavy and graceless.

Elen raised an eyebrow at this evidence of overcaution. She supposed High Justices made enemies, even ones that could come after them on the First Tier; Rasan evidently thought so.

The servant tried to bow her into the trellised waiting area, but she held her ground. "I won't wait. I will see the High Justice immediately."

The servant hesitated, wetting his lips nervously. "I will try, Honored."

It wasn't her he was afraid of, Elen knew. She nodded, and he unlocked the inner gate and disappeared into the cool depths of the house.

Elen waited, standing stubbornly in the sunlit corridor between the court and the veranda until it became apparent that she was meant to wait a long time. She approached the gate and grabbed one of the bars. The vigil on the other side shifted uncertainly, avoiding her eyes. She said, "Open this in the name of the Master Warder." It had worked at the prison, and if everything she suspected was true, this Justice would not dare complain about her high-handedness to Riathen.

The vigil hesitated, looking at the others for help. Elen knew of Warders who could open locks with their power; Seul claimed to be able to though she had never actually witnessed it. Elen turned her inner eye on the lock, tentatively, and almost started back in surprise. For an instant she had been able to "feel" the inside of the lock, sense the position of the tumblers, the oil and dust where they touched. This had never happened to her before. She was lucky to be able to sense the presence of breathing, thinking people, let alone inanimate objects.

Something in her expression must have convinced the vigil, because he was hastily fumbling for a key. Somewhat dazed, she stepped back to let him open the gate, then brushed past him into the house.

The long arched corridor was blessedly cool, with reception rooms on either side. A low voice droning in the distance led her to the back of the house.

It was a large chamber just off the main corridor, with fans moving jerkily in the vaults of the high ceiling and the back wall opening into another inner court, this one far more lush than the one meant for visitors' eyes. The voice she had heard was the High Justice himself, pacing as he dictated to an aged archivist, who was scribbling frantically to keep up. The servant who had let her in was huddled on the floor in a position of abject obeisance that had been outmoded for several generations. Even the Elector's servants weren't expected to abase themselves that way. Elen rather thought some enlightened Elector of the past had issued a decree against it, in fact. She cleared her throat.

Justice Rasan turned with a startled oath. He wore a brief indoor veil, without his bronze mask, but Elen recognized him immediately. His height and build, the way he moved, the rather disquieting sense she had of his soul, all were the same as the man she had confronted in the Trade Inspectors' prison. She smiled and inclined her head politely.

The only sound was the whir of the fans' clockwork and the scratch of pen on paper as the archivist used the pause to catch up. Then Rasan said, "Warder, I don't recall inviting you into my home." His voice was as she remembered it, cold, mocking, and abrasive to the nerves.

"I considered my business too urgent to wait." Elen came further into the room. Perhaps it was euphoria over her success with the lock, but she suddenly found herself enjoying this confrontation. The servant hadn't moved, and she decided she would have a formal denouncement of Rasan written up over the incident. He should appreciate the gesture, since Trade Inspectors were sticklers for every rule of law.

Justice Rasan growled a dismissal, and the servant bolted for the door, the archivist quickly gathering up his pens and inkpots and following. "The Master Warder has sent you here, I suppose?" he said.

Elen decided not to answer that one. She said, "Some time ago the Master Warder came to see you on another matter, and found in your possession a relic of rare beauty, a *mythenin* plaque inlaid with crystal pieces that turned color in the light. You gave it to him. My question is, who gave it to you?"

"Is it the Master Warder who is so interested in this, or is it you?" Rasan went to the stone wine cabinet standing against the wall and drew a cup from the clay jar cooling inside it. "I allowed you to get your creature out of prison—something I would have done for any Patrician lady, no matter what my feelings on her . . . habits—but using the Master Warder's name to satisfy idle curiosity is another matter." He eyed her coldly, obviously expecting some sort of outburst.

Wine, at this time of day, Elen thought. She hoped it made him ill. Really, in the stinking depths of the prison she had thought him menacing. Now she was finding him merely coarse. She sighed a little, as if the only feeling he roused in her was fatigue, and said, "That hardly answers my question. I know that if you aren't a thief yourself, you certainly benefit from their crimes. Your possession of a stolen relic proves that."

He slammed the wine cup down on the cabinet, snarling at her, "I don't believe the Master Warder sent you, child."

"Then let's go and ask him, shall we?" Elen sharpened her voice. Insults hadn't worked, so now he tried anger. He was desperate to be rid of her, perhaps even afraid, and she could have danced for joy. She must be on the right trail. "I already know it was a bribe from relic thieves, but I'm not really interested in your petty greeds and crimes. I want to know who sent you to the Academia last night, I want to know who told you to find another relic, this one a tiny *mythenin* plaque with a winged figure on it, and most of all I want to know who snaps his fingers and makes a High Justice of the Trade Inspectors jump to his bidding!"

Rasan turned away from her, one hand clutching the carved top of the wine cabinet as if to support himself. His other hand was trembling. He said, "You don't know it was a bribe."

He is afraid, Elen thought. There was some satisfaction in hearing that rusty voice convey uncertainty instead of threat or mockery, but there was no time to gloat now. She moved closer, to the low table where the archivist had been working, and glanced down at the scattered papers. Travel orders. Rasan had been making arrangements to leave the city. She smiled tightly to herself. "If you tell us the truth, we can protect you."

"Protect me?" The sneer was back, though she knew it masked fear now. "From your own kind?"

Elen frowned, surprised. "What do you mean?"

"The one she sends with her orders." He turned to face her. "Don't think I don't know who he is, though it's his conceit not to give me his name. I know he's a Warder, I know who his Master is, or one of his masters." His laugh was without a vestige of humor. "She hired the thieves to steal a relic collection from some fool of a court flunky on the Second Tier, and they betrayed her. The idiots didn't realize who she was." He pounded his fist on the cabinet again. "I should have known, I should have known when the fools gave me the plaque and bragged of the Patrician woman they had cheated . . . Then your Master Warder found the plaque, and she learned of my involvement. I had to do as she asked. I found the thieves, but it was too late, the collection had been dispersed. I had to search for the other relics for her. And now . . ." He stared at nothing, his eyes hunted. "Now the relics are found, and my assistance is unnecessary."

Elen thought he was drunker than she had supposed, that he was babbling or having heat visions. The "he" who refused to use his name must be Aristai Constans, but . . . She muttered, "She? Who is—" She caught the image from the surface of Rasan's thoughts. "Oh, no," she said aloud.

"Oh, yes." The Justice nodded.

"We can protect you, I swear it. We'll take you out of the city, tonight, now. Come with me and tell—" A cool breeze scattered the papers on the little table, interrupting her. She glanced at the wall opening into the garden court, then looked again. The flowers and plants were motionless in the hot heavy air. The breeze was inside the room.

Justice Rasan was staring around, fear in his bloodshot eyes. Distracted, Elen hadn't tasted the growing power in the air, but now she realized what was happening. The air spirit that had stalked them at the Academia was here. In the afternoon light it was invisible, but it must have moved just in front of her to stir the papers.

Elen shook back her sleeves and held her hands out, clearing her mind to construct the guard that she had tried to use that night at the Academia. It hadn't held Constans off that well, but there had been no chance to try it on the air spirit. She told Rasan, "Get behind me. I'll try to—"

The Justice cried out suddenly, staggering backward. He must have felt the cold edge of the creature's presence. Elen shouted, "No!" and started toward him, stopping as the deathly cold of the thing enveloped her.

She stumbled back, trying to get her breath, her throat aching with the freezing air she had inhaled. This had happened to her at the fortune-teller's house, when she had unknowingly walked into the ghost. And Radu, who must have had some presentiment of death when he burned bones for her, who had looked as if he had died of fear . . . Rasan was struggling, caught in the thing's invisible grip. He choked, gasping for air, and she watched in shock as his skin turned gray.

Elen backed away. It was happening so quickly. Rasan's terrified eyes were turning dull, his skin chalky. He collapsed, and Elen held up her hands to weave the guard again, fear and desperation giving her faulty power a strength she ordinarily couldn't tap.

The guard formed in front of the doorway to the corridor, a solidification of the air barely visible in the daylight. She felt the air spirit turn toward her; she bit her lip and held her ground as it came closer. Then lines of red light flared briefly as it encountered the guard and retreated.

Elen stumbled back through the door, knowing it was the best she could do. She was trembling with exhaustion, and the edges of her vision were darkening alarmingly, the penalty for having constructed so powerful a working. There was simply no way she could form a guard around the entire room and trap the thing. But this would give her the time to warn the house's other occupants and flee the doomed place herself. She had to tell Riathen what she had learned. She had to warn him.

She darted blindly down the corridor, not seeing the veiled Patrician man waiting for her until she ran right into him. Then it was too late.

Chapter Fifteen

THEY LEFT THE house for the last time an hour or so before dawn, packing the children and the few wicker chests that held all their belongings into a handcart full of bronze pots that its owner was taking down to the docks. The street the carters used was well patrolled, but the man said he would be glad for the company on the long early-morning trip down through the Eighth Tier, and only asked them to pay a few copper bits for the privilege. In the confusion of making arrangements, packing, and herding children, Khat thought to avoid Sagai, but wasn't quite so lucky.

His partner caught him out in the court, when the others were inside and the water keeper was still asleep in his wall cubby. "You do intend to meet us either on the trade road or in Kenniliar, don't you?" Sagai asked without preamble.

"Of course I do." Caught unprepared, Khat couldn't put the casual innocence into that statement that it needed.

"Then why do I have such difficulty believing it?"

Khat shook his head, apparently amazed at this obtuse persistence. His eyes were still dark from the fever yesterday and would not be easily read, even by Sagai. "Are you calling me a liar?"

"The thought crossed my mind," Sagai said mildly. The mildness meant that he wouldn't be drawn into a fight, but he wouldn't back down, either. "What is it you have to do that keeps you from fleeing for your life with the rest of us?"

With real frustration, Khat demanded, "Do you have to know everything I do? What am I, your pet?"

This also failed to distract Sagai. He said, "No, I don't have to know everything you do. But I mean to know if you intend to meet us in Kenniliar, and remember, I can keep this up as long as you can."

Khat looked away, disgusted with himself. And Sagai could keep this up, too. That was how they trained scholars in Kenniliar, standing in the sun arguing a point until someone fainted. It was similar to the debates that went on in the krismen Enclave councils, except they did it in the shade, so the arguing could go on longer. Khat didn't have the strength for it now. He let his breath out, and said, "If there's any way I can, I will."

Sagai studied him for a time, then turned away. "I suppose that will have to be good enough."

They said good-bye only to Ris, who was recognizable now that the swelling and bruises on his face had diminished, and his father and aunt, who were volubly grateful for the gift of the house and sad to see their best neighbors leave. Khat was surprised to feel the parting himself. He hadn't realized how firmly entrenched he had been here, how many ties of friendship had been woven in with the mutually defensive alliances he had formed with the people in this court.

They hadn't gone a few steps down the street when the old water keeper caught up with them. He had been wakened by the commotion and had come to give Khat the tokens he had held for him, water payments that wouldn't be needed now. After a moment's thought, Khat told him to give them to the old woman who lived in the bottom corner of the end house, who wove braid for a living and was always late with her water money.

Khat waited until they were at the docks and Sagai was making the last arrangements with the caravan driver before he faded into the growing crowd. He made his way up to the best vantage point at the top of the docks, where he could sit on the marble base of the First Elector's colossus. He pulled his hood up to make it more difficult to recognize him from below, and watched for over an hour.

He was the one the Trade Inspectors would be after, the one whose silence Riathen would desire the most. The Master Warder had seen Sagai only once, at Arad-edelk's quarters, and if Sagai was out of the city he would discount him. Khat was the one he would want to find, and if the Trade Inspectors might hesitate to leave the city, the Warders would not.

The docks grew gradually more crowded with crewmen, passengers, and street vendors all shouting or trying to get somewhere, with carters unloading goods on the overhead ramps from the warehouses or hauling them into the streets for the long journey up the tiers, while mad beggars gabbled pleas or abuse at everyone. Finally the sun broke over the city, and the shadows fled through the crumbling levels of multistoried warehouses down to the stone piers and finally past the caravan wagons as they rolled out onto the flat expanse of the trade road. It was a relief, really; now Khat had only himself to worry about.

The sun glinted off the marble and polished iron of the colossus and warmed the dirty paving of the steep, narrow walkways below, and Khat felt his fever returning. *So everyone's right, you're sick,* he told himself. There was always some illness sweeping the lower tiers, though none had ever affected him before. It was bound to pass off soon enough.

It was pure luck he saw Ris. The gateway behind the colossus was the main entrance to this section of the dock area, and he saw the boy dodge through the crowd and fight his way to the edge of the street, where he leapt to the top of the stone pediment and shielded his eyes to scan the levels below. Khat swore, and hopped down from the statue's base. Darkness hovered at the edges of his vision, and he had to steady himself before he could cross the street and drag Ris down off the pediment.

Bustling people jostled them, and Khat pulled the boy to a clear space before he shook him and said, "I told you not to come to the Eighth Tier alone. I haven't been gone a quarter day yet and you're already down here?"

"You didn't leave," Ris protested, nonplussed.

"That's not the point."

"But it was important. An Academia scholar came looking for you. We didn't tell him anything, but he said his name was Arad-something and he gave me a whole one-day token—look, here, see?" Ris felt obliged to prove this statement, digging through his grubby robe until he produced the token. "To find you and tell you he had to see you and Sagai right away, it was very important, and to come to the Academia as soon as you could."

Khat looked off across the docks, distracted. Someone had discovered the copy of the text, maybe? It could hardly be anything too bad, or Arad wouldn't have been free to search for him. A trap, maybe? "What did he look like?"

"This tall." Ris held out a hand to indicate an average-sized lower-tier city dweller. "Dark skin, dark eyes, umm . . ."

"Never mind." That described Arad, as well as most of the other inhabitants of Charisat. "Don't tell anyone you saw me, all right? And go home."

Khat stepped back into the crowd, and didn't answer when Ris called after him, "Does this mean you're not leaving?"

The streets up through the tiers had never been so long. The ramps up to the gates had never been so steep. Khat managed to make it past the Seventh Tier to the relative safety of the Sixth without looking too much like someone who was ripe to be murdered. He thought of stopping to rest there in familiar territory, but he didn't want to risk meeting anyone else he knew. Seeing Ris at the docks had been bad enough. He had tried to live on the fringes of the Enclave for a time, after leaving his uncle's guardianship. That had taught him to make clean breaks, if nothing else.

The fever had reached the dangerous point where he wasn't sweating anymore, and his muscles ached as if he had had a thorough beating from an expert at the trade. It made the pain from the cuts on his back seem like a negligible twinge. He was beginning to admit that he knew what caused it.

Hiding the winged relic in his pouch had been a bad idea. If he hadn't done it, he would still be in the Trade Inspectors' prison, but that didn't change what was happening now. People had died this way, most often when something went wrong with the embryo implanted in their pouch and the baby died, and its death poisoned them before they realized what had happened. Kris were just as prone to that kind of danger as the city people, with their far more difficult method of birth.

Later Khat remembered reaching the Academia and arguing with the gate vigil about getting in. He had the feeling the man had already been ordered to admit him, and that he was only delaying to puff up his own importance. The gate was in full sun at this time of day, and Khat was too stubborn to show off his weakness by leaning against the wall or simply sitting down in the street. So when he finally collapsed, it was just inside the gate on the hot flagstones of the entrance court.

He came to in a hazy way when he was being carried into the shade of the gatehouse's porch. The old scholar who had let them in the first time they came to see Arad and who could never keep his veil in place was leaning over him, saying, "Bring water, quickly. Soak a cloth in it."

They had treated it like it was heat sickness, which had probably saved his life. He was surprised they bothered. But it took a certain character to devote your life to collecting old knowledge and searching for new; evidently having that character made it difficult to stand idly by while a life expired on your doorstep.

"This is that krismen the Trade Inspectors came for," someone else said. "Fetch Master Ecazar. He wanted to know when he came back."

No, don't do that, Khat thought. He tried to sit up then, and the inside of his head quietly exploded.

When he opened his eyes again he was in a dark room, lit only by lamplight from the passage outside, all its shadows at unfamiliar angles. It smelled faintly of ink and old paper, and more strongly of someone who had been terribly ill recently. His throat felt raw and dry, though his body remembered being given water only a few moments ago. He lay on something so soft it was difficult to move, tangled up in a heavy blanket. He was shivering from a chill that seemed to come from within, unabated by the hot still air in the room. It had made him dream confusedly of ghosts; that's what had woken him.

Before that he had been dreaming of the Waste and the pirates, of being stretched spread-eagle on the exposed stone of the top level while the heat of it burned into his back and somebody's knife burned a line down his thigh. That was after they had gotten tired of the game of let-him-escape-then-catch-him-again, after the others were dead. Worse dreams had mixed what they had done to him with the vivid images his imagination constructed of what they had done to the others, creating a false memory of seeing the things that in reality he had only been able to hear in the distance. Footsteps were approaching down the passage, but he was drifting off again.

There was another gap of missing time, then suddenly the shadows of three men fell across the band of yellow light in the passage. An unfamiliar voice said, "He has any number of recent wounds, but none appear infected. The tincture of poppies should bring down the fever, but it isn't having any effect. All I can think of is increasing the dosage."

"There is no evidence poppy decreases fever," Arad said, sounding harassed. "As far as I can see, all it does is slow the heart and put the patient into a drugged stupor."

"He is krismen. That's why it isn't working on him. If you would confine yourself to your area of study and let me practice mine—"

"Don't be idiots." Ecazar's dry voice, cutting through the quarrel like a sharp knife. "It's obvious it is no simple fever, and even you, Physician, must admit that you've never treated a kris before. Meddling with tinctures is only going to make it worse. He will either get over it himself or die."

Blunt but probably true. Yes, the Ancient Mages had wrought well. Remnants that still towered over the Waste, roads that cut through it, and kris to live in it. The Waste couldn't poison him, and he couldn't get their dirty little city diseases, either. But he could poison himself.

It was some time later that Khat opened his eyes again. He lay on his side, on a pad of heavy cotton batting, much thicker than anything he normally slept on. A few feet away was a clay jar, water beading on its rounded sides. It looked inviting, and he considered sitting up. *Maybe later,* he thought after a moment. He managed to lift his head enough to look around, and saw this was a bare room, swept clean, and the light coming through the vents high in the wall was the early morning sun. There were some chests in the corner, the expensive kind used to store books. The doorway opened into a passage, unbarred even with so much as a curtain. That was reassuring. *But I'm supposed to be dying,* he remembered. He didn't feel like going anywhere, but he didn't feel like dying, either.

Footsteps in the passage again. This time he stayed awake long enough to see who it was. An old woman, with a plain face above a plain gray kaftan, peered at him through the doorway, then turned back to call out to someone, "He's awake again."

Khat made an effort to push himself up, and everything faded out.

The next time he woke he did sit up, ran a hand through his sweat-matted hair, and knew this time he really was awake. It was the same room, and still morning. Stiff and sore, Khat stretched carefully. He was weak but not light-headed, and not so utterly drained of strength as he had been on his last waking. The fever was blessedly gone. He laid a hand on his pouch, wondering if he had been lucky or if he really had done something permanent to himself. Everything felt all right, and still seemed to work, though when he looked there was a faint trace of redness around the pouch lip.

Noticing that he wore a light cotton robe and nothing else, Khat struggled out of the pallet and found his clothes and boots atop one of the book chests. Even his knife was there.

Dressing, he discovered the cuts on his back had scabbed over. He rubbed his chin and realized he had more than one day's growth of beard. There had been more than one morning, at least.

Arad-edelk appeared in the doorway as he pulled his shirt over his head, saying, "At last. We didn't think you would ever wake."

"How long has it been?"

"You were unconscious three full days. This is the morning of the fourth day since you collapsed," Arad said, watching him worriedly.

"Three days?" Khat stopped to stare at him.

"It was a terrible fever. You're lucky to be alive at all," Arad told him. He didn't look too well either. He wasn't wearing a veil, and his face was tired and worn and his eyes were red, as if he had spent the past few nights working by lamplight. "Where is Sagai? I felt sure he would come to look for you, even if he didn't get my messages."

"He took his family and left the city." Khat tucked his knife through his belt in back and let his shirt hide it. Someone had even cleaned his clothes. At least he had picked a good place to collapse. He supposed Arad had somehow talked Ecazar out of turning him back over to the Trade Inspectors, though he thought he remembered Ecazar being here at one point . . . He also remembered why he had been on his way to the Academia in the first place. "Why did you send for me?" he asked.

The scholar's expression turned grim. He said, "Are you sure you're well enough to hear it?"

"I'm not well enough to stand the suspense. Just tell me."

"It's something in the Survivor text. The most incredible things . . . Come out here."

Khat followed Arad down the passage to his sunlit workroom, where the Ancient mural still lay incomplete in the corner. The rest of the floor was covered with stacks of paper and unfolded journals. Arad had been hard at work on something.

The scholar took up the Survivor text, searching through the fan-folded pages, as Khat eased himself down to the floor. Arad said, "After Sagai showed me the translation method he was taught, the work went much faster."

"You finished it?" Khat asked, surprised. Reading Ancient Script was a painstaking process.

Arad met his eyes, his face serious. "When I began to understand what I was reading, I had no difficulty staying up through the nights." He found the little copper clip that marked his place, and set it aside. "Listen.

"'The Inhabitants of the West were driven back through the doors, but many were left behind. They are beings of light and silence, but deadly. Their voices are music. Once in our world they ride the winds at night, but their embrace is death.' The intonation marker for the type of death means to die from cold, if that's possible. It's talking about air spirits, don't you see? And the creatures we call ghosts. 'Most died in the fire, but some learned to live within it . . .' It goes on like that."

Arad searched for another place in the book, and Khat protested, "Wait. Finish that part." He wanted to rip the text away from Arad, but he was afraid to tear the delicate pages.

"That's not important."

"Not important?"

"Not compared to this." He removed another copper clip and read, "'The Inhabitants of the West came as friends, speaking soft words to all those who would hear'—or know, something like that, it's not clear—'They brought the . . .' Oh, it's complicated, but what it seems to be saying is that the Inhabitants taught the Mages all sorts of new magics, including a type of arcane engine that seems to be what we call a painrod. Doesn't that make a strange kind of sense? The painrods aren't like anything else the Ancients left behind."

"Arad, we'll discuss it later. Keep reading."

The scholar turned more pages, then read, "'The Inhabitants swarmed into our air from the Doors to the West. Driving them back caused the skies to turn dark, the sea to steam and empty, and burning rock rose up from the seabed and drained the water. Strange creatures followed in the wake of the Inhabitants, even as the doors closed, plagues of creatures that burrowed in the blasted earth . . .'" Arad's voice trailed off. He shook his head and fumbled for another page. "'They'—the Mages—'made the'—this word might be translated as 'arcane engine,' but from the context I'm going to recommend 'transcendental device.' I think it's more exact. To close the Western Doors of the sky, to prison the Inhabitants of the West in that dead land between the sky and the stars'—that's why I thought it said the Inhabitants of the West came from the land of the dead, but once I applied the alternate method of reading the intonation markers, the meaning became clear." Arad seemed torn between excitement and horrified doubt. "I know it's hard to believe. What's been going through my mind since I found these passages . . ."

"It can't be true." For some reason Khat didn't want it to be true. He felt cold, as if his fever had come back, and it was making the hair on the back of his neck stand up. He had been comfortable with the mystery of the Ancients. Nibbling away at its edges, uncovering pieces of it one tiny bit at a time, had been his life's work. Having so much of the answer dumped in his lap at once was frightening. It felt as if supposedly solid ground was suddenly shifting under his feet. "Are you sure the book's not just telling some kind of story?"

"I thought that too," Arad assured him. "I thought it was a scribe making up some tale to explain the purpose of the Remnants and the other things the Ancients made that most of the Survivors didn't understand. But that engraving that shows the three relics, so carefully done, the block, the crystal-inlaid plaque, and the one with the winged figure—we know they exist, we've seen them!"

"It was wrong about the block. It said it was four feet long, and the one we found was only three." Khat knew he was being an idiot. Scribes made more errors with numbers than anything else.

"Possibly an error in transcription," Arad said gently, humoring him. "We know at least two copies of the book were made."

Khat still wanted to deny it. Ghosts were ghosts, and air spirits were just a mindless product of the Waste, like spidermites and creeping devil. But there was the one that had come to Radu's house, and stalked them in the Academia . . . "Did you tell Elen about this?"

"I've sent messengers every day, but they were all turned away at the gate. I've been going mad!" Arad shook the book in frustration. "She thought the secrets in this book would explain how to construct arcane engines, so the Warders could further their understanding of the Ancients' magic. It isn't that at all."

"Then what is it?"

Arad set the book down, folding the tattered pages back carefully.

"What it seems to say is that the Inhabitants of the West had corrupted some few of the Mages before they were driven back. That the surviving Mages who constructed the Remnants and the 'transcendental device' wanted to make it extremely difficult to . . . to dismantle, or to make the device stop working. From what I can ascertain, the device must still exist somewhere, perhaps hidden deep in the earth or . . . or even up in the sky, for all I know, but still working, still holding the Inhabitants back in their dead land, wherever it is. The Remnants are the key to it. The Mages raised many of them at a great cost to their power and at a great cost in the lives of the workers who did the building. They built one Remnant for each Western Door, it's clear on that, at least."

"So there's a Door to the West near each Remnant?" Khat asked, thinking, *Hell below, that means there's one somewhere around the Tersalten Flat Remnant.* That was less than a day's travel from Charisat.

"I believe so. Or there was, at any rate. The text says that many of the workers were killed by the heat and the foul airs from the living Waste rock during the building, but in the end, they were successful. Only one Remnant could be used to halt the device, and anyone trying to do so would not only have to know which Remnant, but what to do to it once it was found. Oh, there's some process that has to be gone through, and the three relics seem essential to it. I haven't had the chance to translate that section yet. It's most obscure . . ."

Khat was silent, trying to take it in. He thought of the Tersalten Flat Remnant's antechamber, with all those shapes cut into the walls, just like all the other Remnants. Such a strange thing for the Ancients to do. So deliberately confusing. But if it was part of an arcane engine unlike anything ever discovered before, unlike even the hideously complicated device that had once lived in the deepest level of the Enclave . . .

At the time Khat had thought that they might find a plaque to fit every shape in the antechamber wall and still not have all the pieces of the arcane engine, and he had been wrong. You only needed one plaque, to slide into one shape, in one Remnant. Once you looked at it that way, he could see where the block was meant to be placed too. No telling where the little winged relic went, not yet. But it might become apparent once the other two had been put into place, and if one studied the process Arad spoke of. Khat said, "They should have made it impossible to stop; they should have destroyed those three relics, or never made them. But, you know, they were always so careful. You can't trap yourself inside a Remnant, even if you break the plug that works the door. They must have thought that one day, someone might need to stop the engine. So they left a way to do it."

"And this book is the guide. It gives the clues that any knowledgeable Mage or Warder, or a fakir for that matter, could use to open the Doors of the West, to let the Inhabitants back into our world." Arad rubbed his temples. "Perhaps our philosophers have been wrong. Perhaps this place the Ancients called the West is the land of the dead."

Khat took the book away from him, turning the folded pages thoughtfully but not really seeing the words. Sonet Riathen wasn't wrong about the book at all. Arad had read that part; he just hadn't seen the implications the way the Master Warder would. The book said that the Inhabitants of the West had brought new magics to the Ancient Mages. If Riathen let them back into the world, they would do the same for the Warders.

Right before they killed everyone and made the Waste rock rise again.

The house boasted a cistern and a small room with a basin for bathing, and Khat used it to clean up a bit and to get rid of the three-day beard growth, since looking even more like a foreigner wasn't going to do him any good with anybody. Before he did anything else he wanted to read the key passages in the text for himself, so he took over a corner of the scholar's workroom while Arad went off to take care of his other commitments at the Academia and to send another messenger to Elen.

Arad had two servants, a pimply boy who was plainly terrified of Khat, even when the krismen was doing nothing more alarming than sitting on the floor reading, and the old woman who had looked in on him earlier. She treated him with the casual contempt of a close relation, coming in to threaten him for not eating the pottage she had brought him earlier, and snarling at him when he asked her suspiciously what was in it. He had a good idea who had been in charge of the messier parts of taking care of him.

About midway through the afternoon, when Khat had read enough to badly want to discuss it with Sagai, or Arad, or even Elen, Ecazar arrived.

Khat had heard him coming down the entrance hall and assumed it was Arad-edelk returning. When he looked up Ecazar was already crossing the room, and it was too late. It might have been too late anyway; the house was still surrounded by Academia vigils.

The text was unfolded across his lap, and Khat didn't bother to try to stand. He had borrowed Arad's reading lenses, finding they made the task easier when the light shifted into afternoon, and now pulled them off so he could see Ecazar.

Hard eyes glaring down above a brief veil, the Master Scholar said, "I've spoken to Arad. Is it true?"

"It could be," Khat admitted. "It could also be a collection of mad ramblings."

Ecazar scratched his chin under the veil, eyes narrowing, and said, "What can be done about it?"

You want my opinion? Khat thought, startled and suspicious. At least he assumed the question was directed at him; Ecazar was talking to a spot on the wall about three feet above his head. Wary, he answered, "Nothing, until the Master Warder stops refusing Arad's messengers."

"It isn't only Arad's messengers he refuses; he won't see mine, either." Ecazar hesitated. "There may be something wrong on the First Tier. We have only a few students from the highest families, but none have come down to meet with their tutors since the day before yesterday."

Khat had no reply to that, and felt the conversation lag. He wished Ecazar would go away. To provoke him, he said, "When are you going to call the Trade Inspectors again?"

Ecazar finally met his eyes, angry. "I didn't send for them the first time."

It came to Khat suddenly that Ecazar couldn't have been too suspicious of him, or he would never have allowed Khat and Sagai into Arad's house the first time, when Elen had asked to speak to the younger scholar. If Ecazar had thought him a thief, he would never have allowed Khat to see that mural, to know it existed at all. Still, Khat asked, "If you didn't, then who did?"

The Master Scholar snorted. "I assume it was one of your other criminal associates," he said, turning away. But he hesitated again, and without looking back, added, "I disagreed with Scholar Robelin on any number of points, but handing one of his former assistants over to the Trade Inspectors would be an insult to his memory I do not intend to make."

Khat said nothing, not sure he wanted to believe him because that meant forgiving him, and he wasn't ready for that yet. But he remembered something he wanted to ask. "Wait. What were you looking for that night?"

Ecazar stopped in the doorway, grudgingly. "What do you mean?"

"When you took the relic with the winged figure back to the Porta. What were you looking for?"

The scholar raised an eyebrow, but didn't ask how Khat knew this. He said, "That figure. There was a scholar—I finally discovered it was Ivius-atham—who identified that stylized winged man as a symbol he called the 'seal of the great death,' or alternately the 'seal of the great closing.' His source was a scrap of Ancient Script he discovered bound in with a Last Sea text. I was looking for my notes on his work."

"A death symbol?"

"It's possible he was wrong. I've reread his translation of the scrap, and I suspect it's faulty. I would need the original document to be sure, but that is owned by a collector in Alsea."

Ecazar had unbent as far as he was going to, maybe as far as it was possible for him. He left, and Khat sat there for some time thinking, before he put the lenses on again and went back to the book.

Arad returned late in the day, looking tired, dust-covered, and footsore. "You went to the First Tier," Khat said accusingly.

"I did," Arad admitted, easing himself down onto a stool and putting aside his veil. He accepted a cup of tea from the old servant woman, and said, "The guard at the Master Warder's gate wouldn't admit me, or even take a message in, so I loitered in the street for a long time, and saw no one leave or enter. In fact, I saw no one moving in the house at all," he added.

"No one at all?" Khat asked, thinking of how busy the huge manse had seemed when he had been there. He was worried about Elen. She was a meticulous person, and scrupulous to a fault, and would never have ignored Arad's messengers, no matter what the circumstances. If nothing was wrong, she would have contacted one of them by now.

"No one in the outer court, or on the part of the terrace that I could see over the wall, and no one moved past the windows on the upper floors."

"That was dangerous, Arad."

The scholar shrugged. "I didn't let Master Riathen pay me for the relics he took. Anyone who saw me there might think I had changed my mind, and wished to see him about that. But where would the Master Warder go?"

Khat shook his head. It was easy to imagine Sonet Riathen being called away on some important business; it was not easy to imagine him taking his students, the other Warders who lived in his household, and the servants who kept the place. It didn't explain where Elen had gone. Khat put the book aside and stretched. He hadn't moved except to fold and unfold pages for a long time, and even his hands were cramped.

Either Riathen had been taken away somewhere and all his household dispersed, or he had dismissed them himself and gone somewhere no one could reach him. Khat knew which one he suspected. He just hoped the Master Warder hadn't taken Elen with him.

"I could try approaching one of the other households of Warders," Arad was saying.

"No. There's too good a chance that they would just arrest you first and ask questions later."

"It's a possibility, I suppose." Arad sipped his tea quietly for a moment, then said, "You're going up there, aren't you?"

Khat nodded. There was no point in dissembling.

"If it was dangerous for me to stand in the street, how much more dangerous is it for you to try to enter the house?" Arad protested.

"If you have a better idea, I'd like to hear it."

Arad put his cup aside and rubbed his face, sighing in frustration. "We don't even know if this transcendental device the text speaks of really exists, or where it is. Do you think Riathen's copy named its location?"

"It didn't need to. I know where it is, or where part of it is, anyway. So does Riathen. So do you."

Arad stared. "Where?"

"The first relic Riathen found. It was the plaque that the High Justice had, which was the only piece of the set that was really identifiable as a fragment of an arcane engine. Remember, it fits into the antechamber wall of the Tersalten Flat Remnant. You know," he added pointedly, "the one to the west?"

"Oh. Oh my." The scholar appeared to be suffering from great excitement or physical pain. Khat sympathized; it was the reason he hadn't felt much like eating all day. It was one thing to hypothesize about the existence of arcane engines and "transcendental devices," but quite another to know where one might be found. Arad asked, "Inside the wall, perhaps?"

"Or under it. No one ever thought to look there. Until now."

Chapter Sixteen

IT WAS FULL dark when Khat used the quieter streets to work his way over to the tier wall, past closed shops and sleeping houses, avoiding the noise and light of the area around the theater. He still had Elen's Warder token, but he didn't intend to use it. It would be too easy for someone to order the tier gate vigils to arrest any noncitizens who presented one.

Khat went down one of the narrow courts that dead-ended at the high wall of the rail wagon's corridor, and from there into a narrow alley behind the houses, freezing when he heard a baby cry from inside one of them. The cry died out as the child fretted itself back to sleep. He felt along the fine stone of the rail corridor's wall until he encountered the first handhold. The edges were crumbling, a sign it hadn't been used in a while. That was probably good. Some of these chinks in the wall had been chipped out by earlier entrepreneurs; some he had added himself. Since the rail wagon had been installed, it made a fine way up to the Third Tier, if you were careful.

Khat hauled himself up, silently cursing the loose chips of rock that his boots dislodged. He reached the top and struggled over, dropping down on the other side to land with a crunch on a pile of broken glass. The black wall of the Third Tier was looming above him; some idiot had probably thrown a bottle off the top. He spent the next few moments picking glass out of his boot soles.

The corridor was only about twenty feet across and stank of tar and grease. The other side was set flush against the base of the Third Tier. He made his way down to the bend, where the corridor turned from crossing the width of the Fourth Tier to run parallel to the tier wall and start its long climb up to the Third. The two rails glinted faintly in the moonlight, but it was impossible to see one lone kris hunkered down against the wall. This was the best way to catch a ride on the rail wagon; jumping onto it from above was too obvious. And waiting here, as the wagon came off its straight path and onto the curving one that paralleled the wall, he would be well below the line of sight of the vigils who rode the top.

After a long, uneasy wait, the rails started to shake, and the dull throbbing roar of the approaching wagon echoed up the corridor. Fortunately his timing wasn't off, and it was heading up; it would have been intolerable to have to wait for its return trip.

The glow of the running lamps gradually became visible, and the noise was deafening as the wagon drew near. It was actually three steamwagons linked together, with one steering platform in the front. The big, black iron monster slowed as it reached the bend in the corridor and with grinding gears made the turn. It was close enough for him to study intently how the wheels were fixed onto the rails, how the paneled metal sides, etched with decorative scrollwork, kept out the dust, and for the heat to wash over him with the tang of hot metal that was oddly like the taste of blood. There were vigils up on the topside platforms with air guns, but they were fifteen feet above his head, and were watching the track in front of the wagon. *And lazy,* he thought. Now that the novelty had worn off, only professional thieves used the rail wagon to go from tier to tier anymore, and they were never caught.

The third linked wagon passed, then the first of the tall, boxlike cargo wagons. He would have to catch hold behind the first car; the ones further back were more likely to be dropped off on the Second and Third Tiers. Khat stood, caught the handrail at the back of the first car, and pulled himself up between it and the second car. The space was narrow, the second car ominously close behind him, and after a tense moment he found footing on the protruding undercarriage.

Careful to keep his head down, Khat let out his breath in relief. Now the trick was to hold on and try not to think about what would happen if something went wrong and the two cars slammed together. And hope no one saw him before the wagon reached the First Tier; he had never ridden it that far up before.

The rail wagon groaned like a dying rock demon as it mounted the steep ramp up to the First Tier. It passed through the short tunnel in the tier wall, and Khat buried his head against his arms, choking on the backwash of heat and steam. The tunnel was blessedly short, and the rail wagon came out onto the First Tier, into a wide flat area surrounded by high walls, though undoubtedly they were there to protect the residents from the sight of the ungainly cargo wagons, not to keep anyone out. Lamps and ghostlights hung at intervals from ornate, twisted metal poles, but they didn't eliminate all the concealing pools of shadow.

Khat had been lucky; all the cars except the one behind him and the one he was holding on to had been detached at the Second Tier. The luck was nice, but it left him uneasy, knowing the more he had of it now, the more likely it was to fail spectacularly at some later point.

The rail wagon slowed gradually to a halt now, hissing and groaning. Crewmen waiting on the hard-packed dirt of the yard walked up to the first of the steamwagons, calling greetings to the carters and ignoring the vigils who were clambering awkwardly down from their posts.

Khat slipped off the undercarriage and crossed the ground hurriedly, staying low and dodging the pools of lamplight. He circled behind two enclosed passenger wagons and made it to the outer wall, which was far enough away from the lamps to be well shadowed. Once there, he quickly discovered there was no scaling it without a rope and a grappling hook. Cursing to himself, he moved along it to the gate. This was a big iron barred affair with copper mesh panels to make it more attractive from the outside. There was also a small door cut into it for the use of servants and crew, so they could come and go without the trouble of opening the entire barrier. A gatekeeper was slumped against this side of the wall, either asleep or dozing, with only a weak ghostlamp to light his way.

Khat stood back in the shadow, considering his options, then simply walked up to the smaller door and lifted the latch. Without moving, the gatekeeper grunted an inaudible query at him. Khat grunted back, stepped out, and pulled the door to.

Outside he leaned against the wall, getting his bearings. The gate opened onto one of the First Tier avenues, with a tiled marble colon-nade on the far side. It was quiet and deserted. The smell of a fragrant garden was in the air, and the sound of water running somewhere nearby. After the stink of the rail wagons, it was a welcome relief.

As Khat had discovered on his earlier visit, the First Tier was ri-diculously easy to make your way around in, as long as you stayed away from private houses and kept a respectful distance from the palace environs. There were trees, flowering bushes, fountains, and walkways for strolling Patricians, which also provided plenty of cover for someone who didn't want to be easily observed. Since access was controlled from the gate, the rail yard, and the private entrances like Sonet Riathen's, there were few patrolling vigils.

Khat had to hide behind a bench once, and again in a cluster of persea, as silk- and gold-draped litters passed, each accompanied by a mob of lamp-carrying servants. But even for the First Tier it was oddly quiet. Some of the houses were glowing with lamplight from windows and back terraces, emitting discreet music, loud talk, and laughter. But most were locked up tight, with only a few lit windows. The latter grew more frequent as he neared the area of Riathen's giant manse.

Khat approached it the way he knew best, through the garden where the embassy pavilion stood, where he would have a good view of the raised terrace and the entire back facade. He scrambled over the low wall, brushed through a stand of trees, and found one of the narrow pebbled paths. Staying on it made far less noise than smash-ing through the greenery.

The pavilion itself was dark, and Khat remembered the kris em-bassy would have departed days ago. Riathen's house was just as dark and silent. Moonlight traced the limestone walls, making ghostly shapes out of the flowing carvings on the pediment. He could barely see the outline of the great terrace.

Abruptly Khat halted, crouching down below the level of flower-ing shrubs lining the path. Someone was moving through the under-growth about twenty yards off to his right, softly but purposefully heading in the direction of Riathen's house.

It was too late for a gardener, though not for a lover out looking for a trysting place, but somehow Khat didn't think the other in-truder was either. People were avoiding this area for some reason, and anyone deliberately heading into it was worth talking to.

Khat went down the path, getting slightly ahead of his quarry, then crossed over to the narrow pebbled rim surrounding a pond. Keeping low, he leapt from the end of that to a patch of silversword, and crouched down to wait. From here he should be able to get a good look at the intruder, as whoever it was passed from the heavy bushes into a section of relatively open ground.

Across the little clearing a figure emerged, stepping sideways to free itself from the clinging greenery, glancing around cautiously and not seeing Khat, who was crouched low, just another dark patch on the shadowy ground. It reached the center of the clearing before he recognized it by its walk and build. It was the young Warder Gandin.

And he isn't just out for a stroll, Khat thought. Gandin wore a dark-colored mantle, sensible attire for anyone out sneaking by night. The Warder passed his hiding place unaware, and Khat stood, took one silent step, and caught him from behind, wrapping an arm around his throat. As he expected, Gandin tried to throw him over forward, and was unsettled by Khat's different balance. Khat put pressure on the smaller man's knee joint, yanked backward, and dumped Gandin flat on his back.

He held him down with a knee on his chest, and said quietly, "It's me."

Gandin stopped fighting. "What are you doing here?" he whispered furiously.

"Where's Elen?"

"She's not with you? I was hoping . . ."

"I haven't seen her since you took the relics from the Academia." He decided Gandin was telling the truth, and eased the pressure off his chest a little. Gandin took advantage of the moment to try to overturn Khat, who thumped him back down again. "Don't do that; you'll make me nervous," he told the Warder.

Gandin swore, quite creatively for a Patrician, and added, "Get off me."

"I don't think so. Not yet." Khat could sympathize; he hated being helpless himself, worse than anything, and he hated being bested in a fight, but he didn't intend to beg for information, either. "What happened? Where's Riathen?"

"Under arrest at the palace. All the Warders are under arrest, but most are confined to their homes. Riathen and the others from his household were the only ones taken to the palace."

"Why?"

"I don't know! They would have locked me up too, except I wasn't there when they came for everyone. Will you let me up?"

Khat waited. Frustrated, Gandin swore and added, "Everyone is saying that the Elector tried to have the Heir killed, the way he did her mother, years ago. The Heir escaped and has armed her lictors against him. They say that the palace is an armed camp, with the Elector's lictors and the officials of the court holding parts of it and the Heir and her men holding others. I don't know whether it's true or not. Any other questions, or may I get up now?"

"Why were you going back to the house?"

Gandin didn't answer, setting his jaw stubbornly.

"Did you think the relics were still there, and that Riathen would want you to keep them safe? I'll bet you anything they're gone by now."

Gandin glared up at him. "I had to try. Did Constans take them?"

He doesn't know, Khat thought. Gandin didn't even suspect, like Elen must have. Constans hadn't seen the book. He might know about the engine, Arad's "transcendental device," but he didn't know where it was. Riathen knew that, and he had the relics. He said, "Probably," and let Gandin up, stepping back out of reach.

Gandin eyed him resentfully, and straightened his veil. "What are you doing here?"

Khat didn't have a chance to decide to tell the truth or think up a good lie. Someone on the dark expanse of Riathen's terrace uncovered a lamp. They both crouched down, and Khat scrambled into the cover of the bushes. "You were followed, you idiot," he whispered to Gandin.

"They couldn't follow me; I'd know," he protested. "They must have followed you."

There were moving figures on the terrace, flashes of reflected light on white robes as men dropped over the balustrade into the garden. They must have been First Tier vigils, and wouldn't have uncovered the lamp unless they were already sure their quarry was surrounded. "They wouldn't follow me," Khat pointed out with inescapable logic, scrambling further into the brush. "If they had seen me, they would've shot me by now."

"Well, I would've known they were there if you hadn't distracted me," Gandin argued, following him.

Children, Khat thought in disgust, stopping to listen for anyone ahead. *And Warders who think they know everything.*

There was someone, maybe several someones, moving through the greenery between them and the pavilion. A faint wheeze-click echoed from that direction as well: an air gun's reservoir being pumped up for firing. Khat kicked Gandin to get his attention and whispered, "We'll split up. Get off this tier if you can and go to the Academia."

Gandin nodded, and rose to a crouch, pushing his way through the brush toward the garden wall. Khat took the opposite direction.

He came to a clearing where there was a low coping surrounding a little area of higher ground with a small fountain. He skirted the edge of it, staying low, and almost ran right into the man who stepped suddenly out of a stand of trees.

It was hard to tell who was more surprised. The vigil must have been standing silently in the cover of the trees, watching the clearing, or Khat would have heard him. City-bred, the vigil hadn't heard him moving quietly along the grass verge.

The vigil had a rifle but was too close to use it. Khat saw the barrel swinging toward his head, ducked under it, and tackled. They hit the ground hard, the krismen on top. The vigil still managed to let out a yell. Khat rolled off him, heard running footsteps from all over the garden, cursed, struggled to his feet, and bolted toward the wall. The gun had fallen into the undergrowth somewhere, and he meant to be long gone before the vigil had the chance to recover it.

Khat saw the others clambering over the garden wall in front of him and dodged behind a tree. Three of them, one with a lamp and two with rifles . . .

Then the sand-colored bark about a foot above his head exploded.

He ducked, not realizing what it was, then saw another vigil standing on the higher ground of the little clearing, pointing the long gleaming rifle barrel right at him. Khat froze involuntarily, thinking, *I'm dead.* He was silhouetted against the tree, and the rifle had at least nineteen more shots, depending on how tight the gum seal on the reservoir was. At this distance it was a wonder the man had missed the first time.

The three who had just climbed the wall crashed through the brush and surrounded him. The other two rifles were aimed at him, but strangely enough, nobody was shooting yet. At this close range he would be able to hear the puffs of released air when the guns fired. The one he had tangled with earlier came staggering up from the other direction, cutting off any possibility of escape. One of them lifted the lamp, and Khat winced away from the sudden light.

For the first time he got a good look at them, and his eyes narrowed. These weren't tier vigils; they were Imperial lictors.

"That's him," one of them said. It was a very earnest subcaptain who looked like a young version of Sagai.

They didn't want to shoot him, Khat realized. This was an unusual and not terribly reassuring turn of events. Stepping away from the tree, he said, "Are you sure?"

A couple of them looked startled, probably at the fact that he could talk. He took another step away from the tree, but the one with the lamp shifted to keep him in the circle of light.

The subcaptain was watching him carefully. He said, "You're right, we were ordered to bring you in alive, but Dtrae there can cripple you at this range."

"Cripple" was not a nice word. Khat looked at the indicated lictor, who was carefully sighting down his rifle barrel and did not look nervous.

"Stand still," the subcaptain said, "and put your hands behind your head."

If it was a choice between that and a shattered kneecap . . . Khat looked around one more time. The lictors had tightened the circle around him, and there was still no way out. And this subcaptain was patient, and by no means stupid. He put his hands behind his head.

In moments they were all around him, herding him out into the clearing, dragging his robe off and searching him just as thoroughly as the Trade Inspectors had, if less roughly. They seemed surprised when they found that the only weapon he had was his knife. *What were they expecting, a firepowder bomb?* he wondered.

With rifles still pointed at him they tied his hands behind his back, and he wished he had taken the bullet, but it was too late to balk now. They took him across the park to a gate in the opposite wall, more lictors joining them along the way. When they reached the gate another group came up, and they had Gandin.

The young Warder had fought. The skin around one of his eyes was red and swelling, and the back of his head was bloody. His hands were tied with white cords tipped with red, instead of the ordinary brown cord they had used on Khat. It was something done for Patrician prisoners, a sign of status and a badge of disgrace all in one. The lictors had taken the young Warder's veil, too, which wasn't a good sign either. Despite the possible repercussions, Khat was almost glad Gandin had been caught too; it was what he deserved for letting the lictors follow him.

There were at least thirty of them now. The passage the gate opened into was a wide stone walkway, bare of cover and distractions. Khat tried to work his way over to Gandin and got a poke in the back from a rifle barrel. The young Warder flashed a look in his direction, rueful and angry all at the same time, and got a poke in the back as well.

They were going toward the palace.

They took a new route, avoiding the processional avenue that Khat had gone down with Elen and Gandin days ago, and using instead a narrow alley lined with short flowering trees. The great palace towered over them in the darkness, its hundreds of lamps glowing from windows and terraces.

The alley curved to follow the rounded wall of the palace's first level, and Khat noted the path was slanting downwards. Their way drew closer to the immense structure, so that soon the brilliant limestone facing of the first level wall stretched up above them. They were roughly at the opposite side of the palace from the main entrance, near the face that was turned toward the outer edge of the tier. *A back way in,* Khat thought. Naturally they wouldn't want to drag prisoners in through the front hall.

They came to a little stone-flagged court with an archway in one wall that led back through the gray stone of the foundation level and into the palace. It was guarded by an iron-mesh gate and about twenty well-armed lictors.

They stopped while the gate was unlocked, and Gandin, whose curiosity was overcoming his stoicism, said, "Where are—"

The lictor behind him smacked him in the back with his rifle butt, hard enough to stagger the young Warder. Khat took an instinctive step toward him and ducked to avoid a blow to the head.

"Enough." The subcaptain's voice stopped everyone in their tracks. "That's enough," he said again.

The gate was open, and he led the way through. The lictor behind

Khat gave him a push to get him started, but with his hand, not the rifle. *They're nervous,* Khat thought. *Gandin must be right about the fighting between the Heir and the Elector.* Why else would Imperial lictors be uneasy about entering the palace? *I wonder which side I'm supposed to be on . . .*

Inside was a long corridor with an arched ceiling, all of plain gray building stone, lit by oil lamps in frequent wall niches. Openings led off into branching corridors, and the air was hot and still.

Khat felt a muscle jump in his cheek; it was like being taken into the Trade Inspectors' prison again. Fortunately the place smelled dry and clean, not like the prison at all.

The passage opened into a circular chamber, the hub of several corridors. The floor was a patterned mosaic of palm flowers and suns. Two Patricians stepped out of one of the corridors, as if they had been waiting for the lictors and their prisoners to arrive.

Khat recognized the Heir immediately. She wore jade-colored robes with dark blue scarves flowing like unbound hair from her jeweled cap. The man with her was veiled so heavily he could have been anyone. He wore a long headcloth, layers of veils, and robe piled on robe, all of different colors, red, dark green, brown. It was impossible to even guess who he was. It could have been Sonet Riathen, Khat decided, but somehow he doubted it. The man wasn't nearly tall enough to be Aristai Constans, and besides, Khat had never seen the Mad Warder bother with even a brief veil.

The lictor behind him kicked the back of his knee, and Khat hit the ground hard, barely managing not to fall on his face. He heard Gandin's angry exclamation and knew he must have gotten similar treatment. It was a brutal and effective way to make sure you kneeled for your betters. The lictor jerked him upright with a handful of his shirt, and Khat looked up at their captors.

The Heir folded her arms and studied them both, narrowing her dark eyes. Jade was the gem of choice today; she wore ropes of it around her neck and waist, dangling almost to the floor with beads and bangles, some that might be Ancient work though it was hard to tell at this distance and in this light. Khat hoped Gandin, who was a Patrician and would have no innate instinct of survival in these circumstances, had the sense to keep his mouth shut.

The Heir met Gandin's angry gaze, and said, "You're one of Riathen's Warders."

Gandin said, "Great Lady, what does this mean? What have I done?"

His voice was outwardly respectful, but Khat heard the you-have-no-right-to-do-this-to-me undertone and wondered how the Heir would react to it. The stone floor was hurting his knees, but he knew better than to try to shift around.

"You? You've done nothing." Her smile was almost kind. "You are merely in the wrong place at the wrong time. What has Master Riathen told you about the relics he was searching for? Careful, I know he has all three in his possession now."

"He hasn't told me anything." Gandin threw a quick glance at Khat. "I thought Aristai Constans had stolen them."

The Heir was terribly self-possessed for a woman whose Imperial father had tried to kill her, who was supposedly in danger of losing not only her claim on the Electorate but her life as well. *When Riathen asked for her support she pretended to be hardly interested in the relics at all, and now that's all she seems to want.* Khat looked at the veiled attendant standing next to her and wondered again who it could be. The man wore so many layers of robes you couldn't even see the rise and fall of his breath.

The Heir said, "Constans has other concerns at the moment." She glanced at the veiled man beside her and asked, "Does he know anything of value?"

There was something more than odd about that muffled figure. Khat's attention had been mostly for the Heir when the two had entered the chamber, but now, from this lower vantage point . . . The man's many robes were dragging the ground, and they didn't flow or drape as if there were legs and feet beneath them. Now the veiled form turned toward Gandin, and the young Warder started, rocking back against the lictor behind him. The boy twisted his head away, as if trying to shake something off, then suddenly cried out. He jerked out of the lictor's hold in a desperate effort and fell, his gasp for breath escalating into a scream.

Khat had flinched at the first pain-choked cry. The sounds that were being torn out of the young man's throat were mindless. Gandin was writhing on the floor, helplessly contorting in pain. Khat looked at the Heir: one perfect brow had risen, but her expression hadn't changed.

It went on until Khat thought the boy would surely die. Finally

Gandin went limp, still faintly moaning, his voice rough and raw, as if his throat had been lacerated by the force of his screams.

The veiled man said, "Nothing of importance." His voice was colorless, without accent. He could have been of any tier in Charisat or any city of the Fringe. Khat was good with voices—it was a skill you had to develop when some of the people you did business with covered their faces—but this voice told him nothing.

The Heir nodded. "Take him to the cells," she told the lictors. "Put him in one alone. I don't want him talking to the others."

Khat felt a little relief watching the lictors haul the younger man up off the floor. Presumably that meant Gandin would be able to talk sometime in the near future. If his soul had been ripped out by the roots it couldn't have sounded worse. Then he noticed the Heir was looking at him now.

Khat thought, *Oh, no,* and made an instinctive and useless move backward. The lictor behind him caught a handful of his hair and jerked his head up. The Heir said, "And him?"

Khat waited. A bead of sweat trickled down his neck and past his collarbone. The cords were cutting into his wrists, the lictor's grip on his hair was making his back teeth hurt, and the constriction in his chest was from holding his breath. But nothing happened.

The figure stepped, or drifted, a pace closer to him. The robes brushed the ground, but this time Khat was sure no legs moved beneath the fabric. The thing's motion was utterly inhuman. For an instant he could sense its intense concentration on him, feel it like he could feel a violent Low Season storm approaching across the Waste. Then there was nothing, only the silent room and his own pounding heart.

In that same colorless voice, the figure said, "Kill him."

Nobody moved. In his peripheral vision, Khat could just see the young subcaptain. He was watching the Heir, waiting for her order. Slowly, she said, "I don't think so. Not yet."

The swath of veiling turned to regard her. It said, "If you don't take my advice, I cannot help you."

The Heir's smile was ironic. "Do you want to help me?"

The robes stirred around the figure, but no breeze moved the heavy air in the chamber. The lighter veils lifted, borne up by some undetectable current. Khat felt a cold, sick chill settle in the pit of his stomach. His eyes traveled up the robed figure and saw the veiled head pointed down at him again. It said, "He's of no importance. Kill him."

"Not yet," the Heir said again. "You told me he found the fortune-teller's house, that he took the seal from the Academia for Riathen, and you say he knows nothing of importance?"

Khat had the distinct impression that it didn't like her calling it a liar. The air in the thing's vicinity was suddenly heavier, and it was an effort to take a full breath. Khat knew it wasn't just his fear; the lictors were uneasy, the lamplight flickering on their rifle barrels as they shifted uncertainly. The Heir alone was unmoved, facing the veiled creature as if she wanted the confrontation, as if she was eager to test her hold over it. But it only said, "Remember our bargain," and turned away, moving toward one of the corridors. It remembered to make the skirts of the robes lift when it "walked," but there was something clockworklike about the motion; its body still didn't move like a man's.

The Heir let out her breath and smiled. She nodded to the lictors. "Take him upstairs."

Four watchful lictors took Khat up into the palace. They seemed to be taking back ways, since the staircases and halls they traveled weren't nearly so grand or so well lit as the ones he had seen before. There were armed vigils and lictors everywhere, guarding doors, gathered in corridors, talking in low voices, and peering suspiciously at each other.

Finally they passed through a knot of lictors and into a place he recognized: the anterooms to the Heir's quarters.

They passed through a few connecting chambers, then into a smaller room. Before he could look around one of the lictors tripped him. He fell heavily, the breath knocked out of him, and the lictor's knee came down hard on the small of his back. He tried to twist around and felt a sharp edge rest against the big vein in his wrist. Getting the unequivocal message, he forced himself to relax.

The cords fell away from his wrists, and the lictor stood up. Khat rolled over, bracing for a kick to his ribs or groin, and snarled at the men looking down at him.

Two of them exchanged a disgusted glance; the others merely looked startled. Khat pushed himself back, trying to get a little more room to fight in if they attacked, but they went out through the door behind them, the last one pulling the heavy curtain shut.

They had left him alone. He looked around, saw there was one other door, and leaned down to peer under the curtain. There were booted feet on the other side, at least two sets, and probably more out of sight. He sat up, taking stock of the place and wondering what was next.

It didn't look like a place where prisoners were kept or executions conducted. It was an interior room, without any handy windows to climb out. Woven rugs with a waterbird design meant to simulate Ancient work allowed only a few glimpses of the creamy marble floor. There was a low table of cedar, with inlaid gold and lapis banding its legs, a large couch piled with thick cotton pads and silk cushions, and wall niches holding fragrant candles and onyx vessels filled with dried flower petals. Tiny holes in the sculpted marble ceiling let in a draft that was almost cool. Fan-driven air from outside, probably, that flowed through water-cooled shafts.

A quick search revealed nothing that could be used as a weapon except in the blunt-club sense. There was certainly nothing sharp-edged that he could hide on himself somewhere for future use. A delicate table of gold-inlaid ebony beside the couch held little porcelain jars of unguents, with one that smelled so strongly of myrrh that it made him sneeze, but next to it was a glass decanter of water and a silver tray piled with grapes. He hadn't noticed until this moment how thirsty he was.

The Heir wanted to find out what he knew, and since her veiled friend couldn't find out the hard way, he had an idea how she meant to go about it. It didn't imply much respect for his intelligence, but that was undoubtedly for the best. This wait was probably supposed to help soften him up by giving him time to terrify himself with speculations about his fate.

Khat stretched out on the couch, tucked a silken pillow behind his head, and proceeded to eat the grapes. The cuts across his back were stinging somewhat, the scabs having pulled open during his various struggles tonight. Injuries new and old were aching from the tension in his muscles, but it was nothing to how he would have felt if that creature had torn open his mind the way it had Gandin's. He couldn't think why it hadn't been able to do the same to him, unless it had used up all its strength or power or whatever on the young Warder; it was plain that Gandin had tried to fight it. Or it was the same reason Elen and the other Warders couldn't soul-read him.

He wondered if Elen was a prisoner here, if they had done that to her . . . There was no way to know.

He wondered too if the Heir realized he knew what her companion was, if it had told her not only that it had seen him but that he had seen it three times, or at least felt it once and seen it twice. Outside poor dead Radu's house, and again on the Academia grounds and in the Porta Major. At least now he knew why it had been following him: Riathen had told the Heir he would be the one searching for the relics. But Khat had read the pertinent sections of Riathen's Ancient text, and perhaps the creature's origin was more obvious to him because of that.

Perhaps she didn't know that her companion was an Inhabitant of the West. Perhaps she had never seen it without its concealing robes and veils, when it wasn't pretending to be human.

But Khat remembered the look in her eyes when she challenged the thing, the glint of mixed excitement and fear, and decided she knew exactly what it was that aided her.

Khat frowned at the ornate ceiling. He had to stay alive long enough to tell somebody. He didn't know whom yet, but somebody had to know that the Heir to the Elector's throne kept company with a legendary monster. How it had gotten here was still a mystery, but it was all too easy to guess why it had come: to open the Western Doors and let the others in.

If he could just find Elen . . . She probably wouldn't have any better idea what to do about it than he did, but he could hope. And at least then it would be her problem too and not just his.

The curtains on the first door were pushed open, and the Heir stepped through. With her was a man dressed as an Imperial lictor who looked less like one than Khat did.

Lictors came from the lower houses of Patrician families; this man's pale skin looked as if it had never been touched by the sun, and there was something about the bluntness of his features that suggested the Last Sea coast. He was big, more than a head taller than the Heir, who wasn't a short woman, and he was bulky with muscle, his arms and shoulders straining the seams of his robe. His head was shaved, and the outer flesh of his ears had been trimmed back to featureless lumps, as if they had been eaten away by some disease. His eyes were light blue and dull and maybe a little mad. He made the hackles on the back of Khat's neck rise.

The guard took a step toward him, and Khat slipped off the couch, going to his knees at the Heir's feet.

She touched his face. Her fingernails were long, the edges tipped with gilt to harden and sharpen them. He hated that. She said, "You really are a pretty creature. I regret causing you any harm."

Khat hoped she didn't expect to be thanked for the compliment, because he really didn't think he could manage it, even to save his life. Earnestly, he said, "I'll tell you anything you want to know."

"Really?" She stepped around him and sank down on the couch, propping herself up on one elbow and very much at ease. "That would be very helpful." She patted the edge of the couch in invitation.

He leaned against the cushions, so close to her he could feel her body heat. "But I don't think I know very much."

"We'll see." She touched his hair, as if intrigued by the texture, and asked, "What has Sonet Riathen told you about all this?"

Careful not to be too ingenuous, he kept his eyes on her face, which was really worth looking at if you could only ignore the character behind it. "He said he would kill me if I told anyone about finding the relics. Is he here?"

"No. But I know where he is. When the time is right, I'll remove him." Her fingers were moving through his hair, and this bit of intelligence was so distracting that it took conscious effort to lean his head into the caress and make it look natural. Gandin had said Riathen was under arrest at the palace. But perhaps Gandin only thought so because that was where the other Warders in his household had been taken. *Well, fine,* Khat thought. Now he had to worry again about where the Master Warder was and what he was doing. The Heir asked, "But did Riathen tell you what the relics were for?"

The option to pretend ignorance had been closed when the Master Warder had first brought him here to show off his abilities, but she didn't know he had read the key sections of the Survivor text. He wondered how much she did know. She had probably been the one to arrange the original theft of the relics, and the thieves had been foolish enough to cheat her and disperse the collection on the Silent Market. He said, "They may be pieces of an arcane engine."

"I see. And what were you doing near Riathen's house with Gandin Riat?"

Khat wondered if he dared mention Elen. The chances were good that she was under arrest here somewhere, but he doubted it would help much to have the Heir's attention drawn to her. No, better not. But if the Inhabitant had really read Gandin's soul there was no point in concocting a story. He said, "I wanted to find out what Riathen was doing with the relics. I thought there might be something in it for me." That was enough of the truth not to contradict anything she had learned from the young Warder.

She said, "I appreciate your honesty."

Khat had a bad moment, wondering if she had seen through him so easily, but her hand had moved down to the back of his neck, urging him nearer.

He obediently moved closer, leaning against her knees now, and the feel of a firm thigh beneath the cool silk of her kaftan did terrible things to his concentration. His eyes kept straying to the guard who had accompanied her, who was still a hulking presence beside the door. The Heir noticed his preoccupation and smiled at the glowering figure. "That is Saret," she explained. "He comes from one of the farthest islands of the Last Sea, where their customs are as alien to the Fringe Cities as . . . as you are." Her hand moved lower, down his chest and stomach to explore the raised line of his pouch lip.

Khat's response was tinged with the memory of the fever he had given himself by hiding the little relic there, and he hoped she wouldn't be too adventurous. He said, "He's very . . . distracting."

She hesitated, and then decided to humor him. "Wait outside, Saret."

It wasn't hard to figure out what she wanted. Traditional krismen wisdom on the subject held that leaving marks was rude, but this was an opinion she evidently didn't share. When her long nails tore open one of the scabs on his back he almost bit her with a strength that would have dealt her a permanent scar. She was also disappointed that his anatomy wasn't more unusual, but that was hardly his fault.

Afterwards it was easy to pretend to fall asleep. He was exhausted and still not entirely recovered from the fever, but the thought that she might have everything she wanted from him now and that there was nothing to stop her from having him killed was more than enough to keep him wide awake.

In time he felt her leave the couch, and heard the rustle of silk as she slipped her kaftan over her head and stepped out through the curtain of one of the doorways. He rolled off the couch, found his clothes, and dressed hurriedly and quietly. There would still be guards towards the front of the suite, but he lifted the edge of the curtain on the other door and saw that the lictors who had been there earlier had diplomatically retreated.

Khat stepped through the curtain into another opulent little anteroom, this one with three doors in the far wall. He wasn't sure what he was looking for, other than a way out or a weapon. He just had to keep moving while he had even this limited freedom.

Khat heard the low murmur of voices then, and waited, listening. One of the voices was the Heir's, but the other was familiar as well.

He stepped closer to the middle doorway. The voice was Kythen Seul's.

"She went to Rasan, and the fool told her everything—"

"Did you kill him?" the Heir interrupted.

Khat flattened himself against the wall and tweaked the edge of the door curtain back, just a hairsbreadth. It was the room where Sonet Riathen had had his interview with the Heir days ago, before everyone's life was turned upside down. Kythen Seul stood with his back to the big cedar table, the Heir facing him. The windows behind them showed the lamplit court below, and the gauze drapes were stirring in the warm breeze. Oddly, Seul was dressed as if he had just returned from the Waste, in dun-colored robes kilted up to reveal dusty boots. Presumably his painrod was hidden under his mantle somewhere, to keep anyone from knowing him for a Warder.

"No, your so-useful 'friend' got to him first. But yes, I would have done it. I would have killed a High Justice of the Trade Inspectors for you, killed him as if he were no more than a lower-tier street rat—"

"And did you kill her?" the Heir interrupted again, which Khat thought was just as well. It had been shaping up into quite a self-indulgent little speech.

Elen had suspected a traitor in Riathen's household, and here he was. Khat should have known it was Seul, who had every opportunity to arrange the pirate ambush in the Waste, who had been so conveniently left for dead so he could return to Charisat for help. And who had perhaps bribed the pirates with the mysterious painrods that Riathen had assumed came from Constans? The Survivor text had said that the knowledge to make painrods had come from the Inhabitants of the West. Seul was evidently on good terms with the Heir, who had the willing if not cheerful assistance of an Inhabitant.

Seul hesitated. "She's with Riathen. I've convinced him that she's pressed her power too far and gone mad."

Khat realized with a start that Seul was talking about Elen. *And that son of an Eighth Tier whore was actually thinking of killing her.* He had told Elen to find out about the High Justice, and she must have discovered more than either of them had bargained on. The Heir must have used the High Justice to find the relics in the dispersed collection for her, using whatever tidbits of information Seul managed to get out of Riathen to help the Justice along. And using the Inhabitant too, of course, to follow them, to kill Radu, to chase them through the Academia. Or perhaps that had been its own idea. But when the High Justice was no longer needed she had had her creature kill him.

The Heir touched Seul's face. "You should have killed her."

"There was no need. She can't hurt us now. You've moved against the Elector; it's too late for anything to stop us."

Khat wondered what the Heir thought of that "us" business. Though Seul was probably right; there was no way to stop them now, and her desire to kill Elen was only a reflex action. But the Heir only asked, "They've left the city already?"

"Yes, and he's expecting me to join him again there tonight."

"Well enough. Our friend is becoming impatient. He knows he's served us well, and he wants us to fulfill our part of the bargain and surrender the relics to him. It would be a mistake to put him off any longer."

"Then I should let Riathen go ahead with this?" Seul sounded less certain. "Our 'friend' is dangerous. He could turn on us at any moment."

Khat stepped back from the curtain. The Master Warder was further along in his plans than he had thought. Riathen must already be out at the Remnant. He had heard enough.

So had someone else. Before he could take another step the curtain was yanked violently aside, and he found himself facing the Heir's ugly guard Saret. Ducking back out of reach, Khat grabbed a little alabaster table and slung it at him. The man threw up his arms to shield his head and staggered backward, bellowing wordlessly.

Khat bolted for the nearest door, slammed aside the curtain, and slid to a halt at the sight of half a dozen lictors running toward him.

Guns were pointing at him, so he stayed where he was, and two of them hauled him back into the anteroom. Saret was nursing a bloody nose and looked utterly enraged. Seul and the Heir had come into the room, following the commotion, and the look on Seul's face was almost worth it. "What is he doing here?" the Warder demanded.

The Heir didn't appear particularly put out by either Khat's escape attempt or his eavesdropping. She was watching Seul, as if more interested in his reaction. "He was found near Riathen's house, with one of his Warders. He doesn't know anything of value."

"If he told you that, he's lying," Seul said, glaring at Khat. "Elen told him everything. She was completely taken in by him."

"She was completely taken in by you," Khat said. He could have added to that, but one of the lictors holding him twisted his arm a little more firmly behind his back, and he decided against it.

"She'll thank me when this is over," Seul said, more stung than Khat would've thought. "She'll thank me for her power."

The Heir glanced quickly at him, and if Seul had seen the look in her eyes he might not have been so confident. To stir more trouble, Khat said, "She'll call you a lying bastard traitor and—"

"That's enough." The Heir's voice cut through Seul's angry reply. Pursing her lips thoughtfully, she added, "There's really no need to keep him alive now." She told the lictors, "Take him downstairs to the execution area. I'll come down if I have a moment."

They were already hauling him toward the door. Khat had known this was coming since the lictors had caught him on the First Tier, but that didn't make hearing it any easier. He braced his feet to slow them down, and shouted at her, "I've had better lays in Seventh Tier alleys!" A lictor punched him in the stomach, doubling him over, and he didn't get to see her reaction.

Two lictors and the Heir's private guard took him down several levels, maybe as far down as the belowground entrance where he and Gandin had been brought in. All Khat knew was that for the past few turns of stair and corridor, he had seen no one. The lictors hadn't bothered to speak to him, though they had been pretty free with their speculative comments to each other. Saret hadn't spoken either, and Khat was beginning to think the man didn't have the ability, though it was obvious he could understand well enough.

They came to a doorway barred with a silver-chased panel, and one of the lictors fumbled for a key to unlock it. Khat felt a lump settle into the pit of his stomach. This was it, and he didn't see any way out.

Inside was a sizable room, bare of furniture, lit by a dozen or so bronze lamps, each in a niche high up on the gray-veined marble walls. In the center of the polished stone floor was a pool, round and not much more than twenty feet wide, surrounded by a rim of black tile. The high-ceilinged chamber was round too, except the far end had a section cut out of it for a pillared gallery. Its floor was more than ten feet above the floor of the room, and it seemed to be designed to give a good view of whatever was going on in the pool. The gallery was empty at the moment, and there was no way up to it from this side, so there must be a door back up behind it somewhere. If there was, it was the only other way out.

One of the lictors pushed Khat further into the room. He heard the door close, and the hair on his arms stood straight up. He knew what the pool was for. Patricians were usually strangled with silk, citizens were shot, noncitizens were hanged. Drowning was for foreigners and the worst sort of lower-tier criminals.

The lictors were pushing him forward. Khat got one glance over his shoulder and saw Saret stripping off his robe, leaving himself clad in trousers and a wide leather belt. Now he knew who the executioner was. He planted his feet, but the shove from behind came too quickly, and he went over the side into the pool.

The water was unexpectedly cold, as if it came straight from Charisat's artesian spring and was never warmed by passing through miles of pipes and cisterns. Some Patricians would pay any amount of minted gold for water this cool, and the Heir was wasting it by drowning people in it.

Khat went for the opposite side of the pool, thrashing toward it without bothering to find footing on the bottom. Behind him he heard a splash and saw the displaced water slop out onto the tiles, and knew he wasn't going to make it. He twisted around, throwing a punch, and caught the unprepared Saret just above the jaw. The man jerked his head back with a snarl of angry outrage, as if the idea of resistance had never occurred to him.

The guard avoided the next blow that would have smashed his already injured nose and surged forward with astonishing quickness. Khat threw himself backward. The water dragged at his clothes, and he only managed half the distance he needed; the guard caught him around the waist and pulled him under.

Khat's back bumped against the bottom of the pool. Saret kept his face well twisted away, preventing Khat from going for his eyes or throat. He clawed at the back of the guard's head, but there was nothing on the shaven scalp he could get a grip on. He had a sudden realization how the man had lost the outer flesh of his ears; if there had been anything left he would have torn it off in that moment. He had managed to get one breath before going under and had no idea how long it would last. Logic and the pressure building in his lungs and behind his eyes said not long at all.

The struggling was lifting them off the bottom, giving Khat a little more freedom of movement. Then Saret tried to trap Khat's legs between his, stupidly leaving himself vulnerable, and Khat jerked his knee up. The guard twisted away from him, but Khat caught a blow to the stomach that knocked the last of his air out.

He hit the surface, coughing up water and choking. He was near the edge and grabbed onto the tiled rim to support himself. His eyes stung, and the water had burned a trail through his nose and throat and down into his lungs. He could try to drag himself out of the pool, but there was no way he could move quickly enough to avoid the lictors waiting to throw him back in.

Saret had broken the surface about half the pool's width away, and now spit out some water and smiled at him. Khat showed teeth back at him and had the feeling the man understood the gesture perfectly.

The two lictors had been joined by a man wearing the gilded robes and gold skullcap of a palace steward. He looked faintly disapproving, but not enough to give Khat any hope.

Clearing his throat, the steward announced to the room at large, "The Great Lady has decided she will be unable to attend. She says to finish him."

"If you can," one of the lictors added. His companion laughed and asked him if he wanted to place a wager on the outcome.

Oh, fine, Khat thought, sagging against the pool's edge. That first round Saret had only been playing with him. *And you would think she could at least bother to come down here and watch me be murdered.* He hated to think how she disposed of the prisoners she didn't sleep with.

Saret came toward him again, stalking him through the chest-deep water. The guard was somewhat red-faced from anger at the two lictors, who were still making loud speculations on the outcome. The steward evidently decided he had discharged his duty and beat a hasty retreat, and one of the lictors carefully locked the door after him, still laughing with his companion.

Khat slid away along the side of the pool. One advantage the round contour gave him was that he couldn't be cornered. The guard dived toward him, and Khat pushed off from the side and flung himself out of reach.

Saret repeated this maneuver a few times, trying for him again and barely missing, grinning all the while. Khat shook his dripping hair back out of his face; he felt like he had lead weights tied to his feet and knew the game couldn't go on much longer. His opponent was overconfident; that was one point in his favor. *Of course,* he thought, avoiding a grab by such a bare margin he felt the man's blunt fingers scrape his ribs, *he has every reason to be overconfident.*

The lictors had been calling out advice and suggestions the entire time, which Khat was no longer bothering to listen to. But now one of them called out something that made Saret jerk around and glare back up at them. Khat took the opening without hesitation.

In an instant he was on the bigger man, arm around his throat, trying to get the leverage to crush his windpipe. The guard lifted his feet, taking them both under water, which Khat had expected. Then the man rolled over forward, ending up on top and making Khat lose his grip, which he hadn't expected at all. Before he could thrash away the guard was standing, feet braced on the bottom of the pool, with one arm wrapped around Khat's waist and the other on the back of his neck.

Khat couldn't break that grip, couldn't reach Saret's face, or anything vital. His head was pounding, his lungs at the bursting point. A black wave came in at the edges of his vision as he clawed at the arms holding him, to no effect.

Then suddenly his head broke the surface. Khat thrashed around helplessly. Blindly he found the side of the pool and collapsed on it, letting it support him and coughing up far too much water. Limp and helpless and barely hanging on to the slippery tiles, he drew in a long shuddering breath. He didn't care if the guard came at him again; for this blessed moment he had air.

Gradually the ominous quiet penetrated. No commentary from the lictors, no splashing from his executioner. Khat lifted his head. He looked behind him first, to see if Saret was waiting for him, and saw the man floating facedown, his arms trailing limply, supported only by the water.

He frowned, trying to connect it with his last clear memory, and finally shook his head. He couldn't have done it. He saw the two lictors sprawled on the floor near the door, one still as death, the other making a feeble attempt to move. It was then he noticed Shiskan son Karadon, sitting on her heels beside the pool not five feet away from him.

She was wearing a man's loose shirt and pants, all in black, with a mantle over it. Her sleeves were wet up to the shoulders, but the rest of her seemed dry enough. Her painrod was hanging from her belt, but he could see she had recently put it to good use. She was frowning a little, watching him with a detached concern.

Khat said, "Thank you," and winced. His voice was a weak croak.

She shrugged one shoulder, as if it wasn't worth mentioning, and said, "Constans wants you to come and talk to him. He says it's the least you can do."

Khat considered the request. With Riathen and Seul, the supposedly sane Warders, bent on letting the Inhabitants back into the world, maybe it was time to listen to what the mad Warders had to say. He said, "He's right."

Chapter Seventeen

SHISKAN SON KARADON led Khat to a passage below the execution room, reached by a narrow stair behind an unobtrusive little door in the corridor. At first it was pitch dark, and Shiskan found her way unerringly while he guided himself with one hand on the rough-cut stone of the wall. This was unnerving, but he could tell they were heading away from the palace, toward the outer wall. Finally he detected a graying of the velvet blackness at the end of the passage, and not much later the curved ceiling turned into a stone lattice, with plants and vines twisting through it and allowing an occasional glimpse of the starry sky. They were coming out into one of the garden squares on the inner tierward side of the palace.

Shiskan paused to unlock an iron gate, and the heavy, sweet fragrance of flowering plants and newly watered foliage drifted in on the warm air. The lock gave way, and she pushed the gate open a little and turned to face him. She said, "Constans is in the Citadel of the Winds, with the Elector."

"I thought the Elector was supposed to be holding part of the palace," Khat said. His voice was still hoarse from the near-drowning, and hard to recognize as his own.

"So does everyone else." She glanced back down the passage, not nervously, but with that cool control that was so impenetrable and so annoying. "I have to stay here until sunrise at least. If they don't see any of us, they may suspect he isn't here anymore."

She stood, waiting for him to step out past her and disappear.

Khat found himself reluctant to go, and asked, "Why are you with Constans?"

She didn't seem to find the question odd. "I had Warder talent, and I needed teaching."

"Riathen said he offered to teach you."

Her eyes were dark and serious, despite the irony in her voice. "I've seen how he's 'taught' Elen. She had the potential to be a powerful Warder, but he's kept her where he wants her. Aristai will let me go as far as I can, farther than I should go, probably. Power is everything to us. Whichever Master we follow, whether we let ourselves fall into madness or whether we hold on to sanity by lying to ourselves about our strength, power is everything. Even to Elen."

"You're not mad."

"Not yet." Shiskan pushed the gate open further and stepped out, surveying the lush garden. A fountain bubbled nearby, and the wind stirred leaves, but that was the only sound. "Just go to the Citadel's gate. They'll let you in."

Khat followed, knowing he wasn't going to understand her, no matter how drawn he was to her. "I don't remember saying I'd go there. If they let me in, will they let me out again?"

She glanced at him, one brow raised. "That's a chance everyone takes when they go there. Why should you be any different?"

"I could just leave, too," he said.

"You could."

The least she could have done was acted as if she gave a damn, Khat thought now. He was perched on top of a garden wall, in the deep shadow of an overhanging persimmon tree. Across the wide avenue before him was the gate and front walls of the Citadel of the Winds.

At close range it was still beautiful, even if it had been meant for a prison. Slabs of polished obsidian interlocking in cross and double-cross patterns formed high walls that were slanted back dramatically. Above them the shape of the dome loomed heavy and overpowering in the darkness. The gate was set deep within the sloping wall directly in front of him, a fantastically sculpted edifice of metal with silver bosses and a large rock demon face in the center.

Khat had been hoping that Constans would give in to impatience, and come out. Now not much of the night was left, and Khat had gradually faced the realization that he really was going to have to go in.

His clothes were still damp, though he was no longer leaving a dripping trail on the sand-dusted stone. He had taken a knife from the dead lictor, not that being armed did more than convey a false sense of security. He shifted uneasily and swore under his breath, caught between frustration and self-pity.

The last time his fortune had been truly told, the woman had seen betrayal, of him and by him. He had had the former in plenty, but this was the first time he had really considered the latter.

Sonet Riathen had earned and asked for this betrayal. Gandin Riat was another story. Khat would have helped that young Warder if he could, but he hadn't been competent to get himself out of the Heir's clutches without Shiskan's help; there was simply no way he could free Gandin. But cooperating with Constans would be a betrayal of Elen as well, and it was that he minded. But if he was going to get her free of Riathen and Seul, it was going to be this way. He just wished he knew whether Elen would forgive him for it.

He did have another option. He could walk away.

If the Waste was all that was left of the world after the Inhabitants were done with it again, what did that matter to him? He could survive the Waste, even if stretched out to destroy the Last Sea and all the lowland desert cities. And if what he suspected was true, then the reason the Warders couldn't soul-read him, the reason the Inhabitant hadn't been able to tear his mind open the way it had Gandin's, was because the Mage-Creators of the kris had intended it that way. The Inhabitants were sure to attack the Enclave anyway, but that was none of his concern either.

Khat let out his breath, resigned. *You are just no good at lying to yourself. To everyone else, yes, but not to yourself.* He hopped down off the wall, wiped his sweaty palms off on his damp shirttail, and crossed the avenue.

The sloping walls formed a corridor, the gate set deep within it and stretching up to nearly half their height. It didn't open by itself as he approached, the way gates of similar places in stories always did, when the brainless hero walked up to them to be slaughtered.

Khat banged on the metal panel, and after a short time the right half swung inward. There was no one behind it, which was in keeping with the stories, but the jerkiness of its motion suggested a pulley system, which was only natural on a gate so heavy.

The effort it took to step inside was surprising.

The entrance court was bare of plants or trees, floored with dark tile, with two long shallow reflecting pools framing a wide straight path up to the entrance. Ornamental water notwithstanding, the day's heat would make it a little piece of the Waste, but at night the effect was cool and serene. There was no carving and no paint on the facade, but the way the blocks were set together, and the clean lines and sharp angles of the ribbed projections that ran vertically up the walls, gave it a sere, bleak beauty all its own. Windows covered by stone lattices studded the front, and the door was framed by half a dozen interlocking pointed arches.

Khat sensed movement up on the wall behind him, and the gate began to close. The voice of reason inside his head suggested bolting back out, but he started toward the entrance instead.

The great doors stood open, and he stopped just inside. The entry hall was in the same massive scale as everything else, with a series of hallways leading off from either side. It was lit by too few bronze hanging lamps, bright spots in the dimness, and the draft was almost cool.

At first the entryway was unoccupied; then dark shapes grew out of the shadows, forming into the robed figures of several of Constans's outlaw Warders.

Khat expected to be thrown up against the wall and searched and disarmed, but no one moved. He folded his arms. "So where's the old man?"

There was a brief stirring, maybe of amusement. "This way." One shadow separated from the group and moved up the hall into the darkness ahead.

The place had been lit for Warder eyes, making it dim and secretive. The entry hall opened into a central well, full of the sound of trickling water. Wide stairs curved up around a heavy column of dark stone, and water flowed down it in flickering streams, collecting in a pool at its base. His guide started up the steps, and Khat followed, keeping a distance between them. Khat knew he wasn't as afraid as he should be; he was too numb. *And too stupid,* he thought. *I can't believe you did this.* He shouldn't have come here, but it was too late now.

At this distance, he could see there were thousands of little faces carved into the column, with water running out of their open mouths and eyes. Hard to tell what the artisan had intended in this bad light, but the effect was horrific. The cool air was coming down the shaft as well. There was probably a wind tower arrangement in the dome, drawing the air down inside this column to be cooled by the running water.

They went up past multiple landings, gorgeous dark halls leading off into shadowy depths. There were voices in the distance, some raised in heated discussion.

Finally his guide turned off at a landing and into another hall. Waiting in it, under the pool of light from a lamp stand, were three Imperial lictors with high-ranking chains of office, and two men in the gold robes of court functionaries.

As Khat drew even with them, one of the lictors stepped swiftly forward and grabbed his arm above the elbow. Khat was short on sleep but too nervous to be slow; the man froze when he noticed the knife point just below his chin. The Warder turned back, frowning. Khat got a good look at him for the first time in the glow of the lamp. He was a young man, and veilless, with dark skin and Patrician features, and he didn't look any more insane than anyone else in the corridor. He said, "Let him alone, gentlemen. My master would not be pleased at a brawl in his house."

The lictor pulled away, and Khat let him, stepping back himself and slowly returning his knife to its makeshift sheath. The lictor was an older man, the skin around his eyes lined and gray even in the poor light. His chain of rank proclaimed him an archcommander, the highest rank Khat had ever seen before, if he was reading it correctly. The lictor demanded, "Who is he? Why is he here?"

The Warder said only, "I'm not here to answer your questions," and turned again down the corridor. Khat followed, keeping a wary eye on the other Patricians.

Tall doors opened into a large room, most of which was lost in darkness. Three lamps were suspended from the sculpted ceiling near the room's center, and by their wan light Khat could see a low table, piled with papers and other debris, and bronze cabinets of books back against the right-hand wall. Three large windows studded the far wall, looking down on the flickering lights of the other Patrician manses. In the distance was the tall, glowing column of the palace itself. Each window had a life-sized carving of a rock demon perched above it, the narrow eyes alive with hate, vestigial wings furled and fangs barred, all eerily lifelike under the warm light of the hanging lamps.

Aristai Constans was standing at one of the windows, his dark mantle more threadbare and raglike than ever. The stone claws of the rock demon were gripping the top of the casement over his head, and the wan light struck highlights off the fangs. It was so realistically carved Khat wouldn't have liked to stand beneath it.

Khat's guide had vanished. A breeze moved through the large chamber, making the lamps flicker, stirring papers and dust. Small sounds seemed magnified, as if this wasn't a chamber in a Patrician palace but some huge subsurface cavern. Somebody had to break the silence. Khat said, "I'm here. Are you happy now?"

Constans turned toward him. "It's always gratifying to have a vision fulfilled, but I wouldn't describe myself as happy, no."

His voice was amused, but Khat couldn't read his expression in the half-light. Khat said, "Why did you send her after me?"

"Why did you come here when I asked?" Constans countered.

You mean, why did I come here and put myself completely at your mercy? Khat thought. He said, "All along, you were trying to stop Riathen. That's why you wanted the book."

"I could've wanted it to open the Doors of the West myself."

Khat's mouth was dry, but he had considered that possibility too, while still outside the Citadel. He said, "Why, when all you had to do was wait?"

Constans didn't comment. He stepped forward, under the somewhat brighter illumination of the lamp that hung over the table. Khat had a brief battle with an impulse to back away, though there was still a good fifteen feet between them. Constans was folding a square of paper back into a leather message case. Khat wondered if he had been reading it by starlight. The Warder said, "You've seen the Inhabitant?"

Reminded, Khat glanced at the row of windows, open to the night and the hot breeze.

"No, it can't come here. At least for the moment."

That was as good a reason as any to hold this little meeting on Constans's own terms. Khat answered, "In a fortune-teller's house, at the Academia, at the palace." He hesitated. "And out in the Waste that night, there was an air spirit. Was that it?"

"It was, acting as the Heir's spy." Constans tossed the letter case onto the low table. "Riathen had already shown her the crystalline plaque, hoping to convince her to support him in his search."

The letter case fell among the scatter of papers, landing near a battered iron brazier and a bowl filled with white chips and ash. Seeing it, Khat took an involuntary step backward. *You forgot about that, didn't you,* he told himself. It was easy to imagine what would happen if Constans decided he didn't need his help after all.

Either Constans could soul-read him despite the fact that Khat was kris, or the Warder was just very good at reading faces. "That?" Constans said, one eyebrow arching. "It's a well-kept secret, but the bones that give the very best result in reading the future are the bones of Warders." He smiled. "I never use anything else."

"Oh." *That's so reassuring,* Khat thought, but his heart wasn't pounding against his chest quite so hard now. Considering the source, it was just odd enough to be true. Constans turned away from the table, pacing idly into the dimness, and Khat couldn't tell if he was being given a moment to calm himself or if the old Warder simply felt no sense of urgency. *Well, I do,* Khat thought. He asked, "How long did you know about the Inhabitant?"

He thought Constans wouldn't answer, but when he did his voice sounded oddly matter-of-fact. "Since the Heir first discovered it, roughly two years ago. I felt its presence growing closer many years before that, but I didn't understand what it was that I sensed approaching." Constans spoke as if they had all the time in the world. "The details on how she made her little trader's bargain with it are unclear, but make one she did. It was weak then, and needed her help. Riathen always said she would have made a superlative Warder. But that's Riathen." He paused, not looking back at Khat. "He has everything he needs now, doesn't he?"

Khat hesitated. "Yes."

"For what it's worth," Constans said slowly, "he doesn't realize he's her pawn. He's blinded by sheer greed. Greed for knowledge, for ephemeral power. So is Kythen Seul, for that matter. I detect a theme, don't you?"

Khat didn't care about their motives. He took tight control of his temper, and asked, "Why didn't you tell Riathen?"

"About Seul? I'd given up on rational discussion by the time he became involved. Do you really think Sonet Riathen would have believed me?"

That was a point, much as Khat would have liked to see all this as Constans's fault. He didn't reply.

Constans was silent again for a time, then said, "From the beginning the Heir used the Inhabitant for her own ends. At first as an invisible, undetectable spy among the Patricians at Court. Her defenses against soul-reading are excellent—as are the Elector's; I suppose it's a family trait—so no one realized what she was about. As the creature grew stronger she used it to eliminate her enemies and rivals. We had to send her half-sisters and brother out of the city."

Khat remembered Riathen saying that the Elector's children by his second wife had been sent away. "Then it grew strong enough to make demands on her," Constans continued, pacing again. "She had the relics stolen at its insistence. Then, not knowing who their Patrician employer was, the thieves betrayed her and sold the relics away, necessitating vengeance on her part. The Inhabitant hadn't quite the strength yet to force her to fulfill her part of the bargain, but she must have felt some danger, because she recruited Kythen Seul to help her control it. But within the past ten days its strength has increased a hundredfold. It has even been able to masquerade as human now, for short periods of time."

"I know." Khat shifted uneasily. The increase in strength was evident, even from his short acquaintance with the creature. At Radu's house it hadn't been able to follow them when they ran from it, but a day later at the Academia it had stalked them with ease. And at the palace . . . He asked, "Does she understand what it is?"

"She simply doesn't realize the danger." Constans paused by the center window to lean on the casement, looking toward the palace lights. "She's never seen anything more powerful than a Warder, so she thinks the Warders will be able to control the Inhabitants. She thinks Seul is controlling this one, you see, which is a ludicrous notion. But it allows her—and him—to think so."

Behind Khat there was a hollow bang. He almost jumped out of his skin, spinning around to see the door being thrown open. A man in the court robes and brief veil of a high-ranking Patrician was striding forward into the glow of lamplight, followed by the lictor archcommander who had tried to stop Khat in the corridor, and a dark-robed Warder. The Patrician was saying, "I for one have had enough of waiting. What do you mean to do, Constans?"

Constans came back to the table, regarding them with mild annoyance. "This couldn't wait?"

The mildness was dangerously deceptive, but the Patrician replied angrily, "No, it could not. Your conference with your spy can wait." He threw a glance at Khat, who had backed out of range of the lamps and was glad to be mistaken for someone else. "You must tell us your plans."

Constans's eyes glittered. "And why must I do that?"

The veil hid much of the Patrician's expression, but his voice and his eyes left no doubt of his feelings. He said, "What do you mean to do about the Heir?"

"I mean to stop her."

The Patrician swore in frustration. The archcommander said, "Surely you mean to retake the palace? The Elector will tell us nothing. Does he intend to order the arrest of the Heir?"

"Perhaps he means to let it pass," Constans said, apparently serious. "After all, it was only one small assassination attempt."

"Very well, you warned us and no one heeded you and here we are," the archcommander said, more reasonably. "I admit that. But we must counterattack. You are the only one the Elector listens to."

"Flattering, but hardly accurate."

The talk wasn't telling Khat anything he didn't already know, and he looked around the dim chamber again.

Something about this place was familiar. The fall of starlight through the windows, the height of the ceiling, and the angle and curve of the arches . . . He couldn't remember any of it, but he couldn't shake the feeling that somehow he knew this room. He remembered having the same sense of vague recognition at Radu's house, in the room used for fortune-telling, and he couldn't think where it was coming from. The feeling was far stronger here, almost as if he had mistaken Radu's house for this place . . . Khat shook his head, dismissing that far from comfortable thought.

He was looking toward one of the bronze cabinets stuffed with books, more than tempted to examine a few, just to see what volumes Constans owned. Many of the leather or fabric cases seemed to have been left untied, as if they had been consulted recently.

Then something moved in the shadows near the cabinet.

It was a hunched form, covered with ratty hair like a man-sized dustball. It moved into the light a little, squatting on its haunches and scratching itself.

It was the oracle from Radu's house.

Khat tensed, watching it warily. Naturally Constans wouldn't want to let the creature go to waste, haunting the ghostcallers' quarter. But being Constans, he let it have the run of the house when its services weren't needed.

Its hair was still a mass of tangles, but no longer filth-matted; someone had cleaned it up, or perhaps when it had access to water it cleaned itself. Its wild eyes found Khat, and it started toward him. He pulled his knife half out of the sheath at his back, so the blade caught the light, and the creature halted abruptly, its long nails scrabbling on the floor tile. Taking the hint, it withdrew back into the shadows.

Khat slid the knife back and straightened. This last surprise, mild though it had been in comparison to everything else, was making him feel a little light-headed. This was a fine time for the events of the last few hours to catch up with him. He looked toward the others, wanting to see the Patricians' reactions if they had noticed the creature, and found himself meeting Constans's cold gaze. Khat felt his back stiffen.

Constans looked back to the two men. "That's enough," he said, interrupting the loudest one in midrant. Constans's expression of vague benevolence didn't change, but his presence suddenly seemed to fill the room. He said, "I know you spent two hours with the Elector earlier today, trying to convince him to support you in what I must say is a rather awkward plan to oust the Heir from the palace." The Patrician started in surprise, and Constans smiled. "Of course he told me. He's not a fool, no matter how much he likes to play at being one, and he can see your motives as well as I can. But this is all more serious than you think, and I haven't time to play your petty games."

The Patrician glared, a dangerous mix of anger and indignation. "So this is how you repay the Elector for saving your worthless life."

The archcommander caught his arm and tried to draw him away, counseling caution, but the enraged Patrician shook him off, saying, "He gave you this place that should have been your prison and turned it into a palace, let you work your damned unnatural magics wherever you pleased, let you recruit more of your own kind . . ." The Patrician was confronting Constans rather more aggressively than most people would have thought wise. *Brave, or stupid, or both,* Khat thought. But then he supposed the same thing could be said, and probably was said, about himself.

"And your point is . . . ?" Constans said, cool and mild again.

The Patrician started to answer, but the archcommander caught his arm and shook him sternly, saying, "No, don't press it." The Patrician hesitated, torn between attack and retreat, sense and rage, then turned abruptly and strode toward the door. The lictor followed without a word.

As the two passed through the tall doors, Constans commented, "That man has no sense of humor." He looked to the Warder who had followed them in and was still waiting calmly, and said, "Did I tell you to keep them out of here?"

"You told me not to hurt them," the Warder countered, and Khat recognized the voice of his guide.

Constans eyed him a thoughtful moment, then turned to Khat again, and said suddenly, "This place is familiar to you?"

Khat stepped back into the lamplight, taking a deep breath. Refusing to admit it would be the safest course, but that wouldn't get him an answer. Curiosity overcame caution, and he admitted, "A little."

Constans turned away to the windows again, as if he was watching for something, and perhaps he was. "I've looked into the future again and again, sometimes with Shiskan's help. I saw you when Kythen Seul first approached you to take him into the Waste with Elen. I've seen you in the shadows of all the events leading up to this moment. This establishes a connection between the watcher and the watched. Sometimes the connection can go both ways."

Khat didn't know if he believed that or not, if he even wanted to believe it, or if he had any choice about it at all. He heard the oracle's long nails skitter on the tiled floor in the corner, and said, "Is that how you knew I'd come here?"

"I didn't need to look into the future to know that. You have a combination of intellectual curiosity and courage that makes you dangerous and puts you in constant jeopardy." Constans shrugged and leaned against the casement. "You were bound to end up here sooner or later."

Khat shook his head. *Well, thank you so very much.* "Tell me one thing. Why didn't you destroy the book while you had the chance, out at the Remnant?"

"I suspected it contained the knowledge to open the Doors. I hoped it also included the knowledge needed to close and seal them permanently." He paused. "Did it?"

"Not that I could tell," Khat admitted.

"I see." He didn't even sound mildly disappointed, as if it really mattered little in the end. "The connection between our world and the place we call the West . . ." He looked back at Khat, brows raised. "Why do we call it the West?"

Khat shifted uncomfortably. "We think it's what the Ancients called the land of the dead."

"Ah. The corridor must be a great feat of architecture, existing as it does partly in our world, partly in the West, but mostly in that unknown land in between. I think this particular Inhabitant was trapped in that corridor when the Doors to the West closed, and that it has taken all these past years to travel back here, in the hope that it could reopen the Doors for the others." Constans faced him, looking thoughtful. "The Ancient Mages must have suspected its existence. They left an arcane engine to warn us of its arrival."

Khat looked up, but Constans waited, smiling. Khat cursed under his breath. The last thing he needed now was a guessing game. Then he had it. "The Miracle." It had started to produce its bursts of light twenty years ago, perhaps when the Inhabitant had come close enough to be detected.

"Yes, but by the time it began to deliver its warning there was no one to see who understood."

"Except you."

"Not at first." Constans's gaze seemed to turn inward. "The visions and furies we call ghosts and air spirits . . . they are ghosts, but they are the ghosts of Inhabitants left behind, whose minds were blasted by the closing of the Doors or who degenerated slowly and helplessly over the years when there were no Mages of skill to hear them. When this one arrived, even sadly weak as it was, and drained of its power, it was like lightning on the Waste. It spoke in its true voice to me and to one other."

Constans shook his head with a trace of regret. "It was my fault entirely. He was a friend, and I had convinced him to help me search for the creature. Unfortunately for him, we found it. I listened to it long enough to know its intentions. He listened to it just a little too long. I killed him." He frowned. "If you have to kill one of your friends, I feel it's always better to make it sudden. It's the least you can do. But he has made a strong contribution to my efforts to stop the thing that was partially responsible for his death." His eyes went to the bowl with the bone fragments. Khat followed his gaze, then glanced back to make sure he still had an unimpeded path to the door. Constans continued, "I don't know where Riathen is. I know he intends to open the Doors to the West, but I don't know how or where. I suspect . . . but I don't know for certain. Only you can tell me that."

Khat took a deep breath. Now they had come to it.

One had to keep in mind that Constans was still mad. Perhaps not as dangerous as everyone thought, at least, and not dangerous to the Elector, but still mad. If you felt something frightening and unnatural coming toward you, but no one would believe it existed, if you felt this literally for years, as the whatever-it-was drew slowly and inexorably nearer . . . *What magic does is open the mind to the world,* Elen had quoted to him, so long ago, *and sometimes the world isn't what we think it is . . .*

He could be lying, the voice of reason said again. *Are you going to fall for this just because he's asking you nicely?* Except that it all fit so well with what he knew to be the truth. Khat had no reason under the sky to trust this man. But there was no one else to trust.

He couldn't stand here jittering forever. Khat cleared his throat and said, "The Tersalten Flat Remnant."

For the first time, Constans hesitated. Holding Khat's eyes, he said, "I went there. I felt nothing. Are you sure?"

"I'm sure." It was the only thing he was sure of.

"Very well." There was a pause, and Khat waited, aware he had cast the last die and there was nothing he could do to help himself. Then Constans said, "Estorim."

The young Warder who had remained behind when the Patricians left stepped forward. Khat had forgotten he had stayed in the room.

"Estorim," Constans said again, "conduct our guest out."

Elen was dreaming.

In her dream she lay on the floor of the central chamber of a Remnant, her eyes half-open, her limbs so heavy she couldn't move. It was night, and somewhere a fire was lit. She could hear it and smell it, though it was too far away for her to be bothered by its heat. The stone was gritty with sand, and grated against her cheek, and she could see shadows dance on the walls. Even though her view of the place was limited by her position on the floor, she knew, with the knowledge that comes to one in dreams, that this was the Tersalten Flat Remnant, the one that she had gone to with Khat. But she didn't seem to be dreaming of the time she had spent there; this was something new.

The Remnant felt different to her Warder's senses. It was no longer bare, and empty, and waiting. Something had come to occupy it.

The other odd part of the dream was that she could hear, or almost hear, voices. Soft, musical voices, as if flutes and tambrils were speaking to one another. Sometimes one voice, sometimes several, sometimes hundreds. She couldn't make out the words, because a single deep voice was drowning them out. The single voice sang one low, constant note, and seemed as vast as the Waste and the great sky above it combined. It was preventing her from hearing what the other voices were trying to say. And she knew, with the knowledge that comes to one in dreams, that the single voice was the voice of this Remnant, perhaps of all the Remnants. And that if it ever once faltered and she did hear what the other voices said, something terrible would happen. She knew too, that the voices were coming from that place all power came from, from that place where you sent yourself to see the inner workings of locks, or to see the future, or to soul-read. And that these things were not done inside the mind of a trained Warder, as everyone thought, but in that other place.

Where anything was possible.

How absolutely fascinating, Elen thought, and as soon as the thought was articulated, she realized, *This is not a dream.*

And the voice faltered.

Elen sat bolt upright, hands clapped over her ears, a scream rising in her throat. The scream came out as a coughing fit; her throat was too dry.

By the time she had her breath back the voices were gone. She looked around the Remnant, dazed, trying to understand why she was here. It was night, and there was a small fire, not in the hole in the pit's floor as it should have been but close to the doorway into the ramp chamber. Near it were a couple of travel packs and a clay water jar. The slab on the outer door was down, shutting out the Waste.

Elen had no idea how long she had been unconscious; her limbs were heavy, and her throat might have been stuffed with cotton batting. She flattened her hands on the dusty surface of the stone floor.

It was reassuringly warm and solid. She thought, *This is real. Maybe everything else was a dream.* All she could hear was the natural silence of an isolated place.

She closed her eyes, and carefully extended her senses. Far in the distance, as if separated from her by some great chasm, there was one low voice, singing one deep note . . .

Elen shivered, glancing around the chamber again, making sure she was alone. It was all real, though her dreaming mind could hear it far more clearly than her waking one. Now that she knew where to listen she could hear the resonation of that single voice, just on the edge of her awareness. It meant the other voices were real, too, though she couldn't sense them at all now. And somehow she was very glad of that.

Elen tried to stand, and it took more effort than it should have. Once on her feet she staggered, as if the solid stone of the Remnant had swayed under her. Her head was pounding in rhythm with her heartbeat. She frowned, and felt the back of her skull for knots or matted blood. No, she hadn't been struck there, though she certainly felt like it. *Drugged?* she wondered. It was so hard to think.

She staggered toward the fire and managed to reach the supply packs before her knees gave way. She lifted the lid of the water jar first, and sniffed cautiously. Her nose was city-bred, and she couldn't tell if it was drugged or not, but best not to take chances. Up in the well chamber there was far more water than she would ever need if she had to stay out here for years, and just the thought of it was comforting. When she finished here she would crawl up the ramp and duck her head into the cistern.

She searched the packs slowly and thoroughly, making herself check the inside pockets again when her scattered wits couldn't remember if she had already done it or not. There was not much here except a few packets of travel food, a bronze sextant and compass, and a coil of rope, but the packs were strained at the seams, as if several heavy things had been removed.

Then in one pocket she really had forgotten to search she found a small knife. *Idiots,* she thought, testing the blade carefully. *They probably knew it was here, and just didn't trouble to take it.* She could imagine them saying casually to each other, "Oh, don't bother, she won't know what to do with it." She went to tuck it away into her boot and found herself staring uncomprehendingly at her own dirty toes. *Of course.* Elen bit her lip. She had worn sandals when she went to see Rasan, and someone had taken them, small protection that they were. Her memories of her last trip out here were confusing her.

Elen put the knife away in an inner pocket of her kaftan. There went the half-formed plan of putting all the useful articles in one pack, refilling the jar from the cistern, and striking out for the city. She wouldn't last three steps in the Waste, not dressed like this. Elen frowned, trying to think, wanting to pound her forehead in exasperation but unable to summon the energy.

Aimless, she got to her feet again and stumbled toward the pit.

As she drew near it she could see something was different. Someone had filled in the hole in the floor of it, the cavity that was used as a fire pit. She could see where they had cleaned out the layers of ash and scraped them into a corner.

It had been filled in with a block of dark stone that had a strange metallic sheen, with fine lines in complex circular patterns etched into it.

Her knees trembled, and she sat down hard, muttering to herself, "Oh, I see."

It was their big ugly block, of course. She supposed the crystal plaque that had brought her out here the first time was safe in its place in the antechamber wall, as well.

The ugly block was resonating with the voice of the Remnant. It was so powerful it made her teeth ache.

Someone was coming down the ramp from the well chamber. She felt his footsteps on the stone as if he was walking down the length of her spine. She knew the taste of his mind, too. It was Riathen.

Elen shook her head, wondering at it. The presence of the block in the place meant for it seemed to make it easier to use her power. The humming stone of the Remnant seemed alive and oddly responsive to her inner sense. Perhaps it was also that she had touched that other country of the mind, where the voices came from. The thought was not reassuring.

She felt Riathen cross the chamber, and stop just behind her.

"What is it doing?" she asked him. In a way it was still as if she was dreaming, and she didn't think to question his appearance.

"What it was meant to do," he said. He spoke calmly, as if they were in one of the garden courts of his house, discussing some fine point of power. "There is a tendency to think of arcane engines as engines, as if they resembled steam engines, or clockworks. Oh, some of them did, I imagine. This is rather more sophisticated. It was meant to last a long time, untended, to survive fire and rockfall and other disasters. There is nothing special about the stone in itself, only that it has been imbued with the intent of the most powerful Mages of the Ancients."

Elen gripped the edge of the pit and slid down to the bench, then to the floor. Riathen said nothing to stop her. On her knees, she ran her hands over the block. Its fit into the square cavity was seamless; she couldn't wedge her smallest finger between it and the rock, even if it hadn't been too heavy for her to pry out.

Pry out? she wondered. Why was she so sure it should have been pried out? Her heart froze. The Remnant itself had indicated it to her, in the subtle message carried in its song.

Perhaps it had been so firmly imbued with the intent of the Mages that it had been imbued with life, as well. She looked over her shoulder at Riathen. "It wants you to take it out. Can't you hear it?"

He frowned down at her, concern softening his expression. "You're confused, Elen. Try not to worry."

She snorted, only partly in amusement. "And why is that, I wonder. What did you drug me with?"

"Asphodel. It won't harm—"

"I know what asphodel is," she snapped. It dulled the senses, lulled the victim into a heavy, unnatural sleep. It was also supposed to inhibit arcane power. Trade Inspectors used it on fakirs and ghost-callers when they arrested them, and fortune-tellers were always being accused of slipping it into a rival's tea. It had no effect on the powers of mad Warders, though it made them as dizzy and sick as it did everyone else. Maybe she had gone mad. Or they thought her as weak as a fakir, that the drug would dull what little power she had.

The Remnant wanted the block pried out now. The configuration the stars were assuming was dangerously propitious. Over vast distances she could feel great masses of air, astral bodies, the lines of force that crossed the world, the draw of the tide in the Last Sea, the smoking heat in the belly of a nameless mountain far out into the Waste, all clicking into place like the works of a clock about to strike its hour bell. Soon it would be too late. *I know,* she thought, *I will. I'll do it as soon as I can, I promise, but I can't think if you nag me.*

Elen's awareness of the world as a vast body that she was an infinitesimally small part of gradually faded, leaving her shivering in wonder. She saw Riathen staring at her, his brows drawn together and his eyes worried. She said, "At least try to hear it, can't you?"

His frown deepened, and he didn't reply.

Someone else was coming.

Kythen Seul.

Elen's eyes narrowed. It was Seul who had caught her in Justice Rasan's house, who had forced the first drops of the drug down her throat. The memory of it burned.

Seul came up to Riathen, watching Elen intently. He said, "It's as I thought, then. She's mad."

Riathen shook his head, his face bitter. "No, merely confused. I—"

"She killed a High Justice of the Trade Inspectors," Seul said, as if trying to persuade Riathen to face the sad fact. "You can't deny that."

Elen shook her head, disgusted. So that was his game. "I can deny it." She remembered Rasan clearly, and everything he had said. The Heir was somehow involved in this, in Seul's treachery. She remembered what had really killed Rasan. "What was that ghost?" she demanded. "Did you send it?"

Typically, both men ignored her. Seul kept his eyes on Riathen. For an instant Elen saw past his facade of worried concern to the man beneath, the greed and the guilt, the irritation with Riathen's hesitancy, the barely restrained impatience.

"I never believed it could happen," Riathen was saying, more to himself than to either of them. "Her powers were always so tentative. Certainly I didn't expect it to happen while I—"

All bitter regret, Seul said, "She pushed herself too far. She wanted to serve you too well."

"What are you talking about?" Elen interrupted. They were speaking of her as if she were dead. It was hard to think and she felt awful, but she wasn't dying. Not unless they killed her with asphodel. "Why have you brought me here?"

The Doors of the West, the surface of Riathen's soul said. "For your own good," he replied, gently, aloud. He turned to Seul. "Perhaps when the engine is completed, something can be done for her."

When the engine is completed. Elen's fingers still rested on the block, and it throbbed under her light touch, faster than her heartbeat, urgent, compelling. Its message was more vital than anything the two men said, and her attention drifted.

"Perhaps," Seul admitted.

Elen had a brief glimpse of the Waste from above, as if she looked down on it from some city tower or the top of the Remnant itself. There was a sensation of air rushing past, of an unaccustomed height. The light was the very earliest brush of morning, with stars still visible on the dark horizon.

Something else was there, and its presence was an intrusion, an invasive touch, a disease rotting the body . . .

"Something's coming," she said aloud.

Elen was still looking up at Seul, though her eyes had been temporarily blind. He turned, startled, toward her, then flushed and said, "We should give her more asphodel. If it wears off while we're performing the awakening . . ."

Riathen closed his eyes briefly, as if he was in pain. What Elen read on his soul was relief. He said, "Very well."

Seul pulled a stoppered vial from his mantle, but Riathen didn't comment on this evidence of preparation. He stepped toward her, but the older man stopped him. Riathen said, "I'll give it to her."

Elen gathered her scrambled thoughts, removed her hand from the block to try to shut out its beguiling call. Riathen was kneeling before her, lifting the stopper and holding out the vial. "Please, Elen."

She could dash it from his hand, but she had a better idea. Seul was facing toward the door slab, frowning. Riathen's eyes were on her, and his guard was down.

She took the vial, brought it to her lips, and pushed toward the edge of Riathen's mind an image of her drinking, swallowing. She couldn't prevent a drop or two from rolling over her lips, but the rest went down her chin.

She knew from Riathen's expression he had seen only what she wanted him to see. Elen wiped her sleeve across her mouth to destroy the evidence, making it a little girl's gesture, and smiled at him like a child.

Satisfied, he took her arm to help her up. "Come back here now, and sleep a little. You'll feel better."

She would. She had to rid herself of the last dregs of the intoxicant. Sleeping it off was as good a way as any.

Elen let him lead her to the pallet near the fire. She had tricked the Master Warder with a veiling of sight. She knew she should not have been able to do that. Not ever.

Perhaps they were right. Perhaps she was mad.

She hoped so. It might be the only chance she had.

It was still night when Khat reached the wagon docks, but the sun must be just below the eastern horizon on the far side of the city. The sky was already beginning to gray in that direction.

He made his way out to the end of one of the lesser-used piers, looking back toward the docks for any sign of unusual activity. He had spent the only two copper bits he had to buy a desert robe from a trader in the Seventh Tier market. It smelled of a former owner and itched against his skin, and was probably stolen from a corpse, but he needed some protection in the Waste.

The docks were relatively quiet, the beggars asleep, cargoes piled up for loading onto the early morning wagons, the stokers barely begun warming the engines. But near the center piers were three steamwagons of the light, fast sort used by Imperial couriers and envoys. The cargo space was given over to a larger engine and more room for passengers, and the superstructure was stripped down except for an armored tower with gunports, from which three or four men with air guns could probably hold off a few dozen pirates.

They might be for the Heir; they might also be for Constans. There was no telling. Khat caught hold of a piling and swung down to the loose sand.

The wagons would still be confined to the trade road. He couldn't beat them, but with a head start and taking the overland route directly across the Waste, he might reach the Remnant at roughly the same time. That was the best he could hope for.

Starting the long trek toward the edge of the Waste rock, Khat thought about the time Riathen had already spent in the Remnant.

If it was too late, he was sure they would all find out soon enough.

Chapter Eighteen

The drug was wearing off. Elen sat up against the wall of the Remnant's central chamber, letting the warm stone support her. Riathen and Seul were nowhere to be seen; she remembered they had seemed to spend a great deal of time last night in the upper level, in the anteroom and the well chamber. She tried to struggle to her feet, and gasped, sinking back against the wall again. Her head was one pounding mass of pain; she couldn't stand it. Wetting her dry lips, she started a Discipline of Calm and Silence.

Elen had passed an odd night. Most of it was obscured by the drug, though she had far less of a dose than Riathen and Seul thought. She remembered a strange conversation with Seul, when Riathen had temporarily disappeared.

"You sent the pirates," she had said, wanting to be very clear on that point, for some reason. "You were out there that night, and sent them into the Remnant after us."

"You were lucky. They should have swarmed up onto the roof and overwhelmed you, but I discovered later that a small group betrayed the others and went after you alone, so they could keep the reward to themselves." Seul was confident, indulgent. "But even then they wouldn't have harmed you. I made sure of that."

"No, just mauled me about a bit, and killed Jaq, but they did that anyway."

He had not expected her to be lucid enough to argue, and his eyes had hardened. "Tell Riathen if you wish. He won't believe you."

"Riathen knows already." As she said it she knew it for the truth. Riathen had seen through some of Seul's deceptions, though not all, but he still needed the younger man's help. And what he did with the Ancient relics had become more important to him than the loyalty of his students, the lives of his lictors. It might have been better not to tell Seul this, but there was nothing she could do about it now. The drug and the song of the Remnant reverberating in her soul had given her some strange insights, but it had also made her like some demented oracle, helpless to stop itself from prophesying.

Seul stood abruptly, regarding her with some suspicion. "Maybe you are mad."

Suddenly weary, she had not replied, and watched him walk away.

Elen knew she must have slept then. It had still been dark during that conversation. Now there was early afternoon light falling through the sandtraps, illuminating the chamber with a gentle bronze and gold glow. She pressed her palms against her eyes in relief; the Discipline was lessening the pain, turning it into a manageable ache.

She got to her feet with the aid of the wall, and paused when her vision went black. The drug had done her no good at all. She wished she could treat Seul to a substantial dose of it.

The Remnant's song murmured just beyond her range of hearing, more distant than it had been but still a presence in her thoughts. *I should be terrified of it,* she thought. *What's wrong with me?* She didn't know whether to trust the things that voice had told her or not; so much of the past night was dreamlike. Riathen had said the block was imbued with the intentions of Ancient Mages long dead, and she knew forceful souls could leave vibrant impressions of their thoughts and feelings on stone or metal. She might only be imagining that it actively spoke to her; it might only be a kind of mirror, mindlessly reflecting images from centuries past.

Except that it had shown her the Waste as it was now, today, not with the shallow seas of the Ancients or lakes of fire from the Survivor Time. And it had left her with the strong conviction that whatever Riathen was doing here, it was very dangerous indeed.

Elen had been afraid of that before, afraid that the Survivor text told how to build some powerful arcane engine whose power he meant to keep to himself, or at least to confine to the Warders in his household. *The truth is far worse than that,* she thought. *I know that; I just don't know how I know.*

Her vision gradually cleared, but just as she started to straighten she felt something travel through the stone under her fingers, as if the whole Remnant had trembled. She jerked her hand back, rubbing her uninjured skin, then turned to the empty square of doorway that led to the ramp.

Going for help was impossible. *I have to see what's happening up there,* Elen thought. Whether they killed her for it or not.

Her steps gained strength as she climbed the ramp, as if the blood moving through her veins was washing away the last traces of the asphodel. Looking up, she could see the dim sunlight reflected through the antechamber from the open well chamber, but she could hear nothing, not even muted conversation. She reached the top and paused in the doorway of the antechamber.

The sun filled the open bowl-shaped well chamber with harsh light, and Elen squinted against it, straining to see until her eyes adjusted. The floor had been swept free of sand, or at least the area of open pavement between the door of the antechamber and the heavy stone rim of the cistern was clear of it. Instead of being filled with dust, the grooves that had been carved into the stone floor now glittered with some silver substance that flowed like water. She could see the pattern the grooves formed clearly now: they crossed back and forth between this end of the cistern and the antechamber's door, forming a large square outline composed of overlapping triangles. In the center the pavement was smooth, and Riathen knelt there, motionless and silent, facing away from her toward the cistern.

Elen had no sense of his presence at all now; he might have been a statue dressed in robes.

The sun's sparkle on the water and the myriad reflections of the silvery substance made the air glow. *It must be quicksilver,* Elen realized. Stacked against the corner of the antechamber were several thick-bodied ceramic jugs. She remembered how the seams of the travel packs had been strained and supposed that was what Riathen had carried in them. She didn't need to speculate on why; quicksilver had long been identified as an essential element to the Ancients' arcane constructions.

Something else lay near the jugs. Atop Riathen's folded mantle was the coin-sized relic with the winged figure.

Elen glanced at the door, assuring herself that Riathen was still motionless, then crossed the antechamber in a few silent steps and picked up the little relic. It was warm to her touch, a warmth that seem to flow through her hand, up her arm, and twine right around her consciousness. It was all of a piece with the gradually awakening Remnant; it hardly startled her.

There was power here, contained within the vessel of the well chamber. She shuddered involuntarily with a rush of fear and delight that confused her. Building in the walls, chasing up and down the lines of quicksilver on the floor, humming in the light reflected off the water. The air was thick and heavy with it. A glance at the back wall of the antechamber showed her the crystal plaque was in its place. It was amazing to her that she and Khat and the others had once stood unaffected in this room and examined the text and confronted Aristai Constans.

Elen tucked the little relic away inside her mantle, in the same pocket where she had hidden the knife taken from the packs. What good either object would do her, she had no idea. She moved forward through the waiting silence of the antechamber to the doorway, and stopped there. She sensed Seul's presence just before he caught her arm. He had been standing to one side of the doorway, out of her line of sight. Annoyed, she freed her arm with a twist, and when he reached for her again she met his eyes and pushed at him with her power.

Something in her knew to gather strength from the growing force in the chamber, and Seul stumbled back, astonished. Riathen twisted around. That surprised Elen almost as much as her resistance had surprised Seul; she had thought Riathen in some deep trance.

Riathen's expression was stern. For a moment it seemed as if he didn't recognize her. Elen said, "Don't do this." She still wasn't certain why she had to stop him, but she knew she must.

Riathen tried to assume his old manner, kind and reassuring, but under it she too clearly saw his impatience. "Elen, you are still confused. You don't know—"

"No more games." Elen stepped forward.

Seul muttered, "Careful," but she was cautious of the quicksilver-filled grooves, and her foot came down on firm pavement. She saw

Riathen was holding a small mirror, and the experience gained in her recent apprenticeship told her it was well-polished *mythenin*. It must be part of the working, but she had no idea how. The power gathered here was like a wall before her; moving into it was like pushing her way into a bale of cotton.

Elen said, "I may not understand what you're trying to do here, but I know the consequences will be terrible."

His eyes hardened. "You child, you know nothing. I am turning this Remnant into a source of arcane power that all Warders will learn to tap. That was its purpose; that was why the Ancients constructed it. I'm doing nothing more than using it the way it was meant to be used."

His anger wasn't any easier to face than his condescension. Not pleasant to discover she had been wrong about him all this time, that he treated her like a child not because she was inferior to the other Warders but because that was the way he wanted her. She would save her hurt for later, if there was time. "I know you're playing with forces you don't understand. Yes, the Remnant is coming alive, but something very wrong is happening here, and all you can see is an increase in your power."

"I see an end to madness, I see an end to destroying our own kind. Isn't that worth the risk?"

In a way he was right, it was working. The things he had done here had certainly increased her power, her soul-reading, her Sight, everything. But the one thing all her new abilities told her was that the danger was as acute as a knife to the throat. "You don't know enough to increase our power. You're like a fool playing with a loaded rifle." She caught herself. This was hardly the way to talk him out of anything. She needed cool reason, and all she had was anger. She tried again, keeping a tighter grip on her temper. "Please wait. Can't you hear the Remnant's voice yet? It's warning us that something else is about to happen, something you don't intend—"

Seul said, "Yes." His voice was thick, as if forced out of him against his will. "Yes, Riathen, there's something you don't know . . ."

Elen felt a sense of pressure building, and rubbed her temples, distracted. Concentrating on Riathen and the growing power in the well chamber, she hadn't been listening to the Remnant, but now . . . She realized Seul had stopped speaking, and that Riathen was staring past her into the antechamber. She turned.

Standing there, framed in the doorway, was the Heir. She was dressed in desert robes, a full mantle thrown back over her shoulders. Behind her were three Imperial lictors armed with air rifles and another man whose face was completely obscured with heavy veils. Looking at him, Elen felt a tremor travel through the Remnant, felt that sense of invasion, of revulsion.

The Heir smiled. "I see we're in time."

The sun was high overhead when Khat paused within a half mile of the Remnant. He had traveled mostly on the top level of the Waste to gain time and had stopped only to make a meal out of the pulpy interior of a young jumtree, knowing he would travel faster when he wasn't short on water.

He sat on his heels in the shelter of a crag now, and could see nothing different about the Remnant. It rose up out of the empty vista, the sun striking a golden glow off the steeply slanted stone walls. Still, he knew he wasn't alone out here.

Since Khat had neared the Remnant's vicinity the wind had been bringing him the stink of unwashed human flesh—pirates. Probably the same band that had attacked them the first time, its loyalty purchased by Kythen Seul with food and painrods and who knew what else. He had also heard a steamwagon. None of which told him the best way to approach the Remnant, which was what he was trying to decide on now.

A distant crack startled him. It was a man-made sound, probably an air gun's pellet striking stone. A second crack told him the direction. It was towards the west. *Where the trade road runs nearest the Remnant,* Khat thought grimly. He made for the closest sinkhole and scrambled down it to the midlevel, working his way closer to the sound.

After a short time he could hear shouts, sounds of fighting, echoing oddly up the partially enclosed passages of the midlevel. He was under excellent cover here, but damn it, he wanted to see what was happening. He found a chimney he could climb up; there was light but no direct sun falling down it from the top level, a good sign that there was an outcrop near it that would afford some cover.

Khat climbed up the narrow, rocky passage, the sounds of distant battle growing closer with every hand- and foothold. The chimney broke through the top level amid a tumble of weirdly shaped boulders, the remains of some Survivor Time eruption. Khat scrambled up and worked his way around, belly flat to the dusty stone, until he had a view looking down toward the Ancient-made canyon where the trade road split the Waste.

There was a steamwagon on the road, under attack by a band of maybe as many as forty pirates. The tattered figures were swarming like ants; it was hard to get an accurate estimate of their number. White-robed Imperial lictors were firing down into the mass of pirates; some had leapt off the wagon to take them in hand-to-hand combat. The back platform had been overwhelmed and boarded, but as Khat watched, two pirates fell away, shot by the riflemen atop the wagon's housing. The pirates might not know it yet, but they were all done for. From here Khat could see three more courier wagons rattling up the trade road at full steam.

Khat eased back away from his vantage point and started over the top level toward the Remnant. If the pirates were supposed to be guarding it for Seul they were doing a terrible job. This was really the best distraction he could have hoped for. *Get in, get Elen, and get out,* he reminded himself. *Let Constans deal with Riathen and Seul.*

The rolling waves of rock stretched out to meet the base of the Remnant, and nothing moved anywhere. Still, Khat approached from an angle, out of direct view of the door, making for the south side. He crossed the base quickly and flattened himself up against the wall, then edged to the corner for a quick look. The door slab was up and two Imperial lictors stood before it, arguing, one pointing back toward the trade road.

Khat pulled back, cursing under his breath. They weren't Constans's men, or there would be a Warder or two along. They had to be the Heir's lictors, and there might be more inside. Then a low voice not two feet away said, "I didn't think you could stay away from this."

Khat spun away from the wall, just managing to bite back an exclamation. It was Constans, of course. He had recognized the voice even as he moved.

Constans's dark mantle was covered with dust; he had obviously been walking the Waste, though not as far as Khat had. The three steamwagons Khat had seen arriving in the distance probably belonged to the mad Warder. He must have left them and taken the shorter overland route to the Remnant. "Do be quiet," Constans told him, glancing around the corner to see if the lictors had heard. "They aren't deaf."

You were distracted, Khat told himself, trying to conquer his irritation. Never mind that a city dweller that big, Warder or not, just shouldn't be allowed to sneak up on anybody so silently. "Why aren't you back there killing pirates?" Khat whispered.

"My quarry is here."

Cautiously Khat came back to the wall. Constans said, "There's not much time. Riathen has already done something foolish."

"Is Elen in there?" Khat asked.

"Yes."

The two lictors suddenly came into view, but they weren't after intruders. They were walking away from the west wall, heading determinedly toward the trade road. *No doubt who put that idea in their heads,* Khat thought. Constans slipped around the corner, and Khat followed him.

The Heir stepped further into the well chamber, circling around the quicksilver-filled channels in the stone, smiling at Riathen. Her lictors followed her, spreading out to cover the others with their rifles. The veiled man stayed where he was, motionless, in the doorway of the antechamber.

Elen didn't move. The veiled man was not ten feet away from her, and she could see the hot air seeming to bend and curve around him. She didn't know if she was seeing this with her eyes or with some facility of the mind, awakened by the power in the Remnant. His robes dragged the floor, and his sleeves covered his hands. There was nothing of his body visible, and she had the terrible feeling she knew who this was. Or what it was.

The Heir's attention was all for Riathen. She said, "You must be surprised to see me. But I had more of an interest in your relics than I pretended."

The Master Warder hadn't moved. He was cautiously watching the Heir, but his eyes showed more impatience at the interruption than fear or shock. He said, "I admit to surprise, but now at least I understand Seul's recent desire to spend so much of his time at the palace."

"Ah, yes." The Heir smiled at Seul. "Go on, then, Kythen. You were about to betray me. Or, I should say, to finish betraying me. I assume you ordered the pirates to attack my men, so you could complete this little ceremony without my presence."

"Something's wrong here," Seul said. He glanced uncertainly at

Riathen, then back to the Heir. "The Remnant is filling with power, but there's a sense of danger—"

"You can hear it!" Elen interrupted. "You've heard it all this time, and you're still going on with this? You're madder than Constans."

The Heir sighed. She gestured to the nearest lictor. "Get rid of her."

He made to lift the rifle. Elen pointed at him, feeling the power surge up out of the stone and travel through her body like water through fountain pipes, felt it concentrate in the fragile bones of her hand. At the last instant she managed to direct it away from the lictor's body and toward the delicate mechanism of the rifle.

The rifle's air reservoir burst, and the firing mechanism exploded, spraying metal shards across the chamber. The lictor cried out, dropping the rifle and stumbling backwards, but he was obviously unhurt. The Heir stared, shocked out of her complacency.

Riathen chuckled. To the Heir he said, "Elen has always had a soft heart. Don't imagine I will be so generous."

"If Seul can hear it, you can hear it," Elen whispered.

Riathen looked up at her, and there was regret in his eyes. "Yes, it's been a delicate game we've played the past few days. And you the only one with nothing to hide. As usual."

"Riathen." Seul was watching the veiled man. "Do you know what this creature is? Can you control it?"

The Master Warder studied the unmoving figure. "No, I've never seen its like before, but from my reading of the text I can make an informed guess. This was one part of your deception you managed to keep from me, but I can't see that it matters. With the power of the Remnant, we should be able to control it, and any others of its kind. If they still exist after all these years . . ."

"You can't see that it matters?" Elen shouted. Riathen must have been blinded by power. "I saw it kill a man. I know it's killed others. And the Remnant said . . ." She couldn't put it into words. "It's too dangerous to meddle with."

Riathen didn't seem to hear her. He said again, "With the power of the Remnant at this level, there should be no difficulty."

The Heir was watching in astonishment and growing anger. Her other lictors had backed away in fear, and made no attempt to shoot. She turned to the veiled figure and shouted, "They'll destroy you! Stop them!"

It did nothing.

Elen couldn't catch her breath. The sense of danger was so intense it made her heart pound and her head ache. The harsh light in the well chamber was changing, becoming something of almost solid consistency. She didn't think the Heir and the lictors could see it; they were watching her and Riathen. She said, "Riathen, please, you say you hear the Remnant but you aren't listening! What are you trying to do?"

Riathen glanced up, squinting into the harsh light. The sun seemed to fill the sky. "This will seal the power you now feel into the Remnant forever, accessible by all Warders. This is what the Ancients intended it for." He adjusted the position of the mirror minutely, and the sunlight struck it full on.

The lictors hadn't bothered to close the Remnant's door slab, and no other guards barred the way. Constans disappeared inside without even bothering to look around, but Khat paused in the doorway. The central chamber was empty, but against the wall were the remains of a fire and some scattered supplies and packs. Constans had veered away at once toward the pit. Khat hesitated, then saw what had attracted the Warder's attention.

Their big ugly block had been placed in the hollow square compartment in the center of the pit. Khat went to the edge, looking down at it. He didn't see anything strange or arcane about it. Constans stepped down, stooped as if he meant to run his fingers over the block's surface, then changed his mind abruptly. Stepping back up near Khat, he said mildly, "I believe we're already too late."

"What . . . ?" Khat looked up, but Constans was already halfway across the chamber to the ramp.

Khat swore and bolted after him.

The sunlight struck the *mythenin* mirror in Riathen's hands, and was reflected dazzlingly around the chamber. Elen turned her face away from the glare, and the sudden cessation of the terrible pressure caught her by surprise. She stumbled to the cistern and steadied herself on its rim. The first thing she noticed was that the voice of the Remnant was gone, leaving behind it a curious sense of emptiness. The second was that the light in the chamber had changed drastically. The sunlight was softer, as if it was screened through gauze. She looked up, and blinked.

The open sky and noon sun were gone. It was as if she was standing at the bottom of a tower that stretched up into infinity. It was roughly oblong, following the shape of the well chamber, and the walls were of rough stone, and lined with rocky ledges. Elen frowned, trying to make sense of what she saw. Her eyes followed one of the ridged projections, and she decided that it had once been something like a ramp, or a spiral stair, that had hugged close to the tower's wall, winding up it, leaving the immense central well empty. At one time something large had fallen down that central well, tearing sections out of the ramp way as it passed. *But I see the top of the ramp,* Elen thought, *as if I'm at the top of the tower, looking down, instead of at the bottom looking up.* She shook her head and turned back to the others.

They were all staring upwards, as silent and baffled as she was. Except the veiled figure.

Elen heard it laugh first, echoing in her mind, filling the place where the Remnant's voice had sung. There was something seductive about it that tried to twine around her soul. It seemed to promise all sorts of things—knowledge, skills, power, some beyond her ken and some she understood all too well. *In exchange for what?* Elen thought, derisive and almost amused. She didn't bother to wait for an answer and closed her mind against it, pushing the intrusive presence away.

She came back to herself in time to see the creature's arms come up, flinging away the robes and veils, revealing a mass of air and solid light, hanging there like a small whirlwind. It rose up, flowing toward the well of the tower above them.

The cold wind of its passing was gentle at first; then suddenly it tore at her, twisting her mantle up around her head and stealing the breath from her lungs. Elen tightened her hold on the cistern's rim and tried to crouch down against it but felt her feet leave the pavement. The stone scraped her palms, and water slopped over the edge, drenching her with a cold spray. She hugged the rim tighter, knowing it could only be moments until she lost her grip. She twisted her head free of her mantle, trying to see what was happening. For an impossible moment she thought she saw Khat in the door of the anteroom, and shouted at him to stay back. The shout was lost in the roar of the wind, and she gasped as her hand slipped and she lost her hold on the cistern.

Chapter Nineteen

THE WHIRLWIND TORE through them, tossing them like rag dolls. Howling, roaring, striking with bruising force it swept them away.

Any instant Khat expected to lose consciousness or die; either would have been a relief, but the buffeting went on without respite. Watering eyes kept him from seeing much, but he glimpsed rock walls rushing past at a great distance, as if he were being flung down a tunnel of giant circumference and infinite depth. Then something seemed to shove him toward one side, and a limitless plain of rock wall rushed up at him. Then his shoulder and side struck something solid, and he flattened himself against it, clinging to the precarious safety. He felt Elen still beside him; she had a death grip on his arm. He didn't realize the wind had stopped until he was able to breathe without the gale snatching the air out of his lungs.

Dazed, Khat pushed himself up on his hands and knees and shook his head. They weren't in the well chamber anymore. Fear settled into the pit of his stomach, cold and heavy. The wind was gone, leaving the air dry and cool. The light was softer than daylight, and seemed to come from everywhere and nowhere at once. He could see nothing around him but creamy brown rock. It was rough to the touch and sloped dramatically down.

They should be falling, but the ledge felt as if it was level. Khat's fingers hurt from trying to dig into the rock, and he made himself relax. Elen was huddled next to him. She said something, and Khat shook his head to show he couldn't hear her. From her expression, she hadn't heard herself either; they had both been temporarily deafened by the roaring of the wind. At least, Khat hoped it was temporary.

Behind them a featureless wall stretched up; before them was a gulf of empty space. Across it he could see another wall, curving inward and studded with stone projections like the one they were stranded on, the one they couldn't possibly be holding on to without sliding down into that empty space. *Don't think about it,* he told himself.

This place was something like one of the sinkholes or chimneys of the Waste: a hollow cylinder of stone, its sides lined with outcroppings, but on a scale that was almost unimaginable. Perched here they were like flies on a wall, but without the comfort of wings.

Khat tried to judge the distance to the opposite side, but there was nothing to put it in perspective, no frame of reference; it might have been one mile across or ten. The air was clear, and it smelled of nothing except himself and Elen.

Elen cleared her throat experimentally, and that time Khat heard her, though the sound seemed hollow and distant. He looked down at her in relief and said, "Can you hear me?"

Her face was as bloodless as a corpse, and there was a bruise on her cheek, though that might have come from being slammed into him by the torrent of wind. Her white Warder's robes were stained and dirty, and she was trembling, but then, so was he. She swallowed and said, "Which way is down, do you think?"

Khat closed his eyes to shut out the contradictory evidence of sight, and his stomach almost turned over from vertigo. "Down is this way, the way that looks like up." He didn't want to take his hand off the stone to point, but forced himself. If they were going to do anything other than rot here, they would eventually have to reconcile themselves to letting go of this rock. Down was directly over their heads, the direction their eyes said was up. "Up is below us, the way that looks like down."

"I'll take your word for it," Elen said. Cautiously, keeping a grip on Khat's arm, she lifted her hand from the stone. Her palm was rubbed raw. "We're in the tower I saw. The creature, the ghost brought us here."

"Tower?" He wasn't sure he was hearing her correctly.

She cleared her throat, and in a stronger voice explained, "I looked up, and above the well chamber was a tower, going up . . . forever. There was something like a ramp winding up the sides, but with sections and pieces missing. This stone must be part of it. It doesn't look like much from this angle, but from below I could definitely see it had been a ramp. What I don't understand is where it all came from."

"This is a Doorway to the West." Khat gently pried Elen's fingers off his arm, and edged forward, stretching himself flat to the stone, and looked over the rim.

"It's a what?" Elen asked. Nervously she added, "Careful."

From here he could see what she meant. From this angle, the ledges thrust out from the walls did look like the remains of a ramp that had wound up the inside of the tower, though who could have built it was open to debate. He could also see that this "tower" wasn't perfectly round, but more of an oval shape designed to follow the outline of the Remnant's well chamber. *No,* he corrected himself, *the well chamber was made into an oval to follow the outline of this tower.* But the tower was far larger than the well chamber. "Why aren't we falling?" he asked Elen. "I mean, that's *down,* that's *up.*" He couldn't sense the direction that should be true north, as all krismen could from birth; even trying brought back the vertigo that threatened him whenever he shut his eyes. The absence of that knowledge, the loss of that sense of alignment, was as distracting as a missing front tooth.

"I don't know." Elen's voice was losing its patience. "What is a Doorway to the West?"

Khat told her, as succinctly as he could, what Arad had discovered in the text. As she silently tried to comprehend it he edged forward a little more, giving himself a better vantage point. The air wasn't quite odorless; there was an odd tang to it. *Thunderstorm,* he identified it suddenly. The air smelled of the aftermath of a too-close-for-comfort lightning strike. And he couldn't get over the fact that they weren't falling. "What do you think would happen if we jumped?"

Elen was shaking her head, her mouth set in a bitter line. "Riathen read the text too, but he saw only what he wanted to see in it. And he was right, as far as he went. When the relics are in place the Remnant does help Warders use their power; it even helped me. For a time I was almost as strong as Riathen himself. But he didn't look past that; he wouldn't even acknowledge the thought that whatever came through the Doors might be more than he could handle." Then she frowned at Khat, realizing what he had said. "If we jump? No one's jumping. Don't say that. We'll have to climb to get back."

If we can get back, Khat thought. He didn't need to point that out to Elen; she was just as aware as he was that they were probably dead. "I think Arad's transcendental device is the Remnant itself. Maybe all the Remnants are part of that device, since the text said that each marks a different Door to the West." Khat's eyes were growing used to the odd contours of the place, though he still couldn't judge distance well.

"And the creature we thought was a ghost is the Inhabitant," Elen was saying, more to herself. "I see why it followed us, and why it pretended to let the Heir control it. But why did the Mages leave this Remnant with a Door that could be opened?"

"I don't know, Elen. I got here at the same time you did." Khat reached down and ran his hand over the front of the ledge. This side was perhaps two feet thick, and rough with raw, broken rock. He rolled over on his back so he could look up, or the way that looked most like up. It appeared identical to the way that looked most like down.

"That was a rhetorical question," Elen said, sounding annoyed. "This isn't: can you see any of the others? They must have been brought here too."

"No. Constans went toward Riathen, but that was the last I saw of him." The others Khat didn't give much of a damn about, and he wasn't going to waste effort worrying about Constans. If the old Warder was dead, that was that, but if he was alive he was far better equipped to take care of himself in this situation than they were.

There was a pause, then Elen said, "Constans is here?" Her voice told him this question wasn't an idle one either.

Khat sat up on his elbows so he could see her. She was still crouched against the wall, though the security it afforded was imaginary. He said, "Yes. I told him to come to the Remnant if he wanted to stop Riathen."

Elen was too reasonable to explode, even now, even here. Her face didn't change, and she said only, "Why?"

"When I realized what Riathen wanted to do, I knew someone

had to stop him. Constans already knew about the Inhabitant, and the Doors to the West, and that's why he wanted to take the text away from Riathen and to stop us from finding the other relics. The only reason he didn't let me drop it in the cistern and destroy it that time was because he thought it would tell how to close the Doors. I don't think it does. I looked, but I couldn't find anything about it."

Elen dropped her eyes, one hand twisting the frayed seam of her mantle. She said, "What if he was in league with Seul and the Heir? I know about their part in this."

Khat knew her well enough by now to tell she was angry. Well, he hadn't expected anything else. He said, "He wasn't. It didn't make sense that way. And I had other reasons. I saw him out on the Waste that night, before the pirates came." She looked up at that, startled. "And in the palace when Riathen was meeting with the Heir, in the chamber where the Miracle is kept. And again in the garden outside Riathen's house, the last time you took me there. I didn't understand what he was trying to tell me. He really is mad, just not in the way people think he is. But I didn't really believe him until I went to the Citadel of the Winds, and he let me go again." That was the short version, but he didn't think he had left anything of importance out. She probably hated him for this, and he wasn't sure he could disagree with her. The only reason she wouldn't tell him so was because she had too much sense to rage at her only ally at a time like this. But he wasn't going to beg her to understand; if she couldn't forgive him it was her prerogative.

Elen looked tired more than anything else. "Well, you've been busy, haven't you?" she said.

That was all. Not wanting to press her on it, Khat went back to looking up the center of the tower. It seemed to go on forever. Some distance away he could see a stone platform jutting out from the wall—not the jumbled, random confusion of the broken projections all around them, but something regular, with a curved edge. *Like looking at the underside of a balcony*, Khat thought. A balcony that ran around the entire circumference of the tower. "Come look at this."

Unwillingly Elen crept forward. "Now," she muttered, "I know what spiders feel like." It took her some moments to get used to the perspective, but eventually she saw the strange platform. "Hmm. What do you make of it?"

"I don't know. If the Inhabitants built it . . . But why would they?

They can fly, they don't need ramps and platforms. If people like us built it, they might have been trying to close off this Doorway."

"You mean, build a barrier all the way across so the Inhabitants couldn't get through." Elen edged forward to squint up at the platform. "Does it matter? We should be trying to climb out of here before that Inhabitant comes back for us."

"Which way?"

"What?"

"Which way is out?"

Elen hesitated. "Don't you know?"

"I can tell up and down, but that's it. I don't know which way we came from."

Elen stretched forward to peer up again. "When I looked up, I saw the underside of the broken ramp."

"Elen, look down now. It looks the same either way, up or down."

Elen did, not liking the result. "I thought krismen couldn't get lost," she muttered.

That was unfair. "And I thought Warders knew better than to get sucked into corridors connecting the real world to the land of the dead."

That stopped whatever angry reply she had ready. She met his eyes directly for the first time since he had told her about Constans. "Is the place the Inhabitants come from really the land of the dead?"

"It might as well be as far as we're concerned." Khat took a deep breath, bracing himself, then sat up. It was hard to ignore the sensation that he was about to fall, but closing his eyes was worse. He would just have to get used to it. "We should head for that place that looks like a platform. It's the only thing different we can see."

Elen was silent; then abruptly she twisted around and sat up. She made herself look over the edge again, trying to acclimate herself to the disquieting sense of vertigo. Then she said, "I know you. You just want to die somewhere more interesting than this rock."

That was the first time one of them had actually said it. Barring some friendly god returning to life to rescue them, they were dead. Khat smiled at her, a real smile, no teeth showing. "At least I'll have company."

Elen's mouth twisted wryly. "I'm so honored."

* * *

Once they got used to sitting up, standing was easy.

Getting the hang of standing near the rim of their ledge, stretching up or jumping to catch the edge of the rock above, and hauling yourself up without panicking from the sense that at any instant you were about to plunge into empty space was a different matter. Khat was tall enough to do it without too much difficulty, and was able to help Elen. She managed it by concentrating only on the stone just in front of her, and ignoring where she thought she was and if she should be falling or not. After the first few successful attempts, she stopped and tore her mantle into strips, binding them around her palms and the soft part of her feet, leaving fingers and toes free to feel for holds but affording her some protection.

While she did this Khat leaned out from the edge to look up again, and couldn't tell whether they were any nearer to the platform or not.

It didn't get any easier, but after a time Khat could tell they were making progress. They made frequent stops to rest, but Khat's arms were aching from the strain, and he couldn't close his eyes for even a moment without bringing on an attack of sickening vertigo. Elen wasn't having this trouble, and he didn't know if he was just more susceptible to it than she was or if it had something to do with being kris.

On one of their rest stops they had taken stock of their supplies. Khat had a knife and the clothes he was wearing. Elen had a tiny fruit knife she had stolen with the idea of inserting it in Kythen Seul at some time, and, oddly, the little relic with the winged figure.

"How did you get that?" Khat had asked when she pulled it out of her mantle.

"Riathen left it in the antechamber, with some other things, as if it wasn't part of the ritual. Did the text say anything about it?"

"No, but I didn't have time to study it that closely. Arad might know. Too bad we can't ask him."

She rubbed her thumb over the figure of the faceless winged man. "It still feels warm. It felt alive when I picked it up, but so did every other part of the Remnant I touched. See if you feel anything."

Khat had held it, but it felt like nothing other than inert *mythenin*. Elen had told him something of what she had experienced last night in the gradually awakening Remnant, and though he thought most of it sounded like a dream, he was still willing to believe her. In light of their current predicament, he would have to be a fool not to. And he really didn't know why they bothered to ask each other these questions. *Habit*, he supposed. They had no water, no food, and no hope of getting any, and he couldn't even close his eyes to sleep. They were not going to last long in this strange, empty place.

Khat scrambled over the edge of the next projection, and reached down to help Elen. As he pulled her up beside him she stared at something over his shoulder and gasped, "Look at that!"

He twisted around, reaching for his knife. He had been checking each projection carefully before crawling up onto it, but the repetition and the lack of any sign of anything alive but them had made him careless. But Elen was pointing up at something about a man's height up the wall.

After a moment his tired eyes found it. It was a glyph, the size of his outstretched hand, carved into the wall. Elen must have seen it purely by accident. Khat stood, one hand on the wall for balance, and traced its outline.

Elen demanded, "What does it say?"

There were only a few characters of Ancient Script, but as weary as he was it took him some moments to translate it. "It says 'Aventine-denan, twenty-seventh dynasty, day seventy-one.' " He wished he could copy it; he didn't have anything like paper to do a rubbing or to trace it. He stared hard at it, carefully memorizing the lines; just in case they did survive this, he wanted to be able to reproduce it. "That's in Ancient reckoning. The twenty-seventh dynasty was the last one before the Waste rose. I don't know what 'day seventy-one' is unless he was keeping track of how long he had been here."

"So there were people here," Elen said softly. "Mages, perhaps. Though if Aventine-denan was a Mage, his name wasn't passed down to the Warders. Maybe he found a way out."

They might have passed dozens of glyphs like this one; traveling with their noses to the stone, trying to defeat that paralyzing sensation of falling, they could have missed any number of them. "Maybe," Khat agreed. "But the text said the Inhabitants stole hundreds of people. Maybe they dropped him along the way, like our Inhabitant dropped us, and he stayed here until he decided to see what happened if he jumped."

"You dropped that rock chip to see what would happen and it

fell, just like I said it would. If we jumped, we would fall. No one is jumping."

"All right, all right, I said I wouldn't jump. But . . ." Khat stopped, holding up a hand to keep Elen from replying. Somewhere above them he heard a faint thump, as if something had struck one of the rocks. He thought his hearing was almost back to normal now, though it was hard to tell. The only thing to hear had been their own voices and a distant rushing like wind through a wadi, as if the gale that had carried them here still raged somewhere far away. He wondered if he had imagined the thump.

Then it came again. Khat glanced at Elen and saw from her startled expression that she had heard it too this time. He motioned for her to come toward the wall, and she scrambled to his side.

The next thump was on the ledge directly above them, and they both pressed back against the wall. Khat drew his knife, though he didn't know how much good it would do. An Inhabitant would hardly need to jump from ledge to ledge, but if some of the nastier creatures of the Waste had originally come there through these Doors there was no telling what might live here.

Something dark swung down from the ledge above, and Elen gasped just as Khat realized it was Constans. The Warder landed on their ledge and didn't even have the grace to look surprised to see them. He demanded, "What is taking you so long?"

Khat slumped back against the wall and let out his breath. It was a sure sign your situation was desperate when you were relieved to see Aristai Constans.

Elen stepped forward, confronting the older Warder defiantly. "I hoped you were dead."

"And it's lovely to see you, my dear."

Khat put his knife away. "Where have you been?" He was glad to know the old bastard was alive, but he supposed he would get over that in a moment or two. Hopefully it was only relief at seeing another human face.

"Waiting for you. We can only hold them off so long, and there's something of a language barrier." Constans stepped back, showing a complete disregard for the drop-off behind him, then reached up and caught the rim of the rock overhead. Pulling himself up without apparent effort, he added, "I suggest you hurry."

"We?" Elen repeated, glancing at Khat. "Is . . . is Riathen up there?"

"We're not going anywhere with you until you tell us what's going on," Khat said, folding his arms. He had never been in a position to demand information from Constans before, and he wanted to make the most of it while he had the chance.

Constans appeared again, head hanging down off the ledge. "Riathen is there. Why do you think this corridor hasn't been flooded with Inhabitants, heading for our world? The Doorway we came through is still open."

"What about Seul and the Heir, and the lictors?" Elen persisted.

"They had no resistance to the Inhabitant. They were drawn all the way up, and probably over to the other side."

The other side. Khat felt a cold prickle travel up his spine. Curiosity had always been the bane of his life, but he felt not the slightest urge to see the other side of this Doorway.

Suspicious, Elen said, "I had no resistance to the Inhabitant. Why didn't it draw us all the way up?"

"Elen, you continually underestimate yourself, and I find it intolerable. You haven't even tried to use your power since we came here, have you?"

Elen flushed, caught off guard. "I didn't think it wise, I—"

He cut her off. "Riathen cannot hold the Inhabitants back for long, so I suggest you get over your reluctance and come along."

"Riathen is holding them back?" Elen glanced at Khat, then asked Constans, "You're cooperating with him, and not trying to kill him?"

"There hasn't been time for that." Constans was impatient. "My dear, if I had ever wanted to kill Sonet Riathen, I have had far better opportunities than this."

"I'm not your dear anything. Stop calling me that. And Riathen told me . . ." Elen stopped, wet her lips uncertainly.

"Yes," Constans said. "He told you a great many things, and some of them were true." He pulled his head back, and they heard, "Hurry."

Elen turned away, her hands knotting up into fists. "Damn him," she muttered, "to the highest level of Hell."

"Better make it a little lower," Khat told her, sourly. "He could probably tunnel out of that one." *What did he mean by language barrier?* Khat wondered. Were Constans and Riathen up there trying to reason with the Inhabitants? It would be a strange thing to see if true, considering that Constans and Riathen could barely speak to each other without violence.

They climbed again, moving as fast as they could, not stopping to rest. Khat felt as if they had been doing this forever, but eventually they reached the outcroppings just beneath the platform they had seen from below.

It was an unbroken ring, circling the tower but open in the center. It didn't jut out that much farther than the ledges around them, but the one- or two-foot difference seemed to make the task of climbing up to it almost impossible. Khat didn't see how Constans had made it, except that the Warder was taller than he was and had a complete disregard for his personal survival. He was turning to Elen, about to suggest going from ledge to ledge beneath it, searching for an easier way up, when Constans appeared again, hanging his head down over the edge of the platform.

They both flinched at his sudden appearance, but Constans said, "Finally. Give me your hand, Elen."

Elen looked stubborn. Khat nudged her, gently. "Go on. We don't really have a choice."

Muttering under her breath, Elen approached the edge gingerly, and stretched out her arms. Constans adjusted his position, and said, "Just lean forward."

"Wait." Khat moved up behind her and braced his feet, and put an arm around her waist.

Elen glanced back at him, murmured, "The positions we get into," then leaned forward over empty space. Constans caught her wrist before she could overbalance and Khat let go, and the Warder pulled her up over the edge. In another moment he appeared again.

"Now you."

"I know," Khat said. He could just reach the underside of the platform above, and steadied himself on it. He was considerably heavier than Elen. "You could end up dragging us both over the side, you know."

"I could, but what would be the point of it?"

"Uh, never mind," Khat muttered. He leaned forward and caught Constans's forearm. For an instant, strong as the Mad Warder was, Khat didn't think he would be able to do it. Then Constans's other hand caught the back of his belt and hauled him up and over.

Khat sprawled on the stone, catching his breath, then propped himself up. The platform was smooth, the same cream color and texture as the inside walls of the Remnant. Carved on it was a dizzying pattern of spiraling lines, the same sort of pattern that covered the big ugly block and the Miracle. "The Ancients built this, they must have built the ramps," Khat said, not aware he had said it aloud until he heard his own voice. "How did they get up here?"

"With great difficulty, one assumes," Constans said. "Look up."

Khat did, and had to fight the urge to flatten himself back against the platform. Not more than thirty feet over their heads, if he was gauging the distance properly, the air was thick with the presence of the Inhabitants.

Lines of light marked them, sparking as they struck each other or the walls of the tower in their constant swarming motion. He could feel the freezing cold of the wind that formed their bodies, sense their wish to rush down and destroy. Then Khat saw Riathen, standing perhaps ten feet away near the wall, holding up his hands toward the death in the air above. His face was rapt, and he was motionless, like a statue carved from obsidian. It seemed he might be holding the mass of raging creatures back by will alone, but once Khat looked for it he could see the telltale thickening of the air just below the swirling Inhabitants, the bending of it as if it were heavy with heat.

Elen was standing near Riathen, one hand out as if she didn't quite dare to touch him, for fear she would break that terrible concentration.

Khat turned back to Constans. "How long can he do that?"

"Not long," the Warder said. He was still sitting on the edge of the platform, watching Riathen, his light eyes unreadable. "He isn't the Master Warder by accident, and his power was aided by the Remnant's awakening. But the effort is sure to kill him. I could help him, but he won't allow it. Whether it's an issue of trust, I don't know, but I do know he depends on me to solve this puzzle, and I have been quite unable to do so."

"Solve what puzzle?"

"The puzzle of this place!" Showing real irritation for once, Constans took a swing at him. Khat rolled out of reach. "Obviously this is another part of the Remnant, perhaps meant to close the Door permanently, but just as obviously it isn't working."

"Nothing's obvious when you're dealing with the Ancients,"

Khat snapped. But it was the first time he had seen Aristai Constans agitated by any of this, and it shocked him out of his daze. "That could be why they left the relics to open the Door over this Remnant—they never finished what they were trying to do up here. But they were able to close the Door at the other end. . . . This must do something else." Something important, something worth fighting their way up here, holding back the Inhabitants while they built the ramps and the platform. Whether they used tools and labor or Mages who melted the ramps right out of the walls of the Doorway, it had been no light task. *Aventine-denan, twenty-seventh dynasty, day seventy-one,* he thought, remembering the glyph.

Constans was saying, "I've tried touching his mind, but I can see all the way down into the bottom of his soul, and it's as if there's nothing there, no thought, no feelings. I refuse to believe he's only a shell; I suspect it's some method to keep the Inhabitants from noticing his presence. He's opened his eyes twice, but he doesn't understand a word I've said . . ."

Neither do I, Khat thought. Constans was facing away, looking across the platform toward the opposite side from where Riathen and Elen stood. Khat followed his gaze.

At first he saw nothing but the platform, the cream color of its stone blending seamlessly into the tan and gold of the Doorway's walls. Then his eyes found the figure of a man, seated near the wall.

Khat got to his feet, then stopped abruptly, looking up at the Inhabitants massed overhead. They felt too close for comfort, but standing wasn't really bringing them any closer. He went toward the figure, not quite believing what he saw.

It was a man, seated cross-legged on the platform, covered in dust the same color as the Doorway's walls. He sat so still he might have been a statue. Or a corpse. Khat didn't think he was breathing.

Khat stopped within a few feet of him, and sat on his heels to look more closely. He was a big man, even seated, and Khat thought he might be about his own height or a little taller when standing. His face was finely made, his nose aquiline, and he had the bone structure most people in Charisat thought of as Patrician, though it turned up in the kris Enclave often enough. Khat thought the man was old; the dust coated his face so thickly it obscured even his skin color, but it also marked the hairline tracks of age at the corners of his eyes and the sides of his mouth. He wore robes of an unusual cut, and a headcloth in a strange fashion, wound around his head with the ends tucked in, leaving his neck unprotected.

Constans was standing behind him. Khat glanced up and said, "He's dead."

Constans answered, "Not quite."

The man's eyes opened. Startled, Khat sat back with a thump. Against the dust-rimmed lids and lashes, the man's eyes were a deep liquid brown.

He was looking up at Constans, but without recognition, or any real awareness. The Warder said, "You see, he is alive, and he must be here for some purpose."

"You don't really think he's an Ancient . . ." Khat wasn't aware he had let his words trail off. *What else?* he asked himself. *The Door hasn't been open since the Survivor Time. What else can he be?* His heart was starting to pound, with excitement this time instead of fear. In the Old Menian of the Enclave, he said, "Who are you?"

The eyes moved to him, and for the first time focused.

"That's it," Constans said softly. "I tried in Tradetongue, several of the Last Sea dialects, and what I know of Menian, but I suspect my version was too pidgin to catch his interest." He added, "He's trying to soul-read you."

Khat shook his head, not taking his eyes from the man. "I can't feel anything."

"You wouldn't. Hmm. He's failed."

The man's gaze sharpened, became more aware. His right hand lifted from his lap.

Constans said nothing. Khat was paralyzed.

Moving slowly, as if the muscles had almost forgotten their purpose from long disuse, the man reached out and touched Khat's cheek. Khat felt no impulse to pull away, which was odd in itself. He was wary of just about everybody, and had no reason to trust this man simply because he might be an Ancient Mage. But there was no threat in the gesture, or in the man's eyes. Then the man said, "Success."

Khat was afraid to move, afraid to do anything that might send the man back into his trance. The word had been in Old Menian, but with a pronunciation so different he was surprised he understood him at all. The voice was soft and deep, but with a catch in it from long silence. In the same language, Khat said, "What?"

The old man pulled back his hand, lowered it again to his lap. The touch had been so light, the movement so slow, it had barely disturbed the dust. Almost painfully, he said, "She was the greatest Mage of our time, but when I left, her efforts had produced only monsters. I should have known she would never give up."

It took Khat moments to sort out that sentence, to understand what the old man meant. He asked, "What was her name?"

"Yoane Eveba. Remember it. She was the grandmother of all your kind."

Khat thought the accent on "grandmother" gave it double meaning. Maybe "creator" was a better translation. This was not a trick of the Inhabitants. The names of the Mages who had created the kris had not been preserved, and in Old Menian "krismen" meant only "desert people." But Yoane was a common female name in the Enclave, one that he had never heard in any of the Fringe Cities. Khat's great-aunt had been called Yoane. This man might be a product of his imagination, if he had been driven mad by the Inhabitants, but Constans could see him too, and he doubted they had the same taste in hallucinations. Carefully he asked, "Who are you, and why are you here? How do you live after all this time?"

"I am Sevan-denarin, a Builder. I am here because I failed. There was no point in returning. I do not live, and there is no time here."

I must not be understanding him, Khat thought, frustrated. The kris had always thought their Old Menian was unchanged since the Survivor Time, but obviously some words had shifted in their meaning. Others had strange changes in tone that he knew must signify something. Constans interrupted his thoughts with, "My patience has really been exemplary, but I would like a translation, if you don't mind."

Constans sounded a little dangerous, so Khat repeated what he thought the man had said. Constans said, "I know he tried to soul-read you. Ask him if he is a Mage."

"Are you a Mage?" Khat asked, not thinking the question would be much use. There was no way to be sure if the word had the same sense in Old Menian.

"I was a Builder. I do not live."

"He's a Builder, and he doesn't live," Khat repeated for Constans's benefit. "Now does that clear everything up?"

"Ask him what this place was meant to do."

"I'm getting there," Khat said, annoyed. "This isn't easy." To Sevan-denarin he said, "Did you build this platform? Was it used to close the Door?"

"I Built this, and the Gatehouses beneath each Door. The Gatehouses were only a temporary measure. This was meant to close all the corridors, to seal them on the Other Side, preventing the invaders from ever breaching the barriers into our world again. There was failure. One fought past our defenses and attacked Ashonai, who held the catalyst. She fell down the corridor, and the catalyst was lost. I knew they would have to seal the Door to prevent the invaders from entering our world again, that there would be no time to forge another catalyst or to carry it up here to us. The others returned, or died. I stayed."

The catalyst had been something small enough for a woman-Mage to hold as she stood on this platform. *The seal of the great closing,* Ecazar had said. *Possibly a mistranslation.* Khat was almost afraid to form the thought into words, for fear of tempting fate against them. "This catalyst," he said, giving the word the same odd twist in inflection Sevan-denarin had. "What does it look like?"

Elen shouted a warning, interrupting the old man's answer, and Khat twisted around.

Sonet Riathen had collapsed. Elen was at his side, holding his head. Khat looked up at the swarming Inhabitants above, waiting for them to drop like a rockfall. But the barrier of warped air was still overhead, though he was certain it was lower. He didn't understand. Then he saw Constans, eyes narrowed with concentration, holding his hands up toward the barrier.

He took over whatever Riathen was doing to hold them off, Khat realized, *and we don't have much time.* "Elen! Elen, come here."

She lowered Riathen's head gently, then got to her feet and came toward him. "He's dead. He wouldn't let me help him," she said, her eyes brimming but her voice fiercely angry. "He wouldn't let me even try." She saw Sevan-denarin for the first time and stopped. "What is . . . who is that?"

"This is Sevan-denarin, an Ancient Builder." Khat switched to Old Menian for Sevan's benefit, telling him, "This is Elen son Dia'riadin, a Warder, which is something like one of your Mages, only not as useful."

Sevan's eyes went to Elen, but his gaze was unfocused, disinterested. They were only lucky that the man had thought enough of Yoane Eveba that seeing one of her creations in the flesh was enough to shock him out of his centuries-long sleep. To Elen Khat said, "You've still got the last relic, haven't you?"

She found the winged-figure relic in her robe and handed it to him. Sevan's eyes followed it without interest, and Khat's heart sank. Still, he held it out to the old man, saying, "This isn't the catalyst that was lost?"

Sevan said, "That is not the catalyst Ashonai forged. That is some other's work."

"But we can use it to close all the Doors, forever?"

Sevan met his eyes, and for a brief instant there was nothing distant about his expression at all. "If you wish. I left a ruined world. Is it any better now?"

Khat didn't have an answer for that, at first. When one came to him he was surprised at how little hesitation he had in giving it. *If someone had handed you the opportunity to destroy the world ten years ago, when you had just left the Enclave and you still hated everyone and everything,* he asked himself, *would you have taken him up on it?* Better not to know the answer to that one. He said, "You thought it was worth saving when you built all this. Yoane thought it was worth living in. It's not so much worse off now. It may be a little better."

Sevan held his gaze for a time, while death wailed overhead and no one else moved. Khat didn't need Constans to tell him that the old man was trying to soul-read him again. Maybe trying to make sure that Khat was really what he thought he was. Khat wasn't worried; Yoane had evidently not meant her creations to be vulnerable to the Inhabitants' voices, or to the soul-reading of the other Mages, and she must have told Sevan-denarin her plans. Finally the old man said, "Very well."

Khat let out his breath, not realizing he had been holding it. Maybe he had been a little worried. He said, "How?"

"Give it to the young woman. If she has power, the Will and the Way are to be read from the catalyst."

"You can't even give her a little advice?" Khat ventured.

"If she has power, the Will and the Way are to be read from the catalyst."

Khat sat back. That was all they were going to get. He looked at Elen.

"He's going to help us?" she asked hopefully. Khat hadn't thought about translating for her, and she must have understood only a little of what was going on.

Khat gave her the relic. She had torn her hands during their long climb, and the rags wrapping her palms were lightly stained with blood. He repeated what Sevan had said as best he could in Tradetongue. Elen was aghast. "I can't."

"Why not?"

"I've never been able to . . ." Elen tried to turn away. "My power is weak. I'm terrible at things like this."

Khat grabbed her shoulders and made her look at him. "That was before, when Riathen never let you do anything with it. And you said the Remnant made you almost as powerful as he was."

"You're stronger than you think, Elen," Constans added, startling Khat, who hadn't thought him capable of hearing what went on around him.

"Why don't you do it?" Elen shot back, glaring up at him, anger putting the strength back into her voice. "You're so damn powerful, you save the world."

"I can't do two things at once, and if I let this shield go we are all dead."

"Stay out of this," Khat told him. It might be unfair, considering that Constans was the only thing keeping the Inhabitants back at the moment, but he knew Elen would never listen to him. He said to her, "Just try."

She was silent, staring at the relic in her hand. There was a rush of freezing air from above, and they both ducked instinctively. Khat looked up, and saw the barrier had dropped again. It was no more than ten feet above their heads, if that. Constans said, "A decision soon, Elen, or it will be out of your hands." His voice was drained, exhausted.

Elen glanced back at Riathen's body and wiped her eyes. She glared at Khat. "If I fail, everything terrible that happens next will be my fault. That's the perfect, fitting end to my life, don't you think?"

"If you fail, I promise not to tell anybody," he said.

Elen managed a wry smile that was more than half grimace and got to her feet. She faced the open center of the platform, cradling the little relic in her cupped hands.

Chapter Twenty

ELEN IGNORED THE dizzying drop just below her feet and slowed her breathing, calming her mind, thinking only of the catalyst.

Try, she told herself. *Just try.*

Her mind wanted to wander. Had Riathen subtly encouraged her not to use her power during all his years of teaching? Had she willingly agreed to it, out of her own fear of madness? *Yes, yes, probably; there's nothing you can do about it now.* She sensed an Inhabitant's voice in her thoughts again, subtly persuading this time and not trying to overawe with force. She was a Warder, she could be a powerful one, perhaps the most powerful one. They had always given some humans power; it was jealousy that made the others resist. She could have anything she wanted, it told her.

Maybe this was the same Inhabitant who had tempted Seul so successfully. She thought, *You're lying, of course. You'll kill me like you killed Justice Rasan, and the fortune-teller, and whoever else was in your way.*

No, it said, *I bargain in good faith. The one called Seul would have lived if he had not tried to betray me.* As proof, it offered the secret to constructing the painrods.

Elen felt the knowledge suddenly stream past her consciousness, like a waking dream, but made no effort to remember it. The information was a subtle corruption, and she saw how it must have worked on the Ancients, caught unaware, and perhaps overconfident in their power. A trade of weapons for integrity. Of course, painrods would have no effect on formless beings such as the Inhabitants, only on other humans.

And when the creature said "Betray," she had the clear sense that it had no idea what the word meant. It didn't see her as a person. It couldn't think of killing her as a betrayal, any more than she could think of stepping on an ant as murder. But it had learned to use the word as if it understood it.

You should be the successor to the Master Warder, it said. *But he never thought of you, only of Seul.*

I know that, she thought, *but my power was never strong enough.*

It could be. You could have anyone or anything you ever wanted.

The images it presented were graphic. It had used human lust to manipulate Seul, that was obvious enough. *And what would you know about that, except what you learned from the Heir?* Elen asked the Inhabitant, disgusted with it and herself. *It's all lies, anyway. Riathen lied to me, Seul . . . Oh, Seul lied to everyone. Even Khat lied to me about Constans, and you really expect me to look to* you *for the truth?* Furious, Elen shoved the thing out of her mind. She felt it resist, felt it seem to grow within her mind until her temples throbbed. But the pain fed Elen's anger and she only fought harder, pushing back at it, thrusting it away from her with all her strength. She felt the grip it had on her weaken, then suddenly give way. Its heavy presence was gone and she was alone with her own thoughts again.

The Remnant hadn't lied to her. The single clear note of its song had led her to where power dwelled. Perhaps it hadn't given her power, either; perhaps it had only kindled what was there.

She touched that place in her mind that the Remnant's song had led her to, and the catalyst was suddenly alive in her hands, its warmth enveloping her consciousness. Like a mental map, blazing lines leading her to the goal. One did this, and that, and . . .

Khat watched Elen. The mass of Inhabitants churned like a pot about to boil over, the flashes of red light and swirling clouds of gray air pressing down from overhead. Freezing vapor drifted past the barrier of Warder power, touching bare skin with a chill residue. Khat wondered if it would be like this till the end, no signal of failure, or success, just Constans gradually weakening until the Inhabitants fought their way down to them.

Then the inside edge of the platform glowed molten yellow.

Khat came to his feet. The glowing edge was gradually creeping out toward the open center above the empty well of the Doorway, growing steadily and leaving new, cream-colored stone in its wake. It had gained at least a foot already. Elen flexed her empty hands in wonder. The relic had vanished. She said softly, "I did it."

The wailing of the Inhabitants above increased a hundredfold.

Sevan-denarin was suddenly standing next to Khat. The old man said, "Jump, if you want to live. The Door is closing. The force of it will carry you safely down, if you stay in the center and away from the walls."

Khat translated for the others, having to shout to make himself heard. "What about the Inhabitants?" Elen protested. "If Constans drops the guard, won't they follow us through before the platform closes?"

From behind them, Constans said, "I can make the barrier hold long enough for us to escape, but we won't have much time."

Elen looked over the edge, and then up at the Inhabitants.

"Jump," Sevan said, making an unmistakable gesture.

Khat seconded him, stepping to the edge with her. "Go on Elen, hurry."

She nodded, took a deep breath, then stepped over. "Come on." Khat caught Sevan's sleeve, urging him toward the edge. Sevan pulled away and moved back.

He means to stay here, Khat thought, understanding suddenly.

"I suggest you hurry," Constans said.

Khat looked back. "Then go. Make sure Elen gets out all right."

Constans glanced down at him, then walked over the edge of the shrinking center, disappearing after Elen.

The barrier shivered, but held. The Inhabitants wailed again, outraged. More freezing vapor drifted down, coalescing into water droplets as it passed through the warmer air.

Sevan still hadn't moved. There was perhaps ten feet of empty space left, before the platform would close entirely. Khat said, "If you don't go, I won't."

The old man turned toward him, eyes unreadable, and then moved to the edge.

Khat didn't waste any more time. He grabbed Sevan's arm and pulled the old man over with him.

They were falling, but not headlong. The walls were blurs of gold streaming by, and Khat was too overwhelmed to be frightened. He looked up and saw the platform had closed, blocking the corridor with an unbroken oval of golden light.

Then a cold wind shrieked through him, and a powerful force shoved him toward the wall of the Doorway. Khat caught hold of a ledge, the rough edges tearing at his hands as his full weight came down on his arms. He gritted his teeth and found a foothold, then hauled himself over the edge. He saw Sevan clutching the ledge a few feet away, and hastened to drag the old man up.

Sevan sprawled beside him, and before Khat could ask what had gone wrong a freezing blast of air struck them, knocking them both back against the wall. Khat wiped his eyes and looked up.

Hovering before them was an Inhabitant, its body a swirling whirlwind of dust and air so cold it was opaque, a core of pure bottomless darkness at its heart. It surged toward them again, a tendril stretching out to sweep them off the ledge. Khat ducked under it, flattening himself to the stone, but it caught Sevan, tumbling him head over heels toward the drop-off. Khat threw himself forward and caught the old man's robes, just as Sevan's legs went over the edge.

They hung there, and Sevan was a deadweight. Khat tried to brace himself, his elbows grating painfully on the rough surface. Sevan wasn't helping at all, and he didn't think he could support the big man for long on his own. Then Sevan's other arm gripped the rock, pulling hard, and Khat was able to drag him back up onto the ledge.

Khat collapsed backward. The Inhabitant still hovered there, its malignant attention fixed on them. *This has to be the one from our world, the one that was trapped there all this time,* Khat thought. It hated them too much to be a stranger. *It must have been waiting on this side of the platform for us.*

In a colorless human voice, the voice it had used when it had clothed itself as a human and stood at the Heir's side, the Inhabitant said, "I've trapped you here. The Door to your world closed even as the two Warders passed through it."

Suddenly Khat was furious. "You trapped yourself," he told the creature. It got the pleasure of killing them, but it wasn't going to get the last word if he could help it. "You can't get out either, and you can't get back to your world."

The clouds swirled, red and angry. "My vengeance is better than freedom," it said. "Your company as time travels on to eternity will make my prison bearable." It tore up and away from them, shrieking laughter.

The air warmed around them, and Khat realized his chest ached from breathing in the freezing vapor. His clothes and hair were damp with it. The place was eerily silent, except in the distance he could hear the Inhabitant howling like a remote storm.

Quietly, Sevan-denarin said, "It had no desire to return to its world. They came here because their world is dying, and in their desperation they broke the bonds of it, and found these Doorways that led them to us. They weren't always as you see them now. They are still closely tied to their world, and its protracted death throes have twisted their souls, and only the most fierce survive the journey here. It was the perfect irony that in their battle to conquer us and our struggle to drive them away we both nearly destroyed the land we were fighting over."

That might be true, but Khat knew it wasn't going to stir any sympathy for them in his heart. He pushed away from the wall that was still damp and chill from the Inhabitant's breath. He wouldn't have thought he could last three days here, but that was before he had seen Sevan. *There is no time here*, the old man had said, and Khat was beginning to realize what those words might mean. Trapped here forever, with a being that was all cold death and malice. He asked Sevan, "Was it telling the truth? Are we trapped here?"

Sevan sat up, shaking his head. Much of the coating of dust had rubbed off, and Khat saw for the first time that the old man's skin was as dark as old leather, and that the hair escaping from his wrapped headcloth was white with age. "No," Sevan said, sounding disgusted and weary and really human for the first time. "The mindless thing has forgotten who I am. I'm the Builder, for damnation's sake."

He reached up behind Khat and laid a palm on the wall, frowning in concentration. Then the wall opened up, and they fell through.

Elen felt herself passing through the Door, felt the instant its influence ended and she was falling through the air of her own world. Then she struck water with a stunning impact. She came to the surface, coughing and gasping.

She was in the cistern of the Tersalten Flat Remnant; sunset was streaking the sky overhead. The empty sky. She stared up at it, flailing her arms to keep her mouth and nose above the water. The sky stretched above the well chamber, limitless and open, no Doorway. *It worked,* she told herself, jubilant. *It did work!*

She splashed to the side of the cistern, her clothes dragging at her, and supported herself on the broad stone rim. Her head ached, her hands and feet were cut and bruised, and her exhaustion stretched to the depths of her soul.

Constans was seated on the opposite rim of the cistern, calmly hauling his mantle up and wringing the water out of it. Men in the robes of Imperial lictors, and many of Constans's black-clothed Warders, were running out of the antechamber, carrying lamps, exclaiming in amazement, pointing. Shiskan son Karadon was standing in front of the cistern, her arms folded, unperturbed by what must have been their miraculous appearance. "You're back," she said to Constans. "We were beginning to wonder."

"It was an unusual experience," he told her, "but in the end, there wasn't much difficulty."

The ego of the man, Elen thought. She supposed she might eventually accustom herself to dealing with him, but it wasn't going to be pleasant. She was looking around, at the water, at the open sky above, without really realizing what she was looking for. Then it hit her, as sudden as a blow to the midsection. Khat and the Ancient man were missing. "They aren't here! Khat's not here! They didn't get out." She stared at Constans, horrified.

"I wouldn't wager on that," Constans said. He climbed over the cistern's wall and stood, dripping on the pavement. "Besides Khat's own talents, he had a thousand-year-old Ancient who called himself a Builder with him. If there was another way out to be found, he found it."

Khat had said much the same thing about Constans. Elen closed her eyes and stretched out with her inner senses. Constans and Shiskan and the other Warders were like blazes of light on a dark landscape. The lictors who had accompanied them were less well defined, but still visible as vibrant living souls. Them she ignored, straining past the bounds of the Remnant to the limitless expanse of dead/alive Waste around them. She knew it would be impossible for her to sense Khat, but for an instant she caught a hint of Sevan-denarin's presence, unlike the other Warders, unlike anyone or anything else, but before she could touch it, it was gone again.

So Sevan was here, though he was hiding himself from her detection as he had hidden himself from the Inhabitants. After all that time, it was probably a reflex. It came to Elen suddenly, as the visions from burning bones did, that she would see Khat in Charisat again. She opened her eyes, somewhat reassured. Then she realized what she had done.

Elen looked at her hands, still wrapped in dirty rags. She had cupped the catalyst relic in them, and it had disappeared in a blaze of power, forging the barrier that would trap the Inhabitants in their own world, wherever it was, forever. And now she had soul-read on such a scale as most Warders only dreamed of, seeing for miles around, and she had had a vision of the future without the ritual. It was the same thing she had experienced when the Remnant's voice had whispered in her mind. But the Remnant was silent now, sleeping again, its purpose fulfilled.

Constans had been right; the awakening of the Remnant had changed her. And perhaps he had been right about other things, much as she hated to think it. Well, her own fear had contributed to her reluctance to stretch her power, that she was willing to admit. It seemed a simple matter after everything else.

Elen had her power, but abruptly her much-abused body ceased cooperating, and she needed the help of two lictors to climb out of the cistern.

Khat knew where he was before he opened his eyes. He was curled up on his side, his back against a ridge of burning hot stone. Up and down, along with north, were back where they were supposed to be, and the air was heavy with the searing heat of the Waste. The world felt wonderfully, gloriously right. He lifted his head, then pushed himself up, feeling bruises and scrapes and the protest of strained muscles.

They were on the top level of the Waste, some distance from the Remnant, and the sun was setting in a brilliant haze of red, orange, and gold. To the east the sky had darkened to violet and indigo, though no stars were visible yet. The rock of the top level stretched away in waves, marked by occasional upthrust crags or boulders, all turned the same mellow gold as the fading daylight. Sevan-denarin was standing only a few feet away, facing toward the sunset, the evening breeze pulling at his robes.

Slowly Khat got to his feet, stumbled, and managed to stay upright. They couldn't have fallen far and survived; by his knowledge of the strange geography of the Doorway, Sevan must have managed to bring them out just above the ground. Looking at the old man now, Khat wondered what could possibly be going through his mind: after spending a thousand years in self-imposed exile, to suddenly be released into a world that must bear little resemblance to the one he had left behind. Khat cleared his throat and said, "Well, was it worth saving?"

Sevan turned, his face shadowed by the sun's glare, and said, "It has its own beauty, in a strange fashion. Perhaps it was worth it."

Then Sevan's form seemed to collapse in on itself, and before Khat could move, there was nothing there but dust, scattered over the Waste by the evening wind.

Chapter Twenty-one

KHAT SPENT THE night in a hollow in the wall of a small canyon, not far from the Remnant. It was not a good night, for a number of reasons. He needed to sleep, he needed to think about Sevandenarin's death, and he needed the time alone. The Waste wasn't the best place for this, but it was all he had.

By morning his fever had returned, but so had enough of the will to live for him to start the long walk back to Charisat, with equanimity at least, if not enthusiasm. He kept to the midlevel for the shade, taking his time and foraging along the way. The fever wasn't as bad as it had been before, but it was still enough to make him feel as if his head was stuffed with sand. The relapse had probably occurred earlier, but this was the first chance he had had to notice it.

At the end of the day he holed up for the night in the Fringe, within sight of Charisat. He wasn't much looking forward to reaching it.

Stretched out on top of a wind-smoothed boulder, watching as the sunset turned the sky blood-red and the lamps of the distant city appeared against the growing darkness, Khat had the distinct feeling he had overstayed his welcome in Charisat. His memories of Kenniliar Free City were growing fonder by the hour, and the time alone had given him the chance to come to terms with the idea of visiting there again, at least for a while. He was half tempted to forgo Charisat entirely and strike out along the trade road now; Sagai would be mad to know what had become of the relics, and Khat did have quite a story to tell. If Sagai had managed to buy himself a place in the Scholars' Guild already, the new knowledge might also let him elevate his status within it considerably.

But Kenniliar was a long walk, and while his fever didn't seem to be getting any worse, it wasn't getting any better, either. If he didn't want to send himself into another three-day collapse, he would need a place to recover. He did owe the story to Arad-edelk too, for all his help, and it might be interesting to see Ecazar's reaction. Khat smiled to himself, picturing it. And they might have some news of Elen, of what she would do now that Riathen was dead.

It made more sense to spend a few days in Charisat before starting the journey, and maybe for once he would take the sensible course.

The morning sun was just cresting the city when Khat reached Charisat's docks. Handcarts rolled on the overhead walkways, wagons steamed at the piers, and the changeover from the night's activity to the day's was well under way. At the familiar stench of sewers and hot metal, he almost turned back.

He had climbed the pilings of a disused pier and started toward the ramps when furtive motion at the base of the colossus caught his eye. He hesitated, studying the levels above. The beggars were still asleep, and no one else—loaders, carters, or overseers—was moving with anything but early-hour lethargy. He saw nothing out of the ordinary, and was inclined to shrug it off. He was still unsteady, and his eyes, like his sense of smell, were still attuned to the Waste; it would take time to become accustomed to the city again. Still he took the long way around, going up the carters' ramp at the far end of the docks.

Khat passed the base of the colossus and started up the street that led into the Eighth Tier proper. Not twenty feet ahead, three city dwellers were standing as if they were waiting for something. They were lower-tier, but not as ragged or badly undersized as the usual inhabitants of the Eighth. Reading the tension in their outwardly casual poses, he deliberately slowed his steps.

From behind, someone called his name.

Khat turned, already drawing his knife. At a careful distance down the street were four men. One was Kadusk, whom he knew as an enforcer who worked for Lushan, and two were dockworkers, armed with the long metal bars used to lever bales of cargo on and off wagons. The fourth was the filthy little informer, Ivan Sata.

Khat backed toward the wall. This he didn't need. The street at this point was bordered by black rock walls, above which were warehouses, mostly windowless to prevent thieving, and there was no place to run.

The three men who had waited up the street came toward him, spreading out to block escape, as Kadusk and his dockworkers closed in. They were in full view of the gate to the Eighth Tier, and the vigils there watched with interest. Kadusk had chosen his moment well. This was far enough away from the docks not to constitute an impeding of trade, and Khat didn't look enough like a citizen, even from a distance, for the vigils to stir themselves.

Ivan Sata was hanging behind the other men, watching eagerly but ever-careful of his skin. "How much did they pay you for me, Sata?" Khat called to him.

"Ten five-day tokens," the informer replied. "I earned it. It's hard work following you."

Kadusk grinned. "He lost you for days, then picked you up on the Sixth Tier and trailed you down to the docks. Lushan went mad when we thought you left the city. Wouldn't let us stop watching for you."

Khat put his back against the wall. Ten five-day tokens wasn't that much; he thought it insultingly low, considering the value of a dead kris on the Silent Market, but Ivan Sata had always been an idiot. He must have overheard Khat talking to Caster in the Arcade, but even Sata had probably had more sense than to turn the Silent Market dealer over to Lushan. Caster had friends who would skin Lushan and Sata in slow agony and feed them to spidermites for such an offense. It was too bad no one felt the same about Khat.

One of the enforcers feinted at him. Khat slashed back and ducked under a swing from a loading bar. The enforcer shook his injured hand, cursing, and the first droplets of blood landed on the dusty street.

Kadusk snarled at the others, and they closed in again. Khat ducked under another blow and smashed into the attacker, sending the man staggering back and almost clearing a path for escape. One of the others tackled him before he could take advantage of it, slamming him back against the wall. The breath was knocked out of him, stunning him for precious instants, and someone pinned his knife hand, trying to force him to drop the weapon. The man who had tackled him was still holding him, and with his free hand Khat grabbed a handful of greasy hair and twisted the man's head back sharply. He lacked the leverage to snap the neck, but the man howled and let go of him. Khat tried to push himself up, but his vision blurred and the ground was suddenly unsteady. He slid down the wall, and the last thing he saw was someone's fist coming at him.

He never lost consciousness completely. He dimly realized he was slung head down over someone's shoulder, someone whose robes stank and who was not terribly careful about where he put his hands. Khat's blood was pounding in his ears, and his stomach was trying to crawl up his throat. Splotches of darkness swam before his eyes when he made the mistake of opening them, though there wasn't much to see; his robe had been pulled down to cover his head. The blows hadn't been that devastating; Kadusk and his men had used their fists, fortunately, and not the loading bars, but hanging upside down wasn't helping any, and he kept drifting, unable to break through into real awareness. His instinctive struggles to free himself from whoever was carrying him were ineffective and mostly ignored.

At this time the streets still wouldn't be crowded, and even if a vigil did stop Kadusk all he had to say was that they were carting home a drunken friend. Then Khat heard the far-off bell of the Academia's clock tower and realized they were on the Fourth Tier. That meant Lushan's house, and that shook him back to real consciousness. Once he was inside, there was no hope of escape.

Lushan's house was near the shops; if Khat could put up enough of a fight to draw attention, that might make it an impeding of trade and bring the vigils. It might also mean the Trade Inspectors again, but it would at least buy him some time.

Then the man carrying him stopped abruptly, the sudden change in motion sending Khat into another wave of dizziness. He heard a shout and a scuffle, and decided now was the time to take his chance. He linked his fingers and with doubled fists struck the man in the kidney.

The man cried out and dropped him. Khat hit the ground and rolled over, choking on dust and wincing at the brilliant sunlight. A short distance away two of the enforcers were on the ground too, moaning and holding their heads. A new entrant into the fray was fighting with Kadusk, holding him off with a metal pole from someone's shop awning while the other two tried to get past his guard. Khat couldn't get a good look at his would-be rescuer; the man wore desert robes and a long headcloth, and was moving too quickly for Khat's watering eyes to focus properly. He knew who he thought it was, but that didn't seem possible.

The man who had been carrying him had doubled over, but now straightened painfully up and started toward the fight. Khat twisted around and tripped him with an outstretched leg. The enforcer fell flat, and Khat scrambled forward and leapt on him, getting a stranglehold on his neck.

There was another shout, and someone grabbed the back of Khat's robe and yanked him off the enforcer, sending him sprawling on the street again. Khat found himself looking up at an Imperial lictor subcaptain, who was pointing a rifle at him. "Don't move," the lictor suggested.

Khat decided not to move. The subcaptain took a cautious step closer, studying him carefully, then called over his shoulder, "This is the one, all right."

They were surrounded by at least a dozen Imperial lictors. Kadusk and the enforcers who were still standing were being disarmed. Khat sat up a little, cautiously. It had been close. This was the court just outside Lushan's house.

"This one, too." A lictor pulled the man who had attacked the enforcers out of the group and shoved him towards Khat and his guard. This time, Khat could see who it was.

Sagai knelt next to him, one eye on the subcaptain, muttering, "Out of the pot and into the coals, as usual."

"What are you doing here?" Khat demanded. "You're supposed to be in Kenniliar."

"Looking for you." Sagai was exasperated. "Of course. Caster told me what you'd done to Lushan and that someone had informed on you, so I watched the house in hope of catching sight of you." He let out his breath in a sigh. "I don't know why I bother. It's because the children are attached to you, I suppose."

Khat didn't know whether to be angry or not, considering that Khat himself wasn't where he was supposed to be, either. "How did you get here?" They were both watching the lictor warily, but he didn't seem inclined to shoot them for talking. Sagai was covered with road dust and had taken a couple of knocks in the fight; he looked just as shabby and disreputable as any caravaner.

Sagai explained, "Two days into the journey it became apparent that you weren't coming after us. We were only a day or so out from Kenniliar, and when we passed a caravan going back to Charisat, I thought of returning to look for you. Miram persuaded me she would be all right; she knows Kenniliar well, and has Netta with her. They should be at my uncle's house by now." Sagai hesitated, glanced again at the lictor, and lowered his voice even further. "I spoke to Arad-edelk and looked at the book. He had heard something from Elen about your adventure at the Tersalten Flat Remnant. I could hardly credit it." He hesitated. "Was it true?"

"Every word. But I said if I couldn't leave in time to catch up with the caravan I'd join you in Kenniliar."

"Hell below." Sagai was shaking his head in wonder, not listening to his protest. "Has it anything to do with why we are being arrested by Imperial lictors?"

"I don't know." Khat gave up on the Kenniliar issue. There was no point in arguing about it, anyway. "There are several possibilities."

Some Trade Inspectors arrived, and started to argue with the lictors. They wanted Khat and Sagai as well for fighting near the shops and impeding trade, and not just the others. The lictors wouldn't yield, and the Trade Inspectors collected Kadusk and his men and departed, angry at being deprived of their prey. Khat noticed Lushan hadn't run out of his home to speak for his hirelings, and wondered what the broker was making of all this. Everyone else in the court seemed to be peering out of their windows, pointing and staring.

The other lictors were moving in around them now, and the subcaptain motioned for Khat and Sagai to stand. Khat needed Sagai's help to get to his feet, but once there the swaying world seemed to stabilize, at least for a time. An inquiry as to where they were going might earn a blow to the head with a rifle butt, so Khat didn't ask. There were only two possibilities, anyway. And when they passed the street that led to the High Trade Authority and the prison under it without pausing, that left only the First Tier.

* * *

When they reached the palace Khat was a little relieved to see the lictors were taking them upstairs instead of down. But they went further up than he had been before, until he wondered if they meant to take them all the way to the top, and just what was up there, anyway.

Eventually they reached the seventh level and were taken to a large chamber on the outer wall, with floor-to-ceiling windows, some screened by stone lattices but others with only a low parapet.

The subcaptain stationed a few of his men to guard them and departed, perhaps to report to whoever had wanted them arrested. Khat exchanged a baffled look with Sagai. At least they weren't tied or chained up in some little cell underground.

The unimpeded sunlight heated the room, reflecting off the marble surfaces, but the breeze was stiff, and their captors didn't seem to mind if they moved around. Khat went to the windows first; the view was incredible. The First Tier was laid out like a map below, and they could see the edges of the other tiers, all the way down to the Eighth, where the people and handcarts moved antlike in the streets.

"That is a long way down," Sagai murmured thoughtfully.

Khat leaned out for a better look, and Sagai grabbed the back of his robe. The climb, Khat supposed, was theoretically possible. Each level of the palace stood out farther than the one above it, like a series of steps. But they were awfully tall steps to take without a rope, and they would be in full view of the tier below and anyone who happened to look out of the windows on this side of the palace. "We might do it once it's dark," Khat said softly, mindful of the lictors nearby. "If we're still alive when it's dark," he added.

"We might," Sagai agreed. "Except that I'm old and you're not as healthy as you used to be. You still have that fever? I thought you had gotten over it."

"You're not that old," Khat said, leaving aside the issue of his health. "You weren't having any trouble with the welcoming party Lushan sent for me."

"I was having a great deal of trouble, thank you. It's probably a good thing the lictors came when they did."

"I wouldn't put it that way." Khat had a vivid recollection of the Heir's method of disposing of unwanted guests. At least Saret the executioner was dead, and he needn't worry about running into him again. He turned away from the window and stretched to loosen the tension in his shoulders, wishing they had been taken somewhere with a fountain. His nose wasn't bleeding anymore, but his head was still pounding, and there was a particularly sore spot on his jaw. He had another loose tooth, too.

It would be nice to know who had had them arrested. Khat wondered where Elen was, if they could get word to her, if she could help them. He noticed Sagai still staring out the window, and asked him, "Are you worried about Miram?"

"Somewhat, but . . ." Sagai shook his head, coming away from the parapet. "She knows Kenniliar well, we have family there, and she is both older and wiser than when she so foolishly married me."

Khat winced. It was the worst luck that Sagai had been brought into this at all. "You shouldn't be here anyway," he pointed out. "You should never have turned back."

"Oh, be quiet." Sagai was looking across the room, at the arch where the lictors stood guard. "That mosaic, out in the hall there . . . That's a lovely copy of a Battai mural."

As Khat craned his neck to look at the Battai copy, four more lictors entered their prison, led by an older officer. Khat recognized his chain of rank first. It was the archcommander who had tried to stop him in the Citadel of the Winds, who had been helping the Patrician try to talk Constans into attacking the palace.

The archcommander came toward them, stopping only a bare pace away from Khat. He said coldly, "Well. One of Aristai Constans's spies. But Constans isn't here now."

Khat didn't back away, knowing it would be a mistake. He said, "Are you sure about that?" Constans's ability to appear when least expected must be known in the upper levels of the palace; Khat doubted he was the only one to ever experience it.

The man didn't hesitate. "Oh, I'm sure. He's with the Elector now."

"And will we be told why we have been brought here?" Sagai asked, with polite curiosity.

The archcommander turned his head sharply, startled at hearing someone who looked as Sagai did right now speak with an educated accent. He eyed them both uncertainly and drew back a step, saying, "The Elector ordered it himself."

The Elector, Khat thought. *That can't be right.* Sagai was looking at him for an explanation, and he had none. Before he could suggest that the archcommander was insane, there was a minor commotion in the hall, and the other lictors stepped aside to admit Elen.

She didn't look much the worse for her experience. There were weary shadows under her eyes, but her white mantle and kaftan were pristine, and she wore a painrod at her waist. She looked from Khat to Sagai as she came toward them, her eyes widening at the obvious damage. "Did they do this?" she demanded.

"No, this is from a different fight entirely," Sagai explained.

"Oh." She turned to Khat with an expression of much frustration mixed with concern. "But where were you all this time, and how did you get out of the Doorway? And where is Sevan-denarin?"

The archcommander interrupted before Khat could even begin to answer, demanding, "What are you doing here, Warder?"

Elen faced him as if she was Master Warder. "That's not your concern, Venge," she snapped. "Why did you have these men arrested?"

The lictor looked over at Khat, his eyes hard to read. "The Elector wants to see this one."

Elen said, "That's impossible." It was close to calling Venge a liar, but she didn't appear to care.

"He gave me the orders himself, Warder. The description was exact." Venge kept his temper, but his words were clipped. "And the description of him," he nodded at Sagai, "who was to be questioned on the kris's whereabouts, if we couldn't find him."

"What does this mean, Elen?" Sagai asked, worried. "I thought noncitizens were never admitted to the Elector's presence unless they were with a foreign embassy."

Elen shook her head. "I thought so too, but I suppose it's only custom, and he can see whomever he wants." She turned back to Venge, her eyes narrowed. "What under the great sky does he want to see Khat for?"

With some asperity, Venge said, "I'm not a confidant of his. If I speculated, I would say it had something to do with Aristai Constans."

"Constans?" Elen glared over at Khat. "You'd know about that, then, since he's such a friend of yours."

"He's not an anything of mine. I don't know what's going on," Khat protested. He couldn't quite believe it was happening. Some of his sense of distance from events might be the fever, but most of it was pure shock.

Elen turned on Venge again. "If Sagai was only arrested to be questioned on Khat's whereabouts, and you already have Khat, you can release Sagai now."

Sagai started to protest, and Khat elbowed him in the ribs. Elen was right; if Khat couldn't get out of this, at least Sagai might.

The archcommander wasn't happy, but Sagai's scholarly demeanor, even when he had just been in a fight, was obvious, and Elen seemed to wield more influence here than Khat would have thought possible. Venge forgot protocol so far as to scratch his chin under his veil, and asked grudgingly, "And if the Elector has questions for him as well?" It was the voice of a man willing to be convinced.

"Then release him to me, on my authority," Elen said.

"Very well." Venge motioned the other lictors forward. "But I have to take the kris now."

"Just try not to say very much," Sagai advised Khat in an anxious voice.

"Good-bye," Khat said, getting one look back over his shoulder as the lictors closed in.

Elen followed, somehow managing to edge one of the lictors aside to walk next to Khat. "Don't worry. He isn't a monster."

"You said he was," Khat muttered.

"I did not." Elen glanced self-consciously at Venge. "And I hadn't met him then, had I? I'll see what I can do."

Khat didn't know how she thought she could help. With Sonet Riathen dead, how much influence could a Warder of his household have? The lictors were taking him to yet another set of marble stairs, and Elen stopped, unable to follow further.

Once past the stairs, they led him through a suite of rooms, all high, open, and opulent, and all bare of furniture or anything else practical, as if they existed only for show. There seemed to be no solid walls: stone lattices separated rooms, allowing in daylight and free moving air; mesh screens of copper and bronze served as doors and the pillars were pink marble and porphyry. They passed no other people.

Finally Venge halted in a room that was no more or less beautiful than the others, different in that one wall was only waist-high and looked out over an atrium lush with potted flowers and small trees, with several fountains playing among the greenery. There were a few couches scattered about, draped with silk and gold brocade.

It was also empty except for Aristai Constans, pacing impatiently like a dark specter in the golden room.

Constans came forward, and Khat looked up at him accusingly. "I should have known it was you."

"So am I the bane of your existence?" Constans asked, stopping within arm's reach. The lictors, even archcommander Venge, had cautiously drawn away from the confrontation. Constans didn't look any the worse for his experience either, but then with him it was so difficult to tell anything. "How did you escape from the Doorway?"

"He was a Builder," Khat said, knowing no other way to describe it.

"I see." Constans sounded as if he actually did see. "It may interest you to know that the Miracle is miraculous no longer. It hasn't emitted light since we returned here from the Remnant."

It was a loss and a relief at the same time. The Miracle had been beautiful, but its task was finished. "So it's over," Khat said.

"One would assume."

The room was warm, despite the atrium and the open walls. "Then why am I here?" Khat demanded.

"It doesn't occur to you that it might be out of gratitude?"

Disgusted, Khat turned away, and found himself looking straight at an Ancient mural. It was large, covering the opposite wall, and in beautiful condition, though the subject matter was not as rare as that of the mural in Arad-edelk's care. It was a seascape, showing a rocky promontory that might be the crag where Charisat now rested and a wide sweep of dark foaming water, under a sky of gray churning clouds. A close examination would probably reveal the dynasty. Whoever had had charge of the mounting had resisted the temptation to fill in the missing border pieces with inferior modern work, and the gaps revealed the plain stone of the wall beneath.

Khat didn't realize how long he had stared at it until a firm hand under his chin turned his head back toward Constans, who was watching him narrowly. "I admit, gratitude didn't occur to me either," the Warder said. "You're ill."

Khat jerked away and stepped back. "No." The denial was completely automatic, and Constans did not appear convinced.

The great double doors at the far end of the room began to open, and the Warder turned toward them.

Khat was not entirely sure what happened next. The room, so warmly lit by the sunlight in the adjacent atrium, went strangely dark, and the walls seemed to sway inward. The next thing he knew he was on the floor.

A set of footsteps came near, and someone said, "He looks terrible. What did you do to him?" The voice was an old man's, querulous and annoyed.

"I did nothing." Constans sounded faintly exasperated.

Khat lay sprawled on his back, and such close contact with the cool marble floor revived him a little. He opened his eyes a slit, hoping it would go unnoticed.

The man standing over him must be the Elector. He was as short as a lower-tier dweller; Khat could tell that from even this perspective. He was fat and his features were worse than the portrait on the coins implied, with not even a trace of the aquiline beauty associated with the Patrician class. His robes were fine gold silk trimmed with heavy bands of gilt embroidery, but he wore less jewelry than his chief stewards. It was then Khat noticed he wore no veil. Well, this was the man's own house, technically, and as the one who made the rules, he could do whatever he wanted.

Then Khat realized the Elector was looking down at him, had seen his eyelids flicker. The Elector snorted and turned away.

Khat sat up cautiously. The pounding in his head was worse, making it hard to think. He didn't have any idea of the correct etiquette, though he had the vague idea that as a noncitizen he was supposed to be on the floor anyway. Several of Venge's lictors had staves and stood within easy reach; he knew if he did anything wrong he would find out immediately.

There were other people in the room, some Patricians, others who must be servants, despite the richness of their dress. All were veiled, but their eyes studied him with varying degrees of disgust, curiosity, amusement. *Don't worry about them,* Khat thought grimly. *Worry about yourself.* Constans had settled on the low wall that bordered the atrium, and looked as if he was preparing to watch some entertainment. It didn't matter what Constans did; Khat knew better than to count on help from that quarter. The Elector had taken a seat on the nearest couch. His sharp old eyes weren't on Khat, who was glad of the respite, but on one of the Patricians.

As if continuing an interrupted conversation, the Patrician said, "I am much displeased with the account of the Heir's death."

Khat recognized the voice. He had last heard it shouting at Constans, in the Citadel. It was the Patrician whom Venge had accompanied. The man spread his hands, as if being eminently reasonable.

"The only word we have for it is that of Aristai Constans, and considering that he was always her enemy . . ."

"We also have the word of the new Master Warder." The Elector seemed to be more interested in the set of his rings than the topic of conversation. But now he looked up at the Patrician again, his eyes deceptively sleepy. "She was also present. Surely you do not dispute her account?"

The Patrician hesitated, calculating. "Not if my Honored Lord accepts it."

They are talking about Elen, Khat thought, trying to take it in. *No wonder Venge let Sagai go when she asked it.* He supposed he should find this reassuring. He found himself blaming her for not mentioning it downstairs, though that was idiotic; she hadn't had time.

"Oh, and I do accept it," the Elector assured the Patrician, with an ingenuousness so lightly tinged with sarcasm it might be only imaginary. "You'll forgive me if I send you away, won't you, Adviser? I would so much rather ask my questions in private."

The Patrician bowed, and the room cleared except for Constans, the Elector, and one or two of the silent servants.

"That man is tiresome," Constans said, when the doors had closed. "I can't think why you won't let me kill him."

The Elector frowned at him. "He's obvious. He distracts the others. You know that as well as I do; stop making an exhibit of yourself." He examined his rings again, though there was nothing sleepy about his eyes now, deceptive or otherwise. "What we really brought you here to ask, of course, is what became of the Ancient Sevandenarin? Is he here, in the city?"

Khat realized with a start that this last had been addressed to him. Without thinking, he said, "He died."

"Truly?" The Elector leaned forward. "How?"

Khat tried to answer and found himself coughing helplessly. The Elector lifted a hand, and a servant was suddenly at Khat's side, offering a cup of water. After that, he managed to go on. "He was only here for a few moments, out on the Waste. He died, and the body turned to dust."

The Elector twisted around to consult Constans, who was watching pensively. "It only makes sense," the Warder said. "He was over a thousand years old."

"I see. A great pity," the Elector said slowly, sitting back on the couch. "He could have told us . . . everything."

"Everything might have been too much to know," Constans pointed out dryly. "All at one time, at any rate."

The Elector was eyeing Khat again. "The embassy from the kris-men Enclave asked about any kris living in Charisat. They were very anxious to find someone in particular. It wouldn't have been you, by any chance?"

Khat wasn't far gone enough to admit that. Blank and innocent, he said, "I don't think so."

The Elector looked to Constans again. *He must do it by habit,* Khat realized. With Constans's skill at soul-reading, he would be able to tell when people were telling the truth. Most people, anyway. It must disconcert the Patricians no end.

Smiling, Constans said, "Oh, I doubt they were searching for him. There must be other kris in the city. So many people come and go every day."

Well, thank you very much, finally, Khat thought, careful to let none of it show on his face. *Gratitude, my ass.*

Whether the Elector really believed Constans or simply accepted his judgment on the matter was impossible to guess. He said, "Yes, of course," and gestured at one of the servants. "Tell the lictors he's to be released."

Khat could have fainted again, this time from relief. It had been a very strange experience, taken in all, but not too frightening.

But before the servant had taken two steps to the door, Constans said, "He is ill, however. If he receives no care he will be dead in three days."

"Really?" The Elector frowned. If he noticed the look of pure ha-tred Khat was turning in Constans's direction he gave no sign of it. "Send him to the palace physicians first, then."

A servant brought Venge and the other lictors, and Khat was hauled away. Elen was waiting for him at the stairs down to the sev-enth level. "I told you it would be all right," she said.

"You're Master Warder?" Khat asked her, trying not to make it sound like an accusation.

"Yes." She seemed none too pleased with it. "Constans arranged it. I could kill him. I'm sure it's some sort of trick. What did he say to you?"

"He said I could leave," Khat told her, thinking it was worth a try.

"He said you would see the palace physicians," Venge corrected inexorably.

The physicians were not pleased. They thought he should recover completely from the fever before leaving the palace. The rooms the lictors took him to were on the seventh level, where the marble halls were under constant guard and the large windows that looked out on such a gorgeous view could not be climbed out of, even if Khat had felt up to the challenge. The place might be filled with air and light, but it was just as much a prison as the stinking chambers under the High Trade Authority. His only choice was to submit.

The physicians were too curious for Khat's peace of mind, and the servants were either frightened or disdainful. The first thing they did was take his clothes away, and they were disappointed to discover that he wasn't really that filthy, only from what the past couple of days had done. The robes they gave him in return were silk, but he was in no mood to appreciate it. Most of that first day passed in a dreamlike haze, but by morning he felt well enough to leave. The trouble was in convincing someone to seriously consider the idea.

The physicians said his recovery was not yet complete, and the long day stretched on. Khat's only amusement was that two of the servants were foreigners from the Ilacre Cities, and under the delusion that he couldn't understand their dialect of Menian; listening to what they assumed were private conversations lightened the heavy hours considerably.

The food, of course, was wonderful, and Khat had never been to a place where there was such a lack of concern over where the next dipper of water was coming from. Even in the Academia, where the Elector paid for it, everyone knew water cost coins. Here they didn't seem aware of it at all.

It was, as he told Elen when she came to see him that afternoon, quite the nicest prison he had ever been in.

"It isn't a prison," she argued.

"They won't let me leave," he told her, stretched out on one of the soft cushioned couches. Being treated as a curiosity was better than being treated as garbage, but it weighed just as heavily on the nerves. The Elector could change his mind about releasing him, the lictors could decide to have some fun, a Patrician who equated kris with pirates could walk into the room and shoot him, anything could happen. Elen was the only one he could look to for real help, and it rankled to be dependent on her.

"It's for your own good," she said.

"That's the worst kind of prison."

Elen was there often in the next few days, probably more often than she should have been. Ostensibly it was to keep him company, but she also needed to talk, and at the moment he was all she had. She was finding her abrupt transition to Master Warder a fascinating but sometimes daunting experience. She had better luck dealing with the Elector than Riathen ever had, a fact she couldn't seem to account for. The simple reason that she was both more personable and more open to considering alternatives than her predecessor was something she would come to realize eventually, Khat supposed. That she wasn't playing power games with the Heirs or obsessively committed to furthering the influence of Warders no matter what the consequences probably helped as well.

She had arcane power, which she had always wanted, and she had temporal power, which she had been trained from birth to wield. She had also lost the man who had been a father to her for most of her life, and not only lost him but lost her faith in him. Every memory of Riathen concerned the Warder training that had been her whole world, and every one of those memories was tinged with the knowledge that he had subtly held her back, had manipulated her own fears to control her.

The Warders in her household treated her with cautious courtesy, not understanding her new power and perhaps distrusting her sudden elevation. Gandin Riat was the only one who was genuinely glad for her, but he had seen what the Inhabitant was capable of firsthand, and was the only one who had any real understanding of what had happened.

Khat listened to her, but under Elen's calm surface she was vulnerable, and for some reason that annoyed him no end. He knew she needed him, and had to fight the urge to push her away. Not for the first time, he was glad to be dead to the Warders' soul-reading.

But he wasn't as good at concealing things from her as he thought, and one afternoon Elen said in frustration, "This is so typical of you."

"What?"

"You risked your life to look for me when I went missing, and now you'll barely talk to me."

It wasn't until that moment that Khat understood himself what was wrong. Slowly, he said, "You're Master Warder now, Elen."

"Yes." She had heard the words, but not the meaning behind them. "I don't know how long I'll hold on to it. As long as I can, I suppose. I've never been much of a courtier." She was trying to make it all sound as if it meant nothing, but under the false lightness her voice was bitter. "The only thing I have is my power, and that was handed to me by the Remnant."

Khat was hardly hearing her now, too occupied with his own revelation. Well, maybe it wouldn't matter. Maybe she need never know. He said, "Aren't you ever happy with anything?"

"Well, you're a fine one to say that."

Sagai and Arad-edelk came up the next day and with Elen's help managed to see him, Sagai to make sure he was all right and Arad to hear the story of the Remnant from his point of view. Arad had heard it from Elen, but she hadn't taken as much notice of the details of the Doorway's construction as he would've liked. Khat was glad to see them, no matter how briefly, but it only reinforced his feeling that everyone was off having fun while he was trapped here.

By the fourth day Khat finally persuaded his keepers to give him back most of his own clothes. The things they considered too hopelessly worn to return they replaced with tough plain stuff suitable for the Waste, and that was more reassuring than anything else. It meant that as far as the lower echelon of the palace was concerned, he really was going to be released at some point. The next day Elen came to tell him that the physicians had pronounced him fit to leave the palace, and Khat had never been more relieved in his life.

On the way out, she said, as if making a sudden decision, "There's something I'd like to ask you." They went out to one of the stepped terraces that cut into the lower level of the palace, empty in the afternoon heat, its vine-covered arbor casting alternating bars of light and shadow across the tiles.

Elen leaned against the low wall and was silent for a time, her preoccupied gaze on the court below, tapping her fingers on the stone. Khat didn't interrupt her thoughts; they were far enough out of the palace that he didn't feel trapped, and he suspected he should be in no hurry to have this conversation. Finally Elen said, "Would you . . . consider staying here? I know Sagai's heart is already in Kenniliar, but . . . there's going to be a new study of the Tersalten Flat Remnant by the Academia, and the Warders are to be involved. I've been working it all out with Arad and Ecazar. I would appreciate your help."

Khat looked away, toward the view of Patrician manses and the green squares of their courtyards. It was unfairly tempting. The Academia might even be persuaded to accept him for a time, with Elen's patronage. And he was sure that Arad would help. Arad's world was centered on two things: the Ancients and the scholarly politics of the Academia. He might have noticed Khat was krismen, but it didn't make enough of an impact on his world to make any difference to him, and he would see Khat only as an ally in the latter cause. But Khat could too easily see the problems it would cause for the scholar. And Elen.

Especially Elen.

The other Warders in her household had reacted badly enough when she had worked with him to find the relics. As Master Warder she would have more latitude, but she would have to get along with those men in her household, and his regular presence would make that impossible. But that was really the least important reason.

If his silence rattled Elen she didn't show it, but he knew from experience that the worse the crisis, the calmer she became. She turned to look at him then, resting one hip on the wall and saying more directly, "I think we're friends now, and I suppose I'm not asking for anything more than that. But . . . I'd like the chance to find out if there might be something more than that."

Khat had been propositioned by city people more times than he could remember, but he had never been courted, and never had a request for his company held so much respect for his own feelings. For an instant he almost considered it. He shook his head. "You need me like you needed Kythen Seul, Elen."

She smiled a little. "I don't think you're quite as much of a liability as that." She watched him, taking the refusal as calmly as she had made the offer. "Can you tell me why?"

He could, but didn't want to. He made himself meet her eyes, and it wasn't only the sun's muted glare through the vines that made it difficult. "You said once that you trusted me. Do you still trust me, after I lied to you about Constans?"

Elen didn't like being reminded of it, and dropped her gaze briefly. "I could forgive you that. After all, you were right." She hesitated, as the truth began to occur to her. "Do you still trust me?"

Khat didn't answer, torn between wanting to make her understand and not wanting to hurt her. It would have been easy to lie, to invent an excuse, but she didn't need any more friends to do that to her.

He told her the truth. "You're Master Warder now, Elen."

A breeze came over the balustrade, bringing a blast of smothering heat from the sun-drenched pavement, and the smell of incense and flowers. A group of Patricians with their entourages went by on the walkway just below, perceivable only as chattering voices, soft whipping of robes in the wind, and the jingle of bronze rings on parasols.

Elen had heard the meaning beneath the words this time. She said, "I see."

Her voice was still calm, but the pain was there. Defensive, he said, "I don't tell Sagai everything, either."

"Yes," Elen agreed. "But he expects it, and he's more understanding than I am."

"It isn't you," he said. "It's me. I wish I could trust you."

"I know."

"Sorry."

"Don't be. I'm Master Warder now; that's probably the last dose of honesty I'll get." She pushed herself away from the wall. "I'll walk you down to the Fourth Tier."

They went most of the way in silence, though towards the end it was companionable silence. He had told her the truth, and maybe that was what she needed now, however hard it was to hear.

When they reached the Fourth Tier he kissed her good-bye, and she didn't gasp or change color, though one of the vigils at the tier gate dropped his rifle. She only looked up at him, said, "Good luck," and that was that.

Khat reached the Academia without trouble and found Sagai, who had had a glorious time studying the Survivor text with Aradedelk, but was ready now to go home. It was too late in the day to get passage on a caravan, so they spent the night at Arad's house, but by morning they were at the docks, and ready to leave the dust of the city behind them.